"Young man," Elminst[...] [...] lies in knowing when *not* to use the [...] lands would long ago have become a smoking ruin."

Infamy
She raised the hammer and said the words that she always uttered before a kill: "The Shark sends you to the Nine Hells." Then, in a disgusted tone, she added, "You were too easy."

Magic
Orlando steeled his nerve as the eyes on Jolind's severed head snapped open. The thin-lipped mouth did likewise, and a hissing, hollow scream filled the garden.

The Underdark
There was no shortage of slaves to be had in the Underdark, but the status-conscious dark elves were ever eager to acquire new and unusual possessions. . . .

The Arcane
The Tripartite Orb was a most potent weapon. No fireball would explode in its proximity, no summoning would be effective, no ward would protect, and no magical weapon would gain its weal.

Mystery
I placed my marker in the book, threw the blankets back, and made my way to the front of the church. The sound came again, it struck me as though something was scratching on the outside wall of the building.

The Deep
Morgan felt caught in the grip of some implacable tide, carrying him to the depths of a black abyss. Yet, Avadriel's words rang with truth, and her presence gave him something to hold on to, an anchor in an otherwise tumultuous sea.

Shadow
Melegaunt turned to see a pair of webbed hands clutching the edge of his shadow-walk, between them was a slimy reptilian head shooting up to attack. . . .

Realms of Valor
EDITED BY JAMES LOWDER

Realms of Infamy
EDITED BY JAMES LOWDER

Realms of Magic
EDITED BY
BRIAN M. THOMSEN & J. ROBERT KING

Realms of the Underdark
EDITED BY J. ROBERT KING

Realms of the Arcane
EDITED BY
BRIAN M. THOMSEN & J. ROBERT KING

Realms of Mystery
EDITED BY PHILIP ATHANS

Realms of the Deep
EDITED BY PHILIP ATHANS

Realms of Shadow
EDITED BY LIZZ BALDWIN

Realms of the Dragons
EDITED BY PHILIP ATHANS
December 2004

FORGOTTEN REALMS®

THE BEST OF THE

REALMS

Volume I

**Chosen by Readers
from Anthologies Edited by**

Philip Athans
J. Robert King
James Lowder
Brian M. Thomsen
Lizz Baldwin

THE BEST OF THE REALMS
Volume I

©2003 Wizards of the Coast, Inc.

Distributed in the United States by Holtzbrinck Publishing. Distributed in Canada by Fenn Ltd.

Distributed to the hobby, toy, and comic trade in the United States and Canada by regional distributors.

Distributed worldwide by Wizards of the Coast, Inc. and regional distributors.

Printed in the U.S.A.

Cover art by: Mark Zug
First Printing: November 2003
Library of Congress Catalog Card Number: 2003100835

9 8 7 6 5 4 3 2

US ISBN: 0-7869-3024-1
UK ISBN: 0-7869-3025-X
620-17990-001-EN

U.S., CANADA,
ASIA, PACIFIC, & LATIN AMERICA
Wizards of the Coast, Inc.
P.O. Box 707 1702
Renton, WA 98057-0707
+1-800-324-6496

EUROPEAN HEADQUARTERS
Wizards of the Coast, Belgium
T Hofveld 6d
Groot-Bijgaarden
Belgium
+322 467 3360

Visit our web site at **www.wizards.com**

INTRODUCTION

In January of 2003 a simple online survey was posted on www.wizards.com, asking you, the readers, to vote for your favorite stories from the previous eight FORGOTTEN REALMS® anthologies. After the new setting search, we stopped being surprised by huge, enthusiastic responses to stuff we throw up on the web, and like the setting search, this one was exciting and enlightening—a chance for you to tell us what you want to see, and a chance for us to give it to you.

Of course that survey didn't get there on its own, and all that text from as long as ten years ago didn't get to me via magical sending, so a tip of Jarlaxle's great plumed hat is in order for Kim Lundstrom; Julia Martin; Ramon Arjona; Peter Archer; Marty Durham; Mark Sehestedt; the brilliant editors who were the first to pick these stories out of the mix: James Lowder, J. Robert King, Brian M. Thomsen, and Lizz Baldwin; and of course, the authors themselves.

In this book are fourteen stories, thirteen of which you decided were good enough to be called The Best of the Realms, and one I'm sure you'll agree belongs in that category from now on. Reading through this collection was like a walk through the fabled history of Faerûn itself. Has it really been ten years since the first of these anthologies hit the bookstore shelf? I guess it has been. In that ten years the Realms have lived an epoch, and we've been there every step of the way. Here is a bit of the history of what has become—if you ask me, anyway— the greatest fantasy setting in the genre, and a new story by an author you may have heard of, pointing us toward a very bright, and hopefully very long, future.

—Philip Athans, June 2003

CONTENTS

Originally published in
Realms of the Underdark
Edited by J. Robert King, April 1996

RITE OF BLOOD

Elaine Cunningham

Adolescence has a way of sneaking up on most of us, but for some people, a particular moment or event signals the irrevocable end of childhood. Like many other cultures, the dark elves mark this passage with a coming of age ritual. In this novella-length story, a very young Liriel prepares for the Blooding, the ceremony that celebrates what it is to be a drow.

—Elaine Cunningham, March 2003

Elaine Cunningham has written
fifteen books, including the
New York Times bestseller
Dark Journey, Book Ten in the
STAR WARS® New Jedi Order series.
She is currently working on the first
book in a contemporary dark fantasy
series, as well as a FORGOTTEN REALMS®
book set in Waterdeep and written in
collaboration with Ed Greenwood.
More information about her stories can
be found at
www.elainecunningham.com.

RITE OF BLOOD

CHAPTER 1
JOURNEY INTO DARKNESS

There were in the lands of Toril powerful men whose names were seldom heard, and whose deeds were spoken only in furtive whispers. Among these were the Twilight Traders, a coalition of merchant captains who did business with the mysterious peoples of the Underdark.

There were perhaps six in that exclusive brotherhood, all canny, fearless souls who possessed far more ambition than morals. Membership in the clandestine group was carefully guarded, achieved only through a long and difficult process monitored not only by the members, but by mysterious forces from Below. Those who survived the initiation were granted a rare window into the hidden realms: the right to enter the underground trade city known as Mantol-Derith.

An enormous cavern hidden some three miles below the surface, Mantol-Derith was shrouded with more layers of magic and might than a wizard's stronghold. Secrecy was its first line of defense: even in the Underdark, not many knew of the marketplace's existence. Its exact location was known only to a few. Even many of the merchants who regularly did business there would have been hard pressed to place the cavern on a map. So convoluted were the routes leading to Mantol-Derith that even duergar and deep gnomes could not hold their relative bearings along the way. Between the market and any nearby settlement lay labyrinths of monster-infested tunnels complicated by secret doors, portals of teleportation, and magical traps.

No one "stumbled upon" Mantol-Derith; a merchant either knew the route intimately or died along the way.

Nor could the marketplace be located by magical means. The strange radiations of the Underdark were strong in the thick, solid stone surrounding the cavern. No tendril of magic could pass through—all spells were either diffused or reflected back to the sender, sometimes dangerously mutated.

Even the drow, the undisputed masters of the Underdark, did not have easy access to the market. In the nearest dark elven settlement, the great city of Menzoberranzan, no more than eight merchant companies at any one time knew the secret paths. That knowledge was the key to immense wealth and power, and its possession the highest mark of status attainable by members of the merchant class. Accordingly, it was pursued with an avid ferocity, with complex levels of intrigue and bloody battles of weaponry and magic, all of which would probably earn nods of approval from the city's ruling matrons—if indeed the priestesses of Lolth were inclined to notice the doings of mere commoners.

Few of Menzoberranzan's ruling females—except for those matron mothers who maintained alliances with this or that merchant band—had much interest in the world beyond their city's cavern. Those drow were an insular people: utterly convinced of their own racial superiority, fanatically absorbed in their worship of Lolth, completely enmeshed in the strife and intrigue inspired by their Lady of Chaos.

Status was all, and the struggle for power all-consuming. Very little could compel the subterranean elves to tear their eyes from their traditionally narrow focus. But Xandra Shobalar, third-born daughter of a noble House, was driven by the most powerful motivating forces known to the drow: hatred and revenge.

The members of House Shobalar were reclusive even by the standards of paranoid Menzoberranzan, and they were seldom seen outside of the family complex. At the moment, Xandra was farther from home than she had ever intended to go. The journey to Mantol-Derith was long—the midnight hour of Narbondel would come and pass perhaps as many as one hundred times from the outset of her quest until she stood once again within the walls of House Shobalar.

Few noble females cared to be away for so long, for fear that they would return to find their positions usurped. Xandra had no such fears. She had ten sisters, five of whom were, like Xandra, counted among the rare female wizards of Menzoberranzan. But none of these five wanted her job.

Xandra was Mistress of Magic, charged with the wizardly training of all young Shobalars as well as the household's magically gifted fosterlings. She had a great deal of responsibility, certainly, but there was far more glory to be found in the hoarding of spell power, and in conducting the mysterious experiments that yielded new and wondrous items of magic. If one of the Shobalar wizards should ever try to wrest the instructor's position away, the powerful Xandra would certainly kill her—but only as a matter of form. No drow female allowed another to take what was hers, even if she herself did not particularly want it.

Xandra Shobalar might not have been particularly enamored of her role, but she was exceedingly good at what she did. The Shobalar wizards were reputed to be among the most innovative in Menzoberranzan, and all of her students were well and thoroughly taught.

These included the children—both female and male— of House Shobalar, a few second-born sons from other noble Houses, which Xandra accepted as apprentices, and a number of promising common-born boy-children that she acquired by purchase, theft, or adoption—an option that usually occurred after the convenient death of an entire family, rendering the magically-gifted child an orphan.

However they came to House Shobalar, Xandra's students routinely won top marks in yearly competitions meant to spur the efforts of the young drow. Such victories opened the doors of Sorcere, the mage school at the famed academy Tier Breche. So far every Shobalar-trained student who wished to become a wizard had been admitted to the Academy, and most had excelled in the Art. Their high standard was a matter of pride, which Xandra Shobalar possessed in no small measure.

It was that very reputation for excellence, however, that had caused the problem that brought Xandra to distant Mantol-Derith.

Almost ten years before, Xandra had acquired a new student, a female of rare wizardly promise. At first, the Shobalar mistress had been overjoyed, for she saw in the girl-child an opportunity to raise her own reputation to new heights. After all, she had been entrusted with the magical education of Liriel Baenre, the only daughter and apparent heiress of Gromph Baenre, the powerful Archmage of Menzoberranzan. If the child proved to be truly gifted—and that was almost a certainty, for why else would the mighty Gromph bother with a child born of a useless beauty such as Sosdrielle Vandree?—then it was not unlikely that young Liriel might in due time inherit her sire's title.

What renown would be hers, Xandra exulted, if she could lay claim to training Menzoberranzan's next archmage—the first female to hold that high position.

Her initial joy was dimmed somewhat by Gromph's insistence that the arrangement be kept in confidence. It was not an impossibility, given the reclusive nature of the Shobalar clan, but it was brutally hard on Xandra not to be able to tout her latest student and claim the enhanced status that Baenre favor conferred upon her House.

Still, the Mistress Wizard looked forward to the time when the little girl could compete—and win!—at the mageling contests, and she bided her time in smug anticipation of glories to come.

From the start, young Liriel exceeded all of Xandra's hopes. Traditionally, the study of magic began when children entered their Ascharlexten Decade—the tumultuous passage between early childhood and puberty. During those years, which usually began at the age of fifteen or so and were deemed to end either with the onset of puberty or the twenty-fifth year—whichever came first—drow children at last became physically strong enough to channel the forces of wizardly magic, and well-schooled enough to read and write the complicated drow language.

Liriel, however, came to Xandra at the age of five, when she was little more than a babe.

Though most dark elves felt the stirrings of their innate, spell-like powers in early childhood, Liriel already possessed a formidable command of her magical heritage, and furthermore, she could already read the written runes of High Drow. Most importantly, she possessed in extraordinary measure the inborn talent needed to make a magic-wielding drow into a true wizard. In a remarkably short time, the tiny child had learned to read simple spell scrolls, reproduce the arcane marks, and commit fairly complex spells to memory. Xandra was ecstatic. Liriel instantly became her pride, her pet, her indulged and—almost—beloved fosterling.

And thus she had remained, for nearly five years. At that point, the child began to pull ahead of the Shobalar's Ascharlexten-aged students. Xandra began to worry. When Liriel's abilities surpassed those of the much-older Bythnara, Xandra's own daughter, Xandra knew resentment. When the Baenre girl began to wield spells that would challenge the abilities of the lesser Shobalar wizards, Xandra's resentment hardened into the cold, competitive hatred a drow female held for her peers. When young Liriel gained her full height and began to fulfill her childhood promise of extraordinary beauty to come, Xandra simmered with a deep and very personal envy. And when the little wench's growing interest in the male soldiers and servants of House Shobalar made it apparent that she was entering her Ascharlexten, Xandra saw an opportunity and plotted a dramatic—and final—end to Liriel's education.

It was a fairly typical progression, as drow relationships went, made unusual only by the sheer force of Xandra's animosity and the lengths she was willing to go to assuage her burning resentment of Gromph Baenre's too-talented daughter.

That, then, was the succession of events that had brought Xandra to the streets of Mantol-Derith.

Despite her urgent need, the drow wizard could not help marveling at the sights surrounding her. Xandra had never before stepped outside of the vast cavern that held Menzoberranzan, and the strange and exotic marketplace bore little resemblance to her home city.

Mantol-Derith was set in a vast natural grotto, a cavern that had been carved in distant eons by restless waters, which were still busily at work. Xandra was accustomed to the staid black depths of Menzoberranzan's Lake Donigarten, and the deep, silent wells that were the carefully guarded treasures of each noble household.

In Mantol-Derith, water was a living and vital force. The cavern's dominant sound was that of moving water. Waterfalls splashed down the grotto walls and fell from chutes from the high-domed cavern ceiling, fountains played softly in the small pools that seemed to be around every turn, and bubbling streams cut through the cavern.

Apart from the gentle splash and gurgle echoing ceaselessly through the grotto, the market city was strangely silent. Mantol Derith was not a bustling bazaar, but a place for clandestine deals and shrewd negotiations.

Light was far more plentiful than sound. A few dim lanterns were enough to set the whole cavern asparkle, for the walls were encrusted with multicolored crystals and gems. Bright stonework was everywhere. The walls containing fountain pools were wondrous mosaics fashioned from semiprecious gems, the bridges spanning the stream were carved—or perhaps grown—from crystal, and the walkways were paved with flat-cut gemstones. Xandra's slippers whispered against a path fashioned from brilliant green malachite. It was unnerving, even for a drow accustomed to the splendors of Menzoberranzan, to tread upon such wealth.

At least the air felt familiar to the subterranean elf. Moist and heavy, it was dominated by the scent of mushrooms. Groves of giant fungi ringed the central market. Beneath the enormous, fluted caps, merchants had set up small stalls offering a variety of goods. Perfumes, aromatic woods, spices, and exotic, sweetly scented fruits—which had become a fashionable indulgence to the Underdark's wealthy—added piquant notes of fragrance to the damp air.

To Xandra, the strangest thing about the marketplace was the apparent truce that existed among the various warring races who did business there. Mingling among the stalls and passing each other peaceably on the streets were the stone-colored deep gnomes known as svirfneblin; the deep-dwelling, dark-hearted duergar; a few unsavory merchants from the World Above; and, of course, the drow. At the four corners of the cavern, vast storehouses had been excavated to provide storage as well as separate housing for the four factions: svirfneblin, drow, duergar, and surface dwellers. Xandra's path took her toward the surface dweller cavern.

The sound of rushing water intensified as Xandra neared her goal, for the corner of the marketplace that sold goods from the World Above was located near the largest waterfall. The air was especially damp there, and the stalls and tables were draped with canvas to keep out the pervasive mist.

Moisture pooled on the rocky floor of the grotto and dampened the wools and furs worn by the surface dwellers who clustered there—a motley collection of orcs, ogres, humans, and various combinations thereof.

Xandra grimaced and pulled the folds of her cloak over the lower half of her face to ward off the fetid odor. She scanned the bustling, smelly crowd for the man who fit the description she'd been given.

Apparently, finding a drow female in such a crowd was a simpler task than singling out one human. From the depths of one tentlike structure came a low, melodious voice, calling the wizard properly by her name and title. Xandra turned toward the sound, startled to hear a drow voice in such a sordid setting.

But the small, stooped figure that hobbled toward her was that of a human male.

The man was old by the measure of humankind, with white hair, a dark and weathered face, and a slow, faltering tread. He had not gone unscathed by his years—a cane aided his faltering steps, and a dark patch covered his left eye. Those infirmities did not seem to have hampered his success.

His cane was carved from lustrous wood and ornamented with gems and gilding. Over a silvered tunic of fine silk, he wore a cape embroidered with gold thread and fastened with a diamond neck clasp. Gems the size of laplizard eggs glittered on his fingers and at his throat. His smile was both welcoming and confident—that of a male who possessed much and was well satisfied with his own measure.

"Hadrogh Prohl?" Xandra inquired.

The merchant bowed.

"At your service, Mistress Shobalar," he said in fluent but badly accented Low Drow.

"You know of me. Then you must also have some idea what I need."

"But of course, Mistress, and I will be pleased to assist you in whatever way I can. The presence of so noble a lady honors this establishment. Please, step this way," he said, moving aside so that she could enter the canvas pavilion.

Hadrogh's words were correct, his manner proper almost to the point of being obsequious—which was, of course, the prudent approach when dealing with drow females of stature. Even so, something about the merchant struck Xandra as not quite right. To all appearances, he seemed at ease—friendly, relaxed to the point of being casual, even unobservant. In other words, a naive and utter fool. How such a man had survived so long in the tunnels of the Underdark was a mystery to the Shobalar wizard. And yet, she noted that Hadrogh, unlike most humans, did not require the punishing light of torches and lanterns.

His tent was comfortably dark, but he had no apparent difficulty negotiating his way through the maze of crates and cages that held his wares.

A curious Xandra whispered the words to a simple spell, one that would yield some answers about the man's nature and the magic he might carry. She was not entirely surprised when the seeking magic skittered off the merchant. Either he was astute enough to carry something that deflected magical inquiry, or he possessed an innate magical immunity that nearly matched her own.

Xandra had her suspicions about the merchant's origins, suspicions that were too appalling to voice, but she did not doubt that the "human" was quite at home in the Underdark, and quite capable of taking care of himself, despite his fragile, aged facade.

The half-drow merchant—for Xandra's suspicions were indeed correct—appeared to be unaware of the female's scrutiny. He led the way to the very back of the canvas pavilion. There stood a row of large cages, each with a single occupant. Hadrogh swept a hand toward them, and stepped back so that Xandra could examine the merchandise as she wished.

The wizard walked slowly along the row of cages, examining the exotic creatures destined for slavery. There was no shortage of slaves to be had in the Underdark, but the status-conscious dark elves were ever eager to acquire new and unusual possessions, and there was a high demand for servants brought from the World Above. Halfling females were prized as ladies' maids for their deft hands and their skill at weaving, curling, and twisting hair into elaborate works of art. Mountain dwarves, who possessed a finer touch with weapons and jewels than their duergar kin, were considered hard to manage but well worth the trouble it took to keep them. Humans were useful as beasts of burden and as sources of spells and potions unknown to the Underdark. Exotic beasts were popular, too. A few of the more ostentatious drow kept them as pets or displayed them in small private zoos. Some of those animals found their way to the arena in the Manyfolks district of Menzoberranzan. There, drow who possessed a taste for vicarious slaughter gathered to watch and wager while dangerous beasts fought each other, slaves of various races, and even drow—soldiers eager to prove their battle prowess or mercenaries who coveted the handful of coins and the fleeting fame that were the survivors' reward.

Hadrogh could supply slaves or beasts to meet almost any taste. Xandra nodded with satisfaction as she eyed the collection.

"I was not told, my lady, what manner of slave you required. If you would describe your needs, perhaps I could guide your selection," Hadrogh offered.

A strange light entered the wizard's crimson eyes.

"Not slaves," she corrected him. "Prey."

"Ah." The merchant seemed not at all surprised by that grim pronouncement. "The Blooding, I take it?"

Xandra nodded absently. The Blooding was a uniquely drow ritual, a rite of passage in which young dark elves were required to hunt and kill an intelligent or dangerous creature, preferably one native to the World Above. Surface raids were one means of accomplishing that task, but it was not unusual for the hunts to take place in the tunnels of the wild Underdark, provided suitable captives could be acquired. Never had the selection of the ritual prey been so important, and Xandra looked over the prospective choices carefully.

Her crimson eyes lingered longingly on the huddled form of a pale-skinned, golden-haired elf child. The hate-filled drow bore a special enmity for their surface kindred. Faerie elves, as the light-dwelling elves were called, were the preferred target of those Blooding ceremonies that took the form of a raid, but they were seldom hunted in the Underdark. Accordingly, there would be great prestige in obtaining such rare quarry for the ritual hunt.

Regretfully Xandra shook her head.

Though the boy-child was certainly old enough to provide sport—he was probably near the age of the drow who would hunt him—his glazed, haunted eyes suggested otherwise.

The young faerie elf seemed oblivious to his surroundings. His gaze was fixed upon some nightmare-filled world that only he inhabited. The boy-child would command a fabulous price; there were many drow who would pay dearly for the pleasure of destroying even so pitiful a faerie. Xandra, however, was in need of deadlier prey.

She walked over to the next cage, in which prowled a magnificent, catlike beast with tawny fur and wings like those of a deepbat. As the creature paced the cage, its tail—which was long and supple and tipped with iron spikes—lashed about furiously, clanging each time it hit the bars. The beast's hideous, humanoid face was contorted with fury, and the eyes that burned into Xandra's were bright with hunger and hatred.

Now this is promising! she thought.

Not wishing to appear too interested—which would certainly add many gold pieces to the asking price— Xandra turned to the merchant and lifted one eyebrow in a skeptical, questioning arch.

"This is a manticore. A fearsome monster," wheedled Hadrogh. "The creature is driven by a powerful hunger for human flesh—though certainly it would not be adverse to dining upon drow, if such is your desire. By which," he added hastily, "I meant only to imply that the beast's voracious nature would add excitement to the hunt. The manticore is itself a hunter, and a worthy opponent."

Xandra looked the thing over, noting with approval its daggerlike claws and fangs.

"Intelligent?" she asked.

"Cunning, certainly."

"But is it capable of devising strategy and discerning counterstrategy, to the third and fourth levels?" the wizard persisted. "The youngling mage who will face her Blooding is formidable. I need prey that will truly test her abilities."

The merchant spread his hands and shrugged.

"Strength and hunger are also mighty weapons," he said. "These the manticore has in abundance."

"Since you have not said otherwise, I assume it wields no magic," the wizard observed. "Has it at least some natural resistance to spellcasting?"

"Alas, none. What you ask, great lady, are things that belong rightfully to the drow. Such powers are difficult to find in lesser beings," the merchant said in a tone calculated to flatter and appease.

Xandra sniffed and turned to the next cage, where an enormous, white-furred creature gnawed audibly on a haunch of rothé.

The thing was a bit like a quaggoth—a bearlike beast native to the Underdark—except for its pointed head and strong, musky odor.

"No, a yeti is not quite right for your purposes," Hadrogh said thoughtfully. "Your young wizard could track such a beast by its scent alone!"

The merchant's uncovered eye lit up, and he snapped his fingers.

"But wait! It may be that I have precisely what you require."

He bustled off, returning in moments with a human male in tow.

Xandra's first response was disgust. The merchant seemed a canny sort, too knowledgeable in the ways of the drow to offer such inferior merchandise. Her scornful gaze swept over the human—noting his coarse, dwarflike form, the pale leathery skin of his bearded face, the odd tattoos showing through the stubble of gray hair that peppered his skull, the dusty robes of a bright red shade that would be considered tawdry even by one of the low-rent male companions who did business in the Eastmyr district.

But when Xandra met the captive's eyes—which were as green and as hard as the finest malachite—the sneer melted from her lips. What she saw in those eyes stunned her: intelligence far beyond her expectations, pride, cunning, rage, and implacable hatred.

Hardly daring to hope, Xandra glanced at the man's hands. Yes, the wrists were crossed and bound together, the hands swathed in a thick cocoon of silken bandages. No doubt some of the fingers had been broken as well—

such precautions were only prudent when dealing with captive spellcasters. No matter. The powerful clerics of House Shobalar could heal such injuries soon enough.

"A wizard," she stated, keeping her voice carefully neutral.

"A *powerful* wizard," the merchant emphasized.

"We shall see," Xandra murmured. "Unbind him—I would test his skills."

Hadrogh, to his credit, didn't try to dissuade her. The merchant quickly unbound the human's hands. He even lit a pair of small candles, providing enough dim light so that the man could see.

The red-robed man flexed his fingers painfully. Xandra noted that the human's hands seemed stiff, but unharmed. She tossed an inquiring glare at the merchant.

"An amulet of containment," Hadrogh explained, pointing to the collar of gold that tightly encircled the man's neck. "It is a magical shield that keeps the wizard from casting any of the spells he has learned and committed to memory. He can, however, learn and cast new spells. His mind is intact, as are his remembered spells. As are his hands, for that matter. Admittedly, this is a costly method of transporting magically-gifted slaves, but my reputation demands that I deliver undamaged merchandise."

A rare smile broke across Xandra's face. She had never heard of such an arrangement, but it was ideally suited to her purposes.

Cunning, quickness of mind, and magical aptitude were the qualities she needed. If the human passed those tests, she could teach him what he needed to know. That his mind could be searched at some later time, and its store of magical knowledge plundered for her own use, was a bonus.

The drow quickly removed three small items from the bag at her waist and showed them to the watchful human. Slowly, she moved through the gestures and spoke the words of a simple spell. In response to her casting, a small globe of darkness settled over one of the candles, completely blotting out its light.

Xandra handed an identical set of spell components to the human.

"Now you," she commanded.

The red-clad wizard obviously understood what was expected of him. Pride and anger darkened his face, but only for a moment—the lure of an unlearned spell proved too strong for him to resist. Slowly, with painstaking care, he mirrored Xandra's gestures and mimicked her words. The second candle flickered, then dimmed. Its flame was still faintly visible through the gray fog surrounding it.

"The human shows promise," the Shobalar wizard admitted. It was unusual for any wizard to reproduce a spell—even imperfectly—without having seen and studied the magical symbols. "His pronunciation is deplorable, though, and will continue to hamper his progress. You wouldn't by chance have a wizard in stock who can speak Drowic? Or even Undercommon? Such would be easier to train."

Hadrogh bowed deeply and hurried out of sight. A moment later he returned, alone, but with one hand held palm-up and outstretched so that Xandra could see he had another solution to suggest. The faint light of the fog-shrouded candle glimmered on the two tiny silver earrings in his hand, each in the form of a half-circle.

"To translate speech," the merchant explained. "One pierces the ear, so that he might understand, the other his mouth, so that he might be understood. May I demonstrate?"

When Xandra nodded, the merchant lifted his empty hand and snapped his fingers twice.

Two half-orc guards hastened to his side. They seized the human wizard and held him fast while Hadrogh pressed the rings' tiny metal spikes through the man's earlobe and the left side of his upper lip. The human gave off a string of Drowic curses, predications so colorful and virulent that, astonishment and fear darkening his gray-skinned face, Hadrogh fell back a step.

Xandra laughed delightedly.

"How much?" she demanded.

The merchant named an enormous price, hastening to assure Xandra that the figure named included the magical collar and rings. The drow wizard rapidly estimated the cost of those items, added the potential worth of the spells she would steal from the human, and threw in the death of Liriel Baenre.

"A bargain," Xandra said with dark satisfaction.

CHAPTER 2
SHADES OF CRIMSON

Tresk Mulander paced the floor of his cell, his trailing scarlet robes whispering behind him. It had not been easy, persuading the mistress to provide him with the bright silk garments, but he was a Red Wizard and so he would remain, however far he might be from his native Thay.

Nearly two years had passed since Mulander had first encountered Xandra Shobalar and begun his strange apprenticeship. Though he had not once left the large chamber carved from solid rock, vented only by tiny openings in the ceiling well above his reach, he had not been badly treated. He had food and wine in plenty, whatever comforts he required, and, most importantly, an intense and thorough education in the magic of the Underdark. It was an opportunity that many of his peers would have seized without a qualm, and in truth, Mulander did not entirely regret his fate.

The Red Wizard was a necromancer, a powerful member of the Researcher faction—that group of wizards who sought ever stronger and more fearsome magic. Mulander was somewhat of an oddity among his peers, for he was one of a very few high-ranking wizards whose blood was not solely that of the ruling Mulan race.

His father's father had been Rashemi, and his inheritance from his grandsire was a thick, muscled body and a luxuriant crop of facial hair. From his wizard mother had come his talent and ambition, as well as the height and the sallow complexion that were considered marks of nobility in Thay.

Mulander's cold, gemlike green eyes and narrow scimitar nose lent him a terrifying aspect, and though he conformed to custom and affected baldness, he was rather vain of the thick, long gray beard that set him apart from the nearly hairless Mulan. In all, he was an imposing man, who carried his sixty winters with ease upon his broad, proud shoulders. He was strong of body, mind, and magic. The passing years had only served to thin his graying hair, which he regretted not at all, for it made the daily task of shaving his pate less onerous.

Mistress Shobalar had indulged him in that as well, providing him with incredibly keen-edged shaving gear and a halfling servant to do the honors. Indeed, the drow female seemed fascinated by the tattoos that covered Mulander's head. As well she should have been: each mark was a magical rune that, when activated with the appropriate spell, could transform bits of dead matter into fearsome magical servants. Provide him with a corpse, and he would produce an army. Or *could*, were he able to access his necromantic magic.

Mulander grimaced and slipped a finger under the gold collar that encircled his neck—and imprisoned his Art.

"In time, you will be permitted to remove that," said a cool voice behind him.

The Red Wizard jolted, then turned to face Xandra Shobalar. Even after two years, her sudden arrivals unnerved him, as they were no doubt intended to do.

But that day the implied promise in the drow's words banished his usual resentment.

"When?"

"In time," Xandra repeated. She strolled over to a deep chair and, in a leisurely fashion, seated herself. Two years was not a long time in the life of a drow, but she was obviously well aware of the human's impatience, and she intended to enjoy it.

Enjoyable, too, was the murderous rage, barely contained, in the Red Wizard's eyes.

Xandra entertained herself with fantasies of seeing that wrath unleashed upon her Baenre fosterling. At last, the long-anticipated day was nearly at hand.

"You have learned well," Xandra began. "Soon you will have a chance to test your newfound skills. Succeed, and the reward will be great."

The drow plucked a tiny golden key from her bodice and held it high. She cocked her head to one side and sent the Red Wizard a cold, taunting smile. Mulander's eyes widened with realization, then gleamed with an emotion that went far beyond greed. His intense, hungry gaze followed the key as Xandra slowly lowered it and tucked it back into its intimate hiding place.

"I see that you understand what this is. Would you like to know what you must do to earn it?" she asked.

A shudder of revulsion shimmered down the Red Wizard's spine. Xandra's smile widened and grew mocking.

"Not this time, dear Mulander," she purred. "I have another sort of adventure in mind for you."

She quickly described the rite of the Blooding, the ritual hunt that each young dark elf was required to undergo before being accounted a true drow. Mulander listened with growing dismay.

"And I am to be this prey?"

Anger flashed in Xandra's eyes like crimson fire.

"Do not be a fool," she snarled. "You must prevail! Would I have gone to such trouble and expense otherwise?"

"A spell battle . . ." he muttered, beginning to understand. "You have been preparing me for a spell battle. And the spells you have taught me?"

"They represent all the offensive spells your young opponent knows, as well as the appropriate counterspells." Xandra leaned forward, and her face was deadly serious. "You will not see me again. You will have a new tutor for perhaps thirty cycles of Narbondel. A battle wizard. He will work with you daily and instruct you in the tactics of drow warfare. Learn all he has to teach during the course of this session."

"For he will not live to give another lesson," Mulander reasoned.

Xandra smiled and said, "How astute. For a human, you possess a most promising streak of duplicity! But you are among drow, and you have much to learn about subtlety and treachery."

The wizard bristled.

"We in Thay are no strangers to treachery," he said. "No wizard could survive to my age, much less reach my position, without such skills."

"Really?" the drow asked, her voiced dripping with sarcasm. "If that is the case, how did you come to be here?"

Mulander responded only with a sullen glare, but the mistress of magic did not seem to require an answer.

"You possess a great deal of very interesting magic," she observed. "More than I would have guessed a human capable of wielding, and judging from your pride, more than most of your peers have achieved. How, then, could you have been overcome and sold into slavery, but by treachery?"

Not waiting for a response, Xandra rose from her chair.

"These are the terms I offer you," she said, her manner suddenly all business. "At the proper time, you will be taken into the wild tunnels surrounding this city—as part of your preparations, you will be given a map of the area to commit to memory. There you will confront a fledgling wizard, a drow female with golden eyes. She will carry the key that will release you from that collar. You must defeat her in spell battle—do whatever you must to ensure that she does not survive.

"You may then take the key from her body, and go wheresoever you will. The girl will be alone, and you will not be pursued. It may be that you can find your way to the World Above—if indeed there is still a place for you there. If not, with the spells I have taught you, as well as the return of your own death magic, you should be able to live and thrive in the Underdark."

Mulander listened stoically, carefully masking the sudden bright surge of hope the drow's words awoke in his heart. For all he knew, it could all be an elaborate trap, and he refused to display his elation for the wretched female's amusement.

Or did she perhaps expect him to show fear?

If that was the case, she would also be disappointed. He knew none. The Red Wizard did not for one moment doubt the outcome of the contest, for he knew the full measure of his powers, even if Xandra Shobalar did not.

He was more than capable of defeating an elf girl in spell battle—he would kill the little wench and set himself up in some hidden cavern of the underground world, a place surrounded by warding magic and misdirection spells that would keep even the powerful dark elves from his door.

This he would do, for the Shobalar wizard was right about one thing—there was no welcome awaiting Mulander in Thay, and no welcome for Red Wizards in any land other than Thay. Another of Xandra's thrusts had found its mark, as well: he had indeed been undone through treachery. Mulander had been betrayed by his young apprentice, as he himself had betrayed his own master. It occurred to him, suddenly, to wonder what treachery Xandra's young prodigy might have in store for her mistress.

"You are smiling," the drow observed. "My terms are to your liking?"

"Very much so," Mulander said, thinking it prudent to keep his fantasies to himself.

"Then let me add to your enjoyment," Xandra said softly.

She advanced upon the man and reached up to place one slim black hand against his jaw. His instinctive flinch, and his effort to disguise the response, seemed to amuse her. She swayed closer, her slim body just barely brushing against his robes. Her crimson eyes burned up into his, and Mulander felt a tendril of compelling magic creep into his mind.

"Tell me truly, Mulander," she said—and her words were mocking, for they both knew that the spell she cast upon him would allow him to speak nothing but truth, "do you hate me so very much?"

Mulander held her gaze.

"With all my soul," he vowed, with more passion than he had ever before displayed—more than he knew he possessed.

"Good," Xandra breathed. She raised both arms high and clasped her hands behind his neck; then she floated upward until her eyes were on a level with the much taller man. "Then remember my face as you hunt the girl, and remember this."

The drow pressed her lips to Mulander's in a macabre parody of a kiss. Her passion was like his: it was all hatred and pride.

Her kiss, like many that he himself had forced upon the youths and maidens apprenticed to him, was a claim of total ownership, a gesture of cruelty and utter contempt that was more painful to the proud man than a dagger's thrust. He winced when the drow's teeth sank deep into his lower lip.

Xandra abruptly released him and floated away, suspended in the air like a dark wraith and smiling coldly as she wiped a drop of his blood from her mouth.

"Remember," she admonished him, and she vanished as suddenly as she had come.

Left alone in his cell, Tresk Mulander nodded grimly. He would long remember Xandra Shobalar, and for as long as he lived he would pray to every dark god whose name he knew that her death would be slow and painful and ignominious.

In the meanwhile, he would vent some of his seething hatred upon the other drow wench who presumed to look upon him—him, a Red Wizard and a master of necromancy!—as prey.

"Let the hunt begin," Mulander said, and his bloodied lips curved in a grim smile as he savored the secret he had hoarded from Xandra Shobalar—a secret he would soon unleash upon her young student.

CHAPTER 3
A GRAND ADVENTURE

The door of Bythnara Shobalar's bedchamber thudded solidly against the wall, flung open with an exuberance that could herald only one person. Bythnara did not look up from the book she was reading, did not so much as flinch. She was too accustomed to the irrepressible Baenre brat to show much of a reaction.

But it was impossible to ignore Liriel for long. The dark elf maid spun into their shared bedchamber, her arms out wide and her wild mane of white hair flying as she whirled and leaped in an ecstatic little dance.

The older girl eyed her with resignation.

"Who cast a dervish spell on you?" she inquired in a sour tone.

Liriel abruptly halted her dance and flung her arms around her chambermate.

"Oh, Bythnara!" Liriel said. "I am to undergo the Blooding ritual at last! Mistress just said."

The Shobalar female disentangled herself as inconspicuously as possible as she rose from her chair, and she looked around for some pretense that would excuse her for wriggling out of the younger girl's impulsive embrace. On the far side of the room, a pair of woolen trews lay crumpled on the floor. Liriel tended to treat her clothes with the same blithe disregard that a snake shows its outgrown and abandoned skin. Bythnara was forever picking up after the untidy little wench. Doing so then allowed her to put as much space as possible between herself and the unwanted affection lavished upon her by her young rival.

"And high time it is," the Shobalar wizard-in-training said bluntly as she smoothed and folded the discarded garment. "You will soon be eighteen, and you are already well into your Ascharlexten Decade. I've often wondered why my Mistress Mother has waited so long."

"As have I," Liriel said frankly. "But Xandra explained it to me. She said that she could not initiate the rite until she had found exactly the right quarry, one that would truly test my skills. Think of it! A grand and gallant hunt—an adventure in the wild tunnels of the Dark Dominion!" she exulted, flinging herself down on her cot with a gusty sigh of satisfaction.

"Mistress Xandra," Bythnara coldly corrected her.

She knew, as did everyone in House Shobalar, that Liriel Baenre was to be treated with utmost respect, but even the archmage's daughter was required to observe certain protocols.

"Mistress Xandra," the girl echoed obligingly. She rolled over onto her stomach and propped up her chin in both hands. "I wonder what I shall hunt," she said in a dreamy tone. "There are so many wondrous and fearsome beasts roaming the World Above. I have been reading about them," she confided with a grin. "Maybe a great wild cat with a black-and-gold striped pelt, or a huge brown bear—which is rather like a four-legged quaggoth. Or even a fire-belching dragon!" she concluded, giggling a bit at her own absurdity.

"We can only hope," Bythnara muttered.

If Liriel heard her chambermate's bitter comment, she gave no indication.

"Whatever the quarry, I shall meet it with equal force," she vowed. "I will use weapons that correspond to its natural attacks and defenses: dagger against claw, arrow against stooping attack. No fireballs, no venom clouds, no transforming it into an ebony statue . . ."

"You know that spell?" the Shobalar demanded, her face and voice utterly aghast.

It was a casting that required considerable power, an irreversible transformation, and a favorite punitive tool of the Baenre priestesses who ruled in the Academy. The possibility that the impulsive child could wield such a spell was appalling, considering that Bythnara had insulted the Baenre girl twice since she'd entered the room. By the standards of Menzoberranzan, that was more than ample justification for such retribution.

But Liriel merely tossed her chambermate a mischievous grin. The older wizard sniffed and turned away. She had known Liriel for twelve years, but she had never reconciled herself to the girl's good-natured teasing.

Liriel loved to laugh, and she loved to have others laugh with her. Since few drow shared her particular brand of humor, she had recently taken to playing little pranks for the amusement of the other students.

Bythnara had never been the recipient of those, but neither did she find them particularly enjoyable. Life was a grim, serious business, and magic an Art to be mastered, not a child's plaything. The fact that that particular "child" possessed a command of magic greater than her own rankled deeply with the proud female.

Nor was that the only thing stoking Bythnara's jealously. Mistress Xandra, Bythnara's own mother, had always showed special favor to the Baenre girl—favor that often bordered on affection. That, Bythnara would never forget, and never forgive. Neither was she pleased by the fact that her own male companions had a hard time remembering their place and their purpose whenever the golden-eyed wench was about.

Bythnara was twenty-eight and in ripe early adolescence. Liriel was in many ways still a child. Even so, there was more than enough promise in the girl's face and form to draw masculine eyes. Rumor had it that Liriel was beginning to return those attentions, and that she reveled in such sport with her characteristic, playful abandon. That, too, Bythnara disapproved of, though exactly why that was, she could not say.

"Will you come to my coming-of-age ceremony?" Liriel asked with a touch of wistfulness in her voice. "After the ritual, I mean."

"Of course. It is required."

Bythnara's curt remark finally earned a response—an almost imperceptible wince. But Liriel recovered quickly, so quickly that the older female barely had time to enjoy her victory. A shuttered expression came over the Baenre girl's face, and she lifted one shoulder in a casual shrug.

"So it is," she said evenly. "I faintly remember that I was required to attend yours, several years back. What was your quarry?"

"A goblin," Bythnara said stiffly.

It was a sore spot with her, for goblins were as a rule accounted neither intelligent nor particularly dangerous. She had dispatched the creature easily enough with a spell of holding and a sharp knife. Her own Blooding had been mere routine, not the grand adventure of which Liriel dreamed.

Grand adventure, indeed! The girl was impossibly naive!

Or was she? With a sudden jolt, it occurred to Bythnara that Liriel's last question had hardly been ingenuous. Few verbal thrusts could have hit the mark more squarely. Her eyes settled on the girl and narrowed dangerously.

Again Liriel shrugged.

"What was it that Matron Hinkutes'nat said in chapel a darkcycle or two past? 'The drow culture is one of constant change, and so we must either adapt or die.' "

Her tone was light, and there was nothing in her face or her words that could give Bythnara reasonable cause for complaint. Yet Liriel was clearly, subtly, giving notice that she had long been aware of Bythnara's verbal thrusts, and that henceforth she would not take them in silence, but parry and riposte.

It was well done; Bythnara had to admit that. She found herself at a complete and disconcerting lack for words.

A tentative knock on the open door relieved Bythnara of the need to respond.

She turned to face one of her mother's servants, a highly decorative young drow male discarded by some lesser house. In perfunctory fashion, he offered the required bow to the Shobalar female, and turned his attention upon the younger girl.

"You are wanted, Princess," the male said, addressing Liriel by the proper formal title for a young female of the First House.

Later, the girl would no doubt be accorded more prestigious titles: Archmage, if Xandra had her way, or Mistress of Sorcere, or Mistress of the Academy, or even—Lolth forbid—Matron Mother. Princess was a title of birth, not accomplishment. Even so, Bythnara begrudged it. She hustled the royal brat and the handsome messenger out of her room with scant ceremony and closed the door firmly behind them.

Liriel's shoulders rose and fell in a long sigh. The servant, who was about her own age and who knew Bythnara far better than he cared to, cast her a look that bordered on sympathy.

"What does Xandra want now?" she asked as they made their way toward the apartment that housed the mistress of magic.

The servant cast furtive glances up and down the corridors before answering, "The archmage sent for you. His servant awaits you in Mistress Xandra's chambers even now."

Liriel stopped in mid stride.

"My father?"

"Gromph Baenre, Archmage of Menzoberranzan," the male affirmed.

Once again Liriel reached for "the mask"—her private term for the expression she had practiced and perfected in front of her looking glass: the insouciant little smile, eyes that expressed nothing but a bit of cynical amusement. Yet behind her flippant facade, the girl's mind whirled with a thousand questions.

Drow life was full of complexities and contradictions, but in Liriel's experience, nothing was more complicated than her feelings for her drow sire. She revered and resented and adored and feared and hated and longed for her father—all at once, and all from a distance. And as far as Liriel could tell, every one of those emotions was entirely unrequited. The great Archmage of Menzoberranzan was an utter mystery to her.

Gromph Baenre was without question her true sire, but drow lineage was traced through the females. The archmage had gone against custom and adopted his daughter into the Baenre clan—at great personal cost to Liriel—and promptly abandoned her to the Shobalars' care.

What could Gromph Baenre want of her? It had been years since she had heard from him, though his servants regularly saw that the Shobalars were recompensed for her keep and training and ensured that she had pocket coin to spend at her infrequent outings to the Bazaar. In Liriel's opinion, the personal summons could only mean trouble. Yet what had she done? Or, more to the point, which of her escapades had been discovered and reported?

Then a new possibility occurred to her, one so full of hope and promise that "the mask" dissipated like spent faerie fire. A bubble of joyous laughter burst from the dark elf maid, and she threw her arms around the astonished—and highly gratified—young male.

After the Blooding, she would be accounted a true drow! Perhaps then Gromph would deem her worthy of his attention, perhaps even take over her training himself. Surely he had heard of her progress, and knew that there was little more for her to learn in House Shobalar.

That must be it! concluded Liriel as she wriggled out of the servant's increasingly enthusiastic embrace.

She set out at a brisk pace for Xandra's chambers, spurred on by the rarest of all drow emotions: hope.

No dark elf male took much notice of his children, but soon Liriel would be a child no more, and ready for the next level of magical training. Usually that would involve the Academy, but she was far too young for that. Surely Gromph had devised another plan for her future.

Liriel's shining anticipation dimmed at the sight of her father's messenger: the elf-sized stone golem was only too familiar. The magical construct was part of her earliest and most terrible memory. Yet even the appearance of the deadly messenger could not banish entirely her joy, or silence the delightful possibility that sang through her heart: perhaps her father wanted her at last!

At Xandra's insistence, a full octet patrol of spider-mounted soldiers escorted Liriel and the golem to the fashionable Narbondellyn district, where Gromph Baenre kept a private home. For once, Liriel rode past the Dark-spires without marveling at the fanglike formations of black rock. For once, she did not notice the handsome captain of the guard, who stood watch at the gates of the Horlbar compound. She even passed by the elegant little shops that sold perfumes, whisper-soft silk garments, magical figurines, and other fascinating wares without sparing them a single longing glance.

What were such things, compared with even a moment of her father's time?

As eager as she was, however, Liriel had to steel herself for the first glimpse of Gromph Baenre's mansion. She had been born there, and had spent the first five years of her life in the luxurious apartments of her mother, Sosdrielle Vandree, who had served for many years as Gromph's mistress. It had been a cozy world, just Liriel and her mother and the few servants who tended them. Liriel had since come to understand that Sosdrielle—who had been a rare beauty, but who lacked both the magical talent and the deadly ambition needed to excel in Menzoberranzan—had doted upon her child and had made Liriel the beloved center of her world. Despite that, or perhaps because of it, Liriel had not been able to bring herself to look upon her first home since the day she left it, more than twelve years before.

Carved from the heart of an enormous stalactite, the archmage's private home was reputedly warded about with more magic than any other two wizards in the city could muster between them. Liriel slid down from her spider mount—a distinctively Shobalar means of conveyance—and followed the silent and deadly golem toward the black structure.

The stone golem touched one of the moving runes that writhed and shifted on the dark wall, and a door appeared. Gesturing for Liriel to follow, the golem disappeared inside.

The young drow took a deep breath and fell in behind the servant. She remembered, vaguely, the way to Gromph Baenre's private study. There she had first met her father, and had first discovered her talent for and love of wizardry. It seemed fitting that she begin the next phase of her life there, as well.

Gromph Baenre looked up when she entered his study. His amber eyes, so like her own, regarded her coolly.

"Sit down," he invited her, gesturing with one elegant, long-fingered hand toward a chair. "We have much to discuss."

Liriel quietly did as she was told. The archmage did not speak at once, and for a long moment she was content merely to study him. He looked exactly as she remembered: austere yet handsome, a drow male in his magnificent prime. That was not surprising, considering how slowly dark elves aged, yet Gromph was reputed to have witnessed the birth and death of seven centuries.

Protocol demanded that Liriel wait for the high-ranking wizard to speak first, but after several silent moments she could bear no more.

"I am to undergo the Blooding," she announced with pride.

The archmage nodded somberly and said, "As I have heard. You will remain here in my home until the time for the ritual, for there is much to learn and little time for preparation."

Liriel's brows plunged into a frown of puzzlement. Had she not been doing just that for the past twelve years? Had she not gained basic but powerful skills in battle magic and drow weaponry? She had little interest in the sword, but no one she knew could out-shoot her with the hand crossbow, or best her with thrown weapons. Surely she knew enough to emerge from the ritual with victorious and blooded hands.

A small, hard smile touched the archmage's lips when he said, "There is much more to being a drow than engaging in crude slaughter. I am not entirely certain, however, that Xandra Shobalar remembers this basic fact."

These cryptic words troubled Liriel.

"Sir?"

Gromph did not bother to explain himself. He reached into a compartment under his desk and took from it a small, green bottle.

"This is a vial of holding," he said. "It will capture and store any creature that the Shobalar Mistress pits against you."

"But the hunt!" Liriel protested.

The archmage's smile did not waver, but his eyes turned cold.

"Do not be a fool," he said softly. "If the hunt turns against you and your quarry gains the upper hand, you will capture it in this vial. You can spill its blood easily enough, and thus fulfill the letter of the ritual's requirements. Look. . . ."

He twisted off the stopper and showed her the glistening mithral needle that thrust down from it.

"Cap the vial, and you have slain your prey. All you need do is smash the vial, and the dead creature will lie before you, a dagger—the transmuted needle, of course—thrust through its heart or into its eye. You will carry an identical dagger to the opening ceremony, of course, to forestall any possible inquiries into the weapon that caused the creature's death. This dagger is magical and will dissipate when the mithral needle is blooded, to remove the possibility that it might be found discarded along your path. If pride is your concern, no one need know the manner of your quarry's death."

Feeling oddly betrayed, Liriel took the glass bottle and pressed the stopper firmly back into place. In truth, she found the unsporting solution appalling. But since the vial was a gift from her father, she searched her mind for something positive to say.

"Mistress Xandra will be fascinated by this," she offered in a dull voice, knowing well the Shobalar wizard's fondness for magical devices of any kind.

"She must not know of the vial, or of any of the spells you will learn in this place. Nor does she need to hear of your other, more dubious skills. Please, save that look of wide-eyed innocence to beguile the House guards," he said dryly. "I know only too well the mercenary captain who boasts he taught a princess to throw knives as well as any tavern cutthroat alive. How you managed to slip past the guard spiders Matron Hinkutes'nat posts at every turn, and find your way through the city to that particular tavern, is beyond my imagination."

Liriel grinned wickedly and said, "I stumbled upon the tavern that first time, and Captain Jarlaxle knew me by my House medallion and indulged my wish to learn . . . to learn many things. But it is true that I have often fooled the spiders. Shall I tell you how?"

"Perhaps later. I must have your blood oath that this vial will be kept from Xandra's eyes."

"But why?" she persisted, truly perplexed by this demand.

Gromph studied his daughter for a long time.

"How many young drow die during the Blooding?" he asked at last.

"A few," Liriel admitted. "Surface raids often go wrong—the humans or faerie elves sometimes learn of the attack in time to prepare, or they fight better than expected, or in larger numbers. And it is likely that from time to time a drow dagger slips between a youngling's ribs. In those rites that are taken Below, sometimes initiates become lost in the wild Underdark, or stumble upon some monster that is beyond their skill with magic and weapons."

"And sometimes, they are slain by the very things they hunt," Gromph said.

That was a given. The girl shrugged, as if to ask what the point was.

"I do not desire to see any harm come to you. Xandra Shobalar may not share my good wishes," he said bluntly.

Liriel suddenly went cold. Many emotions simmered and danced deep within her, waiting for her to reach in and pluck one free—yet she truly felt none of them. Her tumultuous responses remained just beyond her touch, for she had no idea which one to choose.

How could Gromph suggest that Xandra Shobalar could betray her? The mistress of magic had raised her, lavishing more attention and indulgent favor upon her than most drow younglings ever dreamed of receiving. Apart from her own mother—who had given Liriel not only life, but a wonderful five-year cocoon of warmth, security, and even love—Liriel believed that Xandra was the person most responsible for making her what she was. And that was saying a great deal. Though Liriel could not remember her mother's face, she understood that she had received from Sosdrielle Vandree something that was rare among her kindred, something that nothing and no one could take from her. Not even Gromph Baenre, who had ordered her beloved mother's death twelve years before.

Liriel stared at her father, too dumbfounded to realize that her churning thoughts were written clearly in her eyes.

"You do not trust me," the archmage stated in a voice absolutely devoid of emotion. "This is good—I was beginning to despair of your judgment. It may be that you will survive this ritual, after all. Now listen carefully as I describe the steps needed to activate the vial of holding."

CHAPTER 4
THE BLOODING

The Blooding ritual took place on the third darkcycle after Liriel's meeting with her father. She was returned to House Shobalar as the day grew old, for all such rituals began at the dark hour of Narbondel.

When the great timepiece of Menzoberranzan dimmed to mark the hour of midnight, Liriel stood before Hinkutes'nat Alar Shobalar, the matron mother of the clan.

The young drow had had few dealings with the Shobalar matriarch, and she felt slightly unnerved by the dark and regal figure before her.

Hinkutes'nat was a high priestess of Lolth, as befitted a ruling matron, and she was typical of those who followed the ways of the drow's goddess, the Spider Queen. Her throne room was as grim and forbidding a lair as anything Liriel had ever seen. Shadows were everywhere, for the skulls of many Shobalar victims had been fashioned into faintly glowing lanterns that threw patterns of death upon every surface and cast ghastly purple highlights upon the dark faces assembled before the matron's throne.

A large cage stood in the middle of the chamber, ready to receive the prey for the Blooding ceremony. It was surrounded on all four sides by the giant, magically bred spiders that formed the heart of the Shobalar guard. In fact, giant spiders stood guard everywhere—in every corner of the chamber, on each of the steps that led up to the throne dais, even suspended from the chamber's ceiling on long, glistening threads.

The throne room was a fit setting for the Shobalar matriarch. The matron resembled a spider holding court in the center of her own web.

She wore a black robe upon which webs had been embroidered in silver thread, and the gaze that she turned upon Liriel was as calm and pitiless as that of any arachnid that had ever lived. She was spiderlike in character, as well: even among the treacherous drow, the Shobalar matron had earned a reputation for the tangled nature of the deals she spun.

"You have prepared the prey?" the matron inquired of her third-born daughter.

"I have," Xandra said. "The youngling drow who stands before you shows great promise, as one would expect of a daughter of House Baenre. To offer her less than a true challenge would be an insult to the First House."

Matron Hinkutes'nat lifted one eyebrow.

"I see," she said dryly. "Well, that is your prerogative, and within the rules set for the Blooding ritual. It is unlikely that recourse will be taken, but you understand that you will bear the brunt of any unpleasantness that might result?" When Xandra nodded grim acceptance, the matron mother again turned to Liriel. "And you, Princess, are you ready to begin?"

The Baenre girl dipped into a deep bow, doing her best to dim her shining eyes and school her face into expressionless calm.

Three days in Gromph's household had not quite destroyed her eagerness for adventure.

"This, then, will be your prey," Mistress Xandra said.

She lifted both arms high, and brought them down to her sides in a quick sweep. A faint crackle vibrated through the damp and heavy air of the chamber, and the bars of the cage flared with sudden fey light. Every eye in the room turned to behold the ritual quarry.

Liriel's heart pounded with excitement—she was certain that everyone could hear it. The light surrounding the cage faded, and she was equally sure that all could feel the hard, cold hand that gripped her chest and muffled its restless rhythm.

Within the cage stood a human male garbed in robes of bright red. Liriel had seldom encountered humans and had few thoughts concerning them, but suddenly she found that she had no desire to slaughter that one. He was too elflike, too much like a real person.

"This is an outrage," she said in a low, angry voice. "I was led to believe that my Blooding would be a test of skill and courage, a hunt involving some dangerous surface creature, such as a boar or a hydra."

"If you misunderstood the nature of the Blooding, it was through no fault of mine," Mistress Xandra retorted. "For years you have heard tales of surface raids. What did you think were slain—cattle? Prey is prey, whether it has two legs or four. You have attended the ceremonies; you know what has been required of those who have gone before you."

"I will not do this thing," Liriel said with a regal hauteur that would have done justice to Matron Mother Baenre herself.

"You have no choice in the matter," Matron Hinkutes'nat pointed out. "It is the part of the mistress or matron to chose the prey, and to name the terms of the hunt.

"Proceed," she said, turning to her daughter.

Mistress Xandra permitted herself a smile and said, "The human wizard—for such he is—will be transported to a cavern in the Dark Dominions that lie to the southwest of Menzoberranzan. You, Liriel Baenre, will be escorted to a nearby tunnel. You must hunt and destroy the human, using any weapon at your disposal. Ten dark-cycles you have to accomplish this. We will not seek you before this time is up.

"But you must take this key," Xandra continued as she handed a tiny golden object to the girl. "I have strung it upon a chain. Keep it on your person at all times. It is not our purpose that you come to grief: with this key, you can summon immediate aid from House Shobalar, should the need arise.

"You have much talent, and you have been well trained," the mistress added in a less severe tone. "We have every confidence in your success."

The older female's apparent concern for her well-being gave Liriel a glimmer of hope.

"Mistress, I cannot slay this wizard," she said in a despairing whisper, letting her eyes speak clearly of her distress.

Surely Xandra, who had trained and fostered her, would understand how she felt and would lift the burden from her.

"You will kill, or you will be killed," the Shobalar wizard proclaimed. "That is the challenge of the Blooding, and it is the reality of drow life."

Xandra's voice was cold and even, but Liriel did not miss the glint in the wizard's red eyes. Stunned and enlightened, Liriel stared at her trusted mentor.

Kill or be killed. There could be little doubt which outcome Xandra preferred.

Liriel tore her gaze away from the vindictive crimson stare and did her best to attend to the ceremony that followed. As she stood silently through the matron's ritual blessing, the girl was struck by a strange and very vivid mental image: somewhere deep within her heart, a tiny light flickered and died—a harbinger, perhaps, of darkness to come. A moment of inexplicable sadness touched Liriel, but it was gone before she could marvel at so strange an emotion. To a young dark elf, such a vision seemed right and fitting—a cause for elation rather than regret. Soon, very soon, she would be a true drow indeed!

CHAPTER 5
KILL OR BE KILLED

On silent feet, Liriel eased her way down the dark tunnel. One of the gifts her father had given her were boots of elvenkind, wondrous treasures crafted of soft leather and dark elven magic. With them, she could walk with no more noise than her own shadow.

She also wore a fine new cloak—not a *piwafwi*, for that uniquely drow cloak was usually worn only by those who had proven themselves by that very ritual. Of course, there were exceptions to that rule, and Liriel did indeed possess one of the magical cloaks of conceal-ment—it played a significant role in her frequent escapes from House Shobalar—but youngling dark elves were not permitted to wear them during the Blooding. The advantage of invisibility removed most of the chal-lenge, and was therefore deemed inappropriate for the first major kill.

Thus Liriel was plainly visible to the perceptive eyes of the Underdark's many strange and deadly creatures, and therefore in constant danger.

The young drow kept keenly alert as she walked. Yet her heart was not in the hunt. She was not entirely cer-tain she still had a heart: grief and rage had left her feel-ing strangely hollow.

Liriel was accustomed to betrayals both large and small, and she was still trying to assimilate her realiza-tion that she must shrug them off and move ahead—albeit with caution. So it had been with Bythnara, whose snippy comments and small jealousies had once pained her deeply. So it had been even with her father, who twelve years earlier had wronged Liriel more deeply than any other person had before or since.

But it would not be so with Xandra Shobalar, Liriel vowed grimly. Xandra's betrayal was different, and it would not go unremarked—or unavenged.

Vengeance was the principle passion of the dark elves, but it was an emotion new to Liriel. She savored it as if it was a goblet of the spiced green wine she had recently tasted—bitter, certainly, but capable of sharpening the passions and hardening resolve. Liriel was very young, and willing to accept and overlook many things in her dark elf kindred. But for the first time, had seen the desire for her death written in another drow's eyes. Liriel understood instinctively that it could not go unpunished if she herself hoped to survive.

But at a deeper, even more personal level, the girl bitterly resented Xandra for forcing her to disregard her own instincts and act against her will.

Liriel rebelled bitterly against the need to submit to her mistress's demands, yet what else could she do if she was to be accounted a true drow?

What else, indeed?

A smile slowly crept over Liriel's dark face as a solution to her dilemma began to take shape in her mind. There was much more to being a drow, her father had admonished her, than engaging in crude slaughter.

The painful weight on the young drow's chest lifted a bit, and for the first time she realized a very strange thing: she did not fear the dreaded wild Underdark. It seemed to her that the wilderness was a wondrous, fascinating place full of unexpected turns and twists. There was danger and adventure and excitement in the very air and stone. Unlike Menzoberranzan, where every bit of rock had been shaped and carved into a monument to the pride and might of the drow, out there everything was new, mysterious, and full of delightful possibilities. There she could carve out her own place. Liriel fell suddenly, deeply, and utterly in love with the vast and untamed Underdark.

"A grand adventure," she said softly, repeating without a trace of irony the words of her own discarded dream. A sudden smile brightened her face, and as she bestowed an affectionate pat upon an enormous, down-thrust spire of rock, she added, "The first of many!"

Without warning, a bright ball of force rounded the sharp corner of the tunnel ahead and hurtled toward her.

The battle had begun.

Training and instinct took over at once. Liriel snapped both hands up, wrists crossed and palms out. A field of resistance sprung up before her an instant before the fireball would have struck. The girl squeezed her eyes shut and tossed her head to one side as the brilliant light exploded into a sheet of magical flame.

Liriel dropped flat and rolled aside, as she'd been taught to do in such attacks. The magical shield could not withstand more than one or two impacts of such power, and it was prudent to get out of the line of fire. To her astonishment, the second blast came in low and hard—and directly toward her. Liriel leaped to her feet and dived for the far side of the tunnel. She managed to put the large stalagmite between herself and the coming blast.

The explosion rocked the tunnel and sent a shower of rock fragments cascading down upon the young drow. She coughed and spat dust, but her fingers darted undeterred through the gestures of a spell.

In response to her magic, the dust and the sulfurous smoke swirled to a central spot of the tunnel and gathered into a large globe. Liriel pointed grimly in the direction of the unseen wizard, and the floating globe obediently rounded the corner toward its prey.

She waited, hardly daring to breathe, for the next attack to come. When it did not, she began to creep slowly and cautiously around the bend. There was no sound in the tunnel ahead, other than the distant drip of water. That was promising: the globe of hot, smoky vapor had been enspelled to seek out and surround its source of origin. If all had gone well, the human wizard would have been smothered by the sulfurous by-products of his own fireball. Liriel picked up her pace. If that was so, she would have a limited amount of time to find and revive him.

The tunnel grew ever brighter as she made her way down its twisting length. The path dipped dramatically, and Liriel saw laid out before her a cavern stranger than any she had ever seen or imagined.

Luminous fungi covered much of the stone and filled the entire cave with a faint, eerie blue glow. Stalagmites and stalactites met in long, irregular pillars of stone, and large crystals embedded in them tossed off glittering shards of light that stabbed at her eyes like tiny daggers.

A brilliant ball of light flashed into being in the center of the cavern. Liriel reeled back, clutching at her blinded eyes. Her keen ears caught the whine and hiss of an approaching missile; she dropped flat as yet another fireball blazed toward her.

The fireball missed her, but barely. Heat assailed Liriel with searing pain as it passed over her, and the smoke and stench of her own scorched hair assaulted her like a blow to the gut. Coughing and gagging, she rolled aside. She blinked rapidly as she went, trying to dispel the lingering sparks and flashes that obscured her vision.

Think, think! she admonished herself. So far she had only reacted: along that path lay certain defeat.

To give herself a bit of time, Liriel called upon her innate drow magic and dropped a globe of darkness over the magic light ahead of her. That leveled the field of battle, but it did not steal the human wizard's visual advantages: there was still plenty of light in the cavern to allow him to see. She had not yet seen him, however.

A suspicion that had taken root in Liriel's mind with the wizard's first attack blossomed into certainty. He had anticipated her responses; he seemed to know precisely how she would react. Perhaps he had been trained to know. Setting her jaw in grim determination, Liriel set out to learn just how well he'd been prepared.

Her hands flashed through the gestures of a spell that Gromph had taught her—a rare and difficult spell that few drow knew of and fewer still could master. It had taken her the better part of a day to learn it, but the effort was repaid in full.

Standing in the center of the cavern, ringed and partially shielded by a circle of stone pillars, stood the human. A stunned expression crossed his bearded face as he regarded his own outstretched hands. The reason for that was all too apparent: a *piwafwi*, which should have granted him magical invisibility, hung in glittering folds over his red-robed shoulders. He had not only been prepared, but equipped.

The human wizard recovered quickly from his surprise. He drew in a deep breath and spat in Liriel's direction. A dark bolt shot from his mouth, then another. The drow's eyes widened as she beheld the two live vipers wriggling toward her with preternatural speed.

Liriel pulled two small knives from her belt and flicked them toward the nearest snake. Her blades tumbled end-over-end, crossing the viper's neck from either side and neatly slicing the head from its body.

The beheaded length of snake writhed and looped for several moments, blocking the second viper's path long enough for Liriel to get off a second volley.

She threw only one knife. The blade plunged into the viper's open mouth and exploded out the back of its head with a bright burst of gore. Liriel allowed herself a small, grim smile, and she resolved to properly thank the mercenary who'd taught her to throw.

It was a moment's delay, but even that much was too long. Already the human wizard's hands were moving through the gestures of a spell—a familiar spell.

Liriel tore a tiny dart from her weapons belt and spat upon it. In response to her unspoken command, the other needed spell component—a tiny vial of acid—rose from her open spell bag. She seized it and tossed both items into the air. Her fingers flashed through the casting, and at once a luminous streak flew to answer the one flashing toward her. The acid bolts collided midway between the combatants, sending a spray of deadly green droplets sizzling off into the cavern.

The human flung out one hand. Magic darted from each of his fingertips, spinning out into a giant web as it flew. The weird blue light of the cavern glimmered along the strands and turned the sticky droplets clinging to them into gemlike things that rivaled moonstones and pearls. Liriel marveled at the web's deadly beauty, even as it descended upon her.

A word from the drow conjured a score of giant spiders, each as large as a rothé calf. On eldritch threads, the arachnid army rose as one toward the cavern's ceiling, capturing the web and taking it with them.

Liriel planted her feet wide and sent a barrage of fireballs toward the persistent human. As she expected, he cast the spell that would raise a field of resistance around himself. She recognized the gestures and the words of power as High Drow. The wizard had indeed been trained for their battle, and trained well.

Unfortunately for Liriel, the human had been schooled *too* well. She'd hoped that her fireball storm would weaken the stone pillars surrounding the wizard, so that they might crumble and fall upon him after the magic shield's power was spent. But it soon became apparent that he had placed the magical barrier in front of the stone formation, thereby undoing her strategy. His shield did not give way before her magic missiles, rather it seemed to absorb their energy. It grew ever brighter with each fireball that struck. It was a drow counterspell, but it was one that she herself had never been taught.

Finally Liriel lowered her hands, drained by the sheer power of the fireballs she had tossed into Xandra's magical web—and the knowledge of the full extent of the Shobalar wizard's treachery.

The human had been trained in the magic and tactics of Underdark warfare and moreover, he knew enough about his drow opponent to anticipate and counter her every spell. He had been carefully chosen and prepared—not to test her, but to kill her. Xandra Shobalar did not content herself with wishing for her student's failure: she had planned for it.

Liriel knew that she had been well and thoroughly betrayed. Her only hope of defeating the human—and Xandra Shobalar—lay not in her battle magic, but in her wits.

Liriel's nimble mind flashed through the possibilities. She knew nothing of human magic, but she found it highly suspicious that the wizard cast only drow spells. He had to have had prior training in order to master such powerful magic; surely he possessed spells of his own. Why did he not use them? As she studied the human, the reason for that became apparent. Her fingers closed around the key that Xandra had given her, and with one sharp tug she tore it from the thin golden chain she'd tied to her belt.

Wrath burned bright in Liriel's golden eyes as she reached for the green vial her father had given her. She pulled off the stopper and dropped the key inside. But before she put the cap back into place, she snapped off the mithral needle and tossed it aside.

Kill or be killed, Mistress Xandra had said.

So be it.

CHAPTER 6
RECURRING NIGHTMARES

Tresk Mulander squinted through his glowing shield toward the shimmering image of his young drow opponent. So far, all had gone as anticipated. The girl was good, just as Mistress Shobalar had claimed. She even had a few unanticipated skills, such as her deadly aim with a tossed knife.

Well enough. Mulander had a few surprises of his own.

It was true that Xandra Shobalar had raped his mind, plundered his vast mental store of necromantic spells. There was one spell, however, that the drow wizard could not touch: it was stored not in his mind, but in his flesh.

Mulander was a Researcher, always seeking new magic where lesser men saw only death. Moldering corpses, even the offal of the slaughterhouse, could be used to create wondrous and fearsome creatures. But his strangest and most secret creation was waiting to be unleashed.

In a bit of unliving flesh—a tiny dark mole that clung to his body by the thinnest tendril of skin, he had stored a creature of great power. To bring it into existence, he had only to make that final separation from his living body.

The wizard worked his thumb and forefinger beneath the golden collar. The enspelled mole was hidden beneath the magical fetter.

Mulander twisted off the bit of flesh, reveling in the sharp stab of pain—for such was a miniature death, and death was the ultimate source of his power. He tossed the tiny mole to the cavern floor and watched with sharp anticipation as the contained monster took shape.

Many of the Red Wizards could create darkenbeasts, fearsome flying creatures made by twisting the bodies of living animals into magical atrocities. Mulander had gone one better. The creature that rose up before him had been fashioned from his own flesh and his own nightmares.

Mulander had begun with the most dreadful thing he knew—a replica of his long-dead wizard mother—and added to it enormous size and the deadliest features of every predator that ever had haunted his dreams. The tattered, batlike wings of an abyssal denizen sprouted from the creature's shoulders, and a raptor's talons curved from its human hands. The thing had vampiric fangs, the haunches and hind legs of a dire wolf, and a wyvern's poisoned tail. Plates of dragonlike armor—in Red Wizard crimson, of course—covered its feminine torso. Only the eyes, the same hard green as his own, had been left untouched. Those eyes settled upon the drow girl—the hunter who had become prey—and they filled with a brand of malice that was only too familiar to Mulander. An involuntary shiver ran through the powerful wizard who had summoned the monster, a response engraved upon his soul by his own wretched, long-gone childhood.

The monster crouched. Its wolflike feet tamped down, and the muscles of its powerful haunch bunched in preparation for the spring. Mulander did not bother to dispel the magical shield. The monster retained enough of a resemblance to his mother for him to enjoy its roar of pain as the force field shattered upon impact.

Enjoyable, too, was the wide-eyed shock on the face of the young drow. She regained her composure with admirable speed and sent a pair of knives spinning into the monster's face. Mulander knew a moment's supreme elation when the blades sank into those too-familiar green eyes.

The monster shrieked with rage and anguish, raking its face with owl-like talons in an effort to dislodge the knives. Long bloody furrows crisscrossed its face before the drow's knives finally clattered to the cave's floor. Blinded and enraged, the creature advanced toward the dark elf girl, its dripping hands wildly groping the air.

The drow snatched a bola from her belt, whirled it briefly, and let fly. The weapon spun toward the blinded creature, and wrapped tightly around its neck. Gurgling, the monster tore at the leather thongs. A sharp snap resounded through the cavern, quickly followed by a grating roar. Sniffing audibly as it sought its prey, Mulander's monster dived with outstretched talons toward the drow girl.

But the drow rose into the air, as swift and as graceful as a dark hummingbird, and the monster fell facedown upon the cavern floor. It quickly rolled onto its back and leaped up onto its feet. A thunderous rush filled the cavern as its batlike wings began to beat. It rose slowly, awkwardly, and began to pursue the drow.

The young wizard tossed a giant web at the monster; the creature tore through it with ease. She bombarded it with a barrage of death darts, but the weapons bounced harmlessly off the creature's plated body.

The drow summoned a bolt of glistening black lightning and hurled it like a javelin. To Mulander's dismay, the bolt slashed downward through one leathery wing. Shrieking with rage, the monster traced a tight spiral to the cavern floor and landed with a stone-shaking crash.

No matter, the magical battle had taken its toll on the drow maid as well. She sank slowly toward the cavern floor, and toward the jaws of the wounded but waiting monster.

Her golden eyes grew frantic and darted toward Mulander's gloating face.

"Enough!" she shrieked. "I know what you need—dispel the creature, and I will give you what you want without further battle. This I swear, by all that is dark and holy!"

A smile of malevolent satisfaction crossed the Red Wizard's face. He trusted no oath from any drow, but he knew that her battle spells were nearly exhausted. Nor was he surprised that she had lost heart for the battle. The girl was pathetically young—she looked to be about twelve or thirteen by the measure of humankind. Despite her fell heritage and magical prowess, she was still a callow lass and thus no match for such as he.

"Toss the key to me," he told her.

"The monster," she pleaded.

Mulander hesitated, then shrugged. Even without the magical construct, he was more than the equal of that elf child. With a flick of one hand, he sent the monster back into whatever nightmares had spawned it. But with the other, he summoned a fireball large enough to hurl the drow against the far wall of the cavern and leave nothing of her but a grease spot. He saw by the fear in her eyes that she understood her position.

"Here—it's in here," the girl said frantically, reaching into a pouch at her waist and fumbling about.

Her efforts were hampered by her own fear. Her breath came in exhausted little gasps and sobs, and her thin shoulders shook with terrified weeping. Finally she took out a tiny silken bag and held it high.

"The key is in here," she said. "Take it, please, and let me go!"

The Red Wizard deftly caught the bag she tossed him, then shook a small glistening sphere into his palm. It was a protective bubble—a bit of magic easily cast and easily dispelled—that contained a delicate vial of translucent green glass. And within that vial was the tiny golden key that promised freedom and power.

Had he glanced at the drow child, Mulander might have wondered why her eyes were dry despite her weeping, why she no longer seemed to have any difficulty maintaining her ability to levitate. Had he taken his gaze from that longed-for key, he might have recognized the look of cold triumph in her golden eyes. He had seen that expression once before, briefly, on the face of his own apprentice.

But pride had blinded him to treachery once before, and had lured him into a mistake that had condemned him to lifelong slavery.

When understanding finally came, Mulander knew that that mistake would truly be his last.

CHAPTER 7
RITUAL

Liriel Baenre returned to Menzoberranzan after a mere two days, battered and bereft of a bit of her abundant white hair, but grimly triumphant. Or so everyone assumed. Not until the ceremony was she required to give formal proof of her kill.

All of House Shobalar gathered in the throne room of Matron Hinkutes'nat for the coming-of-age ceremony. It was required, but most came anyway for the vicarious pleasure to be had in witnessing the grisly relics, and to relive the pride and pleasure of their own first kills. Such moments reminded all present of what it meant to be drow.

At Narbondel, the darkest hour, Liriel stepped forward to claim her place among her people. To Xandra Shobalar, her mistress and mentor, she was required to present the ritual proof.

For a long moment, Liriel held the older wizard's gaze, staring into Xandra's crimson orbs with golden eyes that were cold and fathomless—full of unspoken power and deadly promise. That, too, was something she had learned from her dreaded father.

When at last the older wizard's gaze faltered uncertainly, Liriel bowed deeply and reached into the bag at her waist. She took from it a small green object and held it high for all to see. There were murmurs as some of the Shobalar wizards recognized the artifact for what it was.

"You surprise me, child," Xandra said coldly. "You who were anticipating a 'gallant hunt,' to trap and slay your prey with such a device."

"A child no more," Liriel corrected her.

A strange smile crossed her face, and with a quick, vicious movement, she threw the vial to the floor.

The crystal shattered, a delicate, tinkling sound that echoed long in the stunned silence that followed—for standing before the Mistress of Magic, his green eyes glowing with malevolence, was the human wizard. He was very much alive, and in one hand he held the golden collar that had imprisoned him to Xandra's will.

With a speed that belied his years, the human conjured a crimson sphere of light and hurled it, not at Xandra, but at the dark elf male who stood guard at the rear door. The hapless drow shattered into bloody shards. Before anyone could draw breath, the bits of flesh whirled into the air and began to take on new and dreadful shapes.

For many moments, everyone in the throne room was busy indeed. The Shobalar wizards and priestesses hurled spells, and the fighters battled with arrows and swords winged creatures given birth by their drow comrade's death.

At last, there was only Xandra and the wizard, standing nearly toe to toe and blazing with eldritch light as their spells attacked and riposted with the speed and verve of a swordmasters' dual. Every eye in the throne room, drow and slave alike, was fixed upon the deadly battle, and all were lit with vicious excitement as they awaited the outcome.

Finally, one of the Red Wizard's spells slipped past Xandra's defenses. A daggerlike stab of light sliced the drow's face from cheekbone to jaw. The flesh parted in a gaping wound, deep enough to reveal the bones beneath.

Xandra let out a wail that would have shamed a banshee, and with a speed that rivaled that of a weapons master's death blow, she lashed back. Pain, desperation, and wrath combined to fuel a blast of magic powerful enough to send a thunderous, shuddering roar through the stone chamber.

The human caught the full force of the attack. His smoking body hurtled up and back like a loosed arrow. He hit the far wall near the ceiling and slid down, leaving a rapidly cooling streak on the stone. There was a hole the size of a dinner plate where his chest had been, and his sodden robes were a slightly brighter shade of crimson.

Xandra, too, crumpled, utterly exhausted by the momentous spell battle, and further weakened by the copious flow of blood spilling from her torn face. Drow servants rushed to attend her, and her sisters gathered around to murmur spells of healing. Through it all, Liriel stood before the matron's throne, her face set in a mask of faint, cynical amusement, and her eyes utterly cold.

When at last the Mistress of Magic had recovered enough breath for speech, she hauled herself into a sitting position and leveled a shaking finger at the young wizard.

"How do you dare commit such an . . . an outrage!" she sputtered. "The rite has been profaned!"

"Not so," Liriel said. "You stipulated that the wizard could be slain with any weapon of my choice. The weapon I chose was you."

A second stunned silence descended upon the chamber. It was broken by a strange sound, one that no one there had ever heard before or had ever expected to hear:

Matron Mother Hinkutes'nat Alar Shobalar was laughing.

It was a rusty sound, to be sure, but there was genuine amusement in the matron's voice and in her crimson eyes.

"This defies all the laws and customs of . . ." Xandra began, but the matron mother cut her off with an imperious gesture.

"The rite of Blooding has been fulfilled," Hinkutes'nat proclaimed, "for its purpose is to make a true drow of a youngling dark elf. Evidence of a devious mind serves this purpose as well as bloody hands."

Ignoring her glowering daughter, the matron turned to Liriel and said, "Well done! By all the power of this throne and this House, I proclaim you a true drow, a worthy daughter of Lolth! Leave your childhood behind, and rejoice in the dark powers that are our heritage and our delight."

Liriel accepted the ritual welcome—not with a deep bow, but with a slight incline of her head. She was a child no longer, and as a noble female of House Baenre, she was never to bow to a dark elf of lesser rank again. Gromph had schooled her in such matters, drilling her until she understood every shade and nuance of the complicated protocol. He had impressed upon her that the Blooding ceremony marked not only her departure from childhood, but her full acceptance into the Baenre clan. All that stood between her and both those honors were the ritual words of acceptance that she must speak.

But Liriel was not quite finished. Following an impulse that she only dimly understood, she crossed the dais to the place where a defeated Xandra sat slumped, submitting glumly to the continued ministrations of the House Shobalar priestesses.

Liriel stooped so that she was at eye level with her former mentor. Slowly she extended her hand and gently cupped the older drow's chin—a rare gesture that was occasionally used to comfort or caress a child, or, more often, to capture the child's attention before dictating terms. It was unlikely that Xandra, in her pain-ridden state, would have consciously attached that meaning to her former student's gesture, but it was clear that she instinctively grasped the nuance. She flinched away from Liriel's touch, and her eyes were pure malevolence.

The girl merely smiled. Then, suddenly, she slid her palm up along the jawline of Xandra's wounded cheek, gathering in her cupped hand some of the blood that stained the wizard's face.

With a single, quick movement, Liriel rose to her feet and turned to face the watching matron mother. Deliberately she smeared Xandra's blood over both hands, front and back, and she presented them to Matron Hinkutes'nat.

"The ritual is complete. I am a child no more, but a drow," Liriel proclaimed.

The silence that followed her words was long and impending, for the implications of her action went far beyond the limits of propriety and precedence.

At last Matron Mother Hinkutes'nat inclined her head—but not in the expected gesture of completion. The

Shobalar matriarch added the subtle nuance that transformed the regal gesture into the salute exchanged between equals. It was a rare tribute, and rarer still was the amused understanding—and the genuine respect—in the spidery female's eyes.

All of which struck the young drow as highly ironic. Though it was clear that Hinkutes'nat applauded Liriel's gesture, she herself was not entirely certain why she had done what she did.

That question plagued Liriel throughout the celebration that traditionally followed the ceremony. The spectacle provided by her Blooding had been unusually satisfying to the attending drow, and the revelry it inspired was raucous and long. For once Liriel entered into festivities with less than her usual gusto, and she was not at all sorry when the last bell signaled the end of the night.

CHAPTER 8
HER FATHER'S DAUGHTER

The summons from the Narbondellyn district came early the next day. Gromph Baenre sent word that Liriel's belongings were to be packed up and sent after her.

The young drow received that information stoically. In truth, Liriel did not regret her removal from House Shobalar. Perhaps she did not understand the full meaning of her own Blooding ceremony, but she knew with certainly that she could no longer remain in the same complex as Xandra Shobalar.

Liriel's reception at the archmage's mansion was about what she had expected. Servants met her and showed her to her apartment—a small but lavish suite that boasted a well-equipped library of spellbooks and scrolls. Apparently her father intended for her to continue her wizardly education. But there was no sign of Gromph, and the best the servants could do for Liriel was to assure her that the archmage would send for her when she was wanted.

And so it was that the newly initiated drow spent her first darkcycle alone, the first of what she suspected would be many to come. Liriel found the solitude painfully difficult, and the silent hours crept by.

After several futile attempts at study, the weary girl at last took to her bed. For hours she stared at the ceiling and longed for the oblivion of slumber. But her mind was too full, and her thoughts too confused, for sleep to find her.

Oddly enough, Liriel felt less triumphant than she should have. She was alive, she had passed the test of the Blooding, she had repaid Xandra's treachery with public humiliation, she had even devised a way to keep from slaying the human wizard.

Why was it, then, that she felt his blood on her hands as surely as if she'd torn out his heart with her own fingernails? And what was that soul-deep sadness, that dark resignation? Though she had no name to give the emotion, Liriel suspected that it would ever after cast a shadow upon her blithe spirit.

The hours passed, and the distant tolling of Narbondel signaled that the darkest hour was once again upon Menzoberranzan. It was then that the summons finally came. A servant bid Liriel to dress and await the archmage in his study.

Liriel was less than anxious to face her drow sire. What would Gromph have to say about her unorthodox approach to the Blooding hunt and ceremony? During her three days of preparation, the archmage had repeatedly expressed concern about her judgment and ambition, pronouncing her too trusting and carefree, and he had wondered at the strange bias of her character. It seemed likely to her that he would not approve.

Liriel did as she was told and hastened to her father's sanctum. She had not long to wait before Gromph appeared, still wearing the wondrous, glittering *piwafwi* that held an arsenal of magical weapons, and that proclaimed his power and his high office. The archmage acknowledged her presence with a curt nod and sat down behind his table.

"I have heard what transpired at your ceremony," he began.

"The ritual was fulfilled," Liriel said earnestly—and a trifle defensively. "I might not have shed blood, but Matron Hinkutes'nat accepted my efforts."

"More than accepted," the archmage said dryly. "The Shobalar matron is quite impressed with you. And more importantly, so am I."

Liriel absorbed that in silence then, suddenly, she blurted out, "Oh, but I wish I understood why!"

Gromph lifted one brow.

"You really must learn to speak with less than complete candor," he advised her. "But in this case, no harm is done. Indeed, your words only confirm what I had suspected. You acted partly by design, but partly by instinct. This is indeed gratifying."

"Then you're not angry?" Liriel ventured. When the archmage sent her an inquiring look, she added, "I thought you would be furious upon hearing that I did not actually kill the human."

Gromph was silent a long moment then said, "You did something far more important. You fulfilled both the spirit and the letter of the Blooding ritual, in layers of subtle complexity that did credit to you and to your House. The human wizard is dead—that much was a needed formality. Using Xandra Shobalar as a tool was a clever twist, but washing your hands in her blood was brilliant."

"Thank you," Liriel said, in a tone so incongruously glum that it surprised a chuckle from the archmage.

"You still do not understand. Very well, I will speak plainly. The human wizard was never your enemy. Xandra Shobalar was your enemy. You recognized that, you turned her plot against her, and you proclaimed a blood victory. And in doing so, you demonstrated that you have learned what it is to be a true drow."

"But I did not kill," Liriel said thoughtfully. "Why do I feel as if I had?"

"You might not have actually shed blood, but the ritual of the Blooding has done its intended work all the same," the archmage asserted.

Liriel considered that, and she knew her father's words as truth. Her innocence was gone, but pride, power, treachery, intrigue, survival, victory—all of those things she knew intimately and well.

"A true drow," she repeated in a tone that was nine parts triumph and one portion regret. She took a deep breath and looked up into Gromph's eyes—and into a mirror.

For the briefest of moments, Liriel glimpsed a flicker of poignant sorrow in the archmage's eyes, like the glint of gold shining through a deep layer of ice. It came and departed so quickly Liriel doubted that Gromph was even aware of it. After all, several centuries of cold and calculating evil lay between him and his own rite of passage. If he remembered that emotion at all, he was no longer able to reach into his soul and bring it forth. Liriel understood, and at last she had a name to give the final, missing element that defined a true drow:

Despair.

"Congratulations," the archmage said in a voice laced with unconscious irony.

"Thank you," his daughter responded in kind.

Originally published in *Realms of Valor*
Edited by James Lowder, February 1993

ELMINSTER AT THE MAGEFAIR

Ed Greenwood

This tale was my gleeful chance to show
Elminster and Storm working together. It was
trimmed to fit *Realms of Valor* by omitting snatches
of conversation overheard at the Magefair. So
here are two to put back in, wherever you prefer:

"Of *course* it's not an ordinary dragon! 'Ordinary dragons' don't collect heaps of human skulls
whilst ignoring perfectly good treasure just lying
there for the taking!"

and:

"Well things like that don't just get up and
walk away! With all those claws to drag around,
and the crown, too—it must be hiding somewhere
in your privy! Have any of the maids started
screaming yet?"

—Ed Greenwood, March 2003

Ed Greenwood is the creator of the
FORGOTTEN REALMS, and (thanks to his
antics at conventions) is sometimes
mistaken for the wizard Elminster. An
affable bearded Canadian who lives in
the Ontario countryside with some
eighty thousand books, Ed started
building this shared playground in
1967—and isn't finished yet!

What's more dangerous than a mage out to rule
the entire world? Why, a mage at play, of course. . . .
        –The Simbul, Witch-Queen of Aglarond

ELMINSTER AT THE MAGEFAIR

WARNINGS
The Year of the Dark Dragon (1336 DR)

The rosy light of early morning had scarcely
brightened into the full radiance of day, but the
bard and her gaunt companion had already been
in the saddle for some time.

Storm Silverhand, the Bard of Shadowdale,
was an adventurer of wide experience and fame.
She was also a senior and respected member of
the Harpers, that mysterious band always working for the good of the world. A veteran of many
perilous forays, always alert, she watched her
surroundings constantly as she traveled, hand
never far from the hilt of her sword. Its blade had
run with blood more than once already on that
journey. As she rode, Storm sang softly to herself.
She was happy to be in the saddle again—even
on a ride into known danger.

For two tendays she had ridden beside a
white-haired man as tall as herself, but thinner.

The man was aged and a clumsy rider. He wore simple, much-patched robes covered with old food stains, and trailed sweet-smelling pipe smoke wherever he went.

Though he didn't look it, the old man was an adventurer even more famous than Storm: the Old Mage, Elminster of Shadowdale. More than five hundred winters had painted his long beard white. His twinkling blue eyes had seen empires rise and fall, and spied worlds beyond Toril, vast and strange. He knew more secrets than most wizards—and simpler, more honest men, too—might ever suspect to exist. The years had sharpened Elminster's temper and his tongue, and built his magic to a height that most mages could only dream of.

The great wizard wore old, floppy leather boots, and, most of the time, an irritated expression. At night, on the far side of the fire, he snored like a crawhorn in torment—but he knew it and used magic to mute the noise for the sake of his friend and trail mate. Storm loved him dearly, snores and all, even if he tended to treat her like a little girl.

Despite their friendship, it was unusual for Storm to be riding at the Old Mage's side. When Elminster left Shadowdale on prolonged trips, it was his habit to trust the defense of the dale to the bard. This time, just before the mage's departure, a Harper agent had brought a request from one of Storm's sisters: would she please guard Elminster when he went to the magefair?

In all her years of adventuring, Storm had never heard of a magefair, but the very name sounded ominous. She had been surprised at the easy good humor with which the Old Mage had accepted her announcement that that time, when he left home, she'd be riding with him. In fact, she suspected he'd used horses for the trek, rather than whisking himself across Faerûn in a trice by magic, just to prolong their time together.

Every night Elminster settled himself and his pipe down beside their fire to listen to her pluck a harp and sing old ballads. In return, when she lay down under the watching, glittering stars, he'd softly tell tales of old Faerûn until sleep claimed her. After years of riding the wastes with hearty, hardened warriors, Storm was astonished at how much she'd enjoyed her trip with the odd mage.

But it seemed they had reached their destination, though it was nothing at all like the bard had imagined.

"Why here?" Storm Silverhand asked with tolerant good humor as she reined in beside Elminster on a ridge far from Shadowdale. The bright morning sun cast long shadows from the stunted trees and brush around them. As far as the eye could see, rolling wilderness stretched out, untouched by the hands of man. "We must be halfway to Kara-Tur by now."

The Old Mage scratched his nose.

"Farther," he replied with seeming innocence, "and 'here' because one we seek is close at hand."

As he spoke, a man appeared out of thin air, floating in front of them. The horses snorted and shifted in surprise. Elminster frowned.

The man stood on nothing, booted feet far above the ground. Midnight eyes glowered down out of a thin, cruel white face. He towered impressively over them, clad in a dark and splendid tabard adorned with glowing mystic signs and topped with an up-thrust high collar. A carved, gem-adorned staff winked and pulsed in one of his many-ringed hands.

"Challenge!" he addressed them with cold, formal dignity, raising his empty hand in a gesture that barred the way. "Speak, or pass not!"

"Elminster of Shadowdale," the Old Mage replied mildly, "and guest."

The man's eyes narrowed, and he said even more coldly, "Prove yourself."

"Ye doubt me?" Elminster asked slowly. "Why, Dhaerivus, I recall thy first magefair!" He nodded in reflection and added dryly, "Ye made a most fetching toad."

Dhaerivus flushed.

"You know the rule," he said harshly, waving the staff.

Lights began to race along its length, brightening the crystal sphere that topped it. With slow menace, the floating man brought that glowing end down to point at the Old Mage.

"Aye," Elminster replied. He wagged a finger back and forth and announced lightly, "Nice-ly!"

The staff that menaced them snapped back upright, forced away by the power of Elminster's sorcery. The sentinel who held it gaped at them in astonishment and fear before the muscles of his face rippled and lost their struggle against another dose of the Old Mage's spell-casting.

The magic made Dhaerivus giggle involuntarily for a few moments, then released him. His grin turned rapidly into a scowl of dark anger.

Elminster took no notice. "There ye go," he said jovially to the shaken sentinel as he urged his mount onward. "Happy magic!"

Storm looked back at the furious man as they topped the next ridge. The staff was flashing and flickering like a lightning storm at sea, and the sentinel was snarling and stamping angrily on the empty air.

Storm glanced at Elminster and asked wonderingly, "You cast a cantrip? Making him giggle is 'proving yourself'?"

Elminster nodded and said, "A wizard must prove to a magefair sentinel only that he can work magic. Er, to keep the rabble out."

He rolled his eyes to show what he thought of that attitude and calmly urged his horse down through a tumble of boulders and long grass.

"Guests like thee are exempt from the testing, but each mage is limited to only one such compatriot. No mage can avoid the test and be allowed into the fair. Generally, young bucks cast powerful explosions and the like, or exquisite and—*ahem*—voluptuous illusions, but in this case I, ah, well, ah . . . meant it as an insult."

Storm wrinkled her brow. "I see," she observed carefully, "that I'm going to have to be very careful at this fair."

Elminster waved a hand and replied, "Ah, nay, nay. I must merely get a certain magical key from someone who isn't expected to be insane enough to bring it here—or to have anything at all to do with it—and have a bit of fun. Certain Harpers asked me to come here to protect this friend I must meet. No doubt ye were asked to come along too—to keep a certain Old Mage out of trouble."

He favored her with a level look. Storm smiled and nodded ruefully.

The Old Mage chuckled, "These magefairs are private little gatherings. I haven't been to one in years, and we're far enough from home that my face won't be well known. Certain rules govern those who attend, rules meant to keep things from sinking into a general spell-brawl, but ye'd do well to keep in mind that most everyone here can wield magic—quite well. Walk softly. Drink things that are offered to ye only if I am present and deem it wise. Draw thy magical blade only if ye must. Some come here to gain new spells, but most come to show off what they can do, like children at play. Cruel, over-powerful children, a lot of them."

He scratched at his beard and looked thoughtful.

"As to those who work against us," he added, "the names and faces of their servants at the magefair are unknown to me." He grinned suddenly. "Suspect everyone, as usual, and ye should do all right."

"What is this key we seek?" Storm asked, "and why is it so valuable?"

Elminster shrugged and said, "It's precious only because of what it opens. Its form and purpose ye'll learn soon enough—which is another way of saying I scarce remember what it looks like and haven't the faintest idea why, after so many years, its importance has risen so suddenly and sharply." He cast a dry look at her and added, "Mysterious enough for ye?"

Storm replied with a look that had, over the years, plunged more than one man into icy fear.

Unperturbed, the Old Mage smiled at her as they rode up the heather-clad slope of another ridge.

"Sorry, my dear, but I got quite a lecture last time—from thee, as I recall—on speaking freely about all sorts of little details that should be kept secret in matters like this, so I'm flapping my jaws as little as I can this time around and acting as if only I know the great secret upon which the safety of the entire world rests—oh, there I go. Ye see, I just can't help myself. 'Tis so hard to do all this intrigue and world-saving with grim and solemn seriousness when ye've done it so often down the centuries. Now, where was I? Ah, yes . . ."

There were worse fates, Storm reminded herself with an inward smile, than traveling across half of Faerûn with Elminster. To buoy her spirits, she spent some time trying to remember what some of them were.

That dark reverie took them across several scrub-covered ridges, to the lip of a deep, bowl-shaped valley. A narrow trail wound down into it from somewhere on their right, crossing in front of them to enter a grove of trees. The trees hid the rest of the valley from the two riders.

It was then that a man in rich purple robes sailed into view. Floated would be a more accurate term, since he perched serenely on a carpet that undulated through the air like an eager snake, following the narrow trail far below. And as the bard and wizard watched, the man on the flying carpet sailed into the trees. Their leaves promptly changed color from their former green to a bright coppery hue, and several voices could be heard, raised in cries of praise of the new arrival.

They had obviously reached the magefair.

Far off, on the heights that rose on the other side of the still unseen valley, Storm saw balls of fire bursting in the air.

Elminster followed the direction of her stare and said, "Ah, yes—the fireball throwing contest, d'ye see? Magelings get all excited about it . . . something about impressing their peers. No doubt we'll end up there all too soon. They're allowed to challenge us older dweomer-crafters, ye see, to prove their manly mettles by beating feeble dodderers. Er, womanly mettles too, mark ye, though many maids have sense enough to avoid such vulgar displays of power."

Storm raised an eyebrow and asked, "How does one fireball impress more than another? As the saying goes, aren't all that hit you the same?"

The Old Mage shook his head patiently.

"If a few words of the incantation are changed," he explained, "the spell becomes more difficult to cast and the size and force of its blast mirrors the power and experience of the one throwing it. One wizard can boast that his is bigger than that of the next wizard, y'see. An archmage's firesphere can be quite impressive."

He paused meaningfully, then added, "I mean to get in and get out of the fair, mind ye, with a minimum of dallying. Tossing fire about is more a sport for the green and foolish. Try not to seek out trouble by challenging anyone. Stay close and speak not. It's safer."

And with these melodramatic words the Old Mage kicked his heels and sent his horse galloping down the steep track in reckless haste, raising dust. At the bottom, Elminster plunged his mount into a crowd of laughing, chatting mages. Storm, close on his heels, had time for one stare before she entered the assembled mages.

The gorge was full of folk standing shoulder to shoulder. Their robes formed a moving sea of wild colors, and the chatter was nearly deafening. There were men and women of all shapes, ages, and sizes—and a few whose gender the bard wasn't sure of. Traditional dark, flowing, wide-sleeved robes were amply in evidence, but most of the mages wore stranger, more colorful garments. Storm, who had seen much in the way of garb over many years of wandering, stared in wonder. It is widely held in Faerûn—among non-mages, at least—that those who work Art are all, in varying degrees, crazy. In eccentricity of dress, Storm saw, that was certainly correct.

All manner of strange headpieces and body adornments bristled and sprouted around her, shimmering and sparkling and in some cases shifting shape in fluid movements. One lady mage wore nothing but a gigantic, many-feathered snake, which moved its slow coils continuously around her lithe body. A man nearby seemed clad only in dancing flames. The wizard he was speaking to wore a shifting, phosphorescent fungus, out of which grew small leafy ferns and thistles. Next to them stood a half-elf maiden clad in a flowing gown of gleaming, soft-polished gems strung upon many silken threads. She was arguing with a long-haired dwarf wearing furs and leather upon which a pair of insect-eating lizards crawled ceaselessly, long tongues darting. A snatch of their conversation came to Storm's ears:

"Well, what did the Thayan do then?"

"Blew up the entire castle, of course. What else?"

Other voices crowded in, drowning out the previous speakers.

"What was that? Purple zombies? Why purple?"

"She was bored, I guess. You should have seen the prince's face the next morning. She made a dozen tiny red hands appear out of thin air and pinch him in all the places he had pinched her . . . in front of all the court, too!"

Elminster was riding steadily through the throng. He seemed to know where he was going. Storm followed, past a man who was balancing a full bottle of something dark and red on his large nose and protesting in muffled tones to those watching that he wasn't using any magic to help him. She looked away just before the bottle toppled and spilled all over him, but could not resist looking back at the damp result. She was careful not to smile.

"How many times must I tell thee? First you kiss, *then* cast the spell—or it stays a frog forever!"

Storm shook her head, trying to concentrate on Elminster and ignore such talk. A terrific din of conversation, strange music, humming, and weird little popping noises raged over the crowd. Wizards gestured to impress those they were speaking with, and varicolored smokes and many-hued globes of radiance obediently bobbed or writhed in the air over their heads. Enspelled birds sang complicated melodies, and some flew graceful aerial ballets. Storm peered this way and that, trying to see everything, watching for danger.

Everywhere folk stood talking, arguing, laughing, or dickering, with goblets and flagons of varying sizes and contents in their hands, or floating handily in midair at their elbows. Some sort of rule, Storm guessed, kept the mages themselves from flying, floating, or teleporting about. Mostly they just stood in groups, talking. Storm threaded her mount carefully among them. Three olive-hued tentacles slid out from under a mage's hood as she passed. Small, glittering eyes opened at their ends, surveyed her, and winked. She tried not to show her involuntary shudder as she rode on, past a man with bright green hair and beard who was juggling a ring of hand-sized balls of fire in the air. The lady mage he was trying to impress was in the act of stifling a yawn.

The next group was made up of old and wrinkled crones with cold dark eyes and sinister-looking black robes. They were chuckling and swigging beer from clear glass tankards that didn't seem to empty.

"First babe I ever saw that was born with wings," one was saying delightedly. "Flew around the nursery, giggling, the little scamp. Well, the king nearly swallowed his crown, I tell thee!"

Storm left the women behind, riding across a little open space where rising smoke and ashes suggested someone had experienced a warm and possibly fatal accident very recently. Beyond it, she plunged into the chatter once again.

"You must understand, old friend, that taking the shape of a dragon is an experience that changes one forever—forever, I tell you!"

A mage in florid pink and purple, lace at his wrists and throat, was underscoring that point by flicking a long, forked tongue at the mage he was speaking to—a wizardess with white, furry hair running down her arms and the backs of her hands. Her skin was a deeper purple than the garb of the wizard speaking to her. Her reply to his claims about dragonshaping was an eloquent snort.

Then Storm was threading her way past six enchantingly beautiful half-elf sorceresses, whose heads were bent together in low-voiced intrigue. One looked up alertly, only to relax and give the bard a relieved smile. The others, intent on deal-making, never saw her.

"Well, just change the name and the way you cast it, and he'll never know. I mean, anyone could have come up with a spell like that. Teach it to me, and I'll not tell where

I got it. In return, I'll show you that trick of Tlaerune's, the one that makes men swoon and—"

Shaking her head, Storm hurried on through the magical bedlam, trying to catch up with the Old Mage. Where had he gone? She looked up and down the crowded gorge—there were hundreds of mages there! Yet, thanks to her keen eyes, she managed to find Elminster again. The Old Mage continued to cut through the gathered wizards without slowing or dismounting—until he came to a tree-shaded corner on the far, rocky wall of the gorge. There, in the dappled gloom, a short, stunningly beautiful lady mage was talking with five or six obviously smitten men of the Art.

Storm saw laughing black eyes, flowing black hair, and a gown whose scanty front seemed to be made of glowing, always-shifting flowers.

Then the Old Mage vaulted, or rather fell, straight from his horse into the arms of the lady, with the words, "Duara! My dear! Years have passed! Simply *years!*"

Dark eyes sparkled up into his, and the Old Mage's effusive greetings were temporarily stilled by a deep kiss. Slim hands went around his neck, stroked his tangle of white hair, and moved downward, in a tight, passionate embrace.

After Elminster's glad greetings and the long kiss, Storm heard a low, purring voice replying enthusiastically. On the faces of the men around she saw astonishment, then anger, resignation, or disgust, and finally resigned disinterest. Storm also noticed Duara's fingers at the mage's belt, moving nimbly.

Other eyes had seen it, too—particularly those of a tall, hook-nosed man in a dark green velvet doublet with slashed and puffed sleeves. He'd been watching the Old Mage's affectionate greeting closely, his expression hidden by the smoke from his long, slim clay pipe.

When Elminster finally bid the smiling beauty a noisy *adieu*, the hook-nosed wizard let his pipe float by itself as he strode forward, gesturing wordlessly. In response, Elminster's pouch levitated upward and opened in midair. Silence fell among the mages standing near. It was obvious by their expressions that the green-clad wizard's spellwork was a serious breach of etiquette.

Storm half drew her sword, but Elminster's bony hand stayed her firmly.

In merry tones, he asked, "Lost thy magic, colleague? Want to borrow a cup of this or that?"

The wizard in green looked narrowly at him and at the lone item the pouch held: a twig. "Where is it, old man?"

"The powerful magic ye seek? Why, in here," replied Elminster, tapping his own head with one finger. Unsettled, Storm peered at him; his voice seemed thicker than usual, but his eyes were as bright as ever. "But ye can't get it with a simple snatching spell cast in a moment, ye know. Years of study, it took me, to master even—"

The green wizard gestured curtly. The twig flew toward his open, waiting hand. Before it got there, Elminster snapped his fingers and wiggled his eyebrows. As a result, the twig shot upward, curved in a smooth arc, and darted back toward the Old Mage.

The wizard in green frowned and gestured again. The twig slowed abruptly, but continued to drift toward the smiling face of Elminster. The wizard's hands moved again, almost frantically, but the twig's flight—and Elminster's gentle smile—held steady as the wood settled into the Old Mage's hand.

Elminster bowed to the white-faced, shaking wizard.

Pleasantly, the Old Mage said, "But if it's this magical staff ye want—" the twig instantly became a grand-looking, ten-foot-long, smooth black staff with brass ends wrought in coiling-snake designs—"by all means have it."

And the staff flew gently across empty air to the astonished man's hands.

"But . . . your staff?" Storm asked in wonder as she watched the sweating, dumbfounded wizard in green catch the staff not four paces away. "How will you replace it?"

"Cut myself another one," the Old Mage replied serenely. "They grow on trees."

Clutching the staff and eyeing Elminster anxiously, the velvet-clad wizard reclaimed his pipe, muttered something, and rapidly gestured. Abruptly, he was gone, staff and all, as though he had never been there at all.

Elminster shook his head disapprovingly.

"Bad manners," he said severely. "Very. Teleporting at the magefair! It just wasn't done in my day, let me tell ye—"

"When was that, old man? Before the founding of Waterdeep, I'll warrant," sneered a darkly handsome young man who stood nearby.

Storm turned in her saddle.

The speaker was richly dressed in fur-trimmed silks. His black-browed, pinched face was always sneering, it seemed. Storm recognized him as one of the wizards who'd been speaking with Duara when Elminster arrived.

His voice and manner radiated cold, scornful power as he curled back his lip a little farther and said, "By the way, graybeard, you may call me 'Master.'"

Gripping his own staff—one made of shining red metal, twelve feet long and adorned with ornaments of gold—the dark-browed mage reached for the reins of the Old Mage's riderless horse.

Storm kicked out at his hand from her saddle. The toe of her boot stung his fingers and smashed them away from Elminster's mount. The handsome mage turned on her angrily—to find a gleaming sword tip inches from his nose.

"Heh, heh," chuckled Elminster in thick, rich tones. "Not learned to leave the ladies alone yet, Young Master?"

The mage flushed red to the roots of his hair and whirled away from Storm's blade to face the old man again.

"Why, no, grandsire," he said sarcastically. "Though it's obvious you've been without one for many a year!"

The loud insult brought a few snickers from the younger mages standing near, mingled with gasps and whistles of shocked amazement from older wizards who evidently knew Elminster. The murmuring intensified as some mages shoved closer to watch the coming confrontation, while others suddenly recalled pressing business elsewhere and slipped away to a safe distance.

Elminster yawned.

"Put away thy blade," he said softly to Storm. Then he said more loudly and almost merrily, "It appears boastful striplings still come to magefairs for no greater purpose than to insult their betters."

The Old Mage sighed theatrically and went on, "I suppose, cockerel, that now ye've picked a quarrel and will challenge me, eh? Nay, nay, that's not fair. After all, I've the wisdom of ages with which to make the right choices, whereas ye have only the hot vigor of youth . . . um, pretty phrase, that . . . so I'll even thy odds a trifle: I'll challenge thee! Fireball-throwing, hey? What say ye?"

A cheer arose.

The red-faced mage waited for it to die, then said scornfully, "A sport for children and, I suppose, old lackwits."

Elminster smiled, very like a cat gloating over cornered prey, and said, "Perhaps. On the other hand, perhaps ye are frightened of losing?"

The mage's face grew redder still. He cast a look around at the interested, watching faces, and snapped, "I accept." Then he struck an ostentatious pose and vanished.

An instant later, amid a puff of scarlet smoke, he reappeared on the edge of the gorge and made an insulting gesture at the Old Mage from afar. Elminster chuckled, waved a lazy hand in reply, and climbed clumsily back up onto his long-suffering horse. Storm saw him salute Duara with a wink. Then Duara's eyes met her own, and Storm could read the silent plea in them as clearly as if the young sorceress had shouted it in her ear: *Look after him, lady—please.*

By the time they had ridden up out of the valley to the meadows beyond, many wizards had gathered to watch. Haughty young sorcerers had been hurling fire about all day, but the expectant silence hanging over the scene seemed to indicate that the mage with the red staff had won a reputation at the fair, or many elders remembered Elminster, or perhaps even both.

With more haste than grace, Elminster fell from his

saddle. He hit the ground at a stumbling run, staggered to a halt, and dusted himself off.

Then he saw his waiting opponent and, with obvious pleasant surprise, said, "Well . . . lead off, boy!"

"One side, old man," said the young mage darkly, waving his staff. "Or have you no fear of dying in a ball of flame?"

Elminster stroked his beard.

"Yes, yes," he said eagerly, his mind seemingly far away. "Well do I remember! Oho, those were the days . . . great bursts of fire in the sky. . . ."

The young mage pushed past him.

"Now, how did that one go, eh? Oh, my, yes, I think I recall. . . ." Elminster burbled on, voice thick and eyes far away.

Contemptuously the young mage set his staff in the crook of his arm, muttered his incantation in low tones so the Old Mage could not hear, and moved his hands in the deftly gliding gestures of the spell. An instant later, above the grassy meadow, fire grew from nothingness into a great red-violet sphere. It seethed and roiled, rolled over once, and burst in orange ruin over the meadow, raining down small teardrops of flame onto the grass. Heat smote the watchers' faces, and the ground rocked briefly.

As the roaring died away, the quavering voice of the Old Mage could still be heard, murmuring about the triumphs of yesteryear.

He broke off his chatter for a moment to say mildly, "Dear me, that's a gentle one. Can't ye do better than that?"

The young mage sneered, "I suppose you can?"

Elminster nodded calmly and replied, "Oh, yes."

"Would it be possible to see thee perform this awesome feat?" the mage inquired with acidic courtliness, his voice a mocking, over-pompous parody of Elminster's own thickened tones.

The Old Mage blinked.

"Young man," Elminster said disapprovingly, "the great mastery of magic lies in knowing when *not* to use the power, else all these lands would long ago have become a smoking ruin."

The young mage sneered again and said, "So you won't perform such a trifling spell for us, O mightiest of mages? Is that the way of it?"

"No, no," Elminster said with a sigh. "We did agree, and ye have done thy little bit, so I—" he sighed again—"shall do mine."

He gestured vaguely, then paused and harrumphed.

"Ah, now," the Old Mage said, "how does the rhyme go?"

There were a few titters from the watching crowd as he scratched his beard and looked around with a puzzled air. The young mage sneered at his back, and turned to favor Storm with the same disdain. The bard, who stood close by, hand on the hilt of her sword, met his gaze with a wintry look of her own.

Elminster suddenly drew himself up and shouted:

"By tongue of bat and sulfur's reek,

"And mystic words I now do speak,

"There, where I wish to play my game,

"Let empty air burst into *flame!*"

In answer, the very air seemed to shatter with an ear-splitting shriek. A gigantic ball of flame towered over the meadow, its heat blistering the watchers' faces.

It was like the sun had fallen.

As mages cried out and shaded their eyes, the fireball rolled away from the awed crowd for a trembling instant, then burst in a blinding white flash, hurling out its mighty energies in a long jet of flame that roared away to the horizon. The ground shook and seemed to leap upward, throwing all but the Old Mage to their knees.

When the shaking had died away, Storm found herself lying beside the horses on the turf. By the time she had struggled to her feet and shaken her head clear, the roiling smoke had died away and everyone could see what Elminster's magic had wrought in the meadow. Or rather, what had been the meadow. Where a broad expanse of flame-scorched grass had stretched a moment before, a smoking crater yawned, large and deep and very impressive.

"Umm . . . nice, isn't it?" Elminster said rather vaguely. "I'd forgotten how much fun hurling fire is! How does the spell go again?"

The Old Mage merely waved a finger.

His young opponent, clinging to a red metal staff that had been bent in six places, was just getting to his knees when another ball of flame as big as the first roared over the meadow. That was enough to send him tumbling again, and the young mage soon found himself atop a dazed and rotund Calishite sorcerer. When he could see clearly again, the mage saw a second crater smoking in the distance. Awed murmuring could be heard from the watching wizards all around.

"Now," Elminster said mildly, drawing the stunned young mage to his feet with a firm hand, "was there aught else ye wanted to speak of? Sendings and such, or prismatic spheres—pretty, aren't they? I've always enjoyed them. Or crafting artifacts, say? No? Ah, well then . . . fare thee well in thy Art, Young Master of the Cutting Tongue, and learn a trifle more wisdom, too, if ye've the wits to do so. Until next we meet."

Elminster patted the young mage's arm cheerily, snapped his fingers, and vanished. A moment later he reappeared beside an anxious Storm.

"Mount up," he said cheerily. "We've realms to cross tonight."

"Realms?" asked Storm. As they rode up the ridge and left the magefair behind, she did not look back. "I thought you had to get a key—or was it the twig? Did that mage take the key from you?"

"Oh, no," replied Elminster merrily.

He rode close and touched her forearm. Abruptly the landscape was gone, replaced momentarily by shifting, shadowy grayness. The travelers seemed to be standing on nothing, but the horses trotted as if it was solid ground. Even before Storm could gasp a breath, there was another jolt, and they were somewhere else again—a place of darkness where rocks of all sizes crashed together endlessly, tumbling and rebounding as they hurtled through the emptiness. There was a constant thunder of stone smashing into stone, the scene lit by flashes of phosphorescence from each violent impact.

Storm took one look at the scene and tore her weathercloak from behind her saddle, flinging it over the head of her mount to prevent its rearing and plunging forward off the rather small area of rock they'd appeared on. The Old Mage's mount stood calm, controlled by his magic, no doubt.

Storm stared around at the endless destruction and found herself ducking low as a large, jagged boulder thundered toward them. It was easily as large as four horses and tumbled end over end as it came at them.

Elminster gestured, unconcerned, and the boulder veered off to strike another, larger rock nearby. A deafening crash filled the air, and a shower of stone chips rained down upon the bard. Storm shook her head. Whatever the place was, they were no longer in Faerûn.

"The green-clad dolt thought he had taken our prize," the Old Mage continued casually. "He suspected Duara might pass me the key, but he's found by now that his mighty staff is indeed just a twig. Now he'll have to go on watching her for the rest of the magefair, trying to see if she passes the key on to someone else. And for all he knows, anyone might be me, just wearing another shape. Duara'll lead him a merry dance. She likes hugging young men, and all that." He chuckled. "Shining schemes oft come to naught, ye know."

Boulders rolled and crashed right in front of them. Storm bit her lip to quell an involuntary shriek, shielded her eyes against flying stone shards, and asked, "Duara? You got the key from her, didn't you? I saw her hands at your belt."

Elminster nodded and replied, "Aye, she gave it to me. All three of our foes at the fair saw it, too: the two who challenged me, and one who did not dare come forward."

He fended off six small stones hurtling toward them and continued, "The third mage was there only to watch what transpired, no doubt, and report where we went. I used magic to blind him—and the young master of fire-hurling, too—under cover of my firesphere blast.

They're both fortunate magefair rules prohibit spells that enfeeble the wits, or they'd be staring at nothing for a long time, indeed. The blindness will wear off soon enough, but they'll find us safely gone, and the key with us."

"What—and where—is this key?" Storm asked patiently, reaching into a saddlebag for some cheese. "Why did they not know where you'd hidden it?"

"They saw, but they did not see," the Old Mage replied, using magic to float the cheese she held out deftly to his mouth. "They knew not that Duara and I were old friends—or how quick her wits are."

He reached into his mouth and drew out a small spindle of metal set with a large emerald.

"The key," he said grandly, his voice suddenly its usual clear-edged, fussy self again. "It's been in there since Duara first kissed me." He licked his lips and added, "She still likes almonds."

The waiting cheese slid into his mouth. He chewed, made an approving face, and took Storm's hand. Around them, at his will, the world shifted again.

In the blink of an eye, the darkness and crashing rocks were gone. Their horses stood on a crumbling stone bridge in the midst of a fetid swamp, ringed by vine-hung trees. Slimy stone statues protruded from the still, black waters on all sides. Storm could see they perched on a raised avenue, part of an ancient city that lay drowned in the mire around them.

As Storm glanced behind her, several glistening black tentacles rose lazily from the inky waters and rolled in languid curls across the stone span. After the questing limbs bobbed and swayed—almost as if they sniffed the air—they slid slowly into the water again.

The bard pointed to a trail of ripples, which seemed to mark the path of something large moving toward them just under the water's surface. Elminster nodded, smiled, and waved a hand casually—and they were somewhere else again. The horses were on an old, sunken road in the heart of a dark forest.

Storm sighed.

"The Harpers wanted *me* to protect *you?*" she began to ask.

But when she spied the dull glint of many eyes watching them from dim, shadowed places under the trees, Storm reached for her sword.

Elminster grunted and pitched himself heavily from his saddle. Then he reached up and laid gentle fingers on the wrist of her sword arm.

"Nay," he said softly, " 'Tis more likely, far, they wanted ye to protect others from me."

Storm rolled her eyes. Smoothly she swung herself down from her saddle.

"I shouldn't be here," she said. "Key or no key. This hopping from place to place, world to world, is neither safe nor wise."

Elminster grinned and said, "And coming to the magefair with me was? I've taken us this way home, jumping so often, to give the slip to any mages who might have followed us. Few have the breadth of mind to shift from one world to another as often as we have." The Old Mage patted her arm. "Thanks for thy patience, lass. 'Tis not long now before we'll be at ease, and ye can chat with a good friend."

As Elminster led the way on foot down an uneven path through the trees, bright morning dawned upon the old, unfamiliar forest. The rosy light seemed to make the Old Mage recall something. He turned and gestured behind them. Storm looked back in time to see their horses vanish. She looked at Elminster. He answered her wordless question only with a merry grin and headed back down the path again.

Holding her tongue, Storm followed. And she drew her sword, despite the Old Mage's words; knowing Elminster, his 'friend' could be a blue dragon—or worse.

The path led between two old, moss-covered stones. As they drew near, Elminster reached back and took Storm's hand. They stepped between the stones together, and the bard felt an odd, tingling chill.

They were somewhere else again. Somewhere familiar. Storm knew almost at once that she was in Shadowdale.

Elminster let go of her hand and strode away, reaching into his robes for his pipe. Storm stood staring after him for a moment. Then, in two quick strides, she caught up to him. Setting a firm hand on his shoulder, the bard spun Elminster around.

"Not a step farther," she warned. "Not until you tell me just what's going on. Where are our horses? Why'd we have to ride across half of Faerûn for the key, anyway? Can't this Duara teleport? And wh—"

Elminster laid a finger over her mouth and said, "The need for haste is past. I doubt anyone could have followed us through all the places I took us—not yet. Our mounts have preceded us to the Twisted Tower's stables. Come to my home. There ye'll meet a friend to us both: Lhaeo."

The Old Mage lit his pipe and said not a word more until they were strolling up the flagstone path to the door of his ramshackle stone tower.

It opened at his approach, and he turned and said, "Put away thy blade, Storm, and be welcome."

As they went in, his scribe Lhaeo called from the kitchen, "Tea shortly, Old One!"

"For Storm, too," Elminster said softly.

By some trick of magic, Lhaeo heard his master and called out, "Welcome, Lady Bard!"

"Hello, Lhaeo," Storm replied, looking at the Old Mage with amusement.

Elminster was calmly shoving piles of papers onto the floor, emptying a chair for her to sit in. Dust curled up in thick tendrils. Muttering, he gestured, and it was gone.

"A mite dark in here for me to see beautiful lady guests," the Old Mage murmured, then reached out to touch a brass brazier.

He made a popping sound, and flames flared up, casting a warm, dancing glow on the chair. Elminster gestured with courtly grace, indicating that Storm should sit down. The bard stared at the brazier in puzzlement.

"How does it burn," she asked, "without any fuel?"

"Magic, of course."

Elminster turned away, raising yet another dust cloud on his foray through more piles of parchment.

"Of course." Storm reached out and tapped his shoulder. "Elminster," she said coldly, "talk."

Her tone held the sudden ring of steel.

The Old Mage seated himself calmly on thin air, puffed on his pipe, and grinned at her through the rising smoke.

"Ye deserve to know, lass. Right, then, Duara was briefly an apprentice of mine. She dwells in Telflamm these days, and joined the Harpers a summer back." He puffed his pipe, and a blue-green smoke ring rose slowly up into the low-ceilinged gloom overhead. "She can't use a teleport spell because she hasn't the power yet. Like all young, overeager mages, she took to adventuring to gain magic quickly—and unlike most magelings, came across a dragon's hoard."

Another smoke ring rose up from the pipe. The Old Mage watched its drifting journey, nodded approvingly, and went on.

"Er, the hoard had a dragon attached to it, of course, but that's another tale. Among the baubles, she found my key, so she sent word to me by caravan letter that she had it and would bring it to the magefair if I was interested."

"Who are your mysterious foes, then? How did you lose the key?" Storm asked. "And why was Duara so dim as to send open word to you?"

Elminster shrugged and replied, "She'd no idea anyone save me would be interested in the key—or even know what her letter was about. When I got her note, I used magic to farspeak with her, telling her I'd be coming to the fair. She told me that since sending the letter, she'd been attacked several times, twice found her tower ransacked, and even been threatened one night in her bedchamber by a mysterious whispering voice demanding the key."

Storm rolled her eyes. "So what is this key?"

"The key to this closet, of course," Elminster said calmly, reaching out a long arm into the dusty gloom behind him.

The key gleamed in his hand as it slipped through a slyly smiling dragon head carved into the wall. Lines appeared in the stone around the small carving, outlining a door. It began to swing open by itself.

Elminster pulled the key out and waved it at her.

"This was stolen from me by an unscrupulous man, long ago, who was—very briefly, mind ye—my apprentice. He was an ambitious Calishite, I recall, named Raerlin. I suppose he ended up in the jaws of Duara's dragon."

"Well, what do you keep in there, that mages chase after the key?" Storm asked, looking at the closet's dusty door.

"Old spellbooks, picked up over the years while wandering the world," Elminster replied as the door swung wide.

Storm saw an untidy pile of thick, moldering tomes.

Eerie green and white light flashed suddenly from behind her. As it lit up the Old Mage's face, Storm saw his look of surprise and whirled around, upsetting her chair.

The eerie light came from a flickering oval of flame. It hung upright in the air, in the middle of the tiny, cramped room. Its presence defied the mighty magic that guarded Elminster's tower, magic, Storm knew, that kept the place safe from the archmages of the evil Zhentarim, the Red Wizards of Thay, and worse. No one should have been able to open a gate into the tower.

But the oval of flame was, Storm decided, most certainly a gate. When the bard looked through the flickering magical doorway, she saw a long, stone-lined hall, stretching away into darkness. And something was moving in the gloomy passageway. . . .

Elminster strode forward, frowning, hands weaving spells out of the air.

"Impossible," he murmured.

A shadowy figure was walking slowly toward them, out of the darkness of the phantom hallway. The creature was tall and very thin. Its eyes were two cold, glittering points of light set in dark pits. As it came nearer, Storm could see that the robes it wore hung in tatters, eaten away by rot.

The bard's heart sank. It must have been a lich, a wizard whose magic was so powerful that he lived on, beyond death. Few could fight a lich and hope to survive, few even among the ranks of the great archmages of Faerûn.

The lich came still nearer, and Storm met its fell gaze, staring into the cold, flickering lights of its eyes. They danced in the empty sockets of its skeletal face, measuring her, and turned from her contemptuously to Elminster.

"Death has come for you at last, Old Mage," the lich whispered, its hissing voice surprisingly loud. It was still far down the hallway.

"D'ye know how often I've heard those words? Every murderous fool in Faerûn tries them on me at least once." Elminster raised an eyebrow and added, "Or in thy case, Raerlin, twice."

With one hand he traced a glowing sign in the air.

The lich gave him a ghastly, gap-toothed smile and kept coming. Elminster's other eyebrow went up. His hands moved swiftly in several intricate gestures.

A barrier of shimmering radiance sprang into being across the mouth of the portal. Raerlin's hands moved in response, and the barrier burst into tiny motes of light that scattered like dancing sparks from a campfire, then winked out.

The lich's fleshless skull managed, somehow, to sneer.

"You thought yourself very clever, duping my two servants at the magefair, Elminster," came that hissing whisper again, "but I am not so easily fooled or defeated."

The skull seemed to smile.

"I was at the fair, too," the lich went on. "Your blindness spell failed against me, of course, and you did not even see through my spell-disguise. Are such simple sorceries beyond your understanding now?"

From the kitchen, muted by its stout, closed door, came the sudden rising, incongruous shriek of Lhaeo's kettle coming to a boil.

Elminster's hands were moving again. Storm saw lines of crackling power form between his fingers before he cast forth a bolt at the lich. As the energy flashed away from his hands, it lit up his face in tints of growing worry.

The lich laughed hollowly as Elminster's bolt crackled around its desiccated form. Tiny lightnings spat and leaped around its body, but seemed unable to do any harm. The lich raised a bony hand and cast a spell of its own.

Storm looked back at Elminster in alarm—and saw one of the books in the open closet behind the Old Mage glow suddenly with the same green and white radiance as the flames of the lich's gate. And when she glared at the lich, its eyes glinted at her in triumph. Ghostly gray tendrils of force were moving from the undead mage, toward them both. Raerlin was very close, only paces away from entering the room.

"Flee, Storm!" Elminster snapped. "I cannot protect thee in what will follow!"

His hands were moving in another spell.

Storm shook her head, but stepped back out of the way. Shimmering light burst from the Old Mage's fingers, lancing out to encircle and destroy each reaching tendril in crackling fury. Yet the lich merely shrugged, and its bony fingertips wove another silent spell. The book in the open closet glowed again.

Storm saw a sheen of sweat on Elminster's forehead as his hand darted to his robes and drew forth some small talisman. Then the talisman was gone, vanished right from the Old Mage's hand. As if in reply, a red-glowing band of energy shot out from the lich's shoulders as it stepped over a toppled chair into Elminster's study. The ghostly magical arm reached menacingly forward.

A shield of shimmering, silver-blue force hung in the air in front of the Old Mage, guarding him. The red arm swung easily, almost lazily around it, reaching for—not Elminster, but the closet behind him.

The lich was reaching for the book! Storm's sword flashed out and she slashed at its pages. There was a sudden hissing shriek of horror from the portal, and the red glow rose around her.

The lich's spell-arm clawed at her, trying to hold her back. Leather was torn away, and Storm felt sudden, searing pain across her breast. Thin, dark ribbons of her own blood curled past her eyes, borne upon the energy of the lich's sorcerous arm as it enveloped her.

The Bard of Shadowdale set her teeth and struck

backhanded with her magical blade, trying to free herself from the crimson band of force. There was a sudden flash and a roar. Sparks snapped and flew. The riven shards of her blade glinted brightly before Storm's eyes as she was flung back into a stack of dusty tomes. Blood ran into her eyes, and her breast felt like it was on fire.

Dimly Storm heard Elminster groan. Blinking furiously to clear her sight, she struggled to her feet. The Old Mage was crumpled to the floor, a thin beam of light from one out-flung hand reaching toward her. Behind him, the lich stood triumphant, outlined in a flaming crimson aura. Hands on hips, it laughed hollowly.

The light of Elminster's spell touched Storm, and she felt warm, fresh strength flowing into her. Her fingertips tingled, and the blood was suddenly gone from her eyes and brow.

The lich gestured sharply, and the red cloud around it became a forest of tendrils, overwhelming the darkening spell-shield over the Old Mage. As Storm watched, the shield crumbled and was gone—and the crimson force swirled around Elminster. He gestured weakly, then fell onto his face and lay still.

The blue-white energy of the Old Mage's last enchantment was drawn up into the red cloud. The mystic aura blazed brighter as the lich stepped over the Old Mage's body and strode toward the bard. Raerlin was draining Elminster's magic to power his own dark spells!

Another crimson arm lashed out from that cloud, smashing the bard aside with casual, brutal force. Storm was flung into another pile of books. She saw the red arm reaching in a leisurely manner for the tome inside the hidden room.

Storm got up from the tumbled heap of books as quickly as she could, panting, the smell of her own singed hair strong in her nostrils. Blood still trickled down her chest, and she still held a blackened, twisted sword hilt in her hand. Taking a deep, shuddering breath, she flung the ruined blade at the lich and dived for the tome for which the creature had risked so much. Redness swirled around her, but the book was clenched tightly in her fingers.

Raerlin's voice rose into a hollow, fearful shriek as Storm clutched the book to her bloody chest.

"Myrkul take you, wench!" the lich cried. "You'll ruin it!"

And at last Storm was sure of her course.

She tore at the pages with trembling fingers and thrust the crumpled scraps into the flames of Elminster's magical brazier. The fire flared, and the bard held the parchment in the rising flames, heedless of the searing pain in her hand.

Raerlin's magic struck. Red claws tugged and tore at her. Storm snarled and fought to hold her position, one arm crooked around the brazier. Flames licked greedily at the crumpled pages she held.

Storm felt hair being hauled out of her scalp, yanking her head back. Tears blinded her, and something—her own hair!—tightened around her throat, driven by the lich's magic. The Bard of Shadowdale set her teeth to hold back a scream as she hauled the book up, wrestling against the lich's dark sorcery with all the strength in her arms. And she thrust the tome into the brazier.

There was a hungry roar, and Storm was hurled away. She had a confused glimpse of flying bones and the brass brazier tumbling end over end, away from a rolling, motionless ball of bright flame. Then she crashed again into Elminster's chair with bruising force. Hair blinded her for a moment. Impatiently Storm raked it aside and stared at the ball of fire.

It hung a few feet above the floor of the study, roiling and crackling. At its heart, the blackening, still-glowing book was wreathed in many-colored flames. As she watched, the tome crumbled to ashes and was gone. Off to Storm's left, there was a hissing sound.

She turned in time to see the lich's skull crumble to pieces. The red glow of Raerlin's magic flickered and faded away to nothing. In a moment, the lich was only so much eddying dust.

In the sudden silence, Storm closed weary eyes, wondering when her burned hands would stop trembling.

From somewhere to her right came a loud cough. The

bard blinked her eyes open and tried to rise. Elminster was shaking his head as he got slowly up off the floor, patting at smoldering patches on his robes.

"I must not forget, lass," Elminster said with dignity, "to thank ye properly, at some future time, for once again saving my life."

Storm sputtered in sudden mirth, despite her pain. A moment later, they were laughing in each other's arms, eyes shining. As they shook together in a tight embrace, a door opened, spilling kitchen sounds into the devastated study.

The sudden clatter of crockery was followed by Lhaeo's cheerful voice saying, "Tea's ready! You were making quite a racket in—" He sobered suddenly and blinked at the two singed and wounded friends. "Wh-what happened?"

Elminster pushed Storm away and waved his hands with incredible agility for one so old. An instant later, Storm found herself on her chair again, wearing a splendid gown. The raw pain in her chest and hands was gone. Across a round table set for tea, Elminster sat facing her, clad in splendid silken robes embroidered with dragons. He was smiling gently, his lit pipe ready in his hand.

"Nothing," the Old Mage said airily, "more than a visit between old friends."

As the tea tray descended, Elminster winked at the bard. Storm shook her head, smiling helplessly.

Originally published in *Realms of Shadow*
Edited by Lizz Baldwin, April 2002

DARKSWORD

Troy Denning

When *The Sorcerer* came out, readers kept asking when Melegaunt Tanthul would return. I was a bit surprised by this, since the fate he meets there is not one from which people normally come back. So, when it came time to write a short story for *Realms of Shadow*, I decided to explore a crucial time in his past . . . and in that of the Realms.

—Troy Denning, April 2003

Troy Denning is the author of the
Return of the Archwizards trilogy and
twenty other novels, including the
New York Times best-sellers
Waterdeep, *Star by Star*, and
Tatooine Ghost.

DARKSWORD

20 Flamerule, the Year of the Moat (1269 DR)
Lost on the Road Across the Bottomless Bogs

Out of the fog ahead came mist-muffled voices,
many of them and not far off, mothers singing,
children crying, fathers shouting . . . oxen bellowing, hoarse and weary. Melegaunt Tanthul continued walking as before—which was to say very
carefully—along the road of split logs, which
bobbed on the spongy peat with every step he
took. Visibility was twenty paces at best, the road
a brownish ribbon zigzagging off into a cloud of
pearly white. Not for the first time, he wished he
had taken the other fork at the base of Deadman
Pass. Surely he was still in Vaasa, but whether he
was traveling toward the treasure he sought or
away from it was anyone's guess.

The voices grew steadily louder and more distinct, until the hazy outline of the road ahead
abruptly dissolved into nothingness. Strewn
along a narrow band at the end of the road were

a handful of head-shaped spheres, some perched atop a set of human shoulders with arms splayed wide to spread their weight. Farther back, two sets of nebulous oxen horns rose out of the peat, the blocky silhouette of a fog-shrouded cargo wagon sitting on the surface behind them.

Melegaunt pulled his heavy rucksack off his back and continued up the road, already fishing for the line with which he strung his rain tarp at night. As he drew nearer, the head-shaped blobs seemed to sprout beards and wild manes of unkempt hair. He began to make out hooked noses and deep-set eyes, then one of the heads shouted out, and with a terrible slurping sound, sank beneath the peat. The cry was echoed by a chorus of frightened wails deeper in the fog, prompting the nearest of the remaining heads to crane around and bark something in the guttural Vaasan dialect. The voices fell immediately silent, and the head turned back toward Melegaunt.

"T-traveler, you would do well to s-stop there," the Vaasan said, the frigid bog mud causing him to stutter and slur his words. "The l-logs here are rotted through."

"My thanks for the warning," Melegaunt replied. Still fifteen paces from the end of the road, he stopped and held up the small coil of line he had pulled from his rucksack. "My rope won't reach so far. I fear you have spoiled your own rescue."

The Vaasan tipped his head a little to the side and said, "I think our chances b-better with you out there, instead of in here with us."

"Perhaps so," Melegaunt allowed.

He peered into the fog beyond the Vaasan's tribe, trying in vain to see where the road started again. As annoying as it was in the first place not to know where he was going, the possibility of being forced to turn back before he found out absolutely vexed him.

"Where does this road lead? To Delhalls or Moorstown?"

"Where d-does the road lead?" the Vaasan stammered, his voice sharp with disbelief and anger. "What about my people? After I saved you, y-you are not going to help us?"

"Of course I'm going to help you. I'll do everything I

can," Melegaunt said. Somewhere deeper in the fog, another Vaasan screamed, and sank beneath the bog with a cold slurp. "You might, uh, disappear before I pull you free. If that happens, I'd still like to know where this road leads."

"If that happens, the knowledge w-will do you no good," the Vaasan growled. "Your only hope of reaching your d-destination is to rescue my clan, so that we can guide you wherever you are going."

"Something is dragging your tribe under one-by-one and you are trifling over details?" Melegaunt demanded. He pulled his black dagger, then dropped to his hands and knees and began to probe the logs ahead for rot. "This is no time to negotiate. I won't abandon you."

"Then your patience will be rewarded," the Vaasan said firmly.

Melegaunt looked up, his brow furrowed into a deliberate scowl. "Am I to understand you don't trust me?"

"I trust you to try harder if you have n-need of us."

"An answer as slippery as the bog in which you are mired," Melegaunt snapped. "If I am successful, you will have no need of *me*. How can I trust you to guide me then?"

"You have the word of Bodvar, leader of the Moor Eagle Clan," the Vaasan said. "That is all the trust you need."

"Trust has different meaning for outsiders than for Vaasans, I see," Melegaunt grumbled, "but I warn you, if you go back on your promise. . . ."

"You have nothing to fear on that account," Bodvar said. "You have but to keep yours, and I will keep mine."

"I have heard that before," Melegaunt muttered. "Far too many times."

Despite his complaint, Melegaunt continued to advance up the road, probing ahead for rotten logs. By all accounts, the Vaasans had been a harsh but honest people until the fabled bloodstone mines of Delhalls and Talagbar were rediscovered and the outside world intruded to teach them the value of duplicity and fraud. Since then, save for a few villages like Moortown where a man's word was rumored to be more precious than his life, they were said to be as corrupt and sly as everyone else in a world of liars and cheats.

Melegaunt was beginning to doubt Bodvar's story about the rot when his dagger finally found soft wood. He pressed harder, and the entire log disintegrated, crumbling into red dust before his eyes. Then the one beneath his hands grew spongy, prompting him to push back onto his haunches. The log beneath his knees began to soften as well, and a muddy dome of peat welled up not three feet in front of him, a long line of dorsal barbs breaking the surface as the spine of some huge, eel-shaped creature rolled past.

Melegaunt dropped onto his seat and pushed away, scrambling backward as fast as he could crawl. By the time the wood ceased growing soft, he was five paces farther from Bodvar, distant enough that he could no longer make out even the shape of the Vaasans' heads.

Another clansman screamed, then slipped beneath the bog with a muffled slurp.

"Traveler, are you still there?" Bodvar called.

"For now," Melegaunt replied. He stood and backed away another couple of paces. "Something came after me."

"One of the bog people," Bodvar said. "They are attracted by vibration."

"Vibration?" Melegaunt echoed. "Like talking?"

"Like talking," Bodvar confirmed. "But do not worry about me. My armor muffles the sound—it is made of dragon scales."

"All the same, rest quiet for a while." Melegaunt's opinion of the Vaasan was rising—and more because of the risk he was taking for his tribe than because he wore dragon-scale armor. "I'll get you out. I promise."

"A man should not promise what he cannot be certain of delivering, Traveler," Bodvar said, "but I do trust you to do your utmost."

Melegaunt assured the Vaasan he would, then retreated a few more paces up the road and held his hand out over the road edge. There was not even a hint of shadow. Melegaunt's magic would be at its weakest, and he had already seen enough of his foe's power to know it would be folly to duel him less than full strength—even in a world of decay and rebirth, wood simply did not rot as fast as had those logs.

Doing his best to ignore the occasional screams that rolled out of the fog, Melegaunt removed a handful of strands of shadowsilk from his cloak pocket and twisted them into a tightly-wound skein. In a century-and-a-half of reconnoitering Toril, he had yet to risk revealing himself by using such powerful shadow magic where others might see—but never before had he been given reason to think his long quest might be nearing its culmination. Bodvar was a brave one, and that was the first quality. He was also wary, neither giving oaths nor taking them lightly, and that was the second. Whether he was also the third remained to be seen—and it soon would, if matters went as expected.

Once Melegaunt had twisted the shadowsilk into a tightly wound skein, he uttered a few words in ancient Netherese and felt a surge of cold energy rising through his feet into his body. Unlike most wizards in Faerûn, who extracted their magic from the goddess Mystra's all-encompassing Weave, Melegaunt drew his magic from the enigmatic Shadow Weave. As universal as the Weave itself, the Shadow Weave was less known and far more powerful, if only because the cloaked goddess— she who must never be named—kept it uncompromisingly secret and maddened anyone who revealed its existence.

When he was sufficiently imbued with the Shadow Weave's cold magic, Melegaunt tossed the skein of shadowsilk out over the bog and made a twirling motion with his fingers. The cord began to unwind, but sank into the peat before it finished and continued to spin, drawing long tendrils of fog after it.

An oxen bellowed in alarm, then there was a huge glugging sound followed by the crackle of splintering wood and the shrieks of terrified women and children.

"T-t-traveler?" called Bodvar, sounding weaker and colder than before. "H-have you left us?"

"Stay quiet, Vaasan, or there will be no reason for me to

stay," Melegaunt shouted back. "I am working as fast as I can."

Judging by the restless voices that followed, the clan of the Moor Eagle took little comfort from his assurance. Melegaunt urged them again to be patient. While he waited for his first spell to do its work, he prepared himself for battle, girding himself with magic armor and shields of spell-turning, readying power word attacks and casting enchantments that would allow him to walk on mud or swim through it with equal ease. By the time he finished, his spell had thinned the fog enough that he could see a long line of mired Vaasan men and overloaded wagons curving away toward the jagged gray wall of a distant mountain range. The end of the column was perhaps two hundred paces distant, and fifty paces beyond that, he could see the brownish ribbon of logs where the road resumed again.

Instead of looking impressed or grateful, Bodvar and his equally bearded warriors were all searching the blue sky with expressions of alarmed expectation. Those with free sword arms were holding their weapons ready, while on the wagons, women and old men were stringing longbows and raising spears. Melegaunt glanced around the heavens and found nothing except snow clouds—then heard two loud slurping sounds as another pair of warriors were drawn down into the muck.

He stepped to the end of the log road and held his arm out. Finding that there was enough light to cast a shadow, he swung his arm around until the dark line pointed at Bodvar. Though a good twenty paces remained between them, the fog was so thin that Melegaunt could see that with sapphire-blue eyes and hair as red as bloodstone, Bodvar was both handsome and fair-haired by Vaasan standards.

"You caused this clearing, Traveler?" Bodvar asked.

Melegaunt nodded, then lied, "I like to see what I'm fighting." Actually, he was more comfortable fighting in darkness than light, but if he could keep the Vaasans from pondering the nature of his powers, there was a good chance they would be unfamiliar enough with outsider spells to think he was using normal magic. "The battle goes faster."

"Indeed," Bodvar answered. "Let us hope not too fast. There is a reason the Mountainshadow Bog is crossed only in thick fog."

Melegaunt frowned and asked, "That would be?"

"On its way."

Bodvar raised his hand—the one that was not trapped in the bog—and pointed west. The nearby peaks had grown distinct enough that they resembled a line of snow-capped fangs, and curving down from their summits, Melegaunt saw several lines of pale specks.

"Griffons?" he asked. "Or wyverns?"

"You will wish."

"Well, as long as they're not dragons," Melegaunt said. "Anything else, I can handle."

"You have a high opinion of yourself, Traveler."

"As shall you," Melegaunt replied.

With that, he spoke a few words of magic, and the shadow he had lain across the bog expanded to the width of a comfortable walking trail. Melegaunt stepped off the logs and, continuing to hold his arm out, followed the shadow forward. To prevent the path from vanishing as he moved forward, he had to utter a spell of permanency—and that was when the sodden peat let out an explosive *glub* beside him.

Melegaunt turned to see a pair webbed hands clutching the edge of his shadow-walk, between them a slimy reptilian head shooting up to attack. The face itself was rather broad and froglike, save that its dead black eyes were fixed on Melegaunt's leg and its lips were drawn back to reveal a mouthful of needle-sharp fangs. He lowered a hand and spoke a magic power word, unleashing a cold black bolt that drilled a fist-sized hole through the thing's head. The hands opened, and its lifeless body slipped back into the sodden peat.

"What magic is that?" Bodvar gasped, watching from a few steps ahead.

"Southern magic," Melegaunt lied. He stopped at the

Vaasan's side and stooped down, offering his hand. "You wouldn't know it."

Bodvar was not quick to reach for the shadow wizard's swarthy arm.

"Who would?" he demanded. "We are not so backward here in Vaasa as you may think. We know about the dark magic of Thay."

Melegaunt had to laugh. "You have no idea."

He uttered a quick spell, and tentacles of darkness shot from his fingertips to entwine the Vaasan's wrist.

"Now come out of there," said Melegaunt. "You made a bargain."

Melegaunt stood and drew the tentacles back into his fingers, pulling Bodvar's arm along. A muffled *pop* sounded from somewhere below the peat, and the Vaasan screamed. Though Melegaunt was fairly certain he had just separated the chieftain's shoulder, he continued to pull—pulled harder, in fact. As loud as Bodvar had screamed, the bog people would be after him like a school of snagglesnouts after a waterstrider.

The Vaasan did not budge, and though Melegaunt had the strength to pull the arm off, that would not free Bodvar of the sodden peat's cold clutch. He stopped pulling. Bodvar continued to groan—though less loudly than he had screamed before—and a long ridge of upwelling peat began to snake its way toward the chieftain.

Melegaunt pointed a finger at the head of the ridge and uttered a magic syllable. A ray of black shadow shot down through the peat. The creature was too deep to see whether the attack hit home, but the ridge stopped advancing in Bodvar's direction.

"Be quiet," Melegaunt urged. "See if you can slip free of your boots and trousers."

Bodvar stopped groaning long enough to cast a side-long glance at Melegaunt. "My trousers? My *dragon-scale* trousers?"

"You must break the suction," Melegaunt explained. "It is your trousers or your life."

Bodvar sighed, but struggled to move his free hand under the peat.

"Can you reach them?" Melegaunt asked.

"No, I can't—" Bodvar's eyes suddenly went wide, then he began to yell, "Pull! *Pull!*"

Melegaunt felt the Vaasan being dragged downward and began to haul in the opposite direction. Bodvar howled in pain and rage, his body squirming and thrashing as he struggled to free himself. There was a muffled crunch that sounded something like a breaking bone, then Bodvar finally came free, rising out of the bog with no boots or pants, but a dagger in hand and his sword belt looped over his elbow.

Melegaunt glimpsed a slimy figure slipping down the hole with the Vaasan's trousers trailing from one corner of its smiling mouth, then the bog closed in and concealed it from view. Melegaunt cast a shadow bolt after it, but it was impossible to say whether the spell hit its target or vanished into the bottomless depths without striking anything.

"Hell-cursed mudbreather!" Bodvar swore. "Look what it did to my sword!"

Melegaunt lowered the Vaasan to the shadow-walk, then looked over to find the man naked from the waist down and one arm sagging askew from the shoulder socket, holding the flopping scabbard of a badly shattered sword in his good hand.

"How am I to fight with this?"

"Fight? In your condition?"

Melegaunt glanced toward the mountains and saw that the distant specks had become V-shaped lines, all angling toward the bog where the largest part of the Moor Eagle clan was still trapped. He opened his cloak and pulled his own sword, a slender blade of what looked like black glass, from its scabbard.

"Use this," Melegaunt said, "but with a light hand. It will cut much better than that iron bar you're accustomed to."

Bodvar barely glanced at the weapon.

"I'll use my dagger," said the Vaasan. "That thing'll break the first time—"

"Not likely."

Melegaunt brought his sword down across Bodvar's dagger and sliced through the blade as though it was made of soft wood instead of cold-forged iron, then he flicked the stump out of the grasp of the astonished Vaasan and replaced it with the hilt of his own weapon.

"Be careful not to take off your foot."

Bodvar closed his sagging jaw and, one arm still hanging limply at his side, stepped past Melegaunt and lopped the heads off two bog people emerging from the peat behind him.

"It'll do," he said. Despite the obvious pain from his separated shoulder, the Vaasan did not even clench his teeth as he spoke. "My thanks for the loan."

"Consider it a gift," Melegaunt replied, turning back to the rest of the clan. "I use it so seldom."

To Melegaunt's dismay, the bog people had been far from idle while he was rescuing Bodvar. Half the warriors who had been mired when he arrived had already vanished beneath the surface, while the women and old men were struggling to keep dozens of bog people from clambering onto the cargo wagons with the clan's sobbing children. Melegaunt pulled a handful of shadowsilk from his cloak and flung it in the direction of the wagons, then he spread his fingers and waggled them in a raining motion. A dark pall fell over the six closest wagons, and everyone it touched—Vaasans and bog people alike—fell instantly asleep.

"How did you do that?" Bodvar demanded. "Sleep magic doesn't work against the bog people!"

"Clearly, you have been misinformed." Melegaunt held his arm out toward the nearest wagon, extending the shadow-walk to within three paces of the driver's bench. "Do you think . . ."

Bodvar was already sprinting down the shadow-walk, borrowed sword in hand. When he reached the end, he launched himself into a wild leap over the horns of a mired ox, bounding off its half-submerged shoulders, and came down on the seat between the slumbering driver and the old man slumped beside her. Despite Melegaunt's warning to handle the weapon lightly, he set to work on the sleeping bog people with an ardor that left little doubt about the primitive state of Vaasan weaponsmithing. Melegaunt saw him cut two enemies cleanly apart across the torso and cleave through three of the wagon's sideboards before he could no longer bear to watch and turned his attention to the mired warriors.

The nearest vanished beneath the surface as Melegaunt approached, and two more cried out in alarm. Seeing he had no hope of rescuing even a dozen of the remaining warriors, he tossed his tarp line onto the surface and uttered a long spell. The far end raised itself out of the peat, and the black rope began to slither forward. He pointed at the nearest of the warriors, and the line angled in the man's direction.

"As the rope comes by. . . ."

That was all Melegaunt needed to say. The first warrior snatched the line and, slipping free of his trousers, allowed it to pull him free. He slid across the slippery surface for three paces, then rolled onto his back and began to hack at something beneath the surface with his sword. Seeing that he had at least a reasonable chance of defending himself, Melegaunt directed the rope to the next warrior in line, who also came free without his pants or boots, and there were two Vaasans slashing at their unseen pursuer.

They seemed to slay it after a dozen yards, but by then Melegaunt had three more warriors on the line, and two of them were being trailed by the tell-tale rise of a bog person traveling just beneath the surface. He summoned the rope over to his shadow-walk and used his last shadow bolt to kill one of their pursuers, and the warriors themselves took care of the last one before bounding off after Bodvar to help defend the wagons.

Melegaunt glanced toward the mountains. To his alarm, the distant fliers were so close that he could make out not only the white bodies hanging beneath their wings, but their bandy legs and curved swords as well. Whatever the creatures were—and he had yet to see their like in a century and a half of wandering the world—they were as fast as baatezu. He only hoped they were not as adept as the pit fiends at defeating shadow magic.

Melegaunt sent the rescue rope out again and managed to pull in six more warriors before the bog people claimed the rest. Though he was not happy to fail so many—the number had to be nearly twenty—the Vaasans took their losses in stride, pausing only to grunt a half-understood word of thanks before rushing back to join Bodvar and their fellows in defending the women and children.

Seeing there was no more to be done, Melegaunt retrieved his tarp line and turned toward the mired wagons. With the half-naked warriors he had rescued rushing back to help, the women and old men were holding the bog people at bay with surprising displays of swordsmanship and bravery. No matter how well they fought, though, it was clear that the younger children and older clansmen lacked the agility to leap from wagon to wagon—especially over the heads of panicked oxen—as the warriors were doing.

Melegaunt rushed alongside the caravan, laying his shadow-walk close enough that the trapped Vaasans could jump from their wagons onto the path behind him. The bog people redoubled their attacks, glugging up alongside the walk in a near-solid wall. But all of Bodvar's clansmen were as well-trained and disciplined as his warriors, and they repelled the attacks easily. Though Melegaunt failed to understand why the bog people did not use their rotting magic on the wagons themselves, he was relieved that they were not. Perhaps their magic-user had run out of spells, or maybe the enchantment took too long to cast.

With their panicked masters rushing past, the mired oxen bellowed for help that would never come. Given time, Melegaunt could certainly have freed the creatures and saved the cargo in their wagons, but as things were he would be doing well to lose no more of their masters. As he neared the end of the caravan, he was astonished to see that the bog people had not pulled even one of the beasts from its yoke. Whatever their reason for attacking the Moor Eagles, it had less to do with hunger than wanting to wipe out the tribe.

Melegaunt was twenty paces past the last mired

wagon when a trio of bog people emerged before him, snatching at his legs with their webbed hands. He drilled the middle one with a black shadow bolt, then heard hooked finger-talons clattering off his spell-armor as the other two attempted to slash his legs from beneath him. He brought his boot heel down on a sloping forehead and heard a loud *pop* as the skull caved in, then he caught his other attacker by the arm and jerked it out of the peat. Save that the bog man was covered in slimy brown scales and had a flat, lobsterlike tail in place of legs and feet, it looked more or less humanoid, with powerfully-built shoulders and a navel that suggested it was born rather than hatched.

It slashed at Melegaunt with its free hand several times. When its claws continued to bounce harmlessly off the wizard's shadow armor, it gave up and opened its mouth, attacking with a long, barb-tipped tongue so fast Melegaunt barely had time to tip his head aside and save his eye. He caught the tongue as it shot back toward the creature's mouth, then whirled around to find Bodvar and the rest of the Vaasans staring at him with expressions that were equal part awe and terror.

"Don't just stand there," Melegaunt ordered, "kill it!"

Only Bodvar had possession enough of his wits to obey, slashing the thing across the waist so hard that his borrowed sword came a hair's breadth from opening Melegaunt's ample belly as well. Eyeing the chieftain sidelong, Melegaunt tossed aside the lifeless torso, then pointed at a long line of bog people rising out of the peat beside the gape-mouthed Vaasans.

"Lift your jaws and see to your enemies!"

Without waiting to see whether they obeyed, he turned and extended the shadow-walk the rest of the way to the logs, then he led the way to the relatively solid footing of the road. The bog people had no choice but to give up their attack, for all the Vaasans had to do to be safe was retreat to the middle of the road where they could not be reached.

The creatures flying in from the mountains were another matter. Only a few hundred yards distant, they were close enough that Melegaunt could make out scaly white bodies with long, pointed tails, and also craggy saurian heads with long snouts, swept-back horns, and huge yellow eyes. One of the creatures flung something in their direction and began to make spell gestures.

Melegaunt flattened a ball of shadowsilk between his palms, then flung it toward the approaching dragonmen and uttered a few words in ancient Netherese. A hazy disk of darkness appeared between the two groups and began to bleed black tendrils of shadow into the sky, but Melegaunt had not been quick enough to raise his spell shield. He felt a familiar softening underfoot, and the Vaasans cried out and began to stampede up the road. It was exactly the wrong thing to do. The rotting logs came apart all the faster, plunging the entire tribe to their knees in sodden peat.

In an attempt to spread their weight and slow their descent, they immediately threw themselves to their bellies and splayed their arms. Still standing atop the peat by virtue of the spells he had cast before the battle, Melegaunt cursed and laid his shadow-walk again, then turned to meet the dragonmen.

They were nowhere to be seen, at least not near his spell shield. Pulling another strand of shadowsilk from his pocket, Melegaunt pivoted in a slow circle and—as expected—found them diving out of the sun. Melegaunt allowed himself a tight smile. They were wise to respect his abilities—much wiser, in that regard, than had been better-known foes in the south. He tossed his shadowsilk into the sky and uttered the incantation of one of his more potent spells.

That whole quarter of the sky broke into a shower of shadowy tears. Instead of rolling off when they fell on a body, however, these drops clung to whatever they touched, stretching into long threads of sticky black fiber. Within moments, the entire column of dragonmen had become swaddled in gummy balls of darkness and was plunging headlong into the bog. Melegaunt watched long enough to be certain that none of the fliers would escape, then turned to find the Moor Eagles rushing onto the log road behind him.

They were glancing at him over their shoulders, making signs of warding that might have kept a demon at bay, but that only made Melegaunt feel lonely and unappreciated. Stifling bitter laughter, he walked across the bog to where Bodvar and three more brave warriors stood waiting for him at the edge of the road.

"I'm sorry for your losses, Bodvar," he said. "I might have saved more, but there was much you didn't tell me."

"And much you didn't tell us," Bodvar replied. He laid the hilt of Melegaunt's black sword across his arm and offered it to the wizard. "My thanks."

Melegaunt waved him off.

"Keep it. As I said, I seldom use it anymore."

"I know what you said," Bodvar replied, "but only a fool takes gifts from a devil."

"Devil?" Melegaunt snapped, still not taking his sword. "Is that how you repay my kindness? With insults?"

"What is true is no insult," Bodvar said. "We saw the things you did."

"It was only magic," Melegaunt protested. "Southern magic. If you have not seen its like before. . . ."

"Now it is you who are insulting us," Bodvar said, continuing to offer the sword. "In Vaasa, we are backward in many things—but wisdom is no longer one of them."

Melegaunt started to repeat his protests, then realized he would only anger Bodvar by insisting on the lie—and revealing the truth about the Shadow Weave was, of course, out of the question. If he were lucky enough to avoid being struck dead on the spot, he would lose forever the dark power that had so impressed the Vaasans.

When Melegaunt made no further attempts to argue, Bodvar said, "We will keep the bargain we made." He tipped his chin toward the three warriors with him. "These are the guides I promised. They will take you wherever you wish to go in Vaasa."

Melegaunt started to say that he no longer needed them—then thought better of it and smiled. "*Anywhere*?"

Bodvar looked uncomfortable, but nodded and said, "That was our bargain."

"Good. Then I want them to take me wherever the

Moor Eagles are going." Melegaunt took his sword back and added, "And no tricks, Bodvar. I'm sure we both know what happens to those who play false with devils—don't we?"

Higharvestide, the Year of the Moat
In the Shadows of the Peaks of the Dragonmen

Bodvar came to the island, as Melegaunt had known he would, late in the day, when the sun was sinking low over the Peaks of the Dragonmen and the shadows of the mountains lay long upon the cold bog. What the wizard had not known was that the chieftain would bring his wife, a young beauty with hair the color of night and eyes as blue as a clear sky. She seemed a little thicker around the middle than the last time Melegaunt had seen her, though it was always hard to tell with Vaasan women—their shape tended to vanish beneath all the furs they wore.

Melegaunt watched them pick their way across his zigzagging boulder-walk until a metallic sizzle behind him demanded his attention. He checked the sky to be certain there were no white-scaled fliers diving down to trouble them, then he donned a huge leather mitt and pulled a long narrow mold from the oven he had kept blazing for three days. In the mold, floating on a bed of liquid tin, lay a sword similar to the one he had offered Bodvar all those tendays ago—save that it was still molten and glowing white hot.

Melegaunt placed the sword on a bed of ice—freezes came early to that part of the world—then he waited for the mold to cool. When he was sure the cold would draw the tempering elements down to the underside, he began to lay fibers of shadowsilk on the molten glass, taking care to arrange them first lengthwise, then diagonally in both directions, then lengthwise again so the weapon would have strength and resilience in all directions. Finally, he used his dagger to open another cut on his arm, dripping his warm blood into the mixture and quietly whispering the ancient words that gave the blade its magic thirst.

By the time that was finished, the sword had hardened enough that he could lift it from its mold and plunge it into a vat of slushy water, placed at just the right distance from the furnace to keep it that way. Once the heat had melted all of the slush, Melegaunt removed the sword, then placed it on its bed of hot tin with the opposite side down and returned the mold to the oven again. Such was the art of the shadow blade, heating and cooling a thousand times over, tinting them with shadowsilk until the glass could finally hold no more and began to shed fibers like an unbrushed dog.

A soft boot scuffed the stone at the edge of Melegaunt's work site, then Bodvar called, "I see you are still here, Dark Devil."

"You can see that by the smoke of my furnaces," Melegaunt answered. He pulled the sleeve of his cloak down to hide the cuts on his arm, then turned to glower at the chieftain. "Come for a sword, have you?"

"Hardly," said Bodvar. He cast an uneasy glance at the nineteen weapons racked at the edge of the work site. Though all were completed and honed to a razor edge, they were paler than Melegaunt's sword, with a crystal translucence that still showed the lay of the shadow fibers embedded in the glass. "You are wasting your time on that account."

"Am I?" Melegaunt smirked knowingly and added, "Well, they will be here when you need them."

"Our need will never be that great."

Melegaunt did not argue, only swung an arm toward the furnace behind him and said, "That will be twenty. Twenty warriors is all that remains to you, is it not?"

Instead of answering, Bodvar glanced around the cluttered work area and shook his head.

"Only a devil could live out here alone. It is exposed to every wind that blows."

"It's a safe place to work."

Melegaunt glanced at Bodvar's young wife and smiled. Idona smiled back, but said nothing. Though Vaasan women were hardly shy, he had noticed that most of them preferred to keep their silence around him.

He looked back to Bodvar and said, "The bog people protect every ground approach but one, and the dragonmen are easy to spot from here."

"The dragonmen can watch you," Bodvar countered, "and the bog people have you surrounded."

"Vaasans may see it that way." Melegaunt knelt and began to feed his furnace from the charcoal pile beside it. "The way to destroy an enemy is to make him fight in his home instead of yours."

Melegaunt raised his mitted hand toward a white-hot poker, and Bodvar, not thinking, reached for it—then shrieked in surprise as Melegaunt used a cantrip to summon the utensil and spare him a burned palm.

Idona giggled, drawing an embarrassed, though tender, frown from her husband. Melegaunt shook his head in mock exasperation at Bodvar's clumsiness, and she broke into full laughter.

"You see?" Bodvar complained lightly. "This is what comes of treating with devils."

"Of course, my husband," Idona said. "This bearded one is always saving you from something, the mudbreathing knave."

"That is what worries me," Bodvar said, his tone more serious.

Desperate not to let Bodvar's suspicious nature undermine the unexpected openness his humor had won from Idona, Melegaunt poked at the coals, then changed the subject.

"Speaking of mudbreathers and saving you, Bodvar, you never did tell me why the bog people and dragonmen were trying so hard to wipe out your tribe."

"*Were?*" Idona echoed. "They still are. Why do you think we stay camped at the other end of your walkway? If it wasn't for you—"

"Idona!" Bodvar snapped.

Hiding his delight behind a tolerant smile, Melegaunt tossed the poker aside—it remained hovering in the air—and began to feed more charcoal into the fire.

"I'm only happy to be of use." Melegaunt fixed his gaze on Bodvar and added, "But that still doesn't answer my question."

Bodvar flushed and said nothing.

"Are you going to answer him, Husband," Idona, smirking, asked, "or am I?"

The more Idona spoke, the more Melegaunt liked her.

"By all means, Idona," Melegaunt said, "I would rather hear it from your—"

"I had this idea," Bodvar began. "I wanted to build a fort."

"Fort?" Melegaunt asked.

He stopped feeding the flames and stood.

"For the treasure caravans," Idona said, rolling her eyes. "He actually thought outlanders would give us good coin just to sleep with a roof over their heads."

"And to have us stand guard," Bodvar added defensively. "When we're out hunting, they're always asking to share our camps and fires."

"Do they pay then?" Idona demanded.

Bodvar frowned and said, "Of course not. Who'd pay to pitch his own tent?"

"I see." Melegaunt found it difficult to keep the delight out of his voice. At last, he had discovered something that might move Bodvar to take help from a "shadow devil." "But the bog people and dragonmen prey on the caravans, and they have other ideas?"

Bodvar nodded and said, "The dragonmen sacked our first fort before it was half completed, and when we tried to move south to a more defensible site . . . well, you saw what happened."

Idona took his hand.

"We're better off anyway," she said. "Who wants to live one place the whole year? What happens when the herds move?"

"What indeed?" Melegaunt asked absently.

He was looking over his shoulder toward the granite summit of his little island. On a clear day, it was possible to look across the bog clear to where the log road ended— or began, if the caravan was coming from the mountains with its load of treasure. If he could see the road, then anyone on the road would be able to see the top of the island.

"Melegaunt?" Bodvar asked.

Realizing he had not been paying attention, Melegaunt tore his gaze from the summit and turned back to Bodvar.

"Sorry," he said. "You were saying?"

"He was inviting you to take feast with us," said Idona. "It's Higharvestide, in case you have lost track."

"It's Idona's idea," Bodvar added, though his friendly tone made it clear that he did not object too strenuously. "She says it's only common courtesy."

"And no more than we owe," Idona added, frowning at Bodvar. "Considering all you have done for us."

"All I have done for you?" Melegaunt waved a hand in dismissal. "It's nothing, truly, but I can't join you. Next Higharvestide, perhaps."

"*Next* Higharvestide?" Bodvar scowled at the furnace where the last sword lay on its bed of sizzling tin. "If you're staying to watch over that sword, you may as well come, because—"

"It's not the sword," Melegaunt said. "The sword will be done by nightfall. I must have my rest tonight. Tomorrow will be a busy day for me."

Idona's face was not the only one that fell.

"Then you are leaving?" Bodvar asked. "If you are, be certain to take your swords with you, because they will only—"

"I'm not leaving." Melegaunt had to turn toward the island's granite summit—try as he might, he could not hide his smile. "Tomorrow, I start work on my tower."

"Tower?" Idona echoed.

"Yes." Finally in control of his expression again, Melegaunt turned around. "To watch over the treasure caravans."

But Melegaunt knew he would have no rest that night. He had read in the dawn shadows that it would be the evening when the Moor Eagles moved onto the island with him. His divinations proved correct shortly after dark, when the clan's mead-induced revels were interrupted by the clanging of the sentry's bell. Melegaunt lit a signal beacon he had prepared for the occasion, then went to the front of the work site to inspect the situation.

A cloud of white forms was descending from the peaks of the dragonmen, their wings flashing silver in the moonlight as they spiraled down toward the bog's edge. Their spellcasters were already hurling magic bolts and balls of golden flame at the Moor Eagles, but the rest of the warriors were taking care to forestall counterattacks by keeping their magic-users well screened from Melegaunt's island. A sporadic stream of arrows began to rise from Bodvar's camp and arc into the night, falling pitifully short of their targets.

Melegaunt spread his arms and cast a shadow fog over the camp, more to prevent the Moor Eagles from wasting their time and arrows than to delay the dragonmen. Still, they had not forgotten the sticky rain he had called down on them in the bottomless bog—half their number had sunk beneath the peat and drowned—so they gave the dark cloud wide berth, angling away to land in the foothills on the far side of camp.

Leaving the Moor Eagles to fend for themselves, Melegaunt turned his attention to what he was sure would be the second part of the dragonmen's plan and found a company of bog people slithering up to block his boulder walk. The clan women were gamely rushing forward to meet them, Idona and a few of the others wielding iron swords or wood axes, but most armed with nothing more deadly than fire-hardened spears and cudgels so light Melegaunt could have snapped them over his knee.

"Hold!"

Melegaunt's Vaasan had grown passable enough over the past few months that Idona recognized the command for what it was and called her sisters to a stop. He pointed at a hole in the exact center of the shadow-walk and spoke a single word of magic. A whirling pinwheel of black tentacles erupted from the hole and slashed the bog people into so many chunks of slimy flesh, then withdrew back into the hole.

"*Now* you can come," Melegaunt called, using his magic to project his voice. "And bring those foolish husbands of yours, or the only Higharvestide feast will be that of the dragonmen."

Idona raised her sword in acknowledgement and sent the other women forward with the children, then rushed back into the shadow swaddled camp. Melegaunt waited impatiently for her return. It seemed to take her forever, and he feared the surviving bog people would regain their courage before she could convince her husband to retreat to the safety of the island. Finally, warriors began to stagger onto the boulder walk in twos and threes, often supporting and sometimes carrying each other. Melegaunt thought for a moment that the evening's festivities had simply been proceeding faster than he expected, but then he noticed that one of the men was missing an arm and another had something dangling on his cheek that might have been an eye.

Bodvar came last with Idona at his side, holding an armful of quivers over one arm and a shield over the other, alternately feeding arrows to her husband and stepping forward to intercept the wicked barbs flying their way from somewhere deeper in the camp. Melegaunt allowed them to retreat to the first sharp bend in that fashion, then, speaking a magic command word, he pointed at a crooked crevice bisecting the boulder closest to shore.

A wall of faintly writhing shadows shot up from the fissure, sealing the boulder walk from the Vaasans' camp. Bodvar and Idona turned and raced for the island, moving so fast that they nearly overran the next turn. Only Idona's quick feet—and quicker hands—kept Bodvar from going over the edge and plunging into the cold bog. They took the next corner more cautiously, then reached the island and started up the trail behind the others.

By then, the first wave of dragonmen were flying over and around the shadow wall at the other end of the boulder walk, staying low and close to avoid making themselves targets. It was a bad mistake. As they passed by, the writhing shadows struck out like snakes, entwining anything else they could reach. Whatever they touched vanished, and soon arms, legs, wings, even heads were raining down on the shore and into the bog.

The dragonmen's pursuit stopped cold, and the Moor Eagles' women and children began to pour onto the work site. Melegaunt directed them into the shallow shelters he had hollowed out behind the sword rack. When he turned back to the battle, the tentacles in his shadow wall were swirling outward in three separate cones, each spiraling toward a small cluster of dragonmen hovering over the village. The spinning cones tore through the warrior screen as easily as they had the pursuit fliers a moment earlier, then diced the spell casters they had been trying to shield.

"Try to dispel *my* magic, will you?" Melegaunt called in ancient Draconic. "Come hither. I have more of the same waiting here!"

The last few dragonmen sank behind the shadow and vanished. For a time, Melegaunt feared he truly had defeated the attack that easily. The warriors began to reach his work site and check on their families. There were a handful of anguished cries and panicked calls for missing children, but with Melegaunt's help, the Vaasans had managed their retreat without losing many of their number. Three warriors who were too badly injured to fight were given over to the clan's healing witch, then Bodvar and Idona arrived, breathing hard and supporting each other, but both whole and sound.

"Well, Devil, it seems you have saved us again," Bodvar said. "Whether we like it or not."

Melegaunt spread his hands and said, "I live to serve."

Bodvar scowled and started to make a retort, then someone called, "Whitescales from the east!" and someone else yelled, "And from the west! Thirty at least, coming in low over the bog!"

Melegaunt rushed to the western edge of his work site and saw a long rank of dragonmen approaching the island, their white scales shining like ivory against the dark peat. Their line curved behind the island and, from the cries behind him, continued all the way around to the other side. The clan of the Moor Eagle was surrounded. Struggling to bite back his smile, Melegaunt turned to find Bodvar and Idona standing behind him.

"It seems your faith in me was misplaced," Melegaunt said. "My apologies, Bodvar."

"None necessary. I'm the one who brought this on us," Bodvar said. He fluttered his fingers in the direction of the approaching dragonmen. "Just do what you can."

"I am afraid that will not be much, my friend." Melegaunt spoke loudly enough to be sure that nearby warriors, already gathering to eavesdrop, would be certain to overhear. "Even I have my limits."

"Limits?" Bodvar growled.

"I did not expect this. My magic is all but exhausted."

Bowstrings began to thrum around the perimeter of the work site, but they were too few—and their arrow points too soft—to turn back the dragonmen.

Melegaunt drew his black sword, stepped away from the edge, and said, "But I can still give a good accounting of myself."

As he had hoped, the sight of his darksword proved an inspiration.

"The black swords!" Idona cried, turning toward the rack. "Those will balance the—"

"No." Calm though it was, Bodvar's voice was surprisingly masterful and imposing. "Of all the women in the tribe, Idona, you should know better. A devil's gift is no gift at all."

Idona looked as though she wanted to argue, but her respect for her husband—and for her chieftain—was too strong. She bit her tongue and pointed at the hidden shelter.

"Then we had better fall back," she said, "before there is nothing left to defend."

Bodvar gave the order, and the dragonmen were on them, streaming onto the work site from all sides. They flew headlong into battle, thrusting at their overwhelmed enemies with iron-tipped spears and relying on their size and speed to carry the attacks home. Half a dozen human voices wailed in pain in the first three heartbeats alone, then the second wave came crashing down from the island summit, and it grew clear that the Vaasans hadn't a chance. When they were lucky enough to land a strike, their brittle weapons either bounced off or broke like icicles against the dragonmen's thick scales.

Still, the Vaasans fought bravely and well, falling back toward the shelter behind the sword racks in good order, defending each other and striking at eyes and armpits and other vulnerable areas whenever the chance came. Within moments, there were as many dragonmen lying on the stony ground as there were humans.

And Melegaunt quickly added to the toll. Protected as he was by an aura of impenetrable shadow and holding a sword that would cut through any armor known in Faerûn, he turned and whirled through the dragonman ranks, slashing legs off here and behorned heads there, dancing past spear thrusts and shrugging off claw strikes like a drow blademaster.

One of the huge saurians managed to clasp him from behind in a bear hug, lifting him off the ground and trapping his arms so that it was impossible to wield his sword. Perhaps thinking to take him out over the bog and drop him to his death, the creature spread his wings and leaped into the air. Melegaunt slammed the back of his head into his attacker's snout, smashing it flat and driving one of the bony horns back into the thing's brain. When the wizard dropped back to his work site, the other dragonmen fell over each other to find someone else to attack.

Then it happened.

A trio of dragonmen spotted the hidden shelter and, battering a pair of human defenders aside with their powerful wings, charged for the children. The first warrior scrambled to his feet and rushed after them, shattering his brittle sword against the back of a thick reptilian skull.

The other Vaasan grabbed one of Melegaunt's glass swords. He sliced one dragonman's legs out from beneath him, then cleaved a second's spine on the backstroke and ran the blade through the third one's heart from behind. As the last saurian crashed to his knees, the warrior let out an anguished gasp. He stumbled back clutching at his heart, and one of the women in the shelter wailed in despair, and cried out his name. But he did not fall. Instead, his hair and beard went as white as snow. The swarthiness drained from his face and his skin turned as pallid as ivory, and when he turned back to the battle, his eyes were as dead and black as those of the bog people, and the sword in his hand had lost its crystal translucence. It was as dark and glossy as Melegaunt's, with no hint at all of the shadow fibers embedded in its heart.

A dragonman stepped out of the mad whirl, thrusting at the warrior's heart with an oaken spear. The Vaasan brought his sword up to block and slashed through the shaft as though it was a twig, then he smiled darkly, opened his attacker across the chest, and waded after more victims.

His success inspired another warrior to snatch one of the weapons, and a woman in the shelter grabbed one to defend her children from an approaching dragonman. They killed their first enemies and underwent transformations similar to the first sword-taker, then they, too, began to cut a swath through the attacking saurians. A dozen dragonmen leaped into the air, angling for the rack of deadly swords. They were met by a like number of Vaasans, all pulling weapons off the hangers and putting them to good use.

Bodvar appeared at Melegaunt's side, nearly losing his hand when he made the mistake of grabbing the wizard's shoulder without warning.

"Stop them!"

"How?" Melegaunt asked. He caught a battering wing on his shoulder, then lopped it off and slashed his attacker across the back of the knees. "The choice is theirs. They would rather live than die."

"Not live in your service!" Bodvar objected. "You arranged this."

"Not arranged," Melegaunt replied. He pointed his palm behind the angry Vaasan's head and blasted a would-be attacker with a shadow bolt. "You give me too much credit."

"And you do not give me enough," said Bodvar. The Vaasan stepped close, and Melegaunt felt the tip of a sword pressed to his back. "Release my clan."

Melegaunt glared at the chieftain and said, "At the moment, Bodvar, you have worse enemies than me." Relying on his shadow armor to protect him, he reached back and snapped the steel sword with his bare hand. "If you want them released, do it yourself. All you need do is persuade them to set aside their swords."

Melegaunt shoved the chieftain away and turned back to the battle. With most of the glass swords in hand, the Vaasans seemed to have matters well under control. The dragonmen were being forced steadily away from the shelters, and even when they attempted to use their wings to slip over the defenders, they were met with a flurry of flashing shadow. Finally, they gave up trying and took wing—at least those who could.

Dozens of wounded saurians remained behind with wings too shredded or broken to lift them, yet still strong enough to fight—and ferocious enough to do it well. The Vaasans quickly set to work on them, herding them into a tight ball and driving them toward the cliffs on the east side of the work site. Seeing that only one sword remained, Melegaunt left them to their work and quietly went to the rack and slipped the last sword into his empty scabbard—and that was when Bodvar choose to assert himself again.

"My warriors, look at each other!" he called. "See what Melegaunt's devil weapons have done to you?"

Melegaunt groaned and shook his head in resignation. Were Bodvar not so stubborn and sure of himself, the wizard supposed, he would not be worth the trouble in the first place. He turned to find the chieftain and his loyal wife standing behind their warriors, Idona holding a cloak loaded with an armful of steel swords, which Bodvar was trying none too successfully to press into his clansmen's hands.

"Finish the battle with your own weapons," he said.

One of the sword-takers—Melegaunt thought it was the first—scowled.

"Why would we do that?" He hefted his darksword and said, "These are better."

"Better?"

Bodvar lunged for the sword—and was dropped to the ground by a solid elbow to the face.

"This one belongs to me," the warrior said.

"Does it?" Idona dumped the steel swords on the ground. "Or do you belong to it?"

She glared over her shoulder with a look that sent a cold shiver down Melegaunt's spine, then she grabbed her husband beneath his arms.

"Come, Bodvar." She pulled him to his feet and turned to leave. "We are Moor Eagles no more."

"Leaving?" gasped the warrior who had struck Bodvar. He looked at his darksword a moment, then, as a discontented murmur began to build among his fellows, lowered the weapon. "Wait."

Melegaunt cursed Idona for an ungrateful shrew and, fumbling in his thoughts for some way to salvage the situation, started forward. As usual, it was the dragonmen who saved him. All at once, they burst into action, hurling themselves at the distracted Vaasans. The first sword-taker and another warrior fell instantly, and the work site erupted into a maelstrom of violence even more confused and ferocious than the first. Melegaunt saw pair of saurians springing in Bodvar's direction and took the first out with a bolt of shadow, but the second was too quick. It bowled the chieftain over on the run and lashed out for Idona, then a half-dozen other melees drifted between Melegaunt and the chieftain's young wife, and he lost her.

Melegaunt rushed forward swinging sword and spraying shadow, but the battle was as mad and confused as it was quick. Before he could find Bodvar again, he had to slay two dragonmen and use a spell of shadow-grabbing to keep from being dashed lifeless on the rocks at the base of his own cliff.

When Melegaunt did find the chieftain, he wished he had not been so quick to save himself. Bodvar was standing in the midst of a bloody pile of Vaasans and dragonmen, holding two broken swords of steel and searching the carnage with a look of utter terror on his face.

"Idona?"

Bodvar found a female leg kicking at the ground from beneath a dead dragonman and used a boot to roll the white-scaled corpse away, but it turned out that the leg belonged to another woman.

He turned away from her without comment and called again, "Idona?"

"There," rasped someone. "They've got her."

Melegaunt spun toward the speaker and found a pallid-faced sword-bearer pointing across the work site to a small knot of fleeing dragonmen. They were just starting down the trail toward the boulder walk, each one with a limp Vaasan body slung over its shoulders. The last body in line was that of Bodvar's young wife, her throat ripped out and her head dangling by the spine alone, her blue eyes somehow still locked on Melegaunt's face.

"No!" Melegaunt gasped. He laid a hand on Bodvar's shoulder. "I'm sorry, Bodvar. Sorry beyond words."

"Why? You have what you came for," said Bodvar. He reached down to Melegaunt's scabbard and drew the last darksword, then raced after the dragonmen to reclaim the body of his dead wife. "You have your twenty souls."

Originally published in *Realms of Infamy*
Edited by James Lowder, December 1994

BLOOD SPORT

Christie Golden

You just can't keep a good vampire down.

Elven vampire Jander Sunstar first appeared in the novel *Vampire of the Mists*, and later in the FORGOTTEN REALMS short stories "One Good Bite," "The Quiet Place" and this one, "Blood Sport."

Even though *Vampire of the Mists* has been out of print for many years, I still get email about him at least once a week. He is probably the best-known character I've ever created, and is very dear to my heart.

"Blood Sport" is not so much about Jander and his goodness as what compassion can do to someone whose entire self-image is based on the power of cruelty and hate.

The imagery of the final confrontation, on a stone monument on a snowy night, has been compared to Tim Burton's films, and the moment in which the Shark realizes who the real villain must be is one of the most powerful scenes I've ever written.

I'm proud that one of my stories has been deemed worthy of being included in this anthology.

—Christie Golden, March 2003

Award-winning author Christie Golden
launched her career with
Vampire of the Mists in 1991 and has
gone on to write twenty-two novels
and over two dozen stories in the fields
of fantasy, science fiction, and horror.
Readers are invited to visit her at
www.christiegolden.com

BLOOD SPORT

I understand you're used to being on the other side of these iron bars," said the woman called the Shark. Her black eyes were hard as she gazed through the barred window into the Mistledale prison cell. "Weren't you once captain of the Riders? They called you Rhynn 'the Fair,' right? Oh, but that was before you turned traitor to the people you were sworn to protect."

Inmate Rhynn, an indigo-haired moon elf, did not reply. Only her clenched hands, their slim wrists encircled by metal shackles, betrayed her tension.

The Shark opened the door with the key given her by the new captain of the Riders. She leaned her tall, well-muscled frame casually against the cold stone of the cell. The elf's glare grew more hostile, though she trembled violently. A malicious smile spread across the Shark's tanned face. Her functional, masculine garb—wool tunic, breeches, and cape—kept her warm, even in the middle of the month of Hammer. Rhynn Oriandis was clad only in a shabby tunic that dozens of prisoners before her had worn. Her skin, pale as that of the quarry the Shark hunted, was covered with gooseflesh.

The Shark knelt and brought her tawny face within an inch of Rhynn's.

"It's all come out, Rhynn. I want the vampire."

"I don't care what lies you've heard. He deserved to go free."

"Ah, you elves do protect your own, don't you?" The Shark's lips curled in a sneer. "I've never heard of an elven vampire before. I'm looking forward to this case."

"Race had nothing to do—"

"It had everything to do with your actions!" the Shark interrupted. "What you forgot is that this creature is not an elf any longer and therefore did not deserve your misplaced protection. He's a vampire. They are things of purest evil. They know no race, and the only thing they 'deserve' is a stake through the heart. Give me the information I want, or I'll simply take it from you."

Rhynn's eyes remained steady. "Torture me all you like. I won't break."

"I wouldn't be so sure. They call me the Shark because I'm the predator's predator. I've fought twenty-two vampires and countless humans, and I've always made my kill." Pride colored in her words. "Now—" her hand was a swift blur as she tangled strong fingers in Rhynn's hair—"cooperate, and you come out of this with your sanity and maybe your freedom. Fight me—" she tightened her grip until Rhynn gasped softly—"and you'll have neither."

The Shark chanted an incantation, blunt-nailed fingers digging into Rhynn's skull. Rhynn arched in pain, her shackles rattling furiously, but she could not resist. The Shark's spell tore open the elf's mind.

The woman's emotions had obviously been confused by the vampire's magical charms, for she saw him as a being devoted to good rather than the monster he was. The Shark had probed other minds in that manner before, and always in the victims' memories the blooder was a veritable saint. The Shark concentrated on the elf's appearance, his name, his destination, even as Rhynn tried frantically to secret the information. In her weakened condition, Rhynn could not bear the mental violation. Her mouth opened in a soundless scream, then unconsciousness claimed her.

She's luckier than she knows, thought the Shark; had she resisted further, the struggle to protect the vampire would have destroyed her sanity.

Triumphant, the Shark released her hold on Rhynn. On a whim, she tossed the keys within the elf's reach. Rhynn might revive and free herself before her captors realized it. Maybe she'd escape. Maybe they'd kill her. It didn't really matter. The Shark slipped the hood of her cloak over her head and vanished, thanks to the cape's enchantment. With hardly a thought, she walked out of the small prison and passed the two guards. Her horse was waiting for her behind the jail, out of sight of the guards. Quietly she mounted. Snow muffled the hoofbeats as the Shark headed toward Mistledale's single main gate. The idiot guards there noticed nothing.

According to Rhynn, the monster wanted to return to Evermeet, the elven homeland. The Shark snorted with contempt. Did the blooder actually think he could cross water? No, he'd be stranded along the Sword Coast, probably in Waterdeep. He already had a three month head start. She'd have to ride hard to catch up with him.

The Shark turned her mount westward, toward the place that was becoming known as the "City of Splendors," and kicked the animal savagely.

The hunt was on.

A bawdy song spilled out of the Orc's Head Inn. The Shark, clad in demure feminine attire and appearing deceptively fragile, entered the noisy tavern. She brushed snow off her cape as she observed the noisy, slightly drunken crowd, then unobtrusively seated herself in a shadowed corner. The blooder wasn't there yet, but her sources had assured her he would make an appearance that night.

She had only been seated a moment when a pretty young barmaid plunked a foamy tankard of ale in front of the Shark. The girl was small but full-figured, with a tumble of golden curls cascading down her back.

"On the house tonight," the barmaid explained. "Shallen Lathkule—" the girl gestured to an extraordinarily handsome youth surrounded by merry companions—"is to be wed tomorrow afternoon. He's buying drinks for all, in memory of his lost bachelorhood."

"Well, to Shallen and his bride. He seems to be a popular young man," ventured the Shark, hoping to draw the barmaid into conversation. Perhaps Shallen knew the blooder.

"Oh, he is indeed. Friendly as you'd like. And talented. Crafts the prettiest baubles this side of Evermeet, so they say."

"He's a pretty bauble himself, isn't he?" joked the Shark.

Before the girl could answer, the door opened and the barmaid's eyes lit up with pleasure. The Shark followed her gaze—and her own eyes flashed in excitement.

A slim figure entered, carrying a large crate. He leaned on the door to close it behind him. Though he wore a gray cloak over his blue tunic, his shoulder-length hair was uncovered, brilliant wheat-gold dusted with snowflakes. No hood shadowed his fair features and bronze skin. His eyes perused the scene with subtle caution, a furtiveness that the Shark recognized. The silver gaze settled on her for a moment, then moved on.

Her elf vampire had arrived.

She watched him intently as he moved gracefully to a spot near the door and set down his crate. Unobtrusive as he was, Shallen spotted him.

"There you are!" the young man cried happily, extricating himself from his less sober companions. "Khyrra told me to talk you into coming to the wedding tomorrow."

"I'm afraid I cannot," replied the elf. The Mistledale

folk hadn't exaggerated when they had described the blooder's voice as sweet, like music. "But this might take the sting out of my refusal."

With a small dagger, he cut the rope that had secured the crate and pulled out a small statue. Carved of soft pine, the figurine was a mere eight inches high, but the moment the elf brought it into the light, all eyes were upon him and his work.

Balanced in his golden palm was a miniature of Lliira, Our Lady of Joy. Her long hair flowed about her, merging into her swirling dress as she danced in sheer delight. One hand was raised, palm flat, while the other one curved around her body, following the drape of her garb.

"Her hand is empty, but there's a little hollow right here," the elf pointed out. "Fill it with a jewel that has a special meaning for you and Khyrra. Our Lady of Joy will stand in my stead at your wedding tomorrow."

Shallen's blue eyes were wide and sparkling with tears. The Shark's own eyes narrowed. How easily tricked they were, all of them—Rhynn, Shallen, and probably that little barmaid as well, judging by her reaction to the elf's entrance. Like the vampire who had made it, the gift was beautiful, but surely also dangerous.

"Thank you. I—" Shallen's throat closed up and he turned back to the bar, embarrassed by his emotion.

"Too much ale," quipped a friend.

The awkward moment dissolved into laughter, and the performers resumed their tune. Though the music was loud enough to drown out most conversation in the tavern, the Shark had come prepared to eavesdrop. She rested her chin on her hand, ostensibly engrossed in the singing. As she did, she held a tiny, perfectly formed horn to her ear, easily concealed by her flowing black locks. She whispered a spell, and the voice of the barmaid came clearly to her ears.

"That must've taken you months! What's Shallen done for you that you give him so pretty a thing?"

The elf glanced back at the jeweler and said, "He wears his youth and happiness like a beautiful robe, for all to see and share in. That's enough. When it's time for you to get married, Maia, I promise I'll give you and your husband something even prettier."

Maia's response was an uncertain laugh.

"Don't know as I'll ever have a husband," she said. Slender, nervous hands gestured at her body, a shade too ripe for modesty, and her beautiful face, a touch too hard for innocence. "Most men like uncharted territory, Master Jander, and I'm more like their own fields."

The vampire reached to still her suddenly anxious hands.

Gently, he said, "You told me something of that sort six months ago, when I found you in the City of the Dead. I told you then that your past need not destroy your future. I was right—Kurnin hired you at once, didn't he?"

A sheepish smile played on her full lips.

"Aye," she admitted. "But, Master Jander, none of these people know what I am!"

Her voice had dropped to a near whisper, and the elf's teasing expression grew more solemn.

"You're wrong, Maia. They know what you are. They don't know what you were, and that no longer matters."

"You think so?"

"I know so."

As Shallen had been a moment earlier, Maia seemed close to tears. She blinked them back and allowed herself a true smile, revealing the purity of the beauty that lurked behind the hard facade. "You'd charm the very birds off the trees," she laughed, trying to lighten the mood.

Just as he's obviously charmed you, the Shark thought with a slight sniff of contempt. Charmed you into being his next meal.

Maia left to refill the mugs of the celebrants, and the elf turned his attention to his wares. He carefully emptied the crate of at least a dozen small carvings, turned it over, and spread his cloak over the makeshift table.

The Shark's heart beat faster with anticipation. What she was about to do next was risky, but it was part of the deadly game she loved to play, needed to play. She rose and went to meet her quarry.

The vampire glanced up as her shadow fell across him. The Shark noted, as if she needed further proof, that the undead cast no shadow of his own in the flickering lamplight.

"Your work is impressive," said the Shark.

She met the vampire's gray eyes evenly. There hadn't been a blooder yet that could charm her, but she enjoyed the danger of flirting with the possibility. To her disappointment, the golden vampire didn't even try. He merely continued placing his carvings on the crate.

"Thank you," the blooder replied.

"Do you have your own shop here in Waterdeep?"

"I find it more congenial to work during the day and visit different taverns at night."

I'll bet you do, the Shark noted silently.

She ran a finger along the hull of a tiny, incredibly detailed elven sailing vessel and said, "People are freer with their coin when their throats are wet, I would imagine."

He chuckled politely. "Perhaps they are. Do you like that piece?"

"I do, but I don't have enough with me to buy it tonight," the Shark replied, feigning disappointment. "Could I come to your home tomorrow and purchase it then?"

"I value my privacy when I work," responded the vampire, a touch too swiftly. "I'll be back tomorrow night. Shall I keep it for you?"

"I have an engagement, but I'll send one of my servants for it. Who should she ask for?"

"Jander Sunstar," the elf replied. "And you are?"

"Shakira Khazaar. Thank you for holding the piece for me."

"Standard business practice. I'd hate to lose a sale," Jander answered.

There was a strange expression in those silver eyes, and the Shark felt vaguely uneasy. She had done something wrong. She had gotten careless somehow. The thought was like a slap in the face. She smiled, hoping to allay his suspicion, and was relieved when he returned the gesture with the artless, seemingly genuine smile she had seen him use with the others, his "friends." Still, she felt his eyes boring into her back as she left.

Once outside, the Shark crossed the street and slipped into an alley. After making sure she had not been observed, she drew the hood of the cloak over her head. Woven and ensorcelled by her own hands many years ago, the cloak not only made her invisible, but also disguised the aura produced by her body heat—something vampires could see. The snow-speckled wind was strong, but she maneuvered herself so that it blew directly in her face. Though she was now invisible to the eyes of blooder and human alike, she was not about to risk being betrayed by her scent.

Her wait was not long. Just as the inn closed, the vampire emerged. The barmaid Maia was with him. Carefully, silently, the Shark followed, noting that Jander deliberately left bootprints in the snow, perpetuating the illusion that he was nothing more than an ordinary elf. Too many blooders, used to walking without tracks, forgot that little detail.

Maia and the vampire chatted quietly as he escorted the girl to her home, a single room atop a tailor shop. The Shark waited for the inevitable. The stupid girl, hypnotized by the creature, would invite him in. Of course he would accept, then drink his fill. That was the way it worked, and the Shark never interfered. She knew from a particularly harrowing experience in Suzail that it was unwise to startle a feeding vampire.

Her expectations were fulfilled. Casually, Maia invited the vampire inside, as if she had done so often. Courteously, the blooder accepted. The Shark waited with practiced patience, ignoring the cold. Eventually the vampire emerged, descended the stairs, and turned to stride down the street—still taking care to leave footprints. The hunter followed, slightly puzzled. Rather than assume the form of a bat or dissolve into mist, Jander chose to retain his elf shape and simply walk the distance. He seemed tense, though, and repeatedly glanced over his shoulder.

He thinks someone's following him, she realized suddenly. How could he know?

The Shark's mind raced back to the incident at the inn, and she finally recognized what she had done to arouse the blooder's suspicions. She had not asked the price of the carving. Shame and fear rolled over her, bringing hot blood to her invisible face. Idiot! her mind screamed silently. How could she have jeopardized herself so? Her carelessness could have cost her life—and might still. At that instant, Jander paused to look squarely at her, just for a moment. The Shark's heart lurched. . . . But no, he hadn't seen her. The blooder turned and continued on his way.

At last he stopped in front of a small, stone cottage near the city's outskirts. It wasn't until Jander removed a key and unlocked the door that the Shark understood, with some surprise, that that was the vampire's home. The wooden shingles and door were solid and in good shape. Beneath the shuttered windows stood the winter skeletons of rose bushes, carefully pruned and planted in neat rows. With a final, anxious glance around, Jander carefully knocked the snow from his boots and went inside.

The Shark tasted disappointment like ashes in her mouth. What kind of a challenge was a vampire who planted rose bushes? How could she prove herself against so feeble a foe? Surely something as exotic as an elf vampire ought to push her to her limits, test every bit of cleverness and skill she possessed! She almost felt that she could walk in right then and dispatch the creature without breaking a sweat, but her earlier carelessness tempered her resentment. She would come back the next day and kill him. It would be easy, she knew, yet she still needed to devise a back-up plan just in case something went wrong.

With a final, disgusted look at the cozy cottage that was home to a vampire, she turned and retraced her steps to town. There was one more thing to do that night.

Protected from all eyes by her magical cloak, the Shark arrived at the blooder's cottage the following afternoon.

The vampire's domicile was part of a small row of houses, which all seemed vacant. Shallen Lathkule's wedding, held at the other end of Waterdeep, had indeed drawn a huge crowd. With speedy efficiency, the Shark picked the lock and slipped inside. Closing the door behind her, she allowed her eyes to grow accustomed to the darkness, then looked around.

On the ground floor of the two-story building, she saw nothing sinister, apart from the shutters that were nailed closed and coated with pitch to seal out sunlight. There was a large workbench, with the woodcarver's tools neatly organized. Half-formed carvings sat patiently on shelves. Where they were not covered with shelving, the walls bore lovely paintings and tapestries. In one corner, carefully preserved, was a suit of mail, a sword, and a shield. Relics, no doubt, from the vampire's days as a living being. The stone floor was strewn with fresh rushes. Small squeaking sounds came from behind a curtain toward the back. Senses alert, the Shark moved forward carefully and drew back the curtain.

Dozens of rats milled about in a large pen. She watched them carefully for a few moments, aware that sometimes such simple beasts could be controlled by vampires, but the rats behaved in a perfectly ordinary fashion. Wrinkling her nose at the smell, she let the curtain fall.

"Between meal treats," she said softly. Most blooders kept something of the sort on hand.

She checked the wooden floor for any hidden doors, but found none. The Shark frowned, puzzled, and she glanced at the ladder that led up to the upper floor. Most undead liked their lairs cool and dark, below ground if possible. The Shark shrugged. Upstairs, downstairs—it made no difference to her. Soundlessly, she climbed up to the small loft. She raised her head cautiously, then drew a swift intake of breath.

The vampire had no coffin. Neither did he lie rigid with his hands neatly folded atop his chest. He slept sprawled on the floor, arms and legs bent at unnatural angles. The beautiful features that had smiled in the lamplight the previous night were contorted in what looked like fear. For an instant, the Shark hesitated. She'd never seen a blooder sleep in that position. Could she possibly have been wrong?

No, she decided in the next heartbeat. She had never been wrong where blooders were concerned. Quietly she climbed the rest of the way up and walked carefully over to Jander. No chest movement. He was certainly dead— but why that position? Then it came to her. Blooders slept as they had died, and most had been laid out and buried in coffins. Jander Sunstar had obviously met his vampiric fate in a less tranquil fashion and had never seen a proper ritual burial.

She leaned forward for a better look, and the hood dropped into her eyes. Annoyed, she slipped the hood to her shoulders, instantly becoming visible. It didn't matter. Jander, like every blooder she'd ever slain, was vulnerable, unable to move, let alone fight, during daylight hours. He would die, too. The only question in her mind was how she would kill him. Her strong hands fell to her wide belt, which hosted her tools. Jander's contorted position did not give her a clear shot with her favorite weapon, a small, specially crafted crossbow she could wield with one hand. She had to go with the traditional implements—the stake and hammer.

Straddling the undead body, she placed the tip of the sharpened stake to his breast.

She raised the hammer and said the words that she always uttered before a kill: "The Shark sends you to the Nine Hells." Then, in a disgusted tone, she added, "You were too easy."

A gold-skinned hand seized her left wrist. Silver eyes gazed up at her.

"Not that easy," replied the vampire.

The Shark recovered almost at once from her shock. A quick flick of her wrist liberated a small glass ball from up her sleeve. Liquid—holy water—sloshed within the delicately blown sphere. She shoved it down toward the vampire's face, but he was unbelievably fast. He loosed his grip on her arm, his hand flying up in a blur to protect his face. The glass ball broke, but instead of searing his eyes, the holy water ignited his fingers.

Before the monster could take mist form and flee, the Shark leaped clear, pulled her crossbow from its harness behind her back, aimed, and fired. The slim wooden bolt sank deep into the vampire's chest. Immediately his body began to desiccate; the flesh shriveled and turned from golden to dull tan. Gasping, he dropped to his knees on the wooden floor. The Shark watched eagerly, hungry for the creature's pain. She hadn't expected the vampire to retain so much of his former race that he could move during the day. But she had gotten him, in spite of—

Flailing golden hands closed on the shaft, and the Shark realized that, though the wooden arrow had hit Jander's chest, perhaps even grazed the heart, it had not pierced that most vital of the vampire's organs. With a mighty tug, Jander pulled the shaft free. His golden coloration returned in a rush, and his features took on their normal shape—save that the gentleness was gone from his face.

The Shark scrambled for the ladder, Jander in furious pursuit. She could not defeat him there, not then, and was intent on leaving with her skin intact. Behind her, she heard a savage growl and knew he had taken wolf form. She let go of the rungs and dropped the rest of the way down to the first floor, but not before sharp teeth clicked shut mere inches from her fingers.

She hit the ground running. Shoving her left hand into one of the pouches on her belt, she felt the gooey combination of bat guano and sulfur.

"Twelve feet ahead, three feet high!" she commanded, then pointed her right index finger at the far wall of the cottage.

A small ball of fire appeared at her fingertip, growing in size as it hurtled toward the wall. It exploded on contact, igniting many of Jander's beautiful carvings. Sunlight streamed into the cottage, and the Shark dived headfirst through the opening.

Despite the cushion of snow, she landed hard, and the wind was knocked out of her. For a wild instant, she wondered if the vampire, in addition to being active during the day, was also immune to sunlight. But Jander did not follow her.

The Shark rolled over, gasping for breath. At last she stumbled to her feet and peered in through the hole in the wall. He was nowhere to be seen, of course; he was hiding from the burning light. She was glad that she had taken the time to plan for just such trouble.

"Vampire," she called. Silence. "Vampire! I know you can hear me."

"I hear you." The same voice as the previous night, melodious, but laced with pain and anger. The sound gave her pleasure. He had surprised her up in the loft. But she had a surprise for him.

"I have Maia," she said.

Silence. Then, "You lie."

"I followed you both from the inn last night, then I went back and got her."

A low groan was her reward, and her pleasure grew.

"Don't hurt her. . . . Please. She's innocent. She doesn't know anything about me. I'm the one you want!" The sounds of movement came from within. "I'll . . . I'll come out."

Alarms sounded in her head.

"No!" she cried with more emotion than she had intended.

She'd fallen for that trick before, let a vampire volunteer to die in the sunlight, only to discover that the blooder was also a mage who could cast a sphere of darkness around them both. Unconsciously, her hand went to her throat, touched the healed scar there. She'd been bitten, but she'd won—and had learned a lesson about the treacherous nature of vampires.

But if this blooder was acting, he was quite the thespian. The Shark heard real pain in his voice.

"Why would you want to do that?" she asked. "What is Maia that you would surrender yourself?"

She wanted to hear his answer, but she kept alert for any attack.

From inside, Jander said softly, "She's lovely, and I appreciate beauty."

The Shark snorted. "So you were simply admiring her beauty last night in her room."

A pause, then, "She is untouched. I visit her each night. I'm teaching her how to read."

"Untouched is hardly the term I'd use to describe a two-copper whore. And as for reading . . ."

"What she did to survive does not concern me." Anger thrummed in the rich voice. "What she is now, and what she might be, is what I care about. She is eager to learn. I want to help."

"You want to help, not kill, is that right?"

"Someone once gave me a chance to atone for my past. How can I not do the same for Maia?"

The Shark couldn't help it. Her amusement grew until she actually laughed aloud. He couldn't possibly expect her to believe such a wildly preposterous story.

"You are most entertaining, Master Elf. But I remain unconvinced. If you truly wish to ensure Maia a pleasant future, you'll follow through on your offer. My terms are simple: your unlife for her true life. Meet me tonight, at the monument in the City of the Dead. If you don't show up—well, the slut means nothing to me."

Another pause.

"Most who hunt the nosferatu are holy people," the vampire said at last. "You are not, Shakira Khazaar. Had you been, I would have rejoiced that you had found me, and I would have known why I was hunted. You have asked questions of me, now I ask you: Why would you use an innocent like Maia so? Why do you wish to kill me when I have done no one in this city harm?"

The Shark was taken aback by the unexpected query. No one had ever asked her that before. She killed because that was what she did. She'd done it all her life—first in self-defense, then for coin as a hired assassin. When the pleasure of taking human life paled, she'd turned to stalking the undead. Blooders were a challenge, and everyone wanted them destroyed. She was no longer the thief Shakira, afraid and alone. Neither was she a nameless assassin, who hunted and hid in shadows. She had transformed herself into the Shark, who always caught her prey, whose prowess in the fine art of killing was sought after and widely praised. But those reasons did not come to her lips then.

Instead she spat venomously, "Because Captain Rhynn Oriandis wants you destroyed, you gods-rotted blood-sucker."

Jander's soft gasp made the Shark's hatred-blackened heart skip a beat.

The fool believes me!

Her face contorted in a grimace that she thought was a smile as she left the vampire alone to agonize until nightfall.

For a place of death, the City of the Dead was very pop-ular with the living. Many generations and many classes of Waterdhavians crumbled to dust side-by-side in pauper's graves and gorgeously carved mausoleums: war-riors, sea captains, merchants, commoners. The struggles they had with one another in life ceased to matter as, united in their mortality, they slept the final sleep. Waving grass, shady trees, and beautiful statues lent the place an aura of tranquility. During the day, the little "city" was a peaceful haven for visitors. Night, however, brought a different class of people to the cemetery—those who conducted business best transacted under the vague light of the moon and stars, business handled by people who did not want witnesses.

The centerpiece of the necropolis was a giant monu-ment erected only a few years past. Designed to pay trib-ute to the original settlers of Waterdeep, the statue was a gorgeous work of art. Dozens of individual stone carvings, depicting life-sized warriors battling with all manner of nonhuman adversaries, comprised the sixty-foot high monument. Wide at the base, it narrowed with each level until a lone hero stood atop the fray. Frozen forever at the moment of greatest action, orcs speared their adversaries, doughty swordsmen slew bugbears, and heroes and mon-sters alike died in a variety of dramatic poses.

There the vampire had met Maia several months

before, plying her unsavory trade. There he hoped to see her again that night.

Jander came in elf form, walking, but leaving no footprints. He stopped as he neared the monument. A pale white ring encircled the grand statue, and the pungent scent of garlic filled the cold night air. There came a sound of muffled sobbing, and he glanced upward. With deliberate irony, the Shark had tied the barmaid to a conquering stonework hero, who stood atop the mountain of fighters, arms raised in victory. The girl was lashed securely with rope at hands and feet. A piece of cloth shoved in her mouth stifled words, but not her sounds of fear.

Jander walked slowly around the ring of garlic until he came to a two-foot wide gap in the otherwise unbreachable barrier. He hesitated only an instant before stepping into the circle. It was obviously a trap, but what choice did he have?

At the base of the monument Jander cried out and fell. His foot had been caught in a cleverly concealed, sharp-jawed animal trap made of wood, not steel. And when he hit the ground, a second trap clamped on one of his hands. Holy water soaked the traps' jagged teeth. Steam and blood hissed from the vampire's wounds, glittering black in the moonlight.

With his good hand, Jander splintered the wood that bit into ankle and wrist. On his feet at once, he glanced around, expecting a second attack. None came.

He moved toward the statue more cautiously, his eyes on the snow in front of him rather than the monument itself. There were several more concealed traps waiting to close upon him. Treading delicately, he avoided them.

"I'm here, Maia," he called. "You're safe now."

The stone figure in front of him was a warrior woman with a single braid of long hair. He reached out to it, prepared to begin the climb up to Maia. But the statue smiled and sprang to life. The illusion shed, the Shark drew a small crossbow and fired a wooden shaft directly at Jander's chest. She was no more than two yards away.

Jander grunted at the impact, but the shaft bounced off his body and fell to the grass.

The Shark gasped. The vampire smiled and tapped his chest with a golden forefinger. It clinked. Too late, the Shark recalled the chain mail shirt she had seen in Jander's cottage. She pulled down her hood, safely invisible, and jumped aside. The vampire's hand closed on her cloak, but she yanked it out of his grasp and began to run.

Jander followed without pause.

It took the Shark a moment to realize the blooder didn't need to see her to follow her churning tracks in the snow. At once she leaped straight up, seized the mighty arm of a stone orc, and hauled herself atop it. She scrambled to the left, balanced precariously on a helmeted head and a stone shoulder, then she paused, holding her breath.

For a time, the golden vampire stood as still as a statue himself, gazing about as if he could penetrate the magic that concealed her by sheer force of will. His gaze traveled over and past her. Then Jander turned and began to climb.

When he had gotten halfway up the monument, the Shark lowered herself to the ground as quietly as she could. She readjusted the hood of her cape, making sure it would not slip off as she moved. She hoped she could complete her task before the vampire noticed her telltale footprints.

Hastening to the circle of garlic, she closed the opening with the remainder of the bulbs she had with her. He had no escape—he couldn't even fly over the ring. She returned to the statue and followed the vampire up.

His movements were swift and sure, but not unnaturally so. Jander was taking great care not to reveal his true nature to Maia. Thus far, his deception was to the Shark's advantage. She followed at her own brisk pace, climbing up the battling warriors as easily as if they were limbs of a particularly gnarled tree.

He had reached the top. There was silence, and the Shark knew that the blooder was staring at the holy symbols she'd draped across Maia's body. Carefully, quietly, the hunter continued to climb, listening all the while.

"Lathander, protect me!" came Maia's fear-shrill voice

as Jander pulled the gag from her mouth. "Don't kill me! Please! She—she told me what you are. I'll do whatever you want, but, please, don't kill me!"

Stunned silence. The Shark pulled herself up over a dying archer, awaiting the blooder's response with malicious glee.

"No, Maia," came Jander's voice, filled with an ancient weariness. "I won't kill you. I just . . . here, let me set you free."

The Shark was able to see him. Safely invisible, she watched, tense, as Jander moved to untie the hands of the still-hysterical young girl. He successfully freed her hands and knelt to work at the knots that bound her ankles. Light exploded from the small pink medallion hidden in the folds of Maia's skirts. The Shark's spell had worked beautifully.

The vampire flung his arms up to shield his eyes, stumbled, and hurtled off the monument. The Shark hastened forward. One hand gripping a dying troll, the hunter watched Jander's fall. His body shimmered, recasting itself into a small brown bat. He began to fly back up to the top.

Behind her, the Shark heard Maia sob as she worked loose the knots. Then, whimpering, the barmaid started the climb down from the monument. The Shark ignored her. Maia had served her purpose.

Instead, the hunter kept her attention focused on the vampire. Leaning out precariously over the raised stone swords and braced javelins that pointed up from below, she clung to the troll statue and withdrew a small pouch from her pocket. Grains of wheat fell in a shower over the bat. It was the Shark's favorite trick to play on a vampire in bat form. The grain would confuse the vermin's senses, making it fly wildly. And that would give the Shark a chance to prepare another, more deadly attack.

But Jander did not veer off. The little bat flitted crazily for a moment, then continued moving directly for the Shark's face. No cloak of invisibility could protect her from the heightened senses provided to the vampire in his bat form. She could see the vermin's tiny, sharp-toothed jaws opening as it approached her eyes.

Startled, the Shark ducked. Her foot slipped from the snow-slicked perch, and she dropped toward the upturned stone javelins below. She did not cry out, merely grunted when her death plummet was abruptly cut short. A spear wielded by a bugbear had snagged her cloak. Her throat was bruised from the sudden tug, but she was alive.

The Shark hung, dangling, swinging slightly back and forth. Her mind raced, and she cursed herself. She'd prepared no spells for such an eventuality—no floating, flying, or transformational magic. Grunting with the effort, she reached up, trying to grab the stone spear that held her suspended. She could not reach it. She then stretched to the right as far as she could in hopes of seizing the ugly, porcine face of an orc beating down a hapless stone hero. She grasped only empty air.

More frightened than she had been in decades, the Shark craned her neck to look upward.

The blooder was a silhouette against the star-filled sky as he bent to look at her. Then, slowly, he moved. One arm reached down.

Crying incoherently, the Shark twisted away. Her cloak tore a little, and she dropped four inches. At least the vampire was too far above her to reach her—but, ah gods, he could crawl. . . .

"Give me your hand."

For a moment, she couldn't comprehend the words, so unexpected were they. Jander stretched his hand farther.

"Give me your hand! I can't quite reach you."

The cloak ripped again. The Shark stared down at the next tier of battling warriors and their pointed stone weapons. It was at least a twenty-foot drop.

"I'm coming, Shakira. Hold on."

And indeed, the golden vampire began to climb, head-first, down to reach her.

She suddenly knew, knew with a deep, inner certainty, that Jander Sunstar was not coming to kill her. He was coming to save her life, to pull her back to safety. She, the Shark, the woman who had spent her life perfecting the art of murder, had finally failed to kill. And having failed, she would owe her life to the creature she had sought to destroy. If his forgiving hands closed on her, she would never be able to lift a weapon again. She would cease to be the Shark.

She didn't even have to think. Reaching up, she twined both hands in the cloak.

"The Shark sends you to the Nine Hells," she said aloud, but the words were intended for her own ears.

As the vampire's fingers reached out to her, the Shark smiled like the predator she was, spat at his despairing, beautiful face, and tore the cloak free.

Originally published in *Realms of Magic*
Edited by Brian M. Thomsen and J. Robert King,
December 1995

SIX OF SWORDS

William W. Connors

I've often wondered what happens to characters in a D&D game when their campaign folds. I
mean, they aren't dead, but they don't get to
adventure anymore. Hardly seems fair. I guess
they'd probably just go into retirement, still longing for the thrills of their past lives and spending
an awful lot of time reminiscing. This story was
based on that premise. For those who are interested in trivia, every member of the Six of Swords
is named after one of my favorite baseball players
at the time I was writing. I do that a lot.

—William W. Connors, March 2003

William W. Connors is best known for his work on the RAVENLOFT® game line. He was the designer of the award-winning SAGA® game system and created the DRAGONLANCE: FIFTH AGE® Campaign Setting. He currently works as a freelance artist and writer under the banner of Moonlight Studio and works as the Art/Graphic Director for Fast Forward Entertainment, Inc.

SIX OF SWORDS

I

Moonlight on a silver blade was the last thing Jaybel ever saw.

Fifteen years ago, when he and his closest friends had been adventuring throughout the Western Heartlands, he might have expected such a demise. In those days, he had made his living as an expert picking locks, disarming traps, and unobtrusively eliminating enemies— tasks known for short-lived practitioners. Indeed, on more than one occasion, he'd been snatched from death's dark abyss only by the mystical healing power of the acolyte Gwynn.

In the years since, however, Jaybel had given up the rogue's life. Following the tragedy of his company's last quest, when they had been forced to leave the dwarf Shandt to the so-called mercy of a hobgoblin tribe, the glamour had gone out of that life. Indeed, so terrible had that ordeal been that every member of the Six of Swords had second thoughts about his career.

"I've made my fortune," Jaybel told his comrades. "Now I plan to relax and enjoy it."

With his next breath, he asked Gwynn to marry him, and she hadn't even paused before accepting. The company parted, and he and Gwynn took up residence in the great city of Waterdeep.

With the treasures they had gathered from countless forgotten tunnels and valiant quests, Jaybel and Gwynn had built themselves a modestly elegant home. It included a chapel where she could teach her faith, and a locksmith's shop where he could keep his fingers nimble and his eyes sharp.

For nearly a decade and a half, he and Gwynn had been happy. They had put tragedy behind them and started a new life together. When Jaybel had looked back on those wild days, he always said, "It's a wonder I'm not dead."

Now he was.

II

The metallic ringing of steel on steel fell upon ears so long past ignoring it that they may as well have been deaf. With each impact, sparks filled the night air, streaking upward like startled fireflies, becoming brief ruddy stars, and finishing their fleeting lives with meteoric falls to the stone floor. Thus it went as the sun set and night cloaked the city of Raven's Bluff. Time and time again, Orlando repeated the ritual of his craft. Hammer fell, sparks flew, and the wedge of a plow gradually took shape.

When the farmer's blade was finally completed, the noise ended and the smoldering coals of the forge were left to cool. The brawny, dark-skinned Orlando set about returning his tools to their places, taking no notice of the ebony shape that appeared in the open doorway of his shop.

For a fraction of a second, the shadow filled the doorway, blocking out the stars and crescent moon that hung beyond it. Then, with the grace of a hunting cat, it slipped through the portal and into the sweltering heat of the blacksmith's shop. In the absence of the ringing hammer, the shadow drifted in supernatural silence.

Without prelude, a sepulchral voice wafted from the darkness. Though a whisper, the intonation and clarity of the words made them as audible as any crier's shout.

Jaybel and Gwynn are dead.

Orlando froze, his hand still clutching the great hammer, half-suspended from an iron hook. The voice sent a chill down his spine, raising goosebumps across his body just as it had when he'd last heard it years ago. Orlando turned slowly, keeping the hammer in his hand and trying to spot the source of the voice. As had always been the case when she desired it, Lelanda was one with the darkness.

Relax, Orlando, said the night. *I didn't do it.*

"Then show yourself," said the blacksmith, knowing she wouldn't.

It had been years since Orlando had taken up a weapon aside from a tankard in a tavern brawl. Still, even the passing of the years didn't prevent the well-honed reflexes of his adventuring days from surging back to life. If the witch tried anything, his life wouldn't command a small price. Still, he knew who would walk away from the battle. He doubted Lelanda had given up magic. She was probably even more powerful. So, Orlando's rusty reflexes would provide her only brief entertainment.

To Orlando's surprise, the darkness before him parted. Lelanda's face, crowned with hair the color of smoldering coals and set with emerald eyes that reminded him all too well of a cat's, appeared no more than a yard away from his own. As always, he was stunned by the shocking contrast between her external beauty and her malevolent soul within.

If he struck just then, there was no way the witch could save herself. The muscles in his arm tensed, but he could not bring himself to strike first. He had to hear her out.

"Satisfied?" she asked.

Her voice, no longer distorted by the magical shroud of shadows, seemed gentle and alluring. Orlando knew that, like her beauty, her voice was a deadly illusion. Black widows were beautiful as well. Even knowing the truth, his pulse quickened.

The retired warrior put aside the distraction and asked the only question that made sense: "What happened to them?"

"It wasn't an accident," she said, her eyes lowering to the hammer still in Orlando's hand. He grinned half-heartedly and tossed it toward the nearby workbench. She returned his smile and went on. "Someone killed them."

"You're sure it wasn't you?" he asked.

"Fairly," she said. "I'm on my way to Waterdeep to find out who. We made a lot of enemies in those days."

"We made friends, too," the blacksmith said.

"We lost them as well," said the witch.

Orlando's memory was quick to pull up an image of Shandt, his enchanted battle-axe glowing as it swept back and forth through the ranks of hobgoblins that swallowed him up. It wasn't the way he would have wanted to remember the smiling dwarf.

"If we leave in the morning, we can be there in a few days," said Lelanda. "I know some . . . shortcuts."

"If we leave now, we can be there sooner," said Orlando. "Give me an hour to get ready."

III

Orlando moved through his darkened house without so much as a flickering candle to light his way. Outside, Lelanda sat unmoving on the back of a horse even blacker than the night sky. Orlando knew she was anxious to get under way, and so went from room to room as quickly as possible. The walls of his home were decorated with swords, shields, and other reminders of his adventuring life. Like a thief in his own house, he gathered up three of those heirlooms.

The first of them was Talon, the curved sword that he'd recovered from a dark labyrinth beneath the sands men called the Battle of the Bones. The arcane blade proved almost unstoppable when turned against the living dead. Removed from its traditional place above the hearth, the enchanted blade was returned to the scabbard on Orlando's black leather belt.

The second item removed from his collection was a bronze breastplate. Countless attackers had learned that it had the uncanny ability to turn aside even the most deadly missiles. Arrows, quarrels, and even bullets had all proven impotent against the charms of the bronze armor. Orlando liberated it from the wooden mannequin that guarded an empty first floor hallway. As the yellow-orange armor once again embraced Orlando's muscular chest, he noticed that the passing of his youth made it more snug than he remembered.

With the sword and armor safely recovered, Orlando moved on to the last item he planned to bring with him: a good luck charm. Pausing beside the small shrine adjacent to his bedroom, Orlando slipped a small silver amulet from the hook on which it hung and looped it around his neck. Unconsciously, his fingers ran across its surface, tracing the outlines of the crossed battle-axes that were the icon of the dwarf god Clanggedin Silverbeard. There was no magic in the simple pendant, but it had been a present from Shandt. Since it had been given to him not five hours before the noble dwarf met his fate somewhere in the Underdark, Orlando couldn't look upon it without remembering the broad, crooked smile and gleaming eyes that had made his best friend's countenance so pleasantly memorable. The memory brought Orlando both a smile and a tear.

Locking the door behind him, Orlando left the house and moved to join Lelanda by the stable. She had already saddled Zephyr, his dappled gray horse.

Without a word, the warrior placed his foot in the stirrup, swung himself onto his mount, and nudged the horse into a trot. Many miles passed before either of the old adventurers spoke a word to the other.

IV

Orlando drew back on Zephyr's reigns. The animal, well trained and eager to please its master, slowed quickly from its trot to a full stop. The enigmatic black equine that Lelanda rode did the same, though Orlando saw no sign of a command from rider to mount. The horse seemed always to know what the enchantress expected of it.

"Aren't we going a bit out of our way?" Orlando asked.

"Only slightly," responded the witch. "I thought we might stop at Jolind's estate and tell her what happened. She won't be interested in joining us, of course, but she was one of the Six. She has a right to know."

Orlando was surprised to hear Lelanda speak like that. In their adventuring days, she'd had little use for the individual members of the Six of Swords. To her, they were bodyguards, scouts, and healers who enabled her to explore the mysteries of magic, recover rare spell components, and otherwise practice her arcane art. Perhaps time had softened her heart, or perhaps there was more to the detour than she was telling him.

With the aid of Lelanda's magic, the miles passed as fleeting images in the corner of the eye. Even at that rate, however, it was several hours before the lights of Jolind's tower were visible. When they reached the edge of the clearing in which it stood, both riders brought their mounts to a stop.

"She's done a remarkable job here," said Orlando as his head swept back and forth to indicate the lush forest that rose around them. "I remember when we first found this clearing. The soil was so poisonous that nothing less robust than spitweed would grow here."

"I'll go in first," said Lelanda, ignoring his attempt at conversation. "Jolind always valued her privacy, and I'd hate to have a druid angry at me in the heart of her own forest."

She slipped the hood of her cloak over her head, causing the sunset colors of her hair to vanish into a thick darkness. Even as he watched, Orlando found that he could no longer focus clearly on her. Though he knew exactly where she was standing, he was able to see her only as a fleeting image in the corner of his eye.

I'll be back as quickly as I can, said the darkness.

Before he could respond, Orlando realized he and the horses were alone by the side of the road. He wanted to chuckle, but the chills that her macabre voice had left running along his spine wouldn't let him.

While he waited for his companion to return, Orlando opened the saddlebags draped over Zephyr and pulled out an apple. He fished around for a few seconds more and brought out a small knife. With a deft flick of his wrist, he split the fruit cleanly in two. After wiping off the blade and slipping it back into the leather pouch, he offered one of the halves to his horse and considered the other for a moment. With an unconscious shrug, he reached over and held it before Lelanda's mount. The ebon animal eyed his offering, but then snorted and turned away. Orlando shrugged again and ate it himself. The first hints of dawn were lighting the horizon, and he had an unhappy feeling that the animal's snobbery was to set the tone for the day ahead. He was right.

Jolind is dead, came the too-familiar voice of the darkness. *And the body is warm. The killer must still be nearby.*

V

The inside of the tower stirred Orlando's memories of the time when the Six of Swords had first explored it.

In those days, the surrounding lands had been defiled by the black dragon that made its home there. The entire area had been poisoned by the creature, with pools of acid, swarms of stinging insects, and tangles of slashweed dominating the tortured remnants of the forest. From the moment they'd entered that fell region, the druid Jolind had become solemn and morose. Such destruction, she swore, could not go unpunished.

When they reached the tower—a ruined structure built by an unknown hand centuries before any of the Six were born—Jolind had led their attack against the dragon. Turning the very elements of nature against the creature, she had been instrumental in its destruction.

Eighteen months later, when the company disbanded, she announced her intention to return to that place and restore the forest to its past glory. She had done an outstanding job.

Jolind had not, however, restored the tower. At least, she hadn't done so in the way that Orlando would have. The interior floors and walls had been stripped out, a great glass dome placed atop the tower, and a bubbling fountain set into the ground at its center. The combination of the fish-eye skylight and the dancing water of the fountain made the climate inside the tower hot and sticky.

Under normal circumstances, this would have made the place unbearable. With the careful hand of Jolind to shape the place, however, it had been transformed into a tropical paradise. Great tresses of ivy climbed gracefully up walls dotted with brilliantly colored flowers. Shafts of morning light, shunted downward by the facets of the glass dome, illuminated a dozen trees and the colorful butterflies that flitted between them.

The horrors of the past had been completely banished by the careful hand of the druid. Sadly, they had been replaced by the horrors of the present. At the heart of all this splendor was a copper-smelling pool of red. And at the center of that scarlet expanse lay the body of the druid Jolind. Her head had been cleanly cut from her neck.

It took all the courage Orlando could muster to approach the body. Jolind had been a friend, a companion, and more. For a time, the warrior and the druid had been lovers, seeking escape in each other's arms. Their relationship had lasted less than a year, but in that time, each had learned much about the other's philosophy and profession. For Orlando, that meant a keen appreciation of the ways of nature, the give-and-take of the environment, and an understanding of his place in it. Jolind had not feared death. In her mind, it was nothing more than the end of life. To Orlando, death had always been an enemy to be held at bay. In the end, he knew, death would triumph. For the present, however, he preferred to keep that most final of foes as far away as possible.

"Horrible way to die," he said softly.

The same way Jaybel and Gwynn were killed, said a voice from nowhere.

Though the sound still irritated him, Orlando had already adjusted to the macabre intonations that came from empty air. It was amazing to him how quickly the old ways of thinking returned. Indeed, even as that thought crossed his mind, he realized he had subconsciously drawn Talon from its scabbard. Without the slightest thought, he had made ready to defend himself from Jolind's attacker.

"A pretty fierce struggle," said Orlando, examining the disturbed earth around the pool of blood and beneath the decapitated body. "But something doesn't make sense. All of these footprints were made by Jolind's sandals. Whomever she was fighting didn't make the faintest impression as he moved about."

Perhaps we're dealing with a doppelganger or other form-shifter. If her killer assumed Jolind's shape, you wouldn't be able to tell one set of prints from another.

"I doubt it," responded the warrior. He tilted his head to one side, then to the other. "No, the positioning is pretty clear. Only one person made these prints. What about the undead? Remember that vampire we tracked down near Dragonspear? He didn't leave footprints, throw a shadow, or make any sound when he moved."

As soon as he mentioned that adventure, he wished he hadn't. It was in the ancient crypt where the vampire's coffin had been hidden that Lelanda found the mysterious shroud of shadows.

Possible, responded the enigmatic shadows of the garden, *but unlikely. This place is pretty heavily warded against intrusion by the undead and other unnatural creatures. If the killer is something like that, he'd have to be extremely powerful to enter the tower. For our sakes I'd prefer to believe that isn't the answer.*

Orlando said no more for several minutes. Instead of allowing dark thoughts to dominate his mind, he forced his attention back to the matter at hand. With measured steps, he walked to and fro around the area, using his experience in combat to piece together the puzzle, whose pieces had been scattered in the darkness of the previous night.

After a time, he noticed something and reached into a beautiful but painfully prickly shrub. Cursing and wriggling, he pulled back his arm and drew out a slender, wooden rod some three feet long. Covered in a gleaming white lacquer, it was painfully cold to the touch. From past experience, however, he knew that it was warmer than it should be.

What have you found? inquired the stillest part of the garden.

On some level, Orlando realized it wasn't the fact that he couldn't see Lelanda that bothered him most. It was the spectral nature of her voice while she wore the shroud. There was too much of death and darkness in that place already.

Orlando could stand no more of the one-sided conversation.

"Take off that damned shroud, and I'll show you!" he hissed.

Almost at once, the shadow of a pear tree lightened and the elegant sorceress was standing beside him. She quickly complied with his request, making the hostility in his voice seem suddenly unnecessary.

"I'm sorry," Orlando said softly, "but you have no idea how quickly that thing gets on your nerves."

He expected her to argue the point, just as she would have in the past. To his surprise, her response was quite civil.

"No," she answered, "I suppose I don't. You see, it's been a very long time since I've had a traveling companion. I've gotten rather used to wearing the shroud all the time. I'll try not to use it unless it's an emergency."

There was a brief pause, a moment of still contrast to the violence that had unfolded around them. Orlando searched for something to say, but failed.

Lelanda seemed only slightly more at ease, picking up the frayed threads of conversation.

"I asked you what you had found," she reminded him.

"Looks like a piece of that staff Jolind used to carry with her; feels like it too, almost as cold as those blizzards it could summon up."

Lelanda tilted her head and looked at the broken staff. Her lips pursed as she considered the broken end and several places along its length where something had cut deeply into it.

"There was some pretty powerful magic woven into this thing," she said. "It wouldn't be easy to break. The weapon that hacked these notches out of it and finally broke it must have been every bit as powerful. That doesn't bode well for our future."

Silence fell upon the garden again. Orlando went back to fishing through the shrubs, eventually finding the other section of Jolind's staff.

Lelanda examined the head, looking into the druid's eyes as if she might read the woman's dying thoughts. Then she walked a distance toward Orlando and called to him. He met her halfway between the shrubs and the fallen body.

"We've learned a little bit from an examination of the area and the body, but Jolind can tell us more."

"Necromancy?" asked Orlando, the word sounding just as bitter as it tasted in his mouth. She nodded. He growled. "I suppose there's no choice. Get it over with."

"I'll have to . . ."

"I know," he said.

Two steps brought the witch to the edge of the bloody pool, another to the place where Jolind's severed head had come to land. She looked back at Orlando, flashed him an uncomfortable smile, and raised the hood of the shroud above her head. Instantly, it became difficult for the warrior to focus his eyes on her. Even knowing where she had been standing only a few seconds earlier, he could discern nothing but the faintest impression of the shrouded figure.

The magical energies of death and darkness answered Lelanda's urging. She spoke words of power whose sounds had no meaning to Orlando's untrained ears. He felt the strange tugging of death at his spirit and knew that something stood nearby, hungering for the taste of his soul, contained only by the power of Lelanda's will. If her concentration failed, the consequences could well be disastrous. Then, with a cry of agony from the unseen mage, the spell was completed.

Orlando steeled his nerve as the eyes on Jolind's severed head snapped open. The thin-lipped mouth did likewise, and a hissing, hollow scream filled the garden. Unable to stand the sight, Orlando turned his head away. He felt the need to vomit, but retained control of his traumatized body by remembering that a deadly enemy might lurk nearby.

Jolind, said the spectral necromancer, *can you hear me?*

"Yesss," responded an empty, lifeless voice. "Who are you? Your voice is familiar . . . but distant."

Jolind, this is Lelanda. I'm here with Orlando. We've come to help you.

At that, the disembodied head released a humorless, rasping laugh and said, "You're a little late for that, old friend."

Orlando's nerve buckled, but did not fail him.

I know. We're sorry. But we want to find the person who did this to you. He murdered Jaybel and Gwynn, too. Can you help us? Did you recognize your killer?

"Yes, I know who killed me," whispered Jolind.

Then tell me, Jolind. Be quick; the spell is failing fast, urged Lelanda.

Orlando couldn't decide which was more macabre, the living but unseen spirit of the wizard or the dead, but substantial head of the druid.

"Kesmarex," hissed the head as the eyes slipped quietly shut and the jaw went slack.

The spell had ended, and the spirit of the druid had gone to rest with those of her ancestors.

Orlando hoped she would find peace there. In his heart, he said a last farewell to the woman who had meant so much to him so long ago. It seemed a crime to have drifted away from her. He wondered what mysteries had died with her. A single tear slipped down his bronze cheek.

Kesmarex? said the witch, slipping the hood of the shroud from around her locks and emerging beside the fallen druid. "Who is that?"

"It's not a who," said Orlando. "It's a what. That was the name given to Shandt's battle-axe by the dwarves who forged it. It mean's something like 'Vengeance of the King,' but the words don't translate perfectly into our language."

"But Shandt is dead. . . ." said the witch, her voice trailing off into a haunting silence.

"I know." Orlando exhaled. "He couldn't have survived." After a moment of reflection, he continued, "Tell me more about the wards around this place. Just how certain are you an undead creature couldn't have gotten in here?"

An hour or so later, Orlando still hadn't made sense of Jolind's warning.

"If it was Shandt, he'll be back to get us," said Orlando. "He wasn't one to leave a job undone."

Rather than answer, Lelanda merely poked at the campfire they'd lit at the heart of Jolind's tower.

In the past few hours, her beauty had begun to look worn and haggard. Orlando studied her face, which was still delicate and gentle, with innocent features that belied the cunning viper that lurked within. Still, there was something human showing through the facade she maintained.

"How did you ever become a wandering adventurer?" Orlando asked.

"I don't really know," said the witch. "It just happened, I guess. I was studying in Waterdeep, the usual courses they force on a child of a merchant prince, but they just weren't enough to keep my attention. One of the other students said he was being tutored in magic by an old woman on the outskirts of town. I followed him one day and learned where his teacher lived. When he left, I paid her a visit and demanded she teach me magic. She looked me over carefully and refused.

"I was furious. I guess I was more than a little spoiled in those days. When I tried to pay her for the lessons, she wouldn't take my gold. I'd never met anyone like her before, anyone that gold couldn't buy. It took me tendays of pestering her, but she finally agreed. I guess she wanted proof of my devotion.

"About a year later, I showed up for my lesson and found her dead. She had been murdered by a pack of thieves—assassins, really, in the service of a dark priest. I vowed to avenge her death. That took me another year. By then, I'd gotten used to life on the road, and returning to Waterdeep just didn't seem very palatable to me. I never went back to school or to see my family. I suppose they assumed I'd been killed while trying to avenge my mentor. Somehow, it just didn't matter anymore."

A gust of wind swirled through the tower, twisting the flames that danced above the hearth and lifting a cloud of glowing embers into the air. Lelanda gazed silently at them as if there might be some hidden meaning in their traces.

"How about you?" she asked.

"Ever been a farmer?" he asked in answer.

"No," she said.

"Well, if you had been, you'd understand perfectly."

Lelanda laughed, a clear and sweet sound that Orlando never would have expected from her. There, in the garden where they had once slain a black dragon and had recently buried an old friend, he saw a side of her he had never thought existed. His hand, as if it had a will of its own, reached out and rested atop hers. Her laugh faded away, and her green eyes shifted to meet his.

"Orlando," she said, and a shock went through her body.

Every muscle was rigid for a second, and her eyes bulged. As suddenly as the spasm had struck her, it passed. She went limp and toppled forward, the blade of the great axe Kesmarex buried in her back.

The warrior, his rekindled reflexes already in action,

sprang back. Without conscious thought, he brought the enchanted sword Talon into play, interposing it between himself and whoever might wield the ancient battle-axe.

"Shandt," he cried, "is that you?"

There was no answer, but in a second Orlando knew none would be forthcoming. With a swift and sudden motion, the axe Kesmarex lifted into the air. Lelanda's blood dripped from the blade, but no living hand wielded the weapon.

At last, Orlando understood. He had always known Shandt's blade was enchanted, but had never realized the full extent of its power. But years after the death of its owner, the weapon had tracked down the people it blamed for Shandt's death.

Describing a great arc in the air, Kesmarex swept toward the warrior. He fell back, uncertain how to attack a weapon that had no wielder. He jabbed feebly with Talon, but found that the axe was every bit as maneuverable as it had been in Shandt's hand.

"You don't understand," Orlando cried. "We had no choice!"

The battle-axe chopped at his legs, causing him to leap backward. When his feet touched the ground, he felt the soft earth shift and give way. He had landed squarely on Jolind's grave. Unable to retain his balance, Orlando toppled over and thudded hard on his back. The blade of the axe flashed through the air inches above his nose. Had he still been standing, it would certainly have severed his leg at the knee.

"Shandt was buying us time to escape!" he yelled.

The axe, unheeding, swept upward as if it was being held aloft by its departed master. For a brief second, it hung there. Then, like the blade of a headsman at the block, Kesmarex plunged downward. Orlando tried to roll aside, but the enchanted blade sensed his intention and twisted to follow him. With a metallic crash, it smashed into the warrior's bronze breastplate, tearing through the amber metal and biting into the soft flesh beneath.

Pain burned through Orlando's body as clouds of red rolled across his vision. Talon fell from a nerveless hand, making no sound as it landed atop Jolind's newly dug grave. As the vengeful weapon drew back for its fatal strike, Orlando's hands clutched at the searing wound. His fingers touched jagged metal, exposed flesh, and warm, flowing blood.

And something else. Something smooth and warm and comforting: the amulet of Clanggedin Silverbeard. His fingers closed upon the medallion, and he snatched it clear of his neck. The silver chain upon which it hung stretched and snapped. As the great weapon began to sweep downward, Orlando held the holy symbol high.

"Shandt was my friend!" he cried. "I would have died to save him!"

Moonlight, sifting down from the cloudless sky, struck the glass dome and streamed down into the garden. It fell upon the fallen body of Lelanda, the druid's fresh grave, and the silver axe that sought to avenge its owner's death. Two pinpoints glinted brightly in the shaft of moonlight, one the blade edge and the other the pendant.

VI

Orlando stepped back from the wall. He had returned Talon to its place and cocked his head left and right to make sure it was positioned properly. He reached out and lifted the hilt an imperceptible fraction of an inch.

"Don't worry," said Lelanda from the couch on which she lay. "You've got it right."

Orlando nodded and turned back to the table behind him. With his right hand, he reached tentatively for the great battle-axe Kesmarex, but something stopped his fingers just short of its haft. His other hand slipped to his neck and touched the silver pendant that hung from its recently repaired chain.

His thoughts drifted back to the battle in Jolind's garden. He remembered the great blade falling toward his head, the hollow sound of his voice as it filled the silent garden, and the flash of light that came when the holy symbol was presented. Somehow, the battle-axe recognized the amulet and knew that the silver symbol belonged to the same warrior whose hands had once wielded it. Knowing that anyone who wore that particular crossed battle-axe medallion must be a friend of its owner, it had fallen inert. As far as Kesmarex was concerned, its mission was completed.

He returned to the present as a delicate hand touched his shoulder. He turned and found the emerald eyes of Lelanda scant inches away from his own. The gold band on her finger reflected a greatly distorted image of his own countenance.

"You shouldn't be up," he said, urging her gently back to the couch.

"I'll be all right," she said, "the wound's almost healed. Hang up the axe and come to bed."

Orlando nodded and lifted the magical weapon from its resting place. He turned and elevated it to a place of honor above the hearth. Next to it, he hung the amulet that had saved his life.

"Rest quietly, old friend," said the crimson-haired witch.

Orlando said nothing, but in his heart he knew that Lelanda's wish had been granted.

Originally published in *Realms of Mystery*
Edited by Philip Athans, June 1998

THE ROSE WINDOW

Monte Cook

There is a principal in quantum physics that you cannot measure the qualities of a subatomic particle without, by the very act of observing, changing the particle. With that in mind, I had the odd notion to create a story where the reader, in the act of reading the story, actually changes the story. This is a story that the narrator does not actually want you to read. With that in mind, if you do dare read "The Rose Window," I predict that my own love of tales by H.P. Lovecraft, Clark Ashton Smith, and similar writers, will become quite obvious.

—Monte Cook, April 2003

Monte Cook is a graduate of the
Clarion West Science Fiction and
Fantasy Writer's Workshop
and has written two novels and a
number of short stories. He is also a
professional game designer, having
been one of the designers of the new
DUNGEONS & DRAGONS game as well as
a multitude of other role playing game
products. He owns and operates his
own small game design studio in the
Pacific Northwest with his wife, Sue.

THE ROSE WINDOW

I hope against hope that no one ever reads this.

I suppose I learned the truth the day before yesterday, but it all started a few tendays before that. You see, I was there when the Abbey of Byfor was torn down. I had to go. Loremaster High Tessen had been my mentor. It was like paying my last respects to an old friend.

The late autumn day was overcast and gray, with a cold, northerly wind tearing at us with angry talons. All those attending kept their cloaks tightly wrapped around themselves like armor against the chill. I was surprised at how many had come to take part in the simony that took place.

The abbey was old, and had not actually functioned as a monastery in many years. Nevertheless, until recently, it had still served the surrounding community as a place of worship one day in ten and shelter in times of inclement weather. Now, however, the western wall had begun to collapse and the roof sagged so badly that the local masons claimed the building was no longer safe. A man named Greal had taken over the abbey after the bishop's death a few years earlier. I never was able to determine exactly what station he held in church hierarchy, if any. Greal claimed that he had no coin to instigate the necessary repairs, so he began selling the stone and furnishings alike. He claimed to hope that with the coin he raised he could build a new church, dedicated to Oghma, for the local folk.

I stood outside the decaying edifice and watched as young men carried pews, the lectern and even the stone-topped altar out into the barren, leaf-covered yard. I saw people come and go, purchasing all of the old accouterments that had served the abbey and its parishioners for generations. Later in the day—I had not moved—I saw the young men brandish hammers and tools. Soon, I knew, the stones from the abbey would be taken away and used to build pasture walls and farm houses.

Something—perhaps fate, but now I'm not so sure—bid me to look up to the abbey's tall roof. There, high upon the gable, was the beautiful rose window that I remembered so well from my time as an acolyte there. The round window was fitted with light blue-green glass that formed an extremely complex rose pattern. Though it was dull in that day's gray sky, I knew that in any brighter sunlight it scintillated like a jewel with a brilliant cascade of light.

I left my spot and approached the man called Greal, reaching into an inner pocket in my cloak. I produced a bag of gold—all that I had. He turned toward me with a foul expression.

"Excuse me, sir," I began, "but I understand that you are selling the abbey's, ah, parts." His expression softened, and I continued. "Well, you may not know this, but I once held a position here as a seeker—an acolyte—before I was given my own parish. Loremaster High Tessen was the priest at the time—my mentor."

Greal's dark gray eyes were flat and his mouth was

drawn thin. He folded his arms in front of him, but did not say a word.

"Well," I said, "that old rose window meant a lot to me." I pointed at it, and his eyes followed my gesture. "I would be willing to pay you for it, so that I could put it in my own church."

"Really," he did not ask, but stated.

A light came to his eyes as he turned back toward me. His tight mouth was tense.

"Yes, it would be an excellent . . ." I searched for the right word. ". . . reminder of the Loremaster High and his steadfast faith."

Greal smiled, and I cannot say that I liked it. It was the wide, tight-lipped grin of a predator.

"Yes," he said finally. "An excellent reminder. He was an inspiration to us all."

He held out his hand, and I dropped the purse in it. Emptying the coins into his wide, soft hand, he counted slowly. The sight disturbed me, so I looked up at the window instead. Though it cost me greatly, I knew that I would enjoy the window and the remembrance of Tessen for many years to come.

Satisfied with the price, Greal told the young men to climb up and carefully remove the window for me. I had come to the abbey in my small wagon, and there was room for the window. It all seemed like fate had meant for it to be, for not long after I was driving my team back across the valley to my parish home.

Within a tenday, I had hired some men of my own to come to the church and help me install the window high above the floor of the sanctuary. There I knew it would bring brilliant light down upon the worshipers during each Binding and Covenant, our morning and evening rituals. The window would glorify Oghma as well as the faith of Loremaster High Tessen. I was gladdened. Once it was in place, I noticed that young Pheslan, my own seeker, was transfixed by the window.

"It's so wonderful," he said, "and yet so odd."

I looked up at the window myself, and at the portly Pheslan, and asked, "Odd?"

"Forgive me, brother, I mean no disrespect. It is not odd in an ill fashion. It's just . . . the pattern. Each time I look at it I see something new. Some different facet to the way the glass has been fitted, or some new way the light plays upon the angles. Yes, that's it. It is the angles that are so fascinating."

Looking at the window again, I had to admit that he was right. It was fascinating.

"The workmanship of those days has known no equal since," I said, knowing that such was something that elders always said to the young.

I smiled at the thought, and at the boy as we both bathed in the blessing of sunlight and looked at the beauty of the rose window.

As the next few tendays passed, I became concerned with other things. Oghma, the Lord of Knowledge and the Wise God, bids his servants to spread information and dispense learning as well as watch over the well-being of the worshipers as we guide them toward enlightenment. Thus, the duties of a parish priest are legion, but I suppose that this is not the time to describe them. Let it suffice to say that I was preoccupied—so much so that I paid little attention to the fact that young Pheslan was still enraptured with the rose window. One night, after Covenant, we finished our duties and sat down to our simple meal. He told me that he had seen something strange in the window. I listened only halfheartedly, for I was very tired.

"It must be within the pattern of the glass, or the facets," he explained.

We sat at a small wooden table in the room that lies between our sleeping chambers at the back of the church. It was dark, the only light coming from a lamp on the table at the center of our meager feast.

"What must?" I said, my mouth full of bread.

The young acolyte was too agitated to eat.

"As I said, brother," he said, "there were things that seemed to move in the window as the sun set."

"You mean the light played upon the glass," I said, swallowing.

"Yes, probably." His eyes lowered.

"What do mean, 'probably'?"

"Well, it seemed so real," he replied, looking into my eyes. "They moved."

"What moved?"

"The images in the window. It was as though something was on the other side."

"Perhaps there was something on the other side, Pheslan." I was becoming slightly irritated. "A bird?"

"But I went outside and looked," he said. "There was nothing."

I drank the last bit from my cup and stood.

"Then it was indeed the light of the setting sun playing upon the glass," I concluded. "Enough now, Pheslan. It is time for bed."

With that we retired. Pheslan was nothing if not obedient. It makes me . . .

Well, let me finish the tale first.

Two more days passed, and Pheslan said nothing more about the window. He was quiet, and slow to finish his duties. I knew I needed to talk to him, but I was just too busy. Later, there would be time.

The night of the second day, after retiring, I heard a strange noise. I had been reading in bed as I often did before blowing out my lamp and going to sleep. I heard the noise again. It sounded as if it was coming from outside the church. Perhaps someone was knocking at the door. I placed my marker in the book, threw the blankets back and made my way to the front of the church in my nightclothes. The sound came again, it struck me as though something was scratching on the outside wall of the building.

The stone floor was cold on my bare feet so I hurried through the dark, only my intimate knowledge of the place keeping me from bumping into anything until I entered the sanctuary. There, the light of the full moon shone through the rose window lighting my way to the narthex and the door.

Though there are dangers in the night, even in our peaceful valley, I never bolted the door. The church should always be open, I believed, always there to welcome the poor as well as those in need of knowledge, Oghma's sacred gift. I opened the door and looked out into the dark night. A bitter wind blew dead, brown leaves all around the yard in front of the church.

I could see nothing out of the ordinary.

Again, I heard the scraping. Something was outside scraping against the stone walls of the church. A tree? It had sounded big, so I had thought it best to check. Despite my lack of shoes, a cloak, or a light, I went outside. As I made my circuit of the building I saw nothing. No tree grew so close as to have its branches move against the walls. My eyes spotted no person or animal that could have done it, but my night vision is poor, and it was very dark.

Yet had there not been the light of the full moon coming through the rose window? I looked up. The clouds were thick. Besides, I knew very well—now that my wits were about me—that there was no full moon that night.

I went back inside. Yes, both the sanctuary and nave were full of cool, blue-tinted light and it shone through the rose window. As I looked up at the window, I knew I had to check. So, steeling myself against the cold, I returned to the outside.

No light. I hurried around to the north side of the church, the side that held the rose window. No light. I looked up at the window but it looked perfectly normal, or at least as far as I could see in the dark.

Again, I returned to the sanctuary. Yes, it was still filled with light (was it dimmer now?). I looked up at the window, and down at the lighted church. As I stood there, between the sets of wooden pews in the nave leading up to the altar, the light cast a shadow from the window all around me. To my horror, it was not the rose-shaped shadow it should have been, but that of some great inhuman beast! As I looked down at my feet, I saw that I stood directly in the gaping mouth of the creature's shadow.

I ran. Yelling for Pheslan, I rushed to the back of the church. He came out of his room, his eyes filled with alarm and sleep. Without a word, I grabbed from the night stand the blank scroll that served as a symbol of Oghma's might and led him into the nave.

All was dark.

"Get a light," I commanded with a whisper.

"What is it?"

"Get a light!"

He lit one of the many candles surrounding the altar and brought it forward. It occurs to me now that Pheslan knew the church as well as I did, for he had found the flint in the dark to strike that light. Ah, Pheslan.

In any event, the candle's light illuminated much of the room, albeit dimly. I looked around carefully, first at the floor where the shadow had been, then up at the window.

"Please, Brother," Pheslan said, "tell me what it is."

"I thought I saw something," I said carefully—still looking around.

He replied without hesitation, "In the window?"

"Yes, I suppose. Actually, it was a shadow from a light in the window."

Pheslan looked at me. His eyes were full of questions. I had the same questions.

"I have no idea, my son."

I put my hand on his shoulder and, with one last look around, led him back to our chambers.

I took the candle from him.

"Oghma watches over us, Pheslan," I said. "Just because we do not understand, we can know that he does, for no secret is hidden from him. Besides, while the sights of the night are often frightening, the morning light always dispels the fear they bring. Everything will be fine. I should know better, at my age, than to be scared of shadows."

He smiled and nodded.

After the boy went into his room, I paused. Still holding the candle I went to the front door and bolted it. I did not stop to look at the rose window.

The next day, just to be on the safe side, I performed every blessing and banishment that I've ever been taught, hoping that divine power might cleanse the rose window and the sanctuary itself. Those protective rituals and prayers would surely protect us from any evil that might have been present the night before.

The rest of the afternoon I spent caring for Makkis Hiddle, who had taken ill a few miles down the road. My position as loremaster made me also the most knowledgeable healer in the tiny community. In any event, I did not return until well after dark. Like the previous night, the wind blew from the north and made my trip cold and unpleasant. I unhitched the team and put them in their stalls in the barn behind the east end of the church. They seemed uneasy and stamped and snorted until I calmed them with an apple that I had been saving for myself. As I walked to the front door, I rounded the north side of the building and looked up.

As I watched, a shadow moved across the colored panes of the rose window. It was big—big enough to be a person. My first thought was of Pheslan. Had he climbed up there somehow? I ran into the sanctuary, but all was still. I could see nothing unusual at the window.

The room was lit by a lamp on the altar. Pheslan knew that I would arrive late, and left it for me, as he always did. I knew, too, that I would find some food and wine left waiting for me on the table. I smiled at the thought, and sighed. I was making a fool of myself with all this nonsense. I ate quickly and went to bed.

That night I awoke, startled. The scraping noise was back. It sounded a little like a dog scratching at the door of his master's house, hoping to get in—a big dog. I lit my bedside lamp with a flame from the coals in the brazier that attempted in vain to keep the chill from my room. When I opened my door, I could see that the door to Pheslan's room was already open. I looked in to find it empty. The boy had obviously risen—perhaps awakened by the noise as well?

Then I heard the scream.

I ran into the sanctuary, the flame of my lamp almost going out as it passed through the cold air. I looked frantically about.

"Pheslan?" I called out. My voice was swallowed by the dark emptiness of the room. How had I grown so afraid of my own sanctuary? "Pheslan, boy—where are you?"

No answer came.

My eyes were drawn to the rose window. Dark shapes seemed to move across its surface. Was that light playing against the facets? (How long could I tell myself that?)

I longed for a closer look at the window, but there was no way for me to climb to that height without a ladder, and that would be difficult in the dark. I called out again for Pheslan.

I went outside and checked the barn. The horses and wagon were still there. I checked all around the outside of the building, still calling for my young friend.

"Pheslan!"

By the time I had searched the inside of the church again, the light of dawn was evident, and I blew out my lamp. I knew what I had to do. I returned to the barn and got the ladder. I maneuvered it into the church, despite its weight and size and set it below the rose window. I do not know exactly what I thought I would find up there, but I grabbed a heavy candlestick from the altar and held it tightly in my grip. Taking a deep breath, I began to climb.

When I reached the top, I held on to the top rung of the ladder with one hand, and gripped the candlestick in the other like a weapon. I peered through the window.

I had no idea what I was seeing. I gazed through the rose window and beheld some other place—this was not the churchyard. Instead I saw some infernal realm of shadows and slime-covered things that slithered over a blasted and dreadful landscape. Something flitted across the sky on batlike wings that seemed to leave a trail of greasy residue behind the creature. This window did not look outside. Or rather it did—but not the outside, the Outside. My eyes saw beyond the veil of our world. My mind was besieged by the knowledge that there were places on the other side of the rose window, and they were terrible. The things in those places, I also knew, wanted to get to the inside—to our world.

Gods! I knew all at once that this window was a thing of evil. No longer (or was it ever?) a fine piece of some glazier's workmanship, no longer bits of blue-green stained glass cleverly pieced together. The rose window was a sorcerous, corrupted thing. It gave me a view no man should ever see. But what else did it give? Was it some kind of portal, or doorway?

I raised the candlestick, my eyes tearing with fear and hatred. I was going to smash the window—shatter it and its evil, to erase the loathsome view that it provided. This would be no defilement or desecration, for the window did not actually belong in a holy place, yet still I stopped. One thought came to me (from where?). If I smashed the window, would I destroy it, or would I let in those things that seethed and writhed in that infernal realm? Would shattering the window prevent them from coming through, or would it grant them passage? A burglar in the night often smashes a window to get in. Smashing it for him only makes his entrance easier.

I had to think—but not at the top of that ladder. There, I could still see into that nightmare realm, and worse, I think the things beyond could see me. I climbed down and slumped on the floor next to the altar.

I was at a loss. What could I do? Was Pheslan gone? Was that his scream I had heard, or something else? Had he somehow disappeared into the window? That seemed so impossible. What would Tessen have done in this situation?

My thoughts were always drawn back to my old mentor in times of crisis. I thought of Tessen, and the old abbey, and—

Oghma preserve us.

I saddled one of the horses—I cannot recall which one anymore. I am not much of a rider, but I thought that I could move faster riding just one than in the wagon. I rode through a good deal of the morning, across the valley to the old abbey.

The men had worked fast. Only some of the foundation stones were left. Everything was gone, including any clue I had hoped to find regarding the nature of the rose window. The wall where it had set for over one hundred years had been torn down. The floor where it had cast its shadows was torn apart and covered with rubble, dirt, and leaves.

I stood in the middle of all this and wept. Tessen had committed a sin against Oghma that could never be forgiven. He had kept a secret, and a terrible secret at that. Had he been a guardian over that window, or its servant? I certainly could remember no hint of the malevolence that the window now displayed.

Finally, I could weep no more and I got back on my horse. Perhaps it was just my training in Oghma's priesthood, but I needed information to confront this challenge. When I had been here last, I had learned of one more place that I could go to find the answers I sought. I beckoned my steed back onto the road, and led it into the village nearby, to where I had heard that Greal lived and had set up his temporary new church.

Once I arrived, nearly exhausted now, I slid to the ground. I knocked on the door. When there was no response, I knocked again, pounding now.

"Master Greal?" I shouted.

Still nothing.

"Master Greal, it is Loremaster Jaon."

I continued my pounding, stopping only to confirm that the door was locked.

"I must ask you about the rose window I purchased from you!"

My pounding fist accompanied each word like a drumbeat in some southern jungle ritual.

"I need to ask you about Loremaster High Tessen!"

Completely expired, I collapsed against the door.

"Tell me," I moaned. "Tell me what we were really worshiping in that abbey!"

As I rode back to my parish, I knew that someone had seen me. There had been eyes on me the whole time that I had spent pounding on that door. And as I had sat there, exhausted in the damp soil in front of Greal's home, the autumn leaves blowing around me like dead memories that may very well have been lies, someone watched. No one in that entire town had come when I called out. No one answered their door, but I knew that I was being watched. Even now. . . .

How many of them were there, that had taken part in the foul rites that I could only imagine must have taken place in front of that rose window? Had those rituals gone on even when I had been there? Could I have been so naïve? Could—no, I would not think of it anymore. It was too hard, and too painful, and there were still things that needed doing back in my own church.

Which brings me to right now.

I am writing this the day after I went to the site of the old abbey. I have not yet slept nor eaten. When I came back, I had hoped against hope that Pheslan would be here, and that somehow I would have been wrong. But I was not wrong, and he was not here. I dressed myself in the vestments of my order—white shirt and pants, and the kantlara, a black vest with gold brocade. My kantlara was made for me by my grandmother, who had also been a loremaster. I prepared my holy symbol and brought out the staff that I kept by the door for emergencies—the staff with its ends shod in iron and made for fighting. I prepared to make my move, and take my stand against the evil that I myself had brought to my parish.

But I waited. What if I was wrong, as I had thought

before? What if I let those things through? I somehow told myself that it could not be. An evil thing, like the rose window, must be destroyed. Only good could come from destroying it. Perhaps it could even free Pheslan from whatever held him. If indeed he still lived.

I spent the rest of yesterday at the bottom of the ladder, which I had never moved from its spot below the window. I looked up, but all day long, I saw only the blue-green stained glass. No movement, no shadows, nothing. Somehow, my indecision still prevented me from climbing to even the first rung.

So after so many hours of arguing with myself, pushed farther past exhaustion than I have ever been, I began writing this manuscript on the nightstand in my bed-chamber.

On these few sheets of parchment, penned throughout the night, I have put my story. Now, as I finish, I prepare myself to climb that ladder. I will smash the rose window, and destroy every last shard. If I am right, and the evil is over, I will return here to this manuscript and throw these pages into the fire so that none shall ever learn of these horrible events. But if I am wrong, you are reading this now. If that is the case perhaps you—whoever you are—will know what can be done to right my wrongs.

I am ready.

Originally Published in *Realms of Magic*
Edited by Brian M. Thomsen and J. Robert King
December 1995

THE FIRST MOONWELL

Douglas Niles

One of the most fascinating aspects of fantasy writing is the creation of an environment, an actual ecology, for an imaginary location. The Moonshae Islands under the benign power of the Goddess Earthmother have been a favorite locale of mine for many years, most especially because of that unique ecology. This story attempts to illustrate that intimate relationship in allegory.

—Douglas Niles, March 2003

Douglas Niles had the privilege of
writing the first FORGOTTEN REALMS
novel, *Darkwalker on Moonshae*.
Since then he has revisited the
Realms to write nine novels and a
number of short stories, as well as
contributing more than a dozen books
set in other fantasy worlds.
His most recent work is the Icewall
Trilogy, completed in 2003 for the
DRAGONLANCE line of novels.

THE FIRST MOONWELL

The goddess existed deep within the cocoon of bedrock, an eternal being, formed of stone and silt and fire, her body blanketed by the depths of a vast and trackless sea. In the way of immortals, she had little awareness of the steady progression of ages, the measured pulse of time. Only gradually, over the course of countless eons, did she become aware that around and above her the ocean came to host an abundance of life. She knew the presence of this vitality in all the forms that thrived and grew; from the beginning she understood that life, even in its simplest and most transient forms, was good.

Deep waters washed her body, and the volcanic fires of her blood swelled, seeking release. She was a living thing, and thus she grew. Her being expanded, rising slowly from the depths of the ocean, over millennia spilling along trench and seabed, pressing deliberately, forcefully upward. Over the course of ages, her skin, the floor of the sea, pushed through the realm of black and indigo and blue, toward shimmering reaches of aquamarine and a warmth that was very different from the hot pulse of lava that measured her own steady heartbeat.

Life in many forms quickened around her, first in the manner of simple things, later in larger and more elaborate shapes. Animation teemed in the waters that cloaked and cooled her form. Gashes opened continually in the rocky flesh of her body, and her blood of molten rock touched the chill waters in spuming explosions of steam.

Amid those hissing eruptions, she sensed great forms circling, swimming near, breathing the chill, dark sea. Beings of fin and tentacle, of scale and gill, gathered to the warmth of the earthmother's wounds—wounds that caused no pain, but instead gave her the means to expand, to strive ever higher through the brightening waters of the sea.

And, finally, in the life that gathered to her bosom, she sensed great creatures of heartbeat and warm blood. Those mighty denizens swam like fish, but were cloaked in slick skin rather than scales, and rose through the sea to drink of the air that filled the void above. Mothers nursed their young, much like the goddess nourished her children and her thriving sea. Most importantly, in those latter arrivals the goddess sensed the awakenings of mind, of thought and intelligence.

Unaware of millennia passing, feeling the coolness of the sea against the rising pressure of her rock-bound body, the physical form of the goddess continued to expand. At last, a portion of her being rose above the storm-tossed ocean to feel a new kind of warmth, a radiance that descended from the sky. Periodically this heat was masked beneath a blanket of chilly powder, but the frosty layer yielded itself in a regular pattern to more warmth, to soothing waters that bathed the flesh of the goddess, and more of the golden rays shedding steadily downward from the sky.

The flesh of the goddess cooled, weathered by exposure

to sky. New and different forms of life took root upon her; beings that dwelled in the sea of air turned faces upward to the clouds. Many did not walk or swim, but fixed themselves to the ground, extended lofty boughs upward, creating verdant bowers across the breadth of the land. The growth of those tall and mighty trees, like all forms of life, was pleasing to the goddess. She sensed the fruition and waning of the forests that layered her skin, knew the cooling and warming of seasons with greater acuity than ever before.

It was this awareness that, at last, gave to the earthmother a true sense of passing time. She knew seasons, and in the course of changing climes she learned the pattern of a year. She came to measure time as a man might count his own breaths or heartbeats, though to the goddess each heartbeat was a season, each breath the cycle of the annum. As the years passed by the tens and hundreds and thousands, she grew more vibrant, stronger, and more aware.

The hot blood of earlier eons cooled further; the eruptions from the sea ultimately were capped by solid stone. That firm bedrock, where it jutted above the waves, was layered everywhere in forest, meadow, glade, and moor. Seas and lakes intermixed with the land, keeping the goddess always cool, both fresh waters and brine nurturing the growing populations of living creatures.

Still the goddess maintained communion with the beings of warm blood dwelling in the depths, who swam to the surface and returned, sharing their mind-images of a vast dome of sky, of the sweet kiss of a sea breeze, and the billowing majesty of lofty clouds. Her favorite of those sea creatures was one who had been nourished at her breast from time immemorial, feeding upon the kelp and plankton that gathered to her warm emissions, slumbering for decades at a time in her embrace. She came to know him as the Leviathan, the first of her children.

He was a mighty whale, greater than any other fish or mammal that swam in those seas. His soul was gentle, his mind observant, keen, and patient—as only one who has lived for centuries can know patience. Great lungs filled his powerful chest, and he knew life with a rhythm that the goddess could understand. Sometimes he took a breath of air and settled into the depths, remaining there for a passage of several heartbeats by the reckoning of the goddess—a time of years in the more frenetic pace of the other warm-blooded creatures.

In long, silent communication with the goddess who was his mother, the Leviathan lay in a deep trench on the bottom of the sea, sensing the lingering warmth of her fiery blood as it pulsed and ebbed below the bedrock of the ocean floor. During those times, the great whale passed images he had beheld above the waves, pictures of growing verdancy among the earthmother's many islands, of the teeming array of creatures swarming not only sea and land, but even flocking in the skies.

And he shared, too, his memories of clouds. Those more than anything else stoked the fires of the earthmother's imagination, brought wonder to her heart, and caused curiosity to germinate in her being.

As she communed with the Leviathan, sharing his memories of the things he had beheld, she began to sense a thing about herself: The goddess, unlike so many of the creatures that dwelled upon her flesh, was utterly blind. She lacked any window, any sense through which she could view the world of life flourishing upon her physical form.

The only visual pictures that she knew came from the memory of the great whale, and those were pale and vaporous imitations of the real thing. The goddess wanted to see for herself the sky of cloud and rain and sun, to know the animals that teemed among her forests and glades, the trees that sank their roots so deeply into her flesh.

From the Leviathan, the goddess earthmother had learned about eyes, the orbs of magic that allowed the animals of the world to observe the wonders around them. She learned about them, and desired them . . . and devised a plan to create an eye for herself.

The Leviathan would aid her. The great whale drank from an undersea fountain, absorbing the power and the magic of the earthmother into himself. With easy strokes of his powerful flukes, he drove toward the surface, swimming through brightening shades of water until again his broad back rolled above the waves, felt the kiss of sunlight and breeze.

Swimming strongly, the Leviathan swam to a deep bay, stroking between rocky necks of land into ever narrower waters, toward the western shore of one of the earthmother's cherished isles. Mountains rose to the north, a stretch of craggy highlands crested with snow as the spring warmth crept only slowly upward from the shore. To the south was a swath of green forest, woodlands extending far from the rocky shoreline, blanketing this great extent of the island.

In the terminus of the bay, the land came together from north and south, the waters remaining deep enough for the Leviathan to swim with ease. He came to the place the goddess had chosen, and brought the warm and magical essence of herself through his body. With a great, spuming explosion, he cast the liquid into the air, shooting a shower of warm rain. Precious water splashed onto the rocks of the shoreline, gathered in many streams, flowed downward to collect in a rocky bowl near the gravel-strewn beach.

The essence of the goddess gathered into that pool, milky waters of potent magic. Her presence focused on the skies, on the vault of heavens she had so long imagined. The first thing that came into view was a perfect orb of white, rising into the twilight skies, coursing ever higher, beaming reflected light across the body and blood of the earthmother.

From the waters of her newly made well, the goddess beheld the moon. Alabaster light reflected from the shoals and waves of the shoreline and blessed the land all around. The earthmother saw this light, and she was pleased.

Yet still there was a dimness to her vision, an unfocused haze that prevented her from fully absorbing the presence of the world. The Leviathan lay offshore, rolling in the heavy swell, but the pool was remote from him, bounded as it was by dry ground and rocks. She knew then that it was not enough to have her children in the sea.

The goddess would require a presence on the land, as well.

The wolf, gray flanks lean with hunger, shaggy pelt worn by the ravages of a long hibernation, loped after a mighty stag. The buck ran easily through the spring growth, exhibiting none of the wide-eyed panic that might have driven a younger deer into headlong—and ultimately disastrous—flight. Instead, the proud animal bounded in graceful leaps, staying well beyond the reach of hungry jaws, veering only when necessary to maintain a clear avenue of flight.

In the midst of the keen, lupine face, blue eyes remained fixed upon the lofty rack of antlers. Patience, counseled the wolf's instinct, knowing that the pack could accomplish what one strong hunter could not. As if in response to their leader's thought, more wolves burst from concealment to the side, rushing to join the chase. But the stag had chosen its course well; a long, curving adjustment took it away from the newer hunters, without allowing the big male to draw appreciably closer.

A low cliff loomed ahead, and though no breeze stirred in the depths of the glen, the buck sensed another ambush, canine forms concealed in the thickness of ferns lining the shady depths of the bower. Now the stag threw itself at the limestone precipice, leaping upward with cat-like grace, finding purchase for broad hooves on ledges and mossy outcrops.

With snorting exertion and flaring nostrils, the first outward signs of desperation, the buck scrambled up a rock face three times its own height. A trio of wolves burst from the ferny camouflage below, howling in frustrated hunger as the antlered deer reached the level ground above the cliff and once again increased its speed. Hooves pounded and thundered on the firm ground as, with a flick of a white-feathered tail, the stag raced toward open terrain.

But the leader of the small wolf pack would not, could not, admit defeat. Throwing himself at the rocky face, pouncing upward with all the strength of powerful rear legs, the wolf clawed and scraped and pulled, driven by the desperation of the starving hunter. At last, broad forepaws crested the summit, and the carnivore again loped after his prey, howls echoing after the gasping, thudding noise of the stag's flight.

Others of the wolves tried to follow, though most fell back. Still, a few young males and a proud, yellow-eyed bitch made the ascent. Their baying song added to the din of flight and gave the rest of the pack a focus as smaller wolves raced to either side, seeking an easier way to the elevation above the limestone shelf.

Weariness began to drag at the leader, bringing to his step a stumbling uncertainty that had been utterly lacking before. Yet the scent of the prey was strong, and mingled with that acrid odor came the spoor of the stag's own weariness, its growing desperation. Those signals gave the wolf hope, and he raised his head in a braying summons to the rest of the pack, a cry of anticipation that rang like a prayer through the silent giants of the wood, along the verdant blanket of the cool ground.

But the powerful deer found a reserve that surprised and dismayed the proud hunter. The predator raced through the woods with belly low, shaggy tail extended straight behind. Those bright blue eyes fixed upon the image of the fleeing stag, watching antlers brush overhanging limbs and leaves. Straining, no longer howling as he gasped to make the most of each desperate breath, the wolf pursued in deadly silence.

And in that silence he began to sense his failure. The loping forms of his packmates whispered like ghosts through the fern-lined woodland behind him, but neither were they able to close the distance to the fleeing prey. Even the yellow-eyed female, long jaws gaping in a fang-lined grin of hunger, could not hold the pace much longer.

Then, with an abrupt turn, the stag darted to the left. Cutting the corner of the angle, the leading pair of wolves closed the distance. Soon the male was racing just behind the prey's left quarter, while the powerful bitch closed in from the opposite side. The twin hunters flanked the prey, blocking any attempt to change course.

But the stag continued its flight with single-minded determination, as if it had found a goal. The antlered deer ran downward along the slope of a broad ridge, plunging through thickets, leaping large boulders that would be obstacles only to lesser creatures. The woods opened still more, and the vista showed a swath of blue water, a bay extending between twin necks of rugged land.

Finally the stag broke from the woods to gallop across a wide swath of moor. Soft loam cushioned the broad hooves, and though the deer's tongue flopped loosely from wide jaws and nostrils flared madly with the strain of each breath, the animal actually increased the speed of its desperate flight.

But so, too, did the wolves. More and more of the pack burst from the woods, trailing across the spongy grass-land, running in grim and purposeful silence. If the great male had looked back, he would have noticed a surprising number of canine predators, more by far than had belonged to his pack when they had settled into the den for a winter's rest. And still more wolves came along the shores, gathering from north and south, highland and coast, drawn toward the scene of the hunt, hundreds of gray forms ghosting toward a single point.

The stag finally faltered, but not because of fatigue. The animal slowed to a regal trot, proud antlers held high. The sea was very near, but the buck did not strive for the shoreline. Instead, the forest monarch turned its course along that rocky beach, toward a pool of liquid that rested in the perfect shelter of a rocky bowl.

The pond was too high to be a tidal pool, nor did the water seem like a collection of mere rain or runoff. Instead, the liquid was pale, almost milky-white in color, and it swirled in a hypnotic pattern. The shoreline was steep, but in one place a steplike progression of rocks allowed the buck to move carefully downward.

Wolves gathered on the rocks, surrounding the stag and the pool, knowing that the prey was trapped. Yet some silent compulsion held the hungry predators at bay. Glittering eyes watched with keen intelligence as the stag's muzzle touched the surface of the water; long, panting tongues flopped loosely as the carnivores waited for their prey to drink.

For a long time, the great deer lapped at the waters of the Moonwell, and when finally it had drunk its fill it stepped away, mounting the steps toward the leader. The stag raised its head, baring the shaggy throat, uttering a final, triumphant bellow at the powdery clouds that had gathered in the sky.

When the leading wolf bit into that exposed neck, he did so almost tenderly. The kill was quick and clean, the predator ignoring the red blood that warmed his jaws, that should have inflamed his hunger and passion with its fresh and welcoming scent. Instead, the wolf raised his own head, fixed bright eyes on the same clouds that had been the last things seen by the mighty stag. A long howl ululated across the moor, and the leader was joined by the rest of his pack in a song of joy and worship, in music that hailed their mother and their maker.

When the pack finally fell to feeding, the blood of the stag ran down the rocky steps in crimson rivers. Though the wolves numbered an uncountable throng, there was meat for them all. With a sense of powerful satiation, each predator, after eating its fill, drank from the milky waters of the pool.

The feasting went on for more than a day, and at last the brightness of the full moon rose above the glimmering waters. Pups were born under that light, and youngsters frolicked around the fringes of a mighty gathering.

The red blood mingled with the waters of the Moonwell, and the goddess saw and celebrated with her children. The bold sacrifice of the stag was, to her, a thing of beauty—and with the mighty animal's blood was the water of her Moonwell consecrated.

And the balance of her living children maintained.

Originally published in *Realms of Infamy*
Edited by James Lowder, December 1994

THE GREATEST HERO
WHO EVER DIED

J. Robert King

For my first-ever FORGOTTEN REALMS story, I drew inspiration from a village nestled high in the Snowdownia Mountains in Wales. I had hitchhiked through that little place during college, and its snow-fastness and brutal winds inspired me. When I trudged into the youth hostel, my scraggly beard charged with ice and my shoulders bent beneath an Italian army backpack, I must have seemed a strange and perhaps sinister figure. Thus, the story begins. . . .

—J. Robert King, March 2003

J. Robert King has written nineteen
fantasy novels, most recently
the Onslaught Cycle from
Wizards of the Coast and the
Mad Merlin Trilogy from Tor.

THE GREATEST HERO
WHO EVER DIED

The stormy winds that swept up from the Great Ice Sea often brought unwanted things to lofty Capel Curig. Tonight, in addition to pelting snow and driving gales, the wind brought a hideously evil man.

None knew him as such when he tossed open the battered door of the Howling Reed. They saw only a huge, dark-hooded stranger haloed in swirling snow. Those nearest the door drew back from the wind and the vast form precipitating out of it, drew back as the door slammed behind the dripping figure, slammed, and shuddered in its frame. Without discharging the ice from his boots, the stranger limped across the foot-polished planks of the Reed to a trembling hearth fire. There he bent low, flung a few more logs on the flames, and stood, eclipsing the warmth and casting a giant shadow over the room.

The rumble of conversation in the Reed diminished as all eyes in the tiny pub turned furtively toward the ruined figure.

Silhouetted on the hearth, the stranger looked like some huge and ill-formed marionette. He lacked an arm, for his right sleeve was pinned to the shoulder and his left hand did all the adjusting of his fetid form. Deliberately, that widowed hand drew back some of his robes, but the sodden figure beneath looked no less shapeless. For all his shifting, he did not remove the hood from his head, a head that appeared two sizes too small for his body. Beneath the hood, the man's face was old and lightless, with cold-stiffened lips, a narrow black beard, and a hooked nose. In all, his form looked as though a large man hid within those robes, holding some poorly proportioned puppet head to serve as his face.

He spoke then, and his hollow voice and rasping tongue made the patrons jump a bit.

"Can any of you spare a silver for a bowl of blood soup and a quaff of ale?"

None responded except by blank, refusing stares. Not even Horace behind the bar would offer the stranger a glass of water. Apparently, all would rather dare his wrath than know their charities had provided sustenance to him.

The man was apparently all too acquainted with this response, for he shook his head slowly and laughed a dry, dead-leaf laugh. A few staggering steps brought him to a chair, vacated upon his arrival and still warm from its former occupant. There he collapsed with a wheeze like a punctured bellows.

"In the lands of Sossal, whence I hail, a man can earn his blood and barley by telling a good tale. And I happen to have such a tale, for my land gave birth to the greatest hero who ever lived. Perhaps his story will earn me something warm."

Those who had hoped to dismiss him with bald glares and cruel silence tried turning away and speaking among themselves. Horace, for his part, retreated through a swinging door to the kitchen, to the gray dishwater and the piles of pots.

Unaffected, the shabby wanderer began the telling of his tale with a snap of his rigid blue fingers. Green sparks ignited in air, swirled about him, and spread outward like a lambent palm in the heavy darkness. The sparking tracers lighted on all those seated in the taproom, and each tiny star extinguished itself in the oily folds of flesh between a patron's knotted brows.

The faint crackling of magic gave way to a single, hushed sigh. In moments, the place fell silent again, and the tale began.

"The lands of Sossal were once guarded by a noble knight, Sir Paramore, the greatest hero who ever lived. . . ."

Golden haired, with eyes like platinum, Sir Paramore strode in full armor through the throne room of King Caen. Any other knight would have been stripped of arms and armaments upon crossing the threshold, but not noble Paramore. He marched forward, brandishing his spell-slaying long sword Kneuma and dragging a bag behind him as he approached the royal dais. There the king and princess and a nervous retinue of nobles ceased their conference and looked to him. Only when within a sword swipe of His Majesty did Paramore finally halt, drop to one armored knee, and bow his fealty.

The king, his face ringed with early white locks, spoke.

"And have you apprehended the kidnappers?"

"Better, milord," replied Paramore, rising with a haste that in anyone else would have been arrogance.

He reached into the bag and drew out in one great and hideous clump the five heads of the kidnappers he had slain.

The king's daughter recoiled in shock. Only then did King Caen himself see the wide, slick line of red that Sir Paramore's bag had dragged across the cold flagstones behind him.

"You gaze, my liege, on the faces of the hoodlums you sought," the knight explained.

In the throat-clenched silence that followed, the wizard

Dorsoom moved from behind the great throne, where his black-bearded lips had grown accustomed to plying the king's ears.

"You were to bring them here for questioning, Paramore," said the wizard, "not lop off their heads."

"Peace, Dorsoom," chided the king with an off-putting gesture. "Let our knight tell his tale."

"The tale is simple, milord," replied Paramore. "I questioned the abductors myself and, when I found them wanting of answers, removed their empty heads."

"This is nonsense," Dorsoom said. "You might have simply cut the heads off the first five peasants you saw, then brought them here and claimed them the culprits. There should have been a trial. And even if these five were guilty—which we can never know now—we do not know who assigned these ruffians their heinous task."

"They were kidnappers who had stolen away the children of these noble folk gathered around us," Paramore replied with even steel in his voice. "If anything, I was too lenient."

"You prevented their trial—"

"Still the wagging tongue of this worm," Paramore demanded of the king, leveling his mighty sword against the meddling mage. "Or perhaps these warriors of mine shall do the task first!"

The great doors of the throne room suddenly swung wide, and a clamor of stomping feet answered . . . small feet, the feet of children, running happily up the aisle behind their rescuer. Their shrill voices were raised in an unseemly psalm of praise to Sir Paramore as they ran.

Seeing their children, the nobles emptied from the dais and rushed to embrace their sons and daughters, held captive those long tendays. The ebullient weeping and cooing that followed drowned the protests of Dorsoom, who retreated to his spot of quiet counsel behind the throne. It was as though the sounds of joy themselves had driven him back into the darkness.

Over the pleasant noise, the grinning Paramore called out to the king, "I believe, my liege, you are in my debt. As was promised me upon the rescue of these dear little ones,

I claim the fairest hand in all of Sossal. It is the hand of your beautiful daughter, Princess Daedra, that I seek."

Paramore's claim was answered by a chorus of shouts from the joyous children, who abandoned their parents to crowd the heels of their rescuer. From their spot beside him, the children ardently pleaded the knight's case.

Daedra's bone-white skin flushed, and her lips formed a wound-red line across her face. The king's visage paled in doubt. Before either could speak, though, the children's entreaties were silenced by an angry cry.

"Hush now, younglings!" commanded a thin nobleman, his ebony eyes sparkling angrily beneath equally black brows and hair. "Your childish desires have no say here. The hand of the princess has been pledged to me these long years since my childhood, since before she was born. This usurping knight—" he said the word as though it bore a taint—"cannot steal her from me, nor can your piteous caterwauling."

" 'Tis too true," the king said sadly, shaking his head. He paused a moment, as though listening to some silent voice whisper behind his throne. "I am pressed by convention, Paramore, to grant her hand to Lord Ferris."

Sir Paramore sheathed his sword and crossed angry arms over his chest.

"Come out, wicked mage," said the knight, "from your place of hiding in the shadow of this great man. Your whisperings cannot dissuade my lord and monarch from granting what his and mine and the princess's hearts desire."

With that, Paramore touched the handle of his mighty sword, Kneuma, to dispel whatever enchantment Dorsoom might have cast on the king. Then he snapped his fingers, and the tiny percussion of his nails struck sparks in the air. The king's retinue and the king himself, as though awakening from a dream, turned toward the shadow-garbed mage. Dorsoom sullenly answered the summons and moved into the light.

"Milord, do not be tricked by the puny magic of this—"

"Hush, mage," replied King Caen evenly, regarding Dorsoom through changed eyes. He turned, then, to address the thin nobleman. "Lord Ferris, I know the hand of my daughter has been pledged to you since before you could understand what that pledge meant. But time has passed, as it does, and has borne out a nobler man than thee to take the princess's hand. Indeed, he has taken her heart as well, and mine too, with many great deeds that not a one of them is equaled by the full measure of your life's labors."

"But—"

The king held up a staying hand, and his expression was stern.

"I am now convicted in this matter. You cannot sway me, only spur me to anger, so keep silence." His iron-hard visage softened as he looked upon Sir Paramore. "By royal decree, let the word be spread that on the morrow, you shall wed my darling child."

A cheer went up from all of those gathered there save, of course, Lord Ferris and the mage, Dorsoom. The joyous voices rung the very foundations of the palace and filled the stony vault above.

It was only the plaintive and piercing cry of one woman that brought the hall back to silence.

"My Jeremy!" cried the noblewoman, wringing a light blue scarf in tender, small hands as she came through the doors. "Oh, Sir Paramore! I've looked and looked through all this crowd and even checked with the door guards, and he is not here. Where is my Jeremy?"

Sir Paramore stepped down from his rightful place before the king and, tears running down his face, said, "Even I could not save your son, with what these butchers had already done to him. . . ."

❧ ❧ ❧ ❧ ❧

"And her cries were piteous to hear," the cloaked man muttered low, and the crowd in the pub soaked in the sibilant sound of his voice, "so that even evil Dorsoom shut his ears—"

"That's it, then. No more ale for any of you. I don't care how strong the gale's ablowin' out there; there's a stronger one in here, and it's ablowin' out this stranger's arse!"

It was Horace, fat Horace who'd tended the bar in that tiny crevice of the Kryptgarden Mountains and fed eggs and haggis to the grandfathers and fathers and sons of those gathered there. In all that time, the good folk of Capel Curig had learned to trust Horace's instincts about weather and planting and politics and people. Even so, on that singular night, regarding that singular man, Horace didn't strike the others as their familiar and friendly confidant.

"Shut up, Horace," cried Annatha, a fishwife. "You've not even been listening, back there banging your pots so loud we've got to strain our ears to hear."

"Yeah," agreed others in chorus.

"I hear well enough from the kitchen, well enough to know this monstrous man's passin' garbage off as truth! He makes out King Caen to be a dotterin' and distracted coot when we all know he is strong and just and in full possession of himself. And what of Dorsoom, cast as some malicious mage when in truth he's wise and good? And Lord Ferris, too?"

Fineas, itinerant priest of Torm, said, "I'm all for truth—as you all know—but bards have their way with truth, and barkeeps their way with brandy. So let him keep the story coming, Horace, and you keep the brandy coming, and between the two, we'll all stay warm on this fierce night."

The stranger himself extended that trembling left hand that did the work for two and said with a rasping tongue, "It is your establishment, friend. Will you listen to your patrons' desires, or turn me out?"

Horace grimaced and said, "I'd not throw a rabid dog out on a night like this. But I'd just as soon you shut up, friend. Aside from lyin', you're puttin' a dreamy, unnatural look in these folk's eyes, and I don't like payin' customers to go to sleep on me."

That comment met with more protests, which Horace tried unsuccessfully to wave down.

"All right. I'll let him speak. But, mark me: he's got

your souls now. He's worked some kind of mesmerizin' magic on you with the words he weaves. I, for one, ain't listenin'.'"

Nodding his shadowed and dripping head, the stranger watched Horace disappear into the kitchen, then seemed to study him hawkishly through the very wall as he continued his tale.

"Though Lord Ferris's forked tongue had been stilled that morning before the king and nobles and children, his hands would not be stilled that night when he stalked through the dim castle toward Sir Paramore's room.

"But one other child of the night—the ghost of poor dead Jeremy—was not allied to the sinister plans of Ferris. Indeed, the ghost of Jeremy had sensed evil afoot and so hovered in spectral watch on the stair to Paramore's room. When he spotted Lord Ferris, advancing dark at the foot of the stair, Jeremy flew with warning to the bed foot of his former bosom friend, Petra. . . ."

Petra was a brown-haired girl-child and the leader of the pack of noble children. Jeremy found her abed in a castle suite, for the children and the parents had all been welcomed by King Caen to spend the night. Poor Jeremy gazed with sad ghostly eyes on the resting form of Petra, sad ghostly eyes that had once gazed down on his own still body, lifeless and headless.

"Wake up, Petra. Wake up. I have terrible news regarding our savior, Sir Paramore," the child-ghost rasped.

His phantom voice sounded high and strained, like the voice of a large man pretending to be a child.

And Petra did wake. When she glimpsed her departed friend, her brave girl-heart gave a start: unlike greater ghosts decked in diaphanous gossamers, poor Jeremy had no body upon which to hang such raiment. He was but a disembodied head that floated beyond the foot of her bed, and even then his neck slowly dripped the red life that had once gushed in buckets. So grotesque and horrible was the effect that Petra, who truly was a brave child, could not muster a word of greeting for her dead companion.

"It's Lord Ferris," the ghost-child said urgently. "He plots to slay our Sir Paramore where he sleeps tonight."

Petra managed a stammer and a wide stare.

"You must stop him," came the ghost's voice.

She was getting up from the feather mattress, arraying the bedclothes around her knees. With the sad eyes of small boys—who see small girls as mothers and sisters and lovers and enemies all at once—poor Jeremy watched Petra's delicate hands as she gathered herself.

At last she whispered, "I'll tell Mother—"

"No!" Jeremy's voice was urgent, strident. "Grown-ups won't believe. Besides, Sir Paramore saved your life this morning. You can save his life now, this evening!"

"I cannot stop Ferris alone."

"Then get the others," Jeremy rasped. "Awaken Bannin and Liesle and Ranwen and Parri and Mab and Karn and the others, too. Tell them to bring their fathers' knives. Together you can save our savior as he saved us."

Already, Petra was tying the sash of her bedclothes in a cross over her heart and breathlessly slipping sandals on her feet.

"Hurry," commanded Jeremy. "Even now, Lord Ferris is climbing the stair toward Sir Paramore's room!"

Upon that urgent revelation, Petra gasped, and Jeremy was gone.

Alerted and assembled in the next moments, the children followed Petra to the stair. It was a long and curving stairway that led to the high tower where Sir Paramore had chosen to bed. The steps were dark, lit mainly by a faint glow of starlight through occasional arrow loops in the wall. But when Petra and her child warriors began to climb, they saw ahead of them the vague, flickering illumination of a candle.

"Quiet now," whispered she.

Bannin, a brown-haired boy half her age, nodded seriously and slipped his small hand into hers. The twins Liesle and Ranwen smiled at each other with nervous excitement. Meanwhile, Parri, Mab, Karn, and the others clustered at the rear of the pack and set hands on their knives.

"That's got to be the candle of Lord Ferris," Petra mouthed, indicating the light. "We've got to be quiet, or he'll know we're coming."

The children nodded, for they adored Petra as much as Jeremy had when he lived. And they followed her, doing their very best to be silent and stealthy, though children have a different sense of that than do adults. They proceeded on tiptoes, fingertips dragging dully across the curved inner wall, childish lips whispering loud speculations. As they climbed, the light grew brighter, their fear welled higher, and their voices became froggy from the tension of it all.

With all that muttering, it was no wonder they came around one of the cold stone curves of the stair to find the narrow, black, long-legged Lord Ferris poised above them, his wiry body stretched weblike across the tight passage.

"What are you children doing here?" he asked in an ebon voice that sent a cold draft down the stairs and past the children.

The brave-hearted crew started at that rude welcome, but did not dart.

Petra, who alone hadn't flinched, said stonily, "What are you doing?"

The man's eyes flashed at that, and his gloved hand fell to the pitch-handled dagger at his side.

"Go," he said.

The group wavered, some in the rear involuntarily drawing back a step. But Petra did something incredible. With the catlike speed and litheness of young girls, she slipped past the black-cloaked man and his knife. She stood then, barring the stairs above him.

"We stay. You go," she stated simply.

Lord Ferris's lip curled into a snarl. His hand gripped her shoulder and brusquely propelled her back down the stairs. Her footing failed on the damp stone, one leg twisting unnaturally beneath her. Then came a crack like the splintering of green wood, and a small cry. She crumpled to the stone-edged steps and tumbled limply down to the children, fetching up at their feet and hardly breathing.

They paused in shock. Young Bannin bent, already weeping, beside her. The others took one look at her misshapen leg and rushed in a fierce pack toward the lord. Their young voices produced a pure shriek that adults cannot create, and they swarmed the black-cloaked nobleman, who fumbled to escape them.

They drove their fathers' knives into the man's thighs. He toppled forward onto them and made but a weak attack in return, punching red-headed Mab between her pigtails and, with a flailing knee, striking the neck of Karn, too. The first two casualties of battle fell lifeless beneath the crush, and the steps under them all were suddenly slick with blood.

As though their previous earnestness had been feigned, the children fought with berserker rage. They furiously pummeled and stabbed the man who lay atop them, the once-bold Ferris bellowing and pleading piteously. At one point in the brawl, Parri dropped down to take the crimson dagger from Mab's cold hand, then sunk it repeatedly into the back of the nobleman.

Yet Lord Ferris clung tenaciously to life. His elbow swept back and cracked Liesel's head against the stone wall, and she fell in a heap. Next to go was her twin, Ranwen, who seemed to feel Liesel's death in kindred flesh and stood stock-still as the man's fallen candle set her ablaze. Ranwen, too, was unmade by a clumsy kick.

Aside from the bodies that clogged the path and made it treacherous with blood, Lord Ferris had only poor Parri and two others to battle. His weight alone proved his greatest weapon, for the next children went down beneath him, not to rise again. That left only bawling Bannin and broken Petra below, neither able to fight.

The man in black found footing amidst the twisted limbs of the fallen, then descended slowly toward Bannin and Petra.

"Put the knives away," said he, sputters coming from his punctured lungs.

The boy-child—young, eyes clouded with blood, ears

ringing with screams—drew fearfully back a few paces. Petra could not retreat.

"I told you to go, you little fiends!" growled Lord Ferris. Red tears streaked his battered face. "Look what you've done!"

Bannin withdrew farther, his whimpering giving way to full-scale sobs. But Petra, with a monumental effort, rose. The desperate cracking of her leg did not deter her lunge.

Through bloodied teeth, she hissed, "Death to evil," and drove Parri's blade into the nobleman's gut.

Only then did Sir Paramore come rushing down the stairs, just in time to see wicked Lord Ferris tumble stiffly past a triumphant Petra. She smiled at him from within a sea of scarlet child's-blood, then collapsed dead to the floor.

❀ ❀ ❀ ❀ ❀

The death of the child in the story coincided oddly with the death of the fire on the hearth; the stormy night had reached its darkest corner. But the rapt crowd of listeners, who sat mesmerized in the storyteller's deepening shadow, did not even notice the cold and dim around them. Horace, in the now-frigid kitchen, did.

It was Horace, then, who had to trudge out in the snow for more wood. He wondered briefly why none of the patrons had complained of the chill and dim in the tap-room, as they had tirelessly done in days and years past. As soon as the question formed in his mind, the answer struck him: The stranger's story had kindled a hotter, brighter fire this evening, and by it the people were warming themselves.

Aside from lying slurs on King Caen, Dorsoom, and Lord Ferris—dead now? Horace wondered, fearing that much of the story might be true—no crime had yet been committed by the stranger, not even a stolen bit of bread or blood soup. And his story kept the patrons there when Horace would have thought folks would flee to their lofted beds. But something was not right about the stranger. The hairs on the back of Horace's neck, perhaps imbued by the natural magic of apron yokes and years of honest sweat and aches, had stood on end the moment the man had entered with his swirling halo of snow. As the darkness deepened, as Horace heard snatches of the wicked tale that held the others in thrall, his uneasy feeling had grown to wary conviction. The man was not merely a slick deceiver. He was evil.

Despite that certainty, despite the outcry of every sinew of his being, Horace knew he didn't dare throw the man out or he would have a wall-busting brawl on his hands. Even so, as he bundled wood into the chafed and accustomed flesh of his inner arm, he lifted the icy axe that leaned against the woodpile and bore it indoors with him.

In the taproom beyond, the stranger was bringing his tale to its inevitable end. . . .

There was much that followed the cruel slaying of the innocent children: Sir Paramore's shock at the assassination attempt, the shrieks of parents whose children were gone for good, the trembling praise of the king for the deeds of the fallen, the empty pallets hauled precariously up the curving stair, the filled pallets borne down on parents' backs, the brigade of buckets cleansing the tower, the stationing of guards to protect the princess's betrothed. . . .

And after it all, Sir Paramore prayed long to the mischievous and chaotic heavens, to Beshaba and Cyric and Loviatar, seeking some plan behind the horrific affair. When his shaken mind grew too weary to sustain its devotion and his knees trembled too greatly beneath him to remain upright, Sir Paramore hung the spell-slaying Kneuma on his bedpost and crawled into his sheets to vainly seek sleep.

Without alarm or movement, and as soon as the knight was disarmed and disarmored, the mage Dorsoom stood inside the closed and bolted door. Sir Paramore started, and an approbation rose to his lips as he sat up in bed.

But the mage spoke first, in a sly hiss: "I know what you have done, monstrous man."

Sir Paramore stood up, gawking for a moment in rage and amazement before reaching for his spell-slaying sword. His hand never touched the hilt, though, for in that instant the mage cast an enchantment on him that froze his body like ice.

Seeing Paramore rendered defenseless, Dorsoom said with a cat's purr, "Most folk in this land think you a valiant knight, but I know you are not. You are a vicious and cruel and machinating monster."

Though he could not move feet or legs or arms, Sir Paramore found his tongue: "Out of here! Just as my young knights slew your assassin, I will slay you!"

"Do not toy with me," said the black-bearded mage. "Your sword dispels magic only when in your grip; without it, you can do nothing against me. Besides, neither Ferris nor I am the true assassin. You are."

"Guards! Save me!" cried Paramore toward the yet-bolted door.

"I know how you arranged the kidnappings. I know how you hired those five men to abduct the noblemen's children," said the mage.

"What?" roared the knight, struggling to possess his own body but bringing only impotent tremors to his legs.

The guards outside were pounding and calling for assurances.

"I know how you met with your five kidnappers to pay them for their duties," continued the mage. "But they received only your axe as their payment."

"Guards! Break down the door!"

"I know how you took the clothes of one of the kidnappers you had slain, dressed in them, masqueraded in front of the children as him, and in cold blood slew Jeremy for all their eyes to see. I know how later, in guise of the noble knight you never were, you rushed in to feign saving the rest of the children," said the mage, heat entering his tone for the first time.

The guards battered the bolted door, which had begun to splinter.

Paramore shouted in anguish, "In the name of all that is holy—!"

"You did it all for the hand of the princess; you have killed even children to have her hand. You orchestrated the kidnapping, played both villain and hero, that you might extort a pledge of marriage in exchange for rescuing them."

The tremors in Sir Paramore legs had grown violent; by the mere contact of his toe against the bedpost, his whole pallet shook, as did the scabbarded sword slung on the bed knob.

"I know how you sent this note," the mage produced a crumpled slip of paper from his pocket and held it up before him, "to Lord Ferris, asking him to come up tonight to see you, and knowing that your 'knights' would waylay him."

"It's not even my handwriting," shouted Paramore.

He shook violently, and the rattling blade tilted down toward his stony leg.

Louder came the boot thuds on the door. The crackle of splintering wood grew. With a gesture, though, Dorsoom cast a blue glow about the door, magic that made it as solid as steel.

"And in that bag," cawed the mage, knowing he had all the time in the heavens, "in the bag that late held the five heads of the five abductors lies the head of Jeremy—the head you carved out to form a puppet to appear at the foot of Petra's bed!"

The mage swooped down to the sack of heads, but his hand never clasped it. In that precise moment, the mighty sword Kneuma jiggled free and struck Paramore's stony flesh, dispelling the enchantment on him. A mouse's breath later, that same blade whistled from its scabbard to descend on the bended neck of the sorcerer.

As the razor steel of Paramore sliced the head from the court magician, so too it sundered the spell from the door. The guards who burst then into the room saw naught but a shower of blood, then the disjoined head propelled by its spray onto the bed and Dorsoom's body falling in a heap across the red-stained sack, soaked anew.

Seeing it all awrong, the guards rushed in to restrain Paramore. Whether from the late hour or the outrageous claims of the wizard or the threat of two warriors on one, Sir Paramore's attempt to parry the blades of the guards resulted in the goring of one of them through the eye. The wounded man's cowardly partner fell back and shouted an alarm at the head of the stair. Meantime Paramore, pitying the man whose bloodied socket his sword tip was lodged in, drove the blade the rest of the way into the brain to grant the man his peace.

An alarm went up throughout the castle: "Paramore is the murderer! Stop him! Slay him!"

Sir Paramore watched the other guard flee, then knelt beside the fallen body at his feet. A tear streaked down his noble cheek, and he stared with unseeing eyes upon the sanguine ruin of his life. Determined to remember the man who destroyed it all, he palmed the head of Dorsoom and thrust it angrily into his sack, where it made a thudding sound. Then he stood solemnly, breathed the blood- and sweat-salted air, and strode from the room, knowing that even if he escaped with his life, he would be unrighteously banished.

And he was.

"And that, dear friends," rasped the robed stranger, his left hand stroking his black beard, "is the tragic tale of the greatest hero who ever lived."

The room, aside from the crackle of the hearth fire and the howl of the defiant wind, was dead silent. The people who had once scorned this broken hovel of a man stared toward him with reverence and awe. It wasn't his words. It wasn't his story, but something more fundamental about him, more mystic and essential to his being. Magic. Those who once would have denied him a thimble of water would happily feast him to the best of their farms, would gladly give their husbands and sons to him to be soldiers, their wives and daughters to him to be playthings. And that ensorcelled reverence was only heightened by his next words.

"And that, dear friends, is the tragic tale of how I came to be among you." Even the wind and the fire stilled to hear what had to follow. "For, you see, I am Sir Paramore."

With that, he threw back the yet-sodden rags that had draped him, and from the huge bundle that had been the body of the stranger emerged a young, elegant, powerful, platinum-eyed warrior. His face was very different from the wizened and sepulchral one that had spoken to them. The latter—the dismembered head of Dorsoom—was jammed down puppetlike past the wrist on the warrior's right hand. The dead mouth of the dead wizard moved even then by the device of the warrior's fingers, positioned on the bony palate and in the dry, rasping tongue. Throughout the night, throughout the long telling, the gathered villagers had all listened to the puppet head of a dead man.

The old man's voice came from the young man's mouth as his fingers moved the jaw and tongue.

"Believe him, ye people! Here is the greatest hero who ever lived."

A brown-black ooze clung in dribbles to Paramore's forearm.

Only Horace, stumbling into the taproom, was horrified by the sight; the depravity did not strike the others in the slightest. The simple folk of Capel Curig left their chairs and moved wonderingly up toward the towering knight and his grisly puppet. They crowded him just as the children had done in the story. Cries of "Teach us, O knight! Lead us, Paramore! Guard us and save us from our enemies!" mingled with groans and tongues too ecstatic for human words.

In their center, the beaming sun of their adoration stretched out his bloodied hand and enwrapped them.

"Of course I will save you. Only follow me and be my warriors, my knights!"

"We would die for you!"

"Let us die for you!"

"Paramore! Paramore!"

The praises rose up above the rumble of the wind and the growl of the fire, and the uplifted hands of the people could have thrust the roof entire from the inn had Paramore only commanded it.

The adulation was so intense that none—not even the god-man Paramore himself—saw Horace's flashing axe blade until it emerged red from the knight's gurgling throat.

Originally published in *Realms of the Arcane*
Edited by Brian M. Thomsen and J. Robert King
November 1997

TERTIUS AND THE ARTIFACT

Jeff Grubb

Brian W. Aldiss, in his history of science fiction, *Trillion Year Spree*, connects the very British sensibilities of Tolkien's Middle Earth with the very British sensibilities of P.G. Wodehouse, in particular the latter's tales of Bertie Wooster and Jeeves. Wodehouse wrote a very different type of fantasy than Tolkien—Bertie is an upper class twit of the first water, and Wodehouse's stories inevitably revolve around Bertie getting himself into a pickle, from which he can only be extracted with the aid of his unflappable manservant, Jeeves (You want to know why everyone calls butlers Jeeves? That's why).

In any event, Aldiss's comment stuck with me, and I have as a result always felt comfortable mixing the elite, effete figures of Wodehouse's upper class with the sword and sorcery of the Realms. This has resulted in not one but two figures of the Realms. The first is the relatively hapless Giogi Wyvernspur, who first appeared in *Azure Bonds* and who has in the intervening years grown up, gotten married, sired children, and otherwise transcended his very mortal beginnings. The other was Tertius Wands, who happily remains as cloth-headed today as he was in his first appearance (which was in the ADVANCED DUNGEONS & DRAGONS® comic book, from DC Comics).

With a deep, devoted nod to Wodehouse, a Tertius Wands story will always involve Tertius getting himself into a pickle, from which he may only be extracted with the aid of his unflappable genie/manservant, Ampratines.

For your dining and dancing enjoyment, here's Tertius Wands.

—Jeff Grubb, April 2003

Jeff Grubb builds worlds for a living. A civil engineer by training and a designer of games by profession, writing is his avocation and (not-so) secret joy. He was one of the "First Four"—the initial co-creators of DRAGONLANCE under Tracy Hickman, and was the co-founder, with Ed Greenwood, of the FORGOTTEN REALMS setting.

TERTIUS AND THE ARTIFACT

As I sat on the balcony of the Nauseous Otyugh in Scornubel, suspended between the hangover of the previous evening and the one that was yet to come, I meditated on the phrase "should have stayed in bed." Sound advice, probably postulated first by some spell-flinger after a particularly bad morning of fireballing and lightning bolting and whatnot.

Of course, it did me little good since I was in bed the night before when everything went south. Except me, of course.

Let me explain. It was a little before three bells, and Tertius Wands, yours truly, was blissfully asleep in my quarters at the Otyugh, third floor stateroom with an odorous view of the stables. The Otyugh is one of the new establishments that have popped up after the last Volo's Guide. As a result of Volo's work in popularizing certain locations to travelers, those locations have ceased to be popular to natives, necessitating new inns, dives, and hangouts for adventurers to hang out in. Ampi had at one time suggested that it would be advantageous to follow Volo around, opening new inns in his wake, as the ones he talks about are soon filled to the bursting with warriors and wizards carrying his dratted little tomes.

But I digress. I was setting the scene, dressing the stage, laying the groundwork. Three bells. Bedroom. Otyugh. Then the ceiling exploded.

Well, it did not exactly explode, but the thunderous boom from above was akin to a roof collapsing. I sat bolt upright, and noticed that the bed itself, a stout four-poster of ironwood, was shimmying and jumping like a nervous carrion crawler. Every loose article in the room, from the chamber pot to the steel mirror, joined in this vibrating dance of doom.

I did what any rational man would do—I hid beneath the covers and promised whatever gods would listen that I would never touch Dragon's Breath Beer and death cheese again.

"Tertius Wands!" thundered a frighteningly familiar voice from the direction of the ceiling.

I popped an eye over the edge of the blanket and saw Granduncle Maskar's fiery head. I did not doubt that his head was still attached to his body back in Waterdeep, and he was sending an astral whatsit or a phantasmal thingamabob to address me. At the moment, I was too frightened to care.

Bravely, I faced the mightiest mage of Waterdeep.

"It wasn't my fault!" I shouted, pulling the bed sheets back over my head and hoping I could be heard clearly. "I didn't know she was a priestess of Sune! No one told me about that festhall! I'm innocent!"

"Never mind that!" boomed my granduncle. "I have something important for you to do!"

I peeked over the edge of my covers and managed a kitten-weak, "Me?"

"You," snarled my uncle, his displeasure registering fully on his face. "I had a magical artifact, a remnant of powerful Netheril, which has been stolen from me."

"I didn't do it!" I quickly put in. "Have you checked with Cousin Marcus? He's always picking up things that don't belong to—"

"Silence!" bellowed the fiery, god-sized head floating over my bedpost. "I know who took it—a thief named the Raven, who is heading your way. I want you to get it back. The device looks like three glass spheres, one set floating within the next. Bring it back to me, and you can return to the City of Splendors!"

"Well, that's just it, then," I ventured. "I was thinking about taking up a life on the open road, and . . ."

"Find the Tripartite Orb of Hangrist," said the phantasmal granduncle, "and find it now!"

And with that, Maskar's head exploded in a cascade of fireworks, which succeeded in leaving scorch marks along the wall and shattering the water pitcher. Granduncle Maskar was never one for quiet exits. In fact, in all the years I've known and avoided him, he's never used the door once.

In my nightshirt, I rose unsteadily from my bed and picked up the shattered pitcher. Any thought that I could write this off to some cheese-induced delirium or nightmare was in as many shards as the pottery. Granduncle Maskar wanted something, and wanted me to get it.

And one does not disappoint one's granduncle, particularly when that granduncle could turn one into a toad.

So I whistled up my genie, Ampratines. Well, whistled is a bad word. I more rubbed him up, running my finger over the ring and calling him into being.

Let me make this quite clear: I lack the least bit of magical ability, which makes me an exception in the Wands family, overladened by all manner of conjurers, sorcerers, prestidigitators, and other assorted spellcasters. However, I get by with a genie, attached to a ring I found years ago in a Waterdhavian sewer. But that's a tale for another time.

Ampratines wafted into view like a phantasmal castle suddenly appearing in the desert. The djinn by their nature are a clever race, and Ampi is the cleverest of the lot, with more brain cells per cubic inch than any other creature in Faerûn.

Ampi was dressed as normal, in long blue robes that set off his crimson skin. His black topknot of hair was immaculately greased and mannered, protruding through an azure skullcap like the tail of a championship horse. His solemn mouth was framed by an equally well-mannered beard and mustache.

"What ho, Ampi?" said I. "You heard?"

"Druids in the High Forest heard, I have no doubt," said Ampi calmly, his voice as deep as the crypts of Undermountain and as smooth as a halfling's promise. "It seems your granduncle has need of you."

"Need for a pawn," I muttered, looking around for my pants. Ampi waved a hand, and the missing trousers manifested at the end of his large, well-manicured hand. Genies are wonderful that way, and I think everyone should have at least one. Regardless, I was in no mood to list my djinni's good points after being terrorized by my own flesh and blood. "Why does he need me?"

"I can endeavor to find out," said Ampi smoothly. "It may take me a brief while."

With this he wafted out of view. Butlers, menservants, and members of the guard would pay good coin to learn how to waft as effortlessly as this genie could.

I tried to get back to sleep, but once you've been threatened in bed by a magical projection of the family patriarch, the bliss of slumber is denied. Instead, I paced, worried, and sat up by the windowsill, watching the horses in their paddock and marveling at the simplicity of their lives.

And with the arrival of morning, and the failure of Ampi to return, I chowed down a modest breakfast of snakes in gravy (at least that's what I assumed it was). Then I retired to the portico of the Nauseous Otyugh with orders for the wait staff to send another Dragon's Breath out every half hour, and keep doing so until I was no longer able to send the empties back. I sought to stave off the oncoming hangover from the previous night by launching directly into the next one.

The Nauseous Otyugh, by the way, is a bit ramshackle, a former general store put out of business by Aurora and her catalog. The second floor was set back from the first, creating a wide porch, suitable for the major Scornubel sports of drinking oneself into oblivion and watching others do the same on the street below. I had gotten quite good at both activities for the past two tendays, and was quite prepared to begin my career as a Waterdhavian expatriate, sopping up the sun and the alcohol and telling people about how horrid it was to live in a city like Waterdeep, where every second noble is a mage, and most of those are relatives.

And, of course, now I mentally kicked myself for not leaving Scornubel. Ampi had strongly recommended we keep moving a tenday ago, but I demurred. I would not be like some of my cousins, ordered around by servants, controlled by their butlers, mastered by their own magical homunculi. If I was to be banished from Waterdeep, I had told Ampi at the time, there was no better place to begin my exile than the balcony of old Nauseous, watching the caravans go by. But Scornubel was only a few hundred miles down the Trade Way from Waterdeep, and apparently not far enough from Granduncle Maskar's plots.

My mental wandering was interrupted when I was made aware of a youth to my right, instead of the patient barmaid that had been bringing my drinks. Surely it could not have been noon already, I thought, and the changing of shifts. Someone would have come out with a lunch menu, at the very least.

I strained to focus a bloodshot eye and discovered that the newcomer, bearing ale on a silver plate, was a halfling. His wide ivory grin was visible in the shadows of a badly woven straw hat. I blinked twice, and when he failed to disappear, ventured a conversational gambit.

"Yes?" I asked, that being the soul of wit I could manage at the moment.

"Beggin' yer pardon, sire," said the small demihuman, sweeping off the hat to reveal a tangle of red hair, "but I understand that yer the gentlem'n that was lodgin' on the top floor yesterday eve? The one that had all the thunder and shoutin' and whatever?"

I deeply wished I had some form of native magical ability at the moment, for a comprehend languages spell, or a distill dialect, or whatever would be useful. I chose to stay with a time-proven response: "Yes?"

The halfling shifted uneasily on his furry pads.

"Well, sire, I was outside and heard a lot of it, and the big god-voice said ye was huntin' the Raven."

I nodded slowly, hoping I would appear sage but in reality praying my melon would not pop loose from my shoulders and roll around on the porch.

"And you are . . . ?"

"Caspar Millibuck, at yer servants," the halfling continued. "Well, I'm huntin' the Raven meself, and I figgered that one like ye, with such powerful god-voices, could help one like me, bein' small and short and all, and we could both nab the thief together."

"Uh-huh," said I, banishing most of my foggier thoughts back to the corners of my mind. "And why do you want the Raven?"

I had not just fallen off the spell-wagon, and knew that halflings always had at least three reasons for doing anything, two of which would violate local laws.

The halfling examined his fur-covered pedicure and said, "Well, it's just that the Raven stoled from me family as well, and I'm s'posed to get me coin back. I can't go home till I get it."

Even in its ale-induced state, my heart went out to the small individual, trapped in a similar situation to my own.

"And what did the Raven steal from you?"

"Gold, sire," said the halfling quickly, "all the gold in me orph'nage."

"Orphanage?" I shook my head. "I thought you said it was stolen from your family?"

"Indeed, sire," the halfling bobbed his head up and down rapidly. "Ever'body in my family's an orphan. We're very unlucky."

"Indeed," I muttered, and wondered what the halfling was really after.

Of course, Ampratines was nowhere about, and here it was nearly noon. If I could wrap things up without my erstwhile ally, that would show both the genie and my granduncle I knew a thing or two myself.

"Very well," I said. "Take me to the Raven. We'll sort things out, man to man."

"Ach, ye can't do that," slurred the halfling. "The Raven's no man, but a doppelganger, and can change shape at whim. I think I know where to find him, but ye have to be ready to move, and move quick, when I call. Will ye be helpin' me? For the other orphans, at least?"

With tears in his eyes, he looked up at me, and of course, I said yes. Noble thing to do and all. And besides, this little fellow knew how to find the Raven, and that would make my job all the easier.

I took the ale from the halfling, but did not finish it. I sent the next ale back undrunk as well, and asked instead for a tablet and a stylus, and some of the house stationary. I was in the midst of composing a letter to Granduncle Maskar, telling him everything was under control, when Ampi reappeared. One moment there was nothing to my left shoulder, and the next, there he was—as noble a djinni as ever 'jinned.

"I take it you have something," I snapped, the effects of the long-delayed hangovers coming to the fore. "You've taken most of the morning."

Ampi gave a small quarter-bow from the waist.

"A hundred apologies, Lord Tertius," he said. "It took some doing to ascertain the nature of the device and what exactly happened to it. I finally spoke with a sylph that your granduncle uses to clean out the chimneys. She apparently witnessed most of the news on this unpleasantness."

"Well then, spit it out," I said, impatiently tapping my stylus against the tablet.

"The Tripartite Orb is an artifact of Netheril," said the genie, putting his hands behind his back like a schoolboy reciting his lessons. "Netheril was a kingdom of wizards that fell thousands of years ago, before the founding of Cormyr or Waterdeep. The least of these wizards, it is said, was more powerful than the mightiest mages of the Realms."

"A kingdom of Granduncle Maskars?" I barely suppressed a shudder. "The mind boggles."

"Indeed, it does, milord," said Ampratines. "The Tripartite Orb was apparently a most potent weapon in that kingdom, for it had the ability to kill all magic within its immediate surroundings. No fireball would explode in its proximity, no summoning would be effective, no ward would protect, and no magical weapon would gain its weal. You can see why this would be effective in a kingdom of wizards."

"Right ho," said I. "You get one near it, and they're weak as puppies."

"Effectively so," said the djinni. "So, as a result, most of its history in Netheril consists of mages hiding it in inaccessible places while other mages hired warriors to wrest it from those hiding spots. So it went through most of Netherese history, until the kingdom's fall. It remained hidden until a dozen years ago, when a group of adventurers found it in Anauroch. Your granduncle realized the danger of such a magic-destroying artifact immediately, and acquired it and locked it in his lowest dungeon."

"Far away from any prying eyes or other magics," I put in.

"Quite. The device appears as a set of three crystal globes, one floating within the next, which are made of iridescent crystal, such that they resemble soap bubbles, I am told. As with all artifacts, it is indestructible by most normal means, so your granduncle put it under lock and key in a safe location. And from that safe location, it was stolen two tendays ago by a thief called the Raven, who is apparently heading down the Trade Way to Scornubel."

"Which explains why Granduncle Maskar wants me to recover the thingamabob," I said.

"In part," said the genie. "Also because you are one of the few members of the family without natural magical ability, perhaps he thought you would be less at risk if confronted with a lack of magic entirely."

"Or less of a loss if I ended up dead," I muttered. "Well, at least I have your aid."

Ampratines blanched, which for the genie was a strange thing.

"I fear I can be of less aid than you would prefer. This antimagical sphere will also remove any summoned creatures from the area, including myself. Indeed, its very antimagical nature prevents magical detection. Perhaps it would be to our advantage to notify the local authorities on this matter."

My brow furrowed at the news.

"Local authorities." I shook my head dismissively and said, "If they got their hands on something like this, they'd lock it up under tight guard and magical key, and Granduncle Maskar would be steamed at me until the next Avatar Crisis. No, we can do this on our own."

"But, milord, the antimagical nature precludes . . ."

"No buts." I held up a hand. "While you were questioning a smoky hearth-wisp, I was diligently pursuing my own avenues. Even now, my agents are scouring the city, hunting for this Raven character."

"Your—" Ampratines looked stunned, well, as stunned as a creature made of elemental air could look—"agents . . . ?" He struggled to turn the question into a statement, with some success.

"Indeed," said I, rising unsteadily to my feet. "I will have this small matter solved, with no further involvement on your behalf."

"Milord, I . . ."

"Tut, tut." I touched my hand to my forehead. Both hangovers, long delayed, were now rushing to the fore. "If you say you cannot help, I will not press the issue. Have faith in the Wands family intuition."

The genie looked unconvinced, but said, "As you wish, milord."

I smiled at the djinni. There was no mistaking who was in charge of this relationship.

"But if you could, whip up one of your mystical omelets, tonic to any drinking binge. I think better when the entire Realms isn't pulsing in time with my heartbeat."

Ampratines started a warning, then merely said, "Of course, milord."

He wafted from view.

I stood on the porch of the Nauseous Otyugh, steadying myself on the railing, and tried to look deep in thought. Actually, I was counting the seconds until Ampi's return with the cure to my now-thundering headache.

"That's the Raven?" I asked the halfling. "She's a woman!"

"Hush!" hissed the small red-haired humanoid from beneath the folds of his brown, tattered robe. "She's no more a woman than I'm a red dragon. She be a doppelganger! And she'll notice if ye shout and goggle at her like a fish!"

The woman who was not a woman was seated at a table across the crowded common room. She was dressed in traveling leathers and a blue cape, and she was facing us, which made surreptitious observation difficult. She had a large valise sitting on the table next to her. She cast an errant glance in our direction, and I retreated into the folds of my own brown cloak and hood, turning slightly away from her, trying not to goggle like a fish.

Her companion at the table might have been a hill giant, or perhaps an ogre, for he was as tall as Ampi, and nearly as massive. The companion was dressed in an all-encompassing cloak as well, one of crimson, which made him look like a large sunset at the opposite table.

We were at the Jaded Unicorn, a place that had the unfortunate fate of gaining notice in the aforementioned Volo's Guide. As a result, the place was filled with new-comers, travelers, hardened mercenaries, and dewy-eyed would-be adventurers. As the Unicorn had a bad reputation (according to Volo), the traditional garb was heavy cloaks with the hoods pulled up. It looked like a convention of specters, wraiths, and grim reapers.

The exception was the Raven. She, I mean *it*, had her hood down, showing off golden hair that pooled on her shoulders like spilt ale. She looked as if she had elf blood in her. Her ears were slightly pointed, and her chin tapered to a soft, rounded end. I had to remind myself that all this was an illusion. She—it, I mean—was a shapechanger, and could look like King Azoun or my Granduncle Maskar if it so desired. A doppelganger in its true form was a slender humanoid—sexless, hairless, and pale gray in shade. Altogether an unappetizing thought.

The Raven was in animated conversation with the giant sunset at her table. Her brow became furrowed at one point, and she tapped her oversized case with a slim hand. We were too far away to hear what was being said, but it was obvious they were haggling about something.

And it did not require a master mage to figure out what they were arguing about. The case was about the size and shape that could carry a wizard's crystal ball. Or a Tripartite Orb of the ancients.

Whatever Sunset said seemed to calm her down, for her features cleared. She listened, then nodded, then grabbed the satchel and strode toward the door. Sunset remained at his seat. All eyes were on her, but when she arrived at the doorway, the doppelganger turned and, for the briefest moment, locked eyes with me. I don't know if it was true or not, but I felt as if the world suddenly shifted on its axis and spun in a new fashion.

Then she, it, was gone. I turned back and noticed that the giant Sunset had disappeared as well, probably back to some hidden room with a cabal of Red Wizards of Thay.

"C'mon!" snapped the halfling. "We'll lose 'er if we don' get movin'."

Relieved mildly that my ally was also using the female pronoun for our target, I followed the smaller cloaked figure out of the Unicorn. Our departure did not create any response or commotion, but then, we kept our hoods up.

Night had fallen like a drunken dwarf, and the streets were nearly empty. Those with something to lose were already squirreled away in their beds (unless bothered by their magical granduncles). Selûne was full, however, and reflected like a beacon off our quarry's blond tresses.

We followed her to a small rooming house near the river. A buck-toothed ogre denied us entry, but a few gold coins did buy the information that the young lady (who gave her name as Demarest) had just arrived, always carried the valise, and was staying on the second floor near the back of the inn.

So it was that, almost a full day after Granduncle Maskar first manifested himself, I wore a voluminous robe and edged along a window ledge, a similarly dressed halfling in tow. The breeze off the surrounding plains was brisk, and at several points, I was afraid the cloaks would catch the wind fully and send us spiraling, head over boot heels, over the low buildings of Scornubel like errant paper kites.

For the first time that evening, I regretted giving Ampi the night off. He was most perturbed about my pursuing magic-killing artifacts, so I gave him leave. Even now, he was probably curled up in some merchant's library, digesting some history of the Heartlands, or the *Collected Romances of the Obarskyr Line*, while his master was about to take involuntary flight.

Progress was, therefore, slow. Were we near the front end of the building, we would have undoubtedly been spotted by the watch, in their plate mail and copper helmets. As it was, we did our best to imitate gargoyles when someone passed below us in the alley, and spent the rest of the time inching toward the desired goal: a lit window. As we approached, the occupant within doused the light. We halted for another long moment to ascertain that the faux Demarest had not dimmed her lamp in order to see clearly outside. Then we resumed our onerous march.

The window was latched, a wise precaution even on the second floor in Scornubel. The halfling Caspar produced a long, thin piece of wire that, wedged into the slot between the window halves, sprang the latch easily.

"In ye go, lad," hissed the halfling, smiling with his ivory-white choppers.

"Me?" I whispered back. "I thought you halfling folk would be better at the 'sneaking into someone else's room' sort of thing, being closer to the ground and all."

The halfling gave a disgruntled snort. "Well, I could, but then ye'd be out here on the ledge, twice as big as life, waitin' for the copper-top watch to pick ye off. Of course, if that's yer choice. . . ." He let his voice trail off.

I could see his point. I also realized that if I wanted the Tripartite Orb, I had better get my hands on it before he did.

I slid into the room as silently as I was able, the cloak's ability to muffle my steps offset by its own bulky weight. The moonlight was full in the room, and reduced everything to blue highlights and ebon shadows. Demarest, the doppelganger thief known better as the Raven, was asleep on a wide bed, only her hair, now shining like silver in the moonlight, visible above the wide comforter.

The valise was on a low table across from the bed. It would likely hold the orb, the halfling's gold, or both. It would pay, I thought, to open the satchel and check. If the halfling's gold was not in there, I was sure that I could convince Uncle Maskar to make good their financial loss.

The satchel's large metal clasp opened with a ratcheting click, the bag falling open on the table. There was another click, which at first I thought was an echo.

Then a very steely feminine voice behind me said, "Step away from the bag, or I will drop you where you stand."

I am by nature very good at taking orders, as befits a non-mage in a family of wizards. I put the satchel down on the table and took two steps backward, holding my hands up in clear view. I left the bag open, more from not being told to do otherwise than from any innate curiosity. Within, there was a glint of crystal, not gold.

"Now turn toward me," said the dulcet voice.

I turned slowly, and as I did, I could see Caspar's silhouette at the window. I tried not to flinch, but only hoped that he had planned for this possibility. The woman seated on the bed did not seem to notice him.

The doppelganger was carrying a crossbow, one of those drow-made hand-held jobs that looked every bit as dangerous as it was. She held it level on me and kicked the comforter off her. She was fully dressed beneath the covers, which I realized with both relief and regret.

She regarded me coolly.

"A more foolish disguise than normal, Raven," she said. "Did you mug some fop of a noble for that face?"

"P-Pardon?" I managed, my mind in a bit of a whirl. "I'm sorry, I'm not the Raven. I thought you were. . . ."

I made the mistake of lowering my arms slightly. Raven pointed the crossbow toward my chest, and I raised them immediately.

"Don't even flinch, doppelganger, or I'll drill a new hole through you."

"I'm sorry," I said, wondering if Ampi could hear my silent plea in whatever library he had ensconced himself, "but I'm not the doppelganger here. You are, and if you're confused about it, maybe we should talk about it instead of drilling anyone or anything."

Demarest the not-Raven, not-doppelganger laughed. It was a crystalline laugh, but cold and cruel. She raised the hand crossbow to point at my face, and I closed my eyes. I really did not want my last sight to be a crossbow bolt barreling in on me.

There was a *twang*, but surprisingly no impact or even the slight breeze of a near-miss. Instead, there was a low, feminine cursing. Taking a breath to assure myself I was among the living, I opened my eyes again.

Demarest was back on the bed, clutching with her left hand at the small bolt that had pierced her right front shoulder. Her right arm, though still attached, lay on the bed inert. Of the crossbow I could see nothing. Blood streamed down from the wound along her arm, darkening her blue robes and pooling in a magenta stain on the linens.

I turned to see Caspar amble down out of the window. He was already loading another shot into his own drow crossbow.

I was mildly peeved, and said so. "How long were you going to wait until you made yourself known?" I started, but the halfling raised the crossbow to my face, in much the same way Demarest had done earlier. This was apparently a theme for the evening.

"Step by the woman, fool," snapped the halfling in a very unhalflinglike voice. The voice was sharp, like dried twigs breaking, and apparently used to being listened to.

I took two steps toward the woman, still seated on the bed, her breathing ragged and gasping. Her eyes were turning glassy.

"Poison," said the halfling, keeping the crossbow leveled on me as he moved sideways toward the table. "Not the fastest, but fast enough. Soon you will feel it too."

As he moved, the halfling began to melt like a wax candle and elongate. I know that wax candles don't elongate, but that's what Caspar was doing. The fatty folds of halfling flesh peeled away. The dark cloak turned pale, the head narrowed, and the eyes turned white and pupilless. By the time the halfling reached the table, he was no more a halfling. He was the native form of a doppelganger.

"Raven, I presume," I said, fighting to keep the quivering out of my voice.

"Right for the first and last time," said the creature, keeping the crossbow on me while digging into the bag with his free hand.

He pulled forth a large crystalline globe. Within it floated a second globe of crystal, and within that a third globe. The three globes twinkled in the moonlight of the room.

"You've been very helpful, Tertius Wands," said the doppelganger, smiling with even rows of ivory-colored teeth. "You drew away my former partner's attention so I could get the drop on her. And now you'll serve me again. When they find both your bodies here, the guard will assume that the lady was surprised by a robber and both killed each other, leaving no witnesses to the Tripartite Orb's new owner."

I started to say something about how I could offer a very good price for the orb, but I was drowned out by a low growling. The woman on the bed was fast, faster than I would be in a similar situation—dead of night, bedroom, poisonous bolt in one shoulder. As the Raven and I talked, she had pulled herself into a crouch and now sprang at the doppelganger.

The shapechanger hadn't thought his former partner could shrug off the poison, and had the crossbow leveled at me. He jerked his hand toward the new target as he fired, and his shot was wide. The poisonous bolt buried itself in the woodwork as the woman slammed into him. The globe flew from his hand like a live thing, dancing and spinning in the moonlight.

I dived for it as if it was the last roll at the Highar-vestide feast. My mind told me that after all the aeons, a simple drop would not harm the device, but my heart held the image of Uncle Maskar. My heart drove me to spread forward on the floor, snaring the orb before it touched the carpet.

I caught it with inches to spare, and both I and artifact rolled sideways, away from the sounds of battle. As I rose to my feet, I heard shouts in the distance and felt doors slamming open elsewhere in the inn. Apparently the fight was attracting other attention.

The two thieves, human and doppelganger, brawled in the midst of the room. The doppelganger had already taken Demarest's form in the struggle, so that it looked as if two blond twins were rolling about on the carpet, claw-ing at each other. I looked at them, at the triple orb in my hands, and back at them, and wondered if I could negoti-ate my way around them and out the door. I really did not want to go back out the window and along the ledge.

That was when the door burst open to reveal at least three, and perhaps a dozen, copper-headed watchmen. Each bore a heavy two-handed crossbow, the type that could punch its way through the wall of a stable. Some carried torches and lanterns, and behind them was the giant Sunset in his crimson robes.

The two battling Demarests detangled and slowly rose, regarding the newcomers. I took another step back-ward. The window started looking like a better option all the time.

Sunset reached up and pulled his cowl back, revealing a very familiar, calm face.

Ampratines. Of course. I felt my heart start beating again.

The guards were not as sure as I was, and kept moving their aim from one twin to the next, unsure which was the true danger. Both thieves stood up uneasily, trying to put a few feet of distance between them.

I piped up. "The wounded one is real. The unwounded one is the doppelganger."

The unwounded twin, Caspar/Raven/Doppelganger, wheeled in place and hissed at me, its fangs growing elongated and huge wings sprouting from its back as it did so. It leaped at me, intent on grabbing me as hostage and the globe as a prize.

Two things happened simultaneously. I threw the globe upward, toward the door and Ampi. And there were three or a dozen sharp twangs and the doppelganger collapsed on the floor.

The artifact floated like a soap-bubble across the room, and into the hands of Ampi.

Ampi looked at me, gave a short quarter bow, then dropped the globe.

It hit the ground with a resounding smash, and bits of colored glass spattered in all directions.

It was followed by me, I am afraid, hitting the ground in a dead faint.

❀ ❀ ❀ ❀ ❀

Back on the balcony of the Nauseous Otyugh, I had recovered sufficiently to watch the sun rise over the ramshackle buildings of Scornubel.

"You could have warned me," I said, pouting over an ale.

The djinni produced one more cold compress and placed it over my fevered brow.

"You did not wish any warning," said Ampi. "I pursued matters as I thought I was best able. I have informed the local gendarmes that you realized the doppelganger was a halfling at the start, and played along to discover the location of the missing artifact. Therefore you are held blameless in this matter. The doppelganger is dead, and the thief Demarest, his former partner, has been cleansed of the poison and is ready to accept the town's justice."

"How did you know?"

"I did not know, exactly, though I thought the fact that you received fortuitous aid quite interesting. A word with the wait staff at the Otyugh ascertained that your help was the halfling, and it was not difficult to find a red-headed halfling wearing a straw hat in Scornubel. I noticed he was watching a particular inn, and let it be known at the inn that I was a wizard searching for a particular artifact. Demarest, hoping to unload the item before her partner caught up with her, contacted me for the meeting at the bar, where you saw us. That was when she tried to sell me the fake artifact."

My mind, battered and worn and threatened, skipped a beat, and I said, "Fake artifact?"

"Of course," said the genie. "As I explained to the watch, and took the liberty of putting these thoughts in your name, if the device was truly the described artifact, then I would be unable to get close to it, being a summoned creature myself. The fact that I could sit at the same table with it was sufficient proof that it was a phony, strung up with thin crystals and gases of various densities, such that one sphere would float within the next. At that meeting I purposefully failed to bring the coin she wanted for it. From there it was easy to alert the watch of a possible break-in at Demarest's room. We arrived in time to hear the battle."

I shook my head.

"Fake artifact? Then the doppelganger had the real Tripartite Orb hidden elsewhere?"

"The Raven was probably unaware of the fake as well, since he went to such efforts to recruit you as his pawn. And Demarest, if she had the true globes, would have let the Raven take the fake, convincing him it was the real one. Neither had time to build a replica."

"Then who built the replica?" I said. "Not Uncle Maskar."

"Your granduncle's concern was legitimate as well, I suspect," said the djinni.

"Then if not the thieves, and not Maskar. . ." I took a long sip on my ale bottle. "Uncle Maskar never had the real Tripartite Orb, did he?"

"I don't think so," said the genie. "After all, how do you test an item for magic that supposedly refuses all magic?"

I let a smile crawl onto my face, the first in the past twelve hours.

"So old Granduncle Maskar was hornswoggled in the first place." I chuckled at the thought. "I would love to see the look on his face when he gets my letter explaining that!"

Ampratines made a solemn, low cough. That kind of cough he always makes when he disagrees completely, but cannot bring himself to say something outright. I cast my companion the eye, and he looked up, into the middle distance.

"If your granduncle never had the device," he said solemnly, "that means he would have to now get the device. And who better to get the device than someone who has already gotten the fake one?"

I let that sink into my ale-stained brain. "So the best thing is to not be here at all when he gets the word, eh?"

"Quite."

"Ah, well," I said with a sigh, draining the last of the ale and setting the dead soldier next to the others, "so much for an expatriate life in Scornubel. I think we need to move farther south, farther away from Waterdeep."

"I thought you'd think so," said Ampratines, with a smooth flourish producing our bags, "so I already took the liberty of purchasing the coach tickets. We leave in an hour."

Originally published in *Realms of Magic*
Edited by Brian M. Thomsen and J. Robert King
December 1995

RED AMBITION

Jean Rabe

It seems like I wrote that story a lifetime ago. I was really into Thay at the time, as I'd set my first novel—*Red Magic*—there. Besides, there's just something wonderful about a great bad guy, and with the Red Wizards there was an abundance to choose from. For this particular tale I selected Szass Tam, undoubtedly the biggest, baddest Red Wizard in all of Faerûn. As far as I was concerned, he wrote the proverbial book on evil. Interestingly, my editor on *Red Magic* told me I'd portrayed Szass Tam and his fellow Red Wizards very well. Too well, in fact. He said my villains were deep and rich and left the heroes kind of shallow. It was a long rewrite to beef up the good guys.

Why do I like villains? I think all of us appreciate the likes of Darth Vader, Ming the Merciless, Doctor Doom, and ol' Szass. Normally, I'm a mild-mannered soul, known for pampering puppies and not passing by a Salvation Army Christmas kettle. But Szass, he let me be . . . delightfully malicious . . . if only for a handful of pages.

—Jean Rabe, March 2003

Jean Rabe is the author of a dozen novels and nearly three dozen short stories, and is the happy owner of two wonderful, feet-warming dogs. She lives in Southeastern Wisconsin, where she writes (a lot), reads (not enough), plays with her dogs (never, ever enough), and listens to classical music (too much as far as her rock-n-roll husband is concerned).

In her spare time she pretends to garden, ogles her pretty blue gouramis, and plays D&D.

RED AMBITION

Szass Tam eased himself into a massive chair behind an ornate table covered with curled sheets of vellum and crystal vials filled with dark liquid. A thick candle stood in the middle of the clutter, its flame dancing in the musty air and casting a soft light across his grotesque features.

His pale, parchment-thin skin stretched taut across his high cheekbones, and his wispy hair, the color of cobwebs, spread unevenly atop his age-spotted scalp. His lower lip hung loose, as if there were no muscles to control it, and the fleshy part of his nose was gone, revealing twin cavities. The scarlet robes he wore fell in folds over his skeletal frame and spread like a pool of blood on the floor around his chair.

He absently swirled his index finger in a puddle of wax gathering on the table, letting the warm, oily liquid collect on his skin. He rolled the cooling blob between his thumb and middle finger until it hardened into a ball, then he released the wax and watched it roll across the rosewood finish and come to rest near a decades-old scroll. The piercing points of white light that served as Szass Tam's eyes stared at the parchment. It contained the last enchantment needed to turn his cherished apprentice into a creature like himself—an undead sorcerer . . . a lich. Of course, his apprentice would have to die before the spell could be invoked. Killing her would be no great matter, he decided. Bony fingers grasped the parchment and brought it close to his still heart.

Szass Tam's mortal life had ended centuries ago on a Thayan battlefield a hundred miles north of his comfortable keep. But the magic coursing through him prevented him from passing beyond the land of the living. It bound him to the human realms in a rotting body that pulsed with an arcane power few would dare challenge. The lich considered himself the most formidable Red Wizard in Thay. A zulkir, he controlled the realm's school of necromancy. His apprentice, Frodyne, was also a Red Wizard, one of an august council of sorcerers who ruled Thay through schemes, threats, and careful manipulation. Szass Tam smiled thinly. None were more treacherous than he.

He listened intently. The soft footfalls in the hall were Frodyne's. He placed the scroll in a deep pocket and waited. One day soon he would bless her with immortality.

"Master?" Easing open the door, Frodyne stepped inside. She padded forward, the shiny fabric of her dark red robe dragging across the polished marble floor behind her. "Am I disturbing you?"

Szass Tam gestured to a seat opposite him. Instead, the young woman's course took her to stand beside him. She quickly knelt, placed her delicate hands on his leg, and looked up into his pinpoint eyes. Her clean-shaven head was decorated with red and blue tattoos, fashionable for Thay, and her wide, midnight-black eyes sparkled with a hint of mischief. The corner of her thin lips tugged upward into a sly grin.

Szass Tam had taken her as an apprentice several years before. An amazingly quick study, Frodyne never hid her hunger for spells and knowledge, and she dutifully hung on his every word. The lich thought her loyal, or as loyal as anyone in Thay could be. As she grew in power through the years, he shared horrible designs with her—how to crush lesser wizards under the heels of his skeletal army, how to raise men from the grave, how to steal the souls of the living. He recently confided in her that he was undead, showed her his true, rotting visage, and when she did not shrink from it, he shared with her his plans for dominating Thay. Frodyne had made it clear she wanted to be at his side—forever.

The lich stared at her unblemished, rosy face. Indeed, he thought, she is worthy of passing the centuries at my side. He reached a bony hand to her face and caressed her smooth cheek.

"What brings you here so late?" His deep voice echoed hauntingly in the room.

"I was at the market today, the slave pens," she began. "I was looking over the stock when I discovered a man asking about you and the goings-on in the keep."

The lich nodded for her to continue.

"He was an unusual little man who wore only one tattoo: an odd-looking triangle filled with gray swirls."

"A worshiper of Leira," the lich mused.

"A priest of the goddess of deception and illusions, in fact," Frodyne added. "In any event, I followed him. When he was alone I cast a simple spell that put him under my control. I had to know why he was asking so many questions."

The lich's pinpoint eyes softened, and with his skeletal finger, he traced one of the tattoos on Frodyne's head.

"And what did you learn?"

"Much, Master. Eventually. The priest had a strong will. But before he died he revealed he was worried about one of your armies, the one patrolling Delhumide. There is a ruin in that dead city that a few worshipers of Leira are particularly interested in. The priest believed that deep inside a crumbling temple rests a powerful relic. When your army passed nearby, he feared you had learned of the thing and had sent your army to retrieve it. But when your skeletons did not enter the temple, he was uncertain how much you knew. He came to the city asking about your plans and forces."

The lich gazed into Frodyne's eyes and said, "My skeletons were patrolling. Nothing more. But, tell me, Frodyne . . . why didn't the priest simply enter the temple and take the relic for himself?"

"I wondered that, too, Master." The young apprentice beamed. "I pressed him on the matter. He admitted that while he coveted the relic, he coveted his life more. It seems the Goddess of Liars has guardians and great magic protecting her prize."

The lich stood and drew Frodyne up with him.

"And just what is this relic of Leira?" he asked.

"A crown. The priest said a great energy is harnessed in the crown's gems," Frodyne answered. She smiled thinly and stroked Szass Tam's decaying chin. "And we shall share that crown and energy, just as I shared the priest's tale with you."

The lich stepped back and shook his head slowly.

"I shall send my skeletal army into the heart of the temple and claim the relic as my own."

"Yours, Master?"

"Aye, Frodyne."

"But you would not know of its existence without me." She put her hands on her hips and glared at him. "This is treachery, Szass Tam. I could have claimed the bauble for myself, with you none the wiser. But I chose to share the news with you."

"And in so doing, you chose to abandon your claim to it," the lich replied icily. "The relic will be mine alone. You have done well, my apprentice. I shall have another bauble to add to my hoard."

The comely apprentice strode indignantly to the door, then glanced over her shoulder at the lich.

"But what of Leira, Szass Tam? What if you anger the Patroness of Illusionists and Liars by breaching her temple and stealing something of hers?"

Szass Tam laughed and said, "I have little regard for the goddess of treachery, dear Frodyne. Get some rest. I shall tell you in the morning what my skeletons find in Delhumide."

The lich listened to her footfalls retreat down the hall. Soon she would not need sleep. Or food. Soon she would need none of the things that made men weak, allowing her to one day sit at his side as he ruled all of Thay.

The lich sat straight in his chair and pushed Frodyne from his thoughts. He concentrated on his army of skeletons in Delhumide, stretching his mind across the miles until he made contact with his undead general and directed him to march to Leira's temple. The miles melted away beneath the soldiers' bony feet as they neared the ruined temple of Leira. In an untiring cadence, they approached the temple steps. Then Szass Tam lost contact with them.

The lich cursed and cast himself upon the Thayan winds to fly to Delhumide. As he soared, his form changed. His skin took on a ruddy tint. His cheeks became puffy, and his body thickened to fill out the red silk robes that only moments before had hung on his frame in voluminous folds. His eyes became black, almost human, and his white hair grew thicker and longer, then darkened to match the color of the night sky. The lich added a thin mustache for effect. Few in Thay knew Szass Tam was one of the dead. Outside the confines of his keep he assumed the image of a living man.

The ground passed below him in a blur, the darkness obscuring most of the terrain, but the lich didn't falter in his course. He knew the way to the dead city. He'd been born there.

It was near dawn when he reached the ruined temple. He descended to the rough ground and glared at the crumbling stonework. His eyes smoldered in the gloom and surveyed the carnage. He knew then why he'd lost contact with his army. Strewn about the shattered pillars were more than a hundred skeletal warriors. Their broken bones and crushed skulls gleamed faintly. Near them lay more dead—figures with tattered gray flesh and rotting clothes, things that stank of the grave. The lich knelt near a one-armed zombie and slowly turned the body over. It had little flesh left on its frame. Most of it had been burned away by fire. Szass Tam ran his fingers through the grass around the corpse. Not a blade was singed. Magical fire had killed the army, the lich realized, fire meant for undead.

The hunt for Leira's relic had become very costly. It would take many, many months and considerable effort to raise enough dead to replace those fallen soldiers. Szass Tam stood, silently vowed retribution for the slaughter of his minions, and carefully picked his way toward the crumbling temple stairway. At the base of the steps, the lich spied a twitching form, an undead creature with pasty white flesh, hollow eyes, and protruding broken ribs. The ghoul, lone survivor of the lich's force, tried futilely to rise at the approach of its master.

"Speak to me," the lich commanded in a sonorous voice. "Tell me what happened here."

"Followed your orders," the ghoul rasped. "Tried to breach the temple. Tried to get what you wanted. But they stopped us."

"How many?"

"Three," the ghoul replied. "They wore the robes of Red Wizards."

Szass Tam growled deep in his throat and looked up the stairs. If only three had been able to conquer his force, they must be powerful. He took a last look at his beaten army and padded by the gasping ghoul to carefully select a path up the crumbling steps. Leira's temple lay in ruins like the rest of Delhumide. A once-great city, it was now populated by monsters and was laden with incredible traps—the remaining wards of the nobles and wizards who had once lived there. Creatures roamed freely across the countryside—goblins, darkenbeasts, trolls, and dragons—and they presented enough of a threat to keep the living away.

Szass Tam searched for the magical energies that protected the fallen temple, and he made his way around them to reach the comfort of the shadows inside. The damp coolness of the ruins reminded the lich of a tomb. This was his element. Focusing his eyes, he separated stonework from the darkness. He saw before him a crumbling old hallway that extended deep into the temple and sensed other presences within. He glided toward them.

Eventually the hallway ended, and the lich studied the walls, searching. Nothing. No moving stonework. He scrutinized the bricks by running his fingers over the cool surface to his left and right until he felt no resistance. The bricks before him were not real. Then he heard footfalls, soft and distant. The sound was regular, as of someone walking, and it was coming from far beneath him. He took a step forward and passed through the illusionary wall.

Beyond lay a damp stairway that led down into darkness. The lich cupped his hand and spoke a single word. A globe of light appeared in his palm and illuminated the stairwell. Along the walls and on each step were weathered sigils of various-sized triangles filled with swirling gray patterns—all symbols of Leira. The lich paused to appreciate them. He had little regard for the goddess, but thought the sigils had been rendered by someone with considerable skill.

Most Red Wizards in Thay worshiped one or more malign deities. At one time Szass Tam had, too—but the need to worship some power that might grant eternal life had faded away with the years and with the onset of lichdom. Szass Tam still considered himself respectful of some of the powers, such as Cyric. But not Leira.

Szass Tam was halfway down the steps when he felt a presence approaching. The minutes passed, and the undead zulkir's patience was finally rewarded when a pearl-white phantasm with the face of a beautiful woman formed in front of him. The lich pondered its appearance and decided the thing was nothing more than a hapless spirit tied to the temple.

"Trespasser," the specter whispered in a soft, feminine voice. "Begone from the sacred place of Leira, she who is most powerful. Begone from the Lady of the Mists's temple, the place we are sworn to protect."

The lich stood his ground, eyeing the thing, and for an instant, it appeared the spirit was astonished he did not run.

"I will leave when I am ready," the lich said flatly. He kept his voice low so his quarry deeper in the complex would not hear.

"You must go," the spirit repeated, its voice changing, becoming deeper and sultry. The visage was that of another woman. "This is not a place for those who do not believe. You do not believe in our goddess. You wear no symbol of hers."

"I believe in myself," the lich replied evenly. "I believe in power."

"But not in Leira."

"No. I have no respect for the Lady of the Mists," the lich growled softly.

"Then your bones shall rot here," the specter cursed in a new voice.

The lich stared at the creature. The undead now bore the image of a young man with a long nose, and the voice was strong and masculine. Large ghostly hands reached out and thrust into Szass Tam's chest. The lich stood unmoving, unaffected by the spirit's attack.

"This cannot be! You should be dead!" the spirit shouted with the voice of an old woman. Indeed, the pearl-white form was covered with wrinkles, and the transparent flesh sagged on her cheeks and jaw.

"I am already dead," the lich whispered in reply. "And you will bend to my will—whatever manner of undead you are."

Szass Tam's eyes once more became pinpoints of hot white light. They bore into the old woman's eyes and fixed the diaphanous being in place.

"Who are you?" Szass Tam demanded. "What are you?"

"We are Leira's," the old woman replied. "We are the last of the priests who lived in this temple. When the city fell to the army of Mulhorand, we died. But so strong was our faith in the Lady of the Mists that our wills banded together in one form so we could serve Leira forever."

The lich's lips curled upward slowly and he said, "It is your misfortune you stayed."

His pinpoint eyes glowed brighter, and he concentrated on the ghostly form before him. The spirit moaned in pain, the voice of a young man joining the old woman's.

"No!" the spirit cried in a chorus of voices. "Do not hurt us! Do not send us from the temple!"

"To the Nine Hells I will send you—to join the other priests of the Patroness of Liars," Szass Tam threatened, "unless you serve me and cease your cacophonous whining."

"We serve only Leira," the spirit wailed even more loudly.

"Now serve a better master."

The lich raised a fleshy finger and pointed it at the specter's face. The visage of the young man had returned. A silver beam shot from the tip of Szass Tam's finger and struck the spirit's head, sending the apparition flying backward several feet. The beam pulsed wildly while the spirit convulsed in agony.

"Who do you serve?" the lich persisted.

"Leira," the creature groaned in chorus.

Again the lich struck the creature with a silver beam. The ghostly image wavered and began to spread, as if it was being stretched on a torturer's rack. The spirit's arms and legs lengthened to the corners of the stairwell, and it became as insubstantial as mist.

"Who do you serve?"

"We serve you," the spirit finally gasped in its myriad voices.

Szass Tam's eyes softened to a pale glow. He studied the spirit to make sure it was indeed under his control. The many minds he touched berated him, but they swore their loyalty. Smugly satisfied, Szass Tam willed his human eyes to return.

"Tell me, priests," the lich began. "Were you this ineffectual in stopping the Red Wizards who came before me?"

"The ones below?" the spirit quipped.

The creature's face was that of a beautiful woman, the one the thing had displayed when Szass Tam first encountered it.

"Yes," replied the lich. "The ones below."

"They believe," the ghostly image stated. "They wear the holy symbol of Leira upon their shiny heads. All believers are welcome in this temple. All believers—and you."

"You let them pass freely because they tattooed symbols of Leira on their heads?" the lich queried. "You believed they worshiped your goddess because of a little paint?"

"Yes," the ghostly image answered. "Leira's temple is for Leira's own."

The lich looked past the creature and peered down the stairs.

"You will come with me. You will show me the traps that litter the path before us. And you will show me the relic I seek."

Szass Tam resumed his course down the stairway, the specter at his side pointing out weathered mosaics of its goddess, expounding on the greatness of Leira, and gesturing toward magical wards on every step. The lich passed by the broken bodies of long-dead trespassers as he moved from one chamber to the next. He was so intent on finding the relic that he nearly passed over the only freshly killed corpse. The specter pointed it out to him. The body of a red-robed man, no older than twenty, lay crumpled amid chunks of stone. The man, who wore the painted symbol of Leira on his head, sprawled with his limbs at odd angles. His eyes were wide with terror, and a thin line of blood still trickled from his mouth.

"He was with the other wizards," the specter said in an old man's voice. "Pity he died so young. Though he wore the symbol of the Lady of the Mists and I let him pass, the guardian looked into his heart. His heart betrayed him as an unbeliever. The guardian struck him down."

"Guardian?"

"The Lady of the Mists's eternal servant," the specter replied. "The guardian waits in the chamber beyond."

The lich peered into the black distance and started forward. The spirit of Leira's priests dutifully followed on his heels.

"Kill the thing!" Szass Tam heard a deep male voice cry.

The lich quickened his pace and entered a massive cavern lighted by luminous moss. He stopped and stared at the cavern's three occupants: Frodyne, a Red Wizard he didn't recognize, and a monstrous construct.

"What treachery is this?" the lich's voice boomed.

"Master!" Frodyne squealed.

She was dressed in a soiled and torn red robe, and the triangle she had painted on her scalp was smeared with sweat. Her normally soft features were set in grim determination as she called for her companion to join the fight. The man stayed behind her, ignoring her coarse words, and stared at the great thing before them. Frodyne spread her fingers wide and unleashed a magical bolt of fire at the monstrosity.

Frodyne's foe stood at least thirty feet tall, its head nearly reaching the chamber's roof. The guardian was not undead, but it was certainly not living. The lich eyed the thing from top to bottom. It had the torso of a man and the head of a goat. Its chest bore the symbol of a triangle filled with swirling mists. The thing possessed four eyes that were evenly spaced above the thick bridge of its metallic nose, and its mouth gaped open, exposing pointed teeth made of steel. Four arms as thick as tree trunks waved menacingly at the sides of its body and ended in six-fingered iron claws. Every inch of the creature was gray. The thing's massive legs ended in cloven hooves that created sparks when they stomped on the ground and rocked the cavern. The shockwaves made Frodyne and her companion scramble to stay on their feet.

"It seems you've made it angry, dear Frodyne," Szass Tam said. "Just as you've angered me. You destroyed my army."

"I wanted the crown!" she said as she unleashed another bolt of lightning. "I learned about this temple and the relic, but you said the bauble would be yours. It should be mine!"

The lich watched her nimbly avoid a fist that slammed into the cavern floor where she had been standing.

"I'm sorry!" she yelled. "Help us, please. The crown will be yours. I swear!"

The lich folded his arms and surveyed the battle, not bothering to reply to her plea.

She scowled and brought up her fingers, touching the thumbs together and holding her open palms toward the guardian. She mumbled words Szass Tam recognized as one of the first spells he'd taught her, and icy shards sprang from her hands. The shards flew true and imbedded themselves deep into the breast of the thing. But the attack proved ineffectual, the guardian oblivious. It pulled an arm back to swat her. Frodyne leaped to the side, and the guardian's hand found her companion instead. The sharp metal nails pulled the man's chest open. The wizard was dead before he hit the ground.

"Please, Master," Frodyne begged. "Help me. I'll do anything you ask."

"You destroyed my army," Szass Tam spat. "Your soul can rot here for all I care."

Frodyne raised her hands again and mumbled. A sparkling blue globe appeared in front of her. She blew at it, propelling it magically toward her ebon attacker. The globe impacted just above the thing's waist, popped, and squirted acid on the black metal. Crackling and sizzling filled the chamber, and the guardian bent its head to look at its melting stomach.

"You wield magic well, my sweet," the lich said icily.

"But I need your help to beat this thing!" she cried as she fumbled in the folds of her robe and withdrew a handful of green powder.

Szass Tam slowly shook his head.

"You stopped my skeletons all by yourself. You stopped my plans for having you rule Thay at my side. Surely you can stop this creature."

His voice was gravelly and showed no hint of emotion.

Frodyne started tracing a symbol in the powder in the palm of her hand. The lich turned to watch the construct, which was somehow repairing its stomach. Before Szass

Tam's eyes, metal flowed like water to cover the melted section. In an instant, there was no evidence it had been damaged. It took a step toward Frodyne, its massive foot-fall rocking the cavern and causing her to spill the powder she had intended to use in another spell.

"It could kill her," the specter at Szass Tam's side said simply. It wore the face of the young man. "But she cannot kill it. You cannot kill it. It is Leira's guardian, and it will continue to repair itself until the end of time. It has looked into her heart and discovered she does not honor the black goddess. It cannot rest until she is dead."

"And can it see into my own heart?" the lich posed. "Or perhaps it cannot even see me because the shriveled organ in my chest does not beat."

Frodyne's scream cut off the spirit's reply. The guardian swatted her like an insect, and she flew across the cavern to land on her back. Her red robe was shredded, and blood oozed freely from gouges in her flesh. Her face was frozen in terror, but still she did not give up. The lich had taught her well.

Frodyne withdrew a bit of pitch from the pocket of her ruined garment. Placing it in her bloody palm, she raised her hand until it was in line with the guardian's four eyes. A black bolt of lightning shot forth from her fingers and struck the creature on the bridge of its nose. The guardian stumbled backward from the impact, but was not damaged.

Szass Tam coaxed her, "Think, my lovely apprentice. Cast a spell that will keep it from reaching you. Buy yourself time."

She drew what was left of her robe about her and struggled to her feet. Words gushed rapidly from her mouth, and she pointed her index finger at the cavern floor. The stone beneath the guardian's cloven hooves wavered for a moment, shimmered in the meager light of the chamber, then turned to mud. But the guardian did not fall into the muck. Rather, the gray construct hovered above the great muddy patch, its hooves dangling inches above it in the musty air. Beneath the guardian, the mud hardened and cracked like a dry river bed.

"This cannot be!" Frodyne screamed.

She turned to glance at her mentor.

Szass Tam's hands glowed a faint blue, his long fingers pointed at the ebon guardian. An evil grin played slowly across his face as he returned Frodyne's disbelieving stare. He flicked his wrist, and the guardian floated forward and came to rest on a patch of rock near Frodyne.

"You! You kept it from becoming trapped!" she cried, as she twisted to the side to avoid another blow.

The lich nodded and thrust his hand into the air, mentally summoning an ancient parchment that lay in his tower. His fingers closed around the curled scroll as the guardian reached for Frodyne. Staring at his terrified apprentice, Szass Tam carefully unrolled the parchment.

"I promised you immortality, my dear, a reward for your loyalty. You shall have it."

The lich began to read the magical words, and the construct grabbed Frodyne around the waist. Szass Tam read faster, while the construct lifted her until she was level with its four eyes. The lich finished the enchantment as the guardian squeezed the breath from her lungs and dropped Frodyne's lifeless body like a child would discard a ruined doll.

The parchment crumbled in Szass Tam's fingers, and his apprentice's dead body shimmered with a pale white glow. A moment passed, then Frodyne's chest rose and fell. She took great gulps of air into her lungs and struggled to her feet. She glanced at her mentor, then at the construct, which again reached out to grab her. The thing's fingers closed around her once more and squeezed harder, and Frodyne realized what Szass Tam had done. He had given her eternal life—of a sort.

"No!" she shouted as her ribs cracked and she fell lifeless a second time.

The construct stepped back and waited. Again, the young Red Wizard was resurrected from the dead. Again she struggled to her feet.

"Enjoy your immortality, Frodyne," the lich hissed, as he watched the guardian deliver another fatal blow and witnessed her rise again.

He was pleased Leira's construct would busy itself with Frodyne and leave him alone.

"The relic," the lich pressed the specter. "Show me where the crown is."

The specter gestured to a stony recess. Szass Tam strode to it and took in the mounds of coins and gems. Perfectly faceted emeralds, sapphires, and diamonds glimmered from every cranny. A crown dotted with rubies sat atop the mass. The lich quickly snatched it up and felt the energy pulsing in the metal band.

"Leira's gift," the spirit declared. "The prize of our temple."

Stepping from the alcove, Szass Tam placed the crown upon his head then doubled forward as pain shot through his chest. The lich was caught off guard by the icy hot sensation. He pitched over and writhed on the rocky chamber floor until his frantic movements knocked the crown free.

The painful spasms ended, and the lich slowly stood.

"What manner of power was that, priests?" the lich gasped.

The spirit wore the face of the old woman when it answered, "The power of eternal life. The heart of he who wears the crown will beat forever."

Szass Tam's human form melted away, revealing his skeletal frame and pinpoint eyes.

"My heart does not beat," he said flatly.

"So instead, you felt pain," the woman answered. "The Lady of the Mists is indeed more treacherous than you. Leira lured you here. The priest who tempted your favored apprentice with the relic was merely a pawn."

The lich kicked the crown across the floor and glared at the specter.

"Again the Patroness of Illusionists and Liars struck when your apprentice betrayed you and sought the crown herself. Then my goddess triumphed once more when you lost that which you held dear, a beautiful sorceress who would have spent eternity at your side." The ghostly image pointed at the struggling Frodyne. "You've lost your army, your woman, your ability to trust others. And the prize at the end of your quest was something you can never possess. Who is the more treacherous, Szass Tam?"

The lich threw back his head and laughed, a deep, throaty sound that reverberated off the walls of the cavern. The lich roared loud and long as he padded from the chamber and climbed the stairs.

Originally published in *Realms of Magic*
Edited by Brian M. Thomsen and J. Robert King
December 1995

THE COMMON SPELL

Kate Novak-Grubb

There is a scene in one of Charles Dickens'
novels in which a street urchin wanders London
completely mystified by shop signs. The boy
understands there are people who can magically
decipher their meaning. The confusion of that
illiterate child had a powerful hold on me from
adolescence. Jeff and I had an editor who used to
fret about the high rate of literacy in the Realms
because it wasn't historically accurate. To the
best of my knowledge wizards, women in chain
mail, and dragons were not really part of the
medieval era either. The ability to read and write
is a magic no clever hero can afford to neglect, a
magic I'm grateful to possess, and grateful that
my readers have mastered.

—Kate Novak-Grubb, April 2003

Kate Novak has been happily married
to Jeff Grubb for twenty years.
She has a degree in Chemistry, is an
avid role-playing gamer, and works
part time as a tax preparer where she
puts to use her skills at exploiting the
game rules of the IRS.

THE COMMON SPELL

This is a waste of time. I don't need to learn this," insisted Marl, the cooper's son.

Kith Lias glared at the boy, but she kept her temper in check. Marl was hardly the first to denigrate the skills she was trying to teach. He wouldn't be the last, either. Marl was a big boy, the kind whose lead the other boys would follow. While none of the other students said a word, some of them eyed Marl with admiration that he'd had the courage to voice what many of them were thinking. The rest of the students watched Kith curiously, waiting to see how the teacher would handle his challenge to her authority.

"Even a cooper may need to read and write sometimes, Marl," Kith answered, pushing a strand of her long, dark hair back behind her ear. "You may need to write down the orders for your suppliers and customers so you can remember them better."

The other students nodded at Kith's example, but Marl snorted derisively.

"I'm not going to be a cooper," the boy declared. "Soon as I get enough coin to buy a sword, I'm joining a caravan as a guard. I'm going to be an adventurer."

"A swordling without the common spell," Kith muttered sadly.

"What's a swordling?" asked Lisaka, the tavernkeep's daughter.

"What's the common spell?" Marl demanded.

"A swordling is an adventurer's word," Kith explained, "for a novice sellsword. A mageling is a young mage who hasn't proven herself. The common spell is . . . well, actually it's a story I heard from Alias the Sellsword."

The children in the classroom leaned forward as one. Like all students throughout the Realms, they knew that their teacher could be distracted from the lesson if they encouraged her to reminisce. They were also eager to hear a story about Alias the Sellsword. Alias was a famous adventurer—she rescued the halfling bard Olive Ruskettle from the dragon Mistinarperadnacles and slew the mad god Moander—twice. Only last year she drove the thieves guild from Westgate. A story about Alias would be wonderful.

"Tell us, please," Lisaka asked.

"Yeah, tell the story," Marl demanded.

Kith shrugged and said, "I heard Alias tell this story in the village of Serpentsford in Featherdale. The people there were suspicious of all female strangers who passed through the town, even a hero like Alias, for the village was plagued by a penanggalan."

"What's that?" asked Jewel Weaver, the youngest student in the class.

"It's a female vampire," Marl said with a superior air.

"Not exactly," Kith retorted. "A penanggalan is undead, and it does drink the blood of the living, but there the similarity ends. A penanggalan appears as an ordinary woman in the daylight, and the sun's rays do not destroy it. But at night its head twists away from its body, trailing a black 'tail', which is all that remains of its stomach and guts. The body lies motionless while the head flies off and hunts for its victims. It prefers the blood of women and girls."

Jewel squealed, and several other students shivered. Even Marl looked a little pale.

"The people of Serpentsford had known enough to cremate the victims of the penanggalan so they would not become undead themselves," Kith explained. "But the villagers were beginning to lose hope that they would ever discover the monster, or even any of her secret lairs, for she was very cunning. Alias told this story to raise their spirits."

"So what's the story?" Marl growled impatiently.

Amused at the boy's attentiveness, Kith smiled ever so slightly. She sat back in her chair and folded her hands in her lap. Marl squirmed with annoyance.

Kith began the tale.

"This is a tale of the adventuring party known as the Swanmays. Their members included two swordswomen, Belinda and Myrtle; a pair of rogues, Niom and Shadow; a cleric, Pasil; and a mageling, Kasilith. In the Year of the Worm, the Swanmays wintered in the city of Westgate. Their landlord, a weaver woman, had an apprentice, an orphan girl named Stelly who was thirteen. Stelly and Kasilith, the mageling, became close friends, and Stelly wanted to leave the weaver to join the Swanmays.

"Now, though it was a master's legal obligation, the weaver had not yet taught Stelly to read or write. Belinda, the leader of the Swanmays, wasn't keen on taking responsibility for an illiterate girl whose only skills were with wool, and stealing an apprentice was a crime in Westgate. Yet Belinda liked Stelly. She promised Kasilith that if the mageling taught Stelly to read and write, Belinda would go to the city council, challenge the weaver's claim to Stelly, and petition to take Stelly on as an apprentice swordswoman.

"During the winter, Kasilith taught Stelly how to read and write her letters. Stelly believed what Kasilith was teaching her was actually magic; it was so awesome to the girl that scribbles on paper could mean something.

Kasilith joked that if it was magic, it was the most common spell in the Realms.

"That same winter a penanggalan began to prey on the women of Westgate. Neither the city watch nor any of the adventurers inhabiting the town could discover the creature's lair. In life, the monster had been a noblewoman and her family and their power helped to hide her. By chance or fate, the undead noblewoman came into Stelly's master's shop to have a tear in her cloak repaired and decided to make the weaver her next victim. Explaining she could not call for the cloak until later that evening, the penanggalan made arrangements to meet the weaver after the shop closed.

"A little while later, the weaver learned of Belinda's plan to take Stelly from her. Angrily, the weaver ordered Stelly to repair the noblewoman's cloak, then locked the girl in the workroom. Stelly could hear her master ordering the Swanmays out of her house, then barring the door.

"After crying for a while over her lost chance, Stelly went back to her work. In the pocket of the noblewoman's cloak, the girl discovered an expensive locket engraved with a name. Since Stelly could now read, she recognized the name belonged to a girl who had already fallen prey to the penanggalan. Stelly shouted for her master, but the weaver, thinking the girl was just throwing a tantrum, ignored her cries. Much later in the evening the apprentice heard her master unbar the door to the house and cry out once in fear. The penanggalan had come for the weaver in her true form.

"Locked in the workroom, Stelly could make out the weaver's moans and the sound of the beast slurping up her life's blood. Stelly cowered silently in fear until she became unconscious.

"In the morning the penanggalan, once again in human form, unlocked the workroom door to retrieve her cloak. Pretending concern for the apprentice, the undead noblewoman promised to return and free Stelly after dark. Stelly hid her fear and her knowledge of the woman's true nature. Knowing the penanggalan intended to return after dark to kill her as it must certainly have killed the weaver, Stelly conceived a desperate stratagem. Across the back of the monster's cloak she scrawled 'pnngalin' with a piece of chalk, then folded the cloak carefully so her repair work showed but her markings did not. The noblewoman nodded with satisfaction at the repairs and allowed Stelly to set the cloak about her shoulders. Then the woman left the workroom, locking the apprentice back in. It was the last Stelly ever saw of her."

"Because people spotted the letters . . . and killed the penanggalan," Jewel said excitedly.

"That is how Alias's story ended," Kith said with a nod. "Reading and writing, the common spell, saved Stelly's life."

"Is that all?" Marl asked, obviously not pleased with the tale.

"No, that's not all," Kith retorted, her voice suddenly deeper and more commanding. "The ending Alias gave the tale was a lie."

The students' eyes widened in surprise.

"But why would Alias lie?" Lisaka asked.

Kith shrugged. "She learned the tale from her father, the bard Finder Wyvernspur, and that is how he told it to her. Bards are notorious for manipulating the facts for their own purposes. But I know it was not the tale's true ending. I was staying at the inn in Serpentsford when Alias told the story," Kith explained, "and when she finished a woman in the audience accused her of lying and slapped her."

The students gasped, even Marl.

"The woman had been the Swanmay mageling Kasilith," the teacher explained. "She was only twenty-seven, but she looked fifty at least. She told Alias and the villagers the story's true ending."

"Which was?" Marl prompted.

"Kasilith was supposed to teach Stelly to read and write," Kith said, her voice laden with bitterness, "but instead the two girls spent the winter playing frivolous games with magic and toy swords and their hair and dresses. When Stelly found the locket in the penanggalan's cloak she couldn't read it. The apprentice had no way of discovering that the noblewoman was the penang-galan, and even if she had suspected anything upon hear-ing the weaver cry out that night, the girl did not know enough of her letters to write anything on the back of the monster's cloak. The next night the noblewoman returned to free Stelly. She freed her from her life, by draining all the blood from her body."

"Oh, no," Jewel whispered.

"Oh, yes," Kith replied.

"Did they ever catch the penanggalan?" asked Todd, the baker's son. "Wait a minute!" the boy exclaimed. "I'll bet it was the same penanggalan in Westgate that was in Serpentsford. Kasilith was still hunting her to avenge Stelly's death, wasn't she?"

"That is what she told Alias and her companion, Drag-onbait," Kith answered.

"So, did they catch the penanggalan?" Marl asked.

Kith continued. "Alias had a shard of the finder's stone, an old broken artifact. If you held the stone and had a clear picture of someone or something, the shard sent out a beacon of light in the direction of whomever or whatever you wanted to find. Kasilith said she'd seen the penang-galan's human body once, so Alias gave her the stone. Its light led them to a lair hidden underground, where the penanggalan's torso lay on a bier of fresh pine branches. The monster's head was not there; it would return before dawn, but now it was off hunting.

"With an exalted air, Kasilith used her magic to burn the body. Without its torso the penanggalan would not be able to hide its true nature again. If the head was struck by the sunlight and did not return to its torso within a few hours, it would rot, so the penanggalan would not be able to travel in the daylight anymore, either. The adven-turers hid themselves and waited for the penanggalan's head to return."

"And did it?" Marl asked. He sat on the edge of his seat.

Kith shook her head.

"Then what happened?" Jewel prompted.

"Alias and Dragonbait and the villagers searched everywhere. For days and nights they looked for the penanggalan or its remains. They found no other secret lairs, nor did they find any other victims of the penanggalan. They hoped that the creature had been struck by sunlight and had rotted, but Alias would not give up the hunt until she had positive proof the penanggalan was dead.

"Kasilith did give up, though. She was just about to leave the village when a great snowstorm came down from the northeast. Travel in any direction outside the vale was impossible for nearly a tenday, and so she remained. The mage grew remote and haggard in appearance. The snowstorm broke, but by then Kasilith was so ill she was too weak to leave her bed. Her traveling companion, a pretty foundling girl called Jilly, remained at her bedside.

"Then one night, just as Alias and her companion Dragonbait were about to leave the inn for the hunt, Dragonbait turned about and hissed. Now, Dragonbait came from a strange race of lizard creatures called saurials, but really they're no different from you and me. Dragonbait was a paladin, a champion of the god of justice, and just like a human paladin he could sense the presence of evil. He dashed up to Kasilith's room with Alias hot on his heels. The pair smashed open the door.

"Something lay on Kasilith's chest, nuzzling at her neck. For a moment Alias mistook it for a sleeping toddler. It had silky strawberry blond hair, which Kasilith stroked with one hand. The mage's other hand was wrapped around what appeared to be a child's arm. Then the innkeep came to the door with a lantern, and Alias could see the thing lying on Kasilith was a penanggalan. It was lapping at the blood that oozed from two wounds on the mage's throat, and a glistening black tail attached to the fair head writhed like a snake beneath the mage's hand.

"The innkeep dropped the lantern and fled. Alias gagged in spite of herself, and the penanggalan raised its head and hissed. It had the face of Kasilith's traveling companion, Jilly. Jilly's headless torso lay on the bed beside the mage. The monster rose from the bed, its eyes glowing red, blood gurgling down its throat. In a raspy voice it called out its victim's name and flew toward the window, but its escape was blocked by the saurial paladin and his magically flaming sword. Alias slammed the door shut, trapping the monster in the room with its victim and the two adventurers.

"The penanggalan could fly, but the room's ceiling was low, and Alias's sword was long. She pressed the monster into a corner and was just about to deliver a killing blow when her back exploded with the pain of five magical darts sinking into her flesh. Alias whirled around in surprise. Her eyes widened in shock as she discovered it was Kasilith who'd just attacked her. The mage was not just the penanggalan's victim; she was protecting the undead beast as well.

"Dragonbait threw himself on Kasilith, preventing her from casting any more magic, but the penanggalan, taking advantage of Alias's diverted attention, had turned on its attacker with a vengeance. It swooped down upon the swordswoman and lashed its tail about her neck. Alias flailed her sword awkwardly over her head while she tugged at the creature's tail to keep it from choking her. The tail felt slimy, like a decaying piece of meat, and it stunk of curdling blood. Realizing she hadn't long before the monster crushed her windpipe, Alias tried a desperate measure. She dropped her sword and snatched her dagger from her boot sheath.

"A second later she'd slashed the penanggalan along the length of its tail. Hot blood gushed down on her, momentarily obscuring her vision. The penanggalan sank its teeth into her cheek. Dropping her dagger, Alias grabbed the hair at the monster's temples and ripped it from her, smashing it into the wall over and over, until she had crushed its skull. The tail about her throat went limp and slid from her. Alias dropped the monster on the floor and, retrieving her sword, cleaved its head in two.

"An inky cloud rose from the monstrous head, shrank to a pinpoint of blackness, then vanished. From the bed, Kasilith sobbed out, 'Stelly,' and Alias realized what must have happened."

Kith paused in her story and hung her head for a

moment. She breathed in deeply and let her breath out slowly.

"Jilly was Stelly," Todd cried out. "No one had cremated Stelly's body," the boy speculated, "so she became a penanggalan. But what about the other penanggalan? The one whose body Kasilith destroyed?" the boy asked. "Was that the one that killed Stelly?"

Kith shook her head. "No, the Swanmays did finally find and destroy that one. There was no other penanggalan. Kasilith created an illusion of the body and destroyed it so Alias would think the monster was dead and would go away."

"But Alias was too thorough a hunter, and didn't leave," Marl noted.

"And when Kasilith and Stelly were trapped in Serpentsford by the snow, Stelly had to feed on Kasilith so she wouldn't get caught," Todd added.

"And Kasilith helped Stelly even though she was a penanggalan because she was her friend," Lisaka said.

"A penanggalan isn't the person she was in life. It's just an evil life-force animating her body that knows what she knew," Marl argued. "Right?"

"That's true," Kith said softly.

"But Kasilith didn't know that, did she?" Jewel asked.

"She knew," Kith replied.

"The penanggalan probably hypnotized her into being its slave," Marl said.

Kith shook her head. "No. Kasilith served it willingly. You see, she felt so guilty that Stelly had died because she hadn't taught her to read. So she thought she deserved nothing better for the rest of her life than to serve as the slave to evil because she'd done an evil thing."

"Then what happened to her?" Jewel asked anxiously.

Kith sighed. "Well, she shrieked and cried and ranted and raved for a while. She swore she would never forgive Alias and Dragonbait for freeing her from the penanggalan's enslavement. Still, they attended to her while she was recovering from the penanggalan's wounds."

"More than she deserved," Marl muttered.

"True," Kith agreed. "Alias told the mage that Finder

Wyvernspur had told her so much about Kasilith that she felt she was her friend and would not leave her until she was healed. Kasilith swore she had never met Finder Wyvernspur, but Alias stayed anyway. Finally, one day, something Dragonbait the paladin said made her change her mind about how she felt and about what she should do with her life."

"What did he say?" Jewel asked.

"He told Kasilith that the god of justice abhors punishment for punishment's sake. That we have to find a way to atone for the evil we do, and that we cannot atone for evil with evil, but only with good. He suggested she go out and teach other children who needed to learn to read and write. That way she would honor Stelly's true spirit and maybe bring peace to her own spirit. And that's just what she did."

"So she became a teacher like you?" Jewel asked.

"She became a teacher like me," Kith answered. "She teaches the common spell."

Marl the cooper's son stayed in school another two years before he finally bought his own sword and joined a caravan as a swordling. By then Kith Lias had taught him to read and write the names of every fell creature he might encounter in the Realms and had moved to another dale to teach another village's children. It was during Marl's off-duty hours that the other caravan guards taught him the game anagrams. After that, the cooper's son spent even more time wondering about the mage Kasilith and the teacher Kith Lias.

Originally published in *Realms of Shadow*
Edited by Lizz Baldwin, April 2002

ASSASSIN'S SHADOW

Jess Lebow

Assassin's Shadow was a really fun story to write. Particularly the scenes set in Karsus, the floating city. It's a huge metropolis that runs entirely on magic. Describing the streets and buildings through the eyes of someone who has never experienced such a place was a challenge. Everything is wonderful and exhilarating to Cy. Things that wizards would take for granted seem new and terrifying to him, and so I struggled with the balance between making the streets seem alien from his point of view while at the same time making the residents of the city completely at ease in their surroundings.

—Jess Lebow, March 2003

Jess Lebow lives and works in downtown Seattle.
He has a view of the Space Needle from his apartment (if you lean way out the window and squint), and he sometimes thinks the big pointy thing would make a good tether ball pole for King Kong and Godzilla.

ASSASSIN'S SHADOW

Netheril Year 3392
(The Year of Emerald Groves, -467 DR)

The wet stink of mud hung in the air.

Olostin lowered his foot to the floor at the bottom of a long flight of stairs. The cellar was dark and wet, and rats splashed, unseen, in the far corners of the room.

"You have come," said a voice from out of the darkness.

"As I was directed," replied Olostin.

"You have served us well," came another voice.

"Thank you," replied Olostin.

"And you have prospered from the knowledge and power we have granted to you," continued the first. "Your raiders wreak havoc all over the countryside, and your name strikes fear in the hearts of the common man. Indeed, even the archwizards take notice."

"Your friendship has indeed benefited me greatly. One day I shall bring about the end of the

archwizards' rule, and thus I am forever in your debt."
Olostin bowed toward the sound of the voices.

"Then we have a task for you."

"One that will no doubt be fueled by your hatred of the ruling wizard class," added the second voice.

"Of course," replied Olostin, still bowed. "Tell me only what you require, and consider it done."

"An archwizard by the name of Shadow has been experimenting with a new type of magic," explained the first voice.

"He calls his new source of power the Shadow Weave," interjected the second.

"This Shadow Weave could be the very thing the archwizards need to destroy us."

"How is it that I may serve you?" asked Olostin.

"Kill Shadow before he uncovers too much," affirmed the first voice.

"As you have directed," replied Olostin. He stood and headed back up the stairs.

"In the name of Olostin, submit or meet your doom!"

Cy hurled his torch at a thatch-roofed house and spurred his horse on through the village of Kath. Night had fallen hours before, and the moon was just visible over the high cliffs that outlined one edge of the valley. The sound of almost one hundred horse hooves beat on into the slowly brightening night as the southern border of Kath went up in flames.

The door of a house just in front of Cy burst open, and a man in a nightshift ran into the street, away from the flames and the contents of his house. The side shutters of the same house creaked open and smoke billowed out as a coughing woman, dark streaks of ash lining her face, climbed out with a small child under her arm. The child's head lolled to one side and back in wide flopping arcs with the rhythm of the mother's frantic escape.

Cy rode on, herding the villagers toward the north end of the settlement. There, Kath butted up against a heavily wooded forest, and nearly half of the raiding party waited there for the fleeing villagers.

We'll round 'em up, and rob 'em blind, thought Cy.

He smiled. Rich was definitely going to be a good way to go through life.

Someone screamed ahead. Cy reigned in his horse and stopped in front of a dead-end alleyway. Two other raiders had gotten off their horses and had cornered a village woman. She wore only a light white dress, and she held a tightly bunched section against her chest with one hand. With the other, she was feeling behind her for the wall of the alley, not letting her eyes stray from the men in front of her. Her hair was disheveled, and streaks of dirt or dried blood outlined the curve of her jaw.

"Hey," hollered Cy, getting their attention. "Take your pleasures another time. You heard Lume! Force the villagers to the woods. We don't have time for these games."

The two dismounted men grumbled at Cy and spit toward his horse. They turned their attention back to the woman. She had backed into the corner as far as she could and was pounding on the stone behind her in desperation.

Damn fools, thought Cy, and he spurred his horse down the road.

The village was no more than thirty houses deep from the southern border to the edge of the forest. In the confusion of the raid—the unrelenting thunder of horses, the burning roofs, and the hollering of the bandits—the villagers scattered and quickly fell into the raiders' trap.

Cy spurred his horse toward the forest, and in the next moment, he found himself on the ground, his horse barreling away from him. His tailbone and back hurt from the fall, and his chest burned in a line right across the middle. He shook his head and tried to clear his vision. A large hulking form loomed up out of the night in front of him. The figure raised its arm, and Cy instinctively rolled to one side. A heavy chain impacted the ground. Cy rolled back onto his feet and stood up, pulling his scimitar out of its scabbard as he did.

The man with the chain raised his arms over his head, swinging the heavy links around in a circle, gaining momentum with both hands. Cy's vision cleared some-what, and he got a better look at his attacker. The man had long, ragged blond hair and was wearing only black robes, tied at the waist with a length of rope. He was wearing no shoes. Scars crisscrossed his face and fore-arms. One near his ear was still covered by a dark scab. His shoulders were knotted with lumps of muscle, and his arms easily suspended the weight of the chain. He moved with a quick, considered motion, passing the chain back and forth between his hands, making arcs in the air around his body.

Cy turned his blade in his hand, the metal casting reflected light from the fires on the dark ground. He lunged. Metal clanged, and the tip of his scimitar hit the ground. He just managed to keep his grip on the hilt, but the chain was still moving in quick circles. A crunching thud rang through his ears, and Cy saw stars. His jaw was numb, and he could taste blood. The chain-wielder seemed to grow much, much taller, then Cy realized he was on the ground again. He threw himself flat as the chain whistled by his ear.

Lifting himself up on his hands and feet, Cy crabbed backward, growing the space between himself and the blond man. The chain hit the ground again, throwing dirt in Cy's face. Rolling backward, the raider came up on his feet, sword in front of him. The dark-robed man nodded and closed in, moving the chain back and forth, letting it gain momentum as he changed hands again and again.

This time the chain came in low. Cy jumped and slashed in a flat arc while he was in midair. The tip of his blade tore through the dark robes and cut a deep wound in the blond man's chest. Landing on both feet, Cy leaped backward, narrowly avoiding a blow to his head. The chain was moving faster now. It looked almost like a solid wall of metal as it careened through the air.

Cy pulled his dagger from its sheath. It was the only enchanted weapon he owned. Flipping it over in his left hand, he clutched the tip of the blade between two fingers, then he feigned a lunge with his scimitar. The blond man brought the chain up in a defensive arc, striking at the hilt of the sword. Cy lowered the blade under the flailing chain and brought the dagger up to throw. The chain-wielder was too fast, and he changed directions, throwing Cy off balance. Just barely able to keep to his feet, the raider held onto the dagger but had to lower his arm to keep from falling.

The chain whistled as it came down in an overhead strike. Cy leaped forward, pressing his body as close to his attacker's as possible. Blood spattered his boots as his scimitar cut a deep wound into the blond man's leg. The chain changed directions and hit Cy hard in the back, knocking him straight into the black-robed man. The raider lost his grip on the curved sword as he bounced off a human wall of muscles. The ground came up, and Cy found himself once more on the rocky, hard-packed dirt in the streets of Kath.

This is starting to annoy me, he thought as he got to his feet.

He didn't have time for much more as the chain hit him again right around his midsection. The cold, heavy links wrapped themselves around his body and tangled with the rest of the chain as they made one full circle around Cy's stomach. Just as the dark metal clanked into itself, the raider felt himself lift off the ground. The blond man pulled him clear off his feet, and Cy grunted as all the air left his lungs. Coming down in a heap at the foot of the chain-wielder, Cy struggled to stay conscious. He felt the chain tug and begin to unravel itself from his body. The force of the larger man pulling caused Cy to roll over onto his back as the chain uncoiled. He looked up. The blond man glared back, a crease in his brow, his lips pursed, and hatred in his eyes.

Flinging his arm forward with all of his might, Cy hurled his enchanted dagger at the chain-wielder. The magical metal blade sunk easily into the soft flesh of the neck, and the hilt moved up and down as the man tried to swallow. Blood seeped out around the edges of the wound.

The blond man staggered backward a step and raised his hands to his throat. The look of anger and spite had left his eyes, only to be replaced by a distinct note of fear and uncertainty. Grabbing the hilt of the dagger, the blond man pulled the blade from his neck. Blood poured out in spurting gouts.

Cy slid away, getting slowly to his feet. The raider looked around for his scimitar. It was lying in the dirt a few yards to his right. As he moved to retrieve it, the chain-wielder fell to his knees, bright red blood covering his hands, and a look of complete disbelief filled his eyes. Before Cy had retrieved his blade, the man was facedown on the dirt.

Cy took a deep breath and looked around. The houses were completely consumed by flames. The screaming and chaotic sounds of the raiders riding through the village had stopped. His own horse was nowhere in sight, and he cursed his bad luck for having ridden past this chain-swinging baboon. He felt around his own body to assess the damage. The bruise on his chest where the chain had taken him off his horse had already turned deep purple. His tailbone and back were sore but functional. He had lost a couple of teeth, but his jaw worked well enough for him to be able to enjoy supper around the campfire that night, and that was all he needed to know.

Sheathing his sword, Cy walked over to the blond man. His enchanted dagger lay just past the man's fallen fingertips. The chain-wielder lay facedown in a good-sized puddle of his own cooling blood. Cy wiped the dagger off on the back of the fallen man's dark robes.

The sound of horse hooves lifted over the crackling of the burning thatch roofs. Cy spun around, his dagger in hand.

"That was a nice bit of fighting, if I do say so myself."

Cy recognized the speaker—Lume, the captain of the raiding party. He rode up on his horse and stopped just in front of the fallen man.

"Sir?" Cy looked down at his bruises and bleeding wounds.

"I saw the whole thing. Most of the rest of this scum—" He waved his arm over his shoulder toward the forest and the raiding party—"would be dead after fighting a man like that."

"Thank you, sir."

Cy looked down at the blade of his dagger and twirled it absently.

"If all my men could fight like that, we'd be able to take Karsus without the rest of Olostin's raiders."

Lume dismounted and walked over to the dead man. He kicked him once in the ribs, then rolled him over with his boot.

The man's eyes were open but unfocused. His mouth hung wide as if he were trying to catch a last breath, and blood still trickled down his neck, but it was already starting to harden into scabs.

Lume regarded the dead man for a moment then said, "You know, Cy, I think I might just have a job for you. Stop by my tent in the morning, and we'll discuss the details."

Lume put one foot in a stirrup and swung his weight into his saddle.

"In the meantime," the captain said, "head back to camp. The rest of the party has the villagers well in hand."

Lume turned his horse back toward the village.

"And one more thing, Cy," he said over his shoulder.

"Yes, sir?"

"Enjoy yourself around the campfire tonight, and don't forget to get your share of the booty. We made a good haul this time."

"Thank you, sir, I will."

The evening's festivities were grand. The raiders had made their biggest haul ever. One of the men had ransacked Kath's stock of supplies and come up with several kegs of good red wine and a large cask of mead. There was more than enough in those barrels to make the fifty or so raiders in Cy's party jolly as monks in a vineyard.

The campfire raged. The wine flowed freely. Men told stories of their conquests during the raids. The men they had fought grew larger and more fearsome as the evening wore on. The riches they had stolen became fortunes even the most powerful kings would envy. They laughed and danced and lied to each other until they had all passed out. Then they slept. They would be allowed their excesses for the evening since their booty had been so large. Captain Lume didn't participate in the campfires, but he didn't wake the men early after a good night's haul.

Yes, life as one of Olostin's raiders was very fulfilling for someone like Cy. He had the freedom to do what he wanted, so long as it didn't directly contradict the orders he had been given, and he had the camaraderie of the other raiders. He had riches and wine, and from time to time he even had the affections of a lady or two. All in all, life was good.

❧ ❧ ❧ ❧ ❧

"You're quite fast, Cy," complimented Lume.

Cy had woken just before midday, and after he had dunked his head in a rain barrel and re-bandaged his wounds from the fight the night before, he went to see his captain.

"Thank you, sir."

Cy didn't have a military background, but he believed in giving respect to his elders. Lume was the captain of the raiding party and at least ten years older than Cy, so he figured the man deserved the title of "sir."

"Sit down, please." Lume pointed to a simple chair in the corner of his tent.

Cy nodded and did as he was told.

For a tent, Lume's place was comfortable and well appointed. A hammock stretched from a pole holding up the center of the roof in the middle of the tent to another support forming the corner. A desk sat in the opposite corner with a chair behind it and a large chest beside. Papers were stacked in neat piles on the desk, and a large water pipe sat near them. It was lit, and Lume took a few puffs on it while Cy got comfortable.

The captain leaned forward in his chair, bracing himself against the desk.

"How long have you been with this raiding party, Cy?"

"About a year now, sir."

"Is that all?" he asked.

Cy nodded.

"You know, I hate to admit it, but I've been working for Olostin for fifteen years. I've been leading raiding parties for almost five years now." He leaned back in his chair. "I'm afraid I lose track of all of the young men whom I've seen come and go. I would have thought you'd been with this group longer, but I guess I'm just remembering someone else."

Lume looked at the palm of his hand for a moment.

Cy shifted in his chair.

"Cy, I make no apologies for the mistakes of other men. If a man in my party gets himself killed, then it's his own fault."

He looked the younger man up and down then stared him right in the eyes. Cy held his gaze for a moment, then let if fall.

"If I can't remember how long you've been with this group it's only because I've seen hundreds of others just like you get killed. To tell the honest truth, I can't even remember any of their names. To me, they could have all been named Cy."

Lume chuckled at this. Cy did not.

The captain became serious and once again looked Cy over.

"I'll come to the point, Cy. I have a job for you."

"Sir," he said, not sure what else he could say.

"You're as good with that dagger as I've seen in a long while, and you managed to keep yourself alive last night. I'm hoping," continued Lume, "that you'll manage to get yourself out of this little project alive as well. Tell me, what do you know about our illustrious leader Olostin?"

"Sir, I know he fights to stop the tyranny of the arch-wizards, sir."

"That's a good practiced answer if I've ever heard one."

Cy was startled and began to stand to defend himself.

Lume raised his hand and started to laugh. "It's all right, son," he said. "You've got the basic idea."

Cy settled back down into the chair. He felt as if he had been scolded by his father.

"Do you want to stop the . . . tyranny of the arch-wizards?" asked Lume.

Cy just looked at the captain, wondering where all of this was leading. For a man who said he was going to get to the point, he sure had a round about way of getting there, Cy thought, and all of this questioning of his loyalty and teasing about his age was starting to make him angry.

"Well, Cy?" The captain raised his voice. "Do you believe in what we're fighting for?"

"Yes, sir, I do."

Cy gritted his teeth. He didn't think his performance the previous evening had been as spectacular as the captain seemed to believe, but as Lume himself had said, he was still alive. Surely he didn't deserve a reprimand for killing a skilled fighter in the middle of a raid. This meeting had started so well, and now it seemed as if the captain was accusing him of being a spy or something.

"Well, then, son," Lume said, his voice calm, "I need you to assassinate the archwizard Shadow."

❧ ❧ ❧ ❧ ❧

The journey to the floating city had taken Cy two days on griffonback. The archwizard Shadow lived in Karsus, a city unlike any Cy had ever seen before. It floated, for one thing, but that was the least of the oddities this bustling town had in store.

The streets were lined with small gutters of running water. Brooms moved purposefully along on their own, sweeping dust and debris into the moving water as they went. Bridges lifted streets up over wider rivers, and passersby walked not only on top of the curved stone structures, but on the underside as well. Wizards, carefully carrying parcels of food or armloads of books passed each other and waved as they casually walked upside down. In a city park, four elderly, robed mages rotated freely through the air, their attention focused on a globe the size of a maidensthigh melon that floated between them. Each took turns moving intricately carved gems across the globe and laughing as the result of their moves changed the pitch, angle, or speed of rotation of one of the other wizards playing the game.

It seemed everyone in Karsus used magic, for everything they did defied what little Cy knew about the world and how it was supposed to work. Children played games on the sides of buildings instead of on the ground or in a park. Water flowed uphill, and in some places through thin air. The strange canals that lined the streets didn't start or end anywhere, they just simply continued to flush fresh, clean water through the entire city. People walked adolescent pet dragons through the busy city streets, waving and smiling as they went. Groups of wizards appeared—as if from nowhere—in mid-conversation, apparently unaware that their surroundings had changed. Bags and boxes floated through the air, suspended by nothing, but bound intently for some destination or another.

Cy tried not to gawk as he made his way through the city. Across one bridge and down several blocks, he found a tall, narrow building with dozens of doors stacked one on top of the other all the way up the building's entire facade. A carved wooden sign on street level read: "The Charlesgate Inn," and robed mages floated casually out of the doors on the higher levels, turning around, suspended in midair, to lock the doors behind them.

Cy entered the bottom floor of the inn and rented a room for a few days. He wanted to learn as much about his target as he could before he had to face the man.

Hopefully, Cy thought, Shadow will be so engrossed in his research that he won't see me coming.

It was the young assassin's only hope. In open combat, Cy may have been able to defeat that skilled fighter in Kath, but an archwizard was an entirely different story. If he didn't get a quick, clean, surprise kill, he'd be done for. As he settled into his room, he realized he'd get only one chance at this assassination. He intended to make the most of that chance.

Before Cy had left for Karsus, Lume had opened the raiding party's store of materials and weapons to allow Cy his pick of equipment. They had racks and racks of swords, armor, and bows, and even some things Cy had never seen used before. The job he had been tasked with would be difficult for sure, but extra gear wasn't going to make it any easier. In the end. He simply took with him a small crossbow, some magical leather armor, and his own enchanted dagger. Better to travel light, he decided.

The ornately carved brick tower that Shadow lived in was easy enough for Cy to break into. In fact, there wasn't even a lock on the door. Not wanting to fall prey to overconfidence, the assassin moved through the entry hall very carefully, checking every few feet for traps or magical glyphs. It took him almost an hour to creep slowly down the hall and around the corner. For all of his caution, there were no traps in the long hallway.

At least I wasn't blown to bits, he thought.

Rounding one corner, he entered a very large, grossly wealthy sitting room. The raider in Cy was in awe. Perhaps Lume should have sent him to simply rob the archwizard. The riches held in this one room could have paid for a hundred assassins ten times over. High backed chairs sat around ornately carved wooden tables. Silver sconces with mage-lit stones in them were stationed around the windows, and jeweled candelabras rested on desks, tables, and windowsills. Leather-bound books sat in hundreds of neat rows, arrayed over several dozen large bookshelves lining the walls.

A door swung open on the opposite side of the room. Cy crouched and somersaulted behind one of the high-backed chairs. He pressed himself close to the furniture and held his breath. Heavy footsteps echoed across the hardwood floor. Cy clutched his dagger. So much for surprise.

The footsteps got closer then passed the chair. Cy felt a light breeze pass his cheek, and his vision filled with vivid, swirling colors of magenta, yellow, and silver. The young man blinked, trying to clear his head of the befuddling magic, and the colors passed—but they weren't magic. Cy's vision cleared, and he recognized the hem of a lady's skirts. A young blonde woman, wearing heavy, embroidered linens and carrying a silver tray had passed Cy's hiding place. She walked swiftly past the chair and out into the hall. Her heavy footsteps receded.

Cy stood up, and the door swung open again. Ducking his head behind the furniture, he was certain he'd been seen. Once again, heavy footsteps traveled across the floor. Cy dodged behind the chair, rolling across the floor, around a table, to pop up behind whoever had entered the room. Bringing his dagger down in a broad arc, the young assassin stopped cold. The same blonde, brightly dressed woman who had just passed, only a moment before, was again standing in the middle of the room, only this time she was carrying a large silver jug. The woman's skirts rustled as she continued across the floor, unflinching and unfazed by Cy.

The door opened again. Cy spun around, his dagger out in front of him. The blonde woman was coming out into the sitting room for the third time, but now she had a large box in her hands. Her brilliant blue eyes stared straight ahead as she continued to move toward the young assassin. Two sets of heavy footsteps echoed on the hardwood, one in front and one behind. Shaking his head, certain that he was under magical assault, Cy leaped out of the woman's path, landing hard on a plush leather chair and letting it break his fall as he clattered to the floor.

Spinning around and backing into the corner, Cy scanned the room for any way to escape. Two blonde women—both wearing identical magenta, yellow, and silver linen skirts, one carrying a jug, one a box—continued across the hardwood floor. Neither seemed the least bit interested in Cy. They moved through the room and out into the hallway, intent on carrying their packages to their final destination. The young man watched them as he stood in the corner catching his breath.

The door opened again. Two more blonde, brightly

dressed women—the *same* woman Cy had seen three times already—entered the sitting room and proceeded across the hardwood, their footsteps echoing heavily as they crossed. Cy made no attempt to hide this time, and the women ignored him completely. Picking up a book, the young assassin hurled it at one of the women. It struck with a thud and fell to the floor. Still, the women ignored him.

If they aren't illusions, thought Cy, then they must be constructs.

Convinced that he wasn't under a spell, he continued on his mission.

A set of stairs led down one side of the room. Cy crossed and headed down, avoiding the female golems as he went. The stairway was long, and the air grew cooler as he continued down. The old wooden steps were warped in places, so Cy was careful to transfer all of his weight onto each step slowly, so as to avoid creaking. At the bottom, another hallway continued on. A doorway near the end was partly open, and light spilled out into the hall from the opening. Another of the magenta-skirted women came out of the room and walked down the hall.

Slipping past the unobservant construct, Cy looked through the door. He could see a bed and a night stand in half of a nice, if messy, bed chamber. Someone was shuffling around with a drawer and some papers outside of his field of view. Cy pulled his dagger from his sheath, pressed himself up against the wall, and waited.

Several moments passed. Sweat started to bead on Cy's forehead. The shuffling inside the room continued.

A drawer slammed shut, and a figure came into view and sat on the bed. Square jaw, sandy-brown hair, green eyes, small wire-rimmed glasses, and a tell-tale scar on his left cheek—it was Shadow. Though younger looking than Cy had expected, the man matched the descriptions Lume had given him. The archwizard's attention was focused on a large stack of papers he had in his hands, and he was making marks on them with a piece of charcoal.

Cy took a deep breath and held it. Raising his dagger

up to his shoulder, he burst into the room, hurling the enchanted blade at Shadow as he did so. The wizard didn't even look up from his papers. He simply waved his hand, and the dagger stopped in midair. Worse, Cy stood frozen as well, unable to blink or even wipe the ever-increasing sweat from his forehead.

For quite some time, Shadow simply continued to read his papers. Leafing through them casually as if he didn't have an assassin magically suspended in his bedroom. Eventually, he finished with his work, straightened the papers, and turned his attention to Cy.

"Aren't you a little young to be an assassin?" he asked.

Cy didn't answer. This had been his first assassination, so he really didn't know how the industry worked. He supposed he'd never get the opportunity to find out.

"No matter," reassured the archwizard. "Your age isn't important. What is, however, is the fact that you tried to kill me. So?" He looked Cy right in the eye. "What do you suppose we should do about that?"

Cy tried to spit at the man, to show his indignation and contempt for the wizards who mucked around with the powerful, otherworldly magic that he felt certain would be the doom of all the world, but he was stuck. He couldn't move his lips or even his tongue.

"Well?" asked the archwizard. "Aren't you going to answer me?"

The man chuckled, then he put his hands on his knees and stood up from the bed. He plucked the enchanted blade from where it was suspended in the air.

"Very nice, very nice indeed," he commented. "Don't have much use for these sorts of toys." He walked over to a chest of drawers and placed the dagger on top of it. "I have a few I keep around as souvenirs of the assassins who have most interested me, but I generally don't like to use them. All that blood and such." Shadow rankled his nose. "No, magic is much cleaner."

He picked up a wand with a clear stone attached to the end of it by a leather band.

"And," he added, walking back toward Cy, "far more entertaining and punitive. Just think, if I simply poked you with your blade a few times, sure it would hurt, but in short order you'd die, and the agony you'd feel would be over. With magic—" he brandished the wand—"I can trap you inside this crystal. There you will die slowly as your predecessors sap your strength and tear at your skin."

He smiled warmly at Cy who was still unable to move.

"The best part, however, is that once you've died, your punishment hasn't ended. You will awaken as a shadow, and you'll live out the rest of eternity as an ethereal creature, unable to affect the solid world around you. Doesn't that sound far more horrifying?"

Cy grunted, trying everything in his power to simply move his fingers.

"Yes, I'm sure you'd agree, imprisonment is far worse than simple death."

Shadow turned away from the doorway and started tidying up the room.

"Though, I don't want you to think my trapping you in this wand is at all an easy feat."

Cy continued to struggle, gaining a modicum of hope from the fact that he could already wiggle his toes and clench the muscles in his jaw.

"It's taken me years to be able to perfect this wand," continued the archwizard. "True, the imprisonment spells are simple enough, as you are now, I'm sure, painfully aware."

Shadow continued to fiddle in the room.

"No, it's the transformation from human flesh to the insubstantial that has proven tricky, though not impossible."

Cy could feel warmth spreading through his arms and chest, and he was able to shuffle his feet a little.

Shadow looked at the wand with reverent awe.

"This little device right here represents most of my life's work. You know," he said, speaking not really to Cy but rather to himself, "I've lived a long time, and it seems to me that as we've grown, things just keep getting smaller and smaller." He chuckled. "I guess that's what we call progress."

Cy almost had control of his body back. If Shadow

continued to amuse himself for just a few more minutes, he might be able to make a break for it, and he'd much rather get killed fleeing than just standing there like a stupid jackass.

"Anyway, enough with the chit chat." The archwizard turned his attention back to the young assassin and leveled the wand at him. "I suppose I should figure out who hired you to kill me before I dispose of you. I don't suppose you came of your own accord. You're too young for that."

The wall behind Shadow exploded outward into the room. What had appeared to be solid stone was actually a secret door made of wood, and the splinters of stone-colored door sprayed out at the two men. Two gigantic ogres stood at the top of a set of stairs in the space where the door used to be.

Cy was thrown to the floor next to the bed. Shadow, too distracted with the first assassin to protect himself from the two new ones, was also knocked face-first to the floor. The ogres didn't waste any time, and they rushed into the room to clobber the fallen archwizard. Ham-sized fists began to beat the mage. The two beasts worked together, pummeling the man simultaneously with opposing blows. Then one stopped pounding the wizard and unsheathed a large sword off its back. The blade slid out of the scabbard with an oily grind.

Cy had regained control of his body, and he got to his feet, pulling the larger splinters from his skin. The ogres were completely ignoring him, but they were pounding Shadow into a bloody pulp right in the middle of the door-way. He glanced over toward the passageway.

If the ogres got in that way, then there must be a way out, he thought.

He took a deep breath and steadied himself. In the moment he took to compose his thoughts, his mind reeled. What if there were more ogres down there? What if they had used magic to get into the lower chamber? If he went down there would he be trapped?

"Lift him up," shouted the ogre with the sword.

The other grunted and stopped beating the archwizard

long enough to bend down and grab the man by the robes.

Cy turned back toward the doorway, deciding to take his chances with the ogres he knew of rather than whatever could be dwelling down the stairs. While they prepared to behead Shadow, the young assassin charged the door, hoping to slip behind the busy brutes and the doomed archwizard on his way to freedom.

He took two large steps and dropped into a crouch, trying to ram right through. The ogre holding Shadow took a half step back at that precise moment, crashing into the charging human as he barreled across the room. The two assassins got tangled in each other's limbs, and they both hit the floor with a crash—Cy tumbling head over feet into the hallway, and the ogre against the doorframe. Shadow came to his feet, being pulled from the floor by the ogre and gaining momentum from the great brute's fall.

Wand still in his hand, he shouted, "*Shadominiaropalazitsi,*" and leveled the crystal end at the standing ogre.

A dark gray stream fired out of the wand in a direct line at the ogre assassin. As it approached the ogre's upright form, the stream spread out and began to curve and split. It formed a whirlwind of darkness around the beast, and the gray areas started to separate and take on individual, humanlike shapes. The shadows had narrow, elongated heads, and spindly, malformed limbs, and they flew in ever-quickening circles around the ogre. For his part, the assassin stood, his sword poised over his head, and gawked in awe and horror.

The shadows attacked, diving toward the armed figure and tearing at him with claws that seemed to form out of thin air. Cy could hear the ogre howl as if he was in great pain, but no blood issued forth. Instead, the ogre dropped his sword and slowly sank to the floor, landing on the ground with a thud like a sack of horse manure.

Cy gained his feet and turned up the steps. He'd seen enough. As fast as he'd ever felt himself move, he was up the stairs, dodging brightly dressed constructs as he fled out the front door. Never did he turn around, and it wasn't until he was on his griffon on the way back to report to Lume that he realized he no longer had his enchanted dagger.

Arriving in camp by sunup the second day, Cy entered Lume's tent at a run.

"Sir, I have terrible, urgent news."

Lume was sitting at his desk eating his morning meal, and the young man's frantic entrance startled the captain, causing him to cough up a mouthful of food.

"In the name of all the gods, what do you think you're doing?" he screamed. Then, abruptly, his tone changed. "Oh, Cy!" Lume stood up. "What is it lad? Did you kill the archwizard?"

"No, sir, I did not."

Lume slammed his hand on the desk. "Then what are you doing here?"

Cy proceeded to intone to Lume all the details of his assassination attempt. He left out nothing, and the captain listened intently to the entire story. Then it was Lume's turn to talk.

"Are you certain they were shadows that came out of the wand?" he asked.

"Yes, sir, I'm absolutely positive."

"Gods. A wand with that kind of power could . . ."

Turning around and placing his hands to the sides of his head, he paced out from behind the desk and moved around the tent. After a few moments, he came out of his reverie. He looked at Cy and shook his head.

"But you failed. I should have known that chain-wielder wasn't an adequate challenge to determine if you could kill an archwizard."

"Sir?"

Lume whirled, blurting out his words. "The chain-wielder, son! I sent him to test you. How else do you think a man of that skill ended up in such a backwater village as Kath?"

"*You* sent the blond man after me, sir? But, I . . . I don't understand."

"Are you stupid, boy? I planted the man in Kath and paid him to attack you," replied Lume.

"But . . . but why? That man almost killed me."

"To see if you were up to this assassination," he explained, "but obviously it was a poor test."

Cy stood with his arms limp and his mouth open wide.

Lume paced back and forth for a while longer, then he caught sight of Cy. "Child, stop your bemoaning. You lived. All that matters now is that we go back to kill Shadow and get that wand." Lume walked over to the young man and put his hand on his shoulder. "Despite the fact that you failed, you've provided us—provided our great leader Olostin himself—with a real opportunity to reclaim our world from the haughty archwizards."

Cy just stared, fuming at Lume.

"Son, if we get that wand," explained the captain, "we could use it against Shadow and all of his kind. We've been trying to kill that man for years, and now we might finally have an opportunity to use his own research against him. Wouldn't that be beautiful?" He smiled and slapped Cy on the shoulder. "You know something Cy, I've sent a countless number of assassins after Shadow over the years, and you're the first to come back alive. You should take pride in that. You're one in perhaps a thousand, and now you'll get another chance to complete your mission."

Cy pulled away from the captain. "You do what you want, but I'll have no part of it."

Lume narrowed his gaze. "You'll do what I tell you, or you'll be dead."

He stepped toward Cy and lowered his hand to his saber. Cy stood his ground.

"You sent me to die once already. I'm not going back."

The captain brought his sword up in a quick arc, hitting Cy squarely under the jaw with the pommel as the blade scraped out of its scabbard.

The young assassin fell back, and he held his hand to his face, trying to stop the flow of blood as he stared up at his captain from the floor. Two armed guards came through the tent flap, their swords drawn.

"Take him back to his tent," Lume instructed the men, "and make sure he doesn't go anywhere." He turned back to the young man on the floor. "He'll be needed shortly—to finish his failed duties."

Two days later, Lume sent a group of men to escort Cy to the party's armory. The captain was there briefing a small group of men on the coming assassination.

"I will personally accompany you men to make sure that this time we succeed where Cy failed," intoned Lume. He smiled at Cy as the guards untied the younger man's bonds. "Cy will go along, under my personal supervision, to provide the necessary details about Shadow's home and habits." He looked out at the crowd of assembled assassins. "If this man—" he pointed to Cy—"attempts to escape or in any other way avoid his duty to this group, he is to be executed. Do I make myself clear?"

Every head in the group nodded assent.

Each of the assassins was given special boots that masked the sound of their footsteps and special cloaks that made them more difficult to see, and each was issued an amulet that made them less susceptible to the effects of Shadow's magic.

"These won't protect you from the shadows," explained Lume, "but they will make you less of a target for the archwizard."

Cy gritted his teeth. This whole mission might not be necessary had he had one of those amulets on the first attempt.

Then Lume gave each of the men a light crossbow with a single bolt, and a small dagger, and they left for Karsus. The plan was for Cy to lead the other assassins into Shadow's bedchamber where they would overwhelm him with sheer numbers.

"The archwizard won't try to use anything too deadly inside the small confines of that room," strategized the captain. "He'll more likely try to subdue us as he did Cy, or enspell the whole group to make us think he is our ally, and deal with us individually at his leisure. We're not going to let that happen. As soon as we get in sight, we unload with the crossbows. The bolts I gave you are magically enhanced to ensure a perfect strike. You only have one, because if you fail, there won't be an opportunity for another shot. Keep him distracted, so he can't use his magic, and we should all live through this." Lume looked at each of the assassins in turn. "Once Shadow is dead, we find his wand, and we get out of there and celebrate."

The other raiders let out a loud whoop at their captain's confidence. Cy kept his mouth shut. It wasn't going to be that easy, and he knew most of these men, himself included, weren't coming back. He just hoped that one of those who wasn't going back to camp would be Captain Lume.

❧ ❧ ❧ ❧ ❧

At the entry to Shadow's opulent home, Lume jabbed the end of his saber into Cy's ribs and said, "Now, be a good lad and show us in."

Cy lead the silent, nearly invisible band of assassins down the long hallway into the decadent siting room. In complete silence, the entire troop weaved through the blonde constructs and marched down toward the bedchamber.

Just as before, the door at the end of the hall was ajar and a light was on inside the room. Cy beckoned the other assassins ahead of him and pressed himself against the wall. The raiders complied and moved around him, taking up positions on either side of the door. Lume came up behind Cy, and he nodded to the waiting troops. One of them held his hand out and silently counted to three with his fingers, then he charged through the door, the others following him in.

From where he was standing, Cy could only see the men leave the hall. With the boots they were wearing, he couldn't even hear them move. He and Captain Lume waited for the sounds of a scuffle or of magic being cast, but they never came. After several moments of silence, one of the men came back into the hall and waved the two men in. Lume pushed Cy by the shoulder, and he moved around the door in front of his captain.

The bedchamber was still in a shambles, but the wall was once more intact where the ogres had burst into the room. The other assassins stood around, casting nervous glances back and forth as if something invisible might sneak up on them. Cy moved over toward the wall, stopping briefly at the chest of drawers where his enchanted dagger was still resting.

I'd rather die with this in my hand, he thought. He picked up the blade.

When he reached the section of wall where the secret door had been, he placed his hand where he thought the doorframe might begin. His fingers slipped through the wall. The archwizard hadn't fixed the broken section, he had simply cast a spell over the opening. It would be a simple matter of stepping through the illusion to get to the stairs beyond.

Cy straightened up and headed out into the hall, motioning to Lume as he did.

The captain glared at Cy and asked, "What's going on?"

"Shadow has a laboratory in the basement behind that wall. He's cast an illusion over the opening to make us think the wall is solid, but if I were him, I'd have other defenses in place as well. I think we're better off hiding out here and waiting for him to come out."

Lume nodded and pushed Cy back through the door. The captain arranged the assassins in strategic positions around the room, then he went back into the hallway, dragging Cy with him.

Hours passed. The assassins waited. Finally, the wall wobbled as the illusion allowed someone to pass through. Shadow was looking down at a contraption in his hands and not at all paying attention to his surroundings. The wand was stuck in the belt of his robe, and he didn't appear to have any of the bruises or scars that a man who had been brutally beaten by two ogres should have.

Two steps into the bedroom, the archwizard realized

that something was wrong, and he began to cast a spell. The assassins unloaded their crossbows, and the man screamed, dropping the gadget in his hands and stumbling toward the bed, his spell lost on his lips.

Cy watched as the wizard fell to his knees, and Lume let out an excited yelp and bolted into the room, his dagger in hand. Shadow was holding his hands against his chest and looking at the ground. He was bleeding quite heavily.

"Well, well, well," intoned Lume. He was standing a few feet away from the archwizard with a large smile on his face. "If it isn't the mighty archwizard Shadow. Do you have any idea how long I've been trying to kill you?"

The man looked up from his position on the floor, and he finished mouthing the lasts words of another spell. He glared up at the captain as the magical bolts jutting from his body shot back out, sailing across the room and striking the assassins who had shot them. Every one of them fell to the floor, dead with a bolt buried in his forehead. Shadow continued to bleed, and he put his hand out to steady himself. His skin turned quite pale.

"No. Frankly," said the wizard, "you have a lot of competition when it comes to assassinating me."

Lume didn't waste any time. He crossed to the wizard and pushed him to the floor, taking the wand from his belt with one hand and placing the edge of his dagger to Shadow's throat with the other.

"Well allow me to introduce myself. My name is Lume, and I work for Olostin."

"Yes—" Shadow coughed hard—"Yes, I recognize the name. Pleasure to make your acquaintance."

"Believe me, the pleasure is all mine." He turned to Cy. "Is this the wand you spoke of," he asked, holding up the crystal-tipped rod.

"It appears to be, yes."

The captain took a step back and turned again to the archwizard.

No longer under the watchful eyes of a band of assassins, Cy lunged at Lume with his dagger.

"Die, you pig!"

The captain sidestepped the blow, but he stumble-stepped to one side.

Cy swung again at the older man's back. The enchanted blade sliced through Lume's leather armor, opening a long, bloody gash in the captain's side.

"You stupid fool," Lume hissed.

Pulling his saber is a flash, the captain made two quick slashing attacks.

Cy parried the first blow, but the second landed just below his wrist, knocking his dagger from his hand. Lume swung again, and Cy struggled backward, avoiding the blade but falling back over the bed. Cy landed on the floor against Shadow, cradling his wrist where Lume had cut him.

The captain leveled the wand at the two men on the floor.

The archwizard struggled to breathe, but he laughed anyway.

"You can't use that," he said. "You don't know the command word."

"You're wrong, wizard, and now I'm going to destroy you with your own toy." Lume smiled down at Shadow. "Ironic that you could spend so much of your life perfecting a tool such as this—" he shook the wand—"only to be killed by it in the end."

"You don't know what sort of forces you're messing with." He coughed, blood trickling down the corner of his mouth.

"Neither did you." Lume straightened his arm and spoke the word Cy had repeated for him back at camp. "*Shadominiaropalazitsi.*"

Once again a column of rushing dark gray plasma flowed out of the wand. It headed straight for the prone archwizard, coalescing into humanlike forms along the way. As it jetted forward, the stream of shadows split into a curling mass. Shadow raised his hand instinctively to protect his face, but this time, the shadows broke into individual swirls, and twisted, wavering forms spread out all over the room. They filled every corner and place of darkness.

Now spread out, the shadows began to collect again, forming a cyclone around Captain Lume.

Lume screamed, "What's happening? What's going on?"

"Don't you see, you fool?" explained the archwizard. "Don't you recognize any of those shadows?"

"No, no, I don't." He swung his saber in wide, swooping arcs. "Stay away from me," he screamed. "Stay away, you hear?"

Shadow lifted himself off the floor.

"Is that any way to treat your previous assassins?" asked the archwizard.

Lume's face dropped, and his swinging momentarily slowed.

"That's right." Shadow smiled. "I punished your assassins by turning them into shadows and trapping them in that wand, and you just released them to seek vengeance on you for earning them an eternity of suffering."

The shadows wasted no time, diving in to touch the stunned captain while he listened to the archwizard.

Lume's knees went weak, and he began his frantic swinging again.

"But you were the one who sent them to their deaths," he screamed.

"They don't blame me for defending myself from assassination. They blame you for sending them to kill an archwizard. You should learn to not mess with forces beyond your control."

Lume was getting tired, and his defense was weakening. His wild arcs with his saber were slowing, and the shadows were touching him repeatedly. He dropped to the ground, lifting his head to speak again to Shadow.

"Those are fine words, coming from the likes of you."

Lume collapsed, his head hitting the wooden planks of the floor with a decided thud.

The shadows spun around in a pack over the limp body on the floor. A dark shape formed around the captain's corpse, then it coalesced into a humanlike shadow and lifted into the air, joining the swirling mass above. As a group, they dived toward the wand still gripped in Lume's dead hand. The dark gray stream narrowed as it approached the crystal, and as quickly as they had come forth, the shadows disappeared.

The archwizard reached into the sleeve of his robes and pulled forth a large purple bottle. Uncorking the vial, he swiftly drank down the contents. A strange white glow surrounded his skin, and the bleeding stopped. He looked much better, though not quite whole and hearty.

He looked at Cy, who was still on the floor cradling his bleeding wrist, and said, "As I said before, you are entirely too young to be an assassin. I suggest you find another line of work."

With that, he turned around and went back through the illusionary wall.

Cy looked down at the dead body of Captain Lume and nodded, then he turned around and headed back up the stairs, dodging a pretty blonde golem on his way out.

Originally published in *Realms of the Deep*
Edited by Philip Athans, March 2000

AND THE DARK TIDE RISES

Keith Francis Strohm

Around the time I sat down to write this story, I was deep in the grip of my enduring fascination with all things Celtic. I had recently watched *The Secret of Roan Inish* and happened to find myself right in the middle of a book called *Island Cross Talk*, a fascinating collection of reminiscences and stories told by a fisherman of the Blasket Islands, an island chain off the southwest coast of Ireland. So, the images and cadences of Irish fishing life and speech were in the forefront of my brain.

With the Threat From the Sea storyline about to make such major "waves" in the FORGOTTEN REALMS universe, I found myself focusing on how the start of the war would effect the simple folk of Faerûn, and how heroism isn't simply a quality for plate mail girded knights. The resultant story, one of my first, still makes me think of peat fires and fog-bound islands.

—Keith Francis Strohm, April 2003

Keith Strohm lives and writes in
Seattle, Washington. During his time
at Wizards of the Coast he worked as
the Brand Manager for
DUNGEONS AND DRAGONS, as well as the
Category Manager for both
Roleplaying Games and Miniatures—
eventually leaving the company after a
stint as the Vice President of the
Pokemon Product Group. When asked
of his current projects, he just nods
and smiles enigmatically.

AND THE DARK TIDE RISES

7 Eleint, the Year of the Gauntlet

The last rays of the setting sun spun out over the waters of the Inner Sea, transforming its rippled surface into shimmering gold. Umberlee's Fire, the sailors called it, and considered it a good omen, a sign that the Sea Queen had blessed their work. Morgan Kevlynson stood on the bow of the sea-worn fishing dory that had served his family for years and ignored the spectacular display. Absently, he pushed a strand of coal-black hair from his face, blown there by the swirling, salt-flecked fingers of the wind, and let his thoughts wander beneath the fiery skin of the sea.

Darkness surrounding, like a cocoon, the wild impulses of the deep; blue-green presences where sunlight caresses sea-halls.

There were mysteries here. He knew that as surely as he knew his own name. The sea held an ancient wisdom—wild and untamed; carried dark promises upon its broad back. And sometimes, when he sailed the waters in silence, they called to him.

Today was such a time.

Morgan closed his eyes, absorbed in the dance of wind and wave and foam. He felt a familiar emptying, as if some inner tide receded; his heartbeat pulsed to the rhythm of the sea, slow and insistent, like the whitecaps that struck the side of the dory, until everything became that rhythm—heart, boat, sky—the world defined in a single liquid moment.

That's when he saw her: eyes the color of rich kohl, skin as green-tinted as the finest chrysoberyl, and blue-green hair that flowed more freely than water itself. Yet, there was a sadness, a vulnerability about this creature that set an ache upon him more fierce than any he had ever felt. He was about to ask what he could do to set a smile back upon her face when she opened her mouth and—

"*Tchh*, laddie! Lay off yer sea-dreamin' and give us a hand." The voice was deep, resonant, and rough as coral, worn smooth only by the companionable lilt of the fishermen of the Alamber coastline.

Morgan opened his eyes and spun quickly to face the sound, only just catching himself as his sudden movement set the dory rocking. Angus, his grandfather, sat athwart the starboard gunwale stowing line with the ease of long practice. The old man's sun-burnished skin covered his face and hands like cracked leather. A thick shock of silver hair crowned the ancient fisherman's bowed head, and his rough woolen clothes were worn thin and dusted with dried salt. Despite the weathering of years, Angus showed no signs of slowing down. His wits and his grasp remained firm, as was the way of those who spent their entire lives fishing the rough shores and islands of Alamber.

Despite himself, Morgan smiled at the thought of his grandfather ever needing anyone's assistance.

"But Granda, I was just—"

" 'Tis sure I knew what you were about, lad," the old man interrupted. "Moonin' over the water. 'Tis not natural.

The sea'd just as soon swallow you up as leave you be. Never doubt the right of that, boyo. She's a fickle lover, she is, and a man cannot hope to understand her."

Morgan sighed, moved to the small wooden mast at the center of the boat, and carefully folded up the coarse cloth that made up the dory's only sail. He had heard this same lecture at least three hundred times. His grandfather would never tire of it. The old man's voice droned on as the young fisherman gathered up the now-thick bundle of sailcloth. It was difficult to keep the irritation out of his movements. Morgan was sure that he felt his grandfather's disapproving stare when he dropped the cloth a bit too forcefully into its storage area beneath the prow.

Still, the old fisherman continued his lecturing. It was not fair, really. Morgan had lived nearly eighteen summers—and had sailed for most of those. He was no land-bred lackaday, ill-prepared for work upon a fishing boat, nor was he a pampered merchant's son come to the Alamber coast on holiday. He was a fisherman, born into one of the oldest fishing families on the Inner Sea. Yet his fascination with the sea seemed to frighten his grandfather—and the close-knit inhabitants of Mourktar.

Thinking back, he knew the reason why. The superstitious villagers had never really accepted him. His mother dead from the strain of childbirth, his father lost in grief so deep that he sailed out into the Inner Sea one winter night, never to return, Morgan had grown up wild, spending many a sunset running across the rocks and cliffs that jutted out over the water, listening to the song of the waves and breathing in the salty musk of the wind. "Sea-touched," they had called him. Changeling. Pointing to his black hair and fair skin, so different from the sun-golden complexion and reddish hair of Mourktar's natives, as outward proof of the very thing they whispered softly to each other in the deep of night, when the wind blew hard across the shore. Even now, Morgan knew that many still made the sign of Hathor behind his back if he gazed too long out at sea or sat on Mourktar's weathered quay in deep thought.

He searched for signs of bitterness, for some resentment

of his reputation, but found none. He had grown up with the simple reality that no one understood him. He had friends, conspirators who were happy to while away the time between childhood and manhood by stealing a mug or two of frothy ale from old Borric's tavern or playing at war amid the scrub-choked dunes, and there were evenings enough of stolen kisses beneath the docks. But no one truly knew what went on in his deepest core, that silent part of him that heard the measured beat of the sea's heart, that felt its inexorable pull like a vast undertow of need. No one could know these things—except perhaps his father.

Morgan shuddered at that thought and shook himself free of his reverie. His frustration and resentment drained out of him, leaving behind only emptiness and a numbing chill. The sun had nearly fallen beneath the horizon, and he looked up to find his grandfather staring expectantly at him in the purplish haze of twilight, his discourse apparently finished.

"I said, 'tis a fierce storm'll blow tonight, and we'd best be finishing soon." The old man shook his head and muttered something else under his breath before opening the waterproof tarp they used to cover the boat.

Morgan *hmmphed* guiltily and moved to help his grandfather, threading a thin rope through the small holes around the tarp's edge and running it around the metal ringlets attached to the sides of the boat. In truth, not a single cloud floated anywhere in the twilit sky, but the coastal breeze had picked up, bringing with it a sharpening chill. He had long ago stopped doubting his grandfather's ability to guess the weather.

Once he'd finished securing the tarp, the old man spat and walked down the quay toward Mourktar.

"Come lad, we've a fair catch to bring home, and there's a dark tide running in. Besides, I've a yearning for some of yer gran's fish stew."

Morgan bent and hefted the sack of freshly caught fish over his shoulder, thanking the gods that they had sold the rest of the day's catch to the merchants earlier. As he turned to look one last time at the dory, rising and falling to the swelling of the waves, he caught sight of a furtive movement near the boat. He was about to call to his grandfather, fearing the mischievous vandalizing of a sea lion, when he caught sight of a head bobbing just above the surface of the water. Morgan couldn't make out any more of this strange creature, but that didn't matter. Staring at him in the fading light, he saw the face of his dream.

In a moment, she was gone, and he turned back to his grandfather. Though the two walked back to the village in silence, Morgan's mind was a jumble of confusion and disbelief.

❖ ❖ ❖ ❖ ❖

The storm raged throughout the night, battering the rough thatch of the simple hut. Morgan tossed fitfully under his thick quilt while the wind howled like a wolf through the dirt lanes and footpaths of Mourktar. His grandparents slept deeply in the main room. He could hear their throaty snores, a rough counterpoint to the storm's fury. Sleep, however, refused to grant Morgan similar relief. Instead, he lay there curled up into a ball, feeling lost and alone, and very small against the night.

It had been like that the entire evening. When he and Angus had arrived at their family's hut for supper, storm clouds had already blotted out the newly shining stars. Morgan had barely noticed. The vision of the sea woman's face had flared brightly in his mind since he'd left the docks, and his thoughts burned with her unearthly beauty. Everything else seemed dull in comparison, hollow and worn as the cast off shell of a hermit crab.

He had sat through supper mostly in silence, distracted by the rising song of the wind. Several times he had almost gasped in horror, for he heard in that mournful susurrus the slow exhalation of his name ushering forth from the liquid throat of the sea. His grandparents had borne this mood for as long as they could. Morgan's muttered responses to his gran's questions, however, had finally earned him a cuff from Angus. Though even that blow had felt more like an echo of his granda's anger, a memory of some past punishment. Frustrated, the old fisherman stormed away from the driftwood table, cursing. Morgan mumbled some excuse soon after and staggered to his cot, seeking relief in the cool release of sleep.

He failed.

Thoughts of *her* consumed him, and his skin burned with the promise of her touch. She wanted him, called to him in a voice full of moonlight and foam and the soft, subtle urging of the sea. He lay there for hours, trying to hide from her, trying to retreat into the hidden places of his mind. But she followed, uttering his name, holding it forth like a lamp.

Morgan, come!

Come, my heart-home!

Come!

Briefly, irrationally, he wondered if his father had heard the same voice on the night he stole a boat and, broken by grief, sailed out to his death on the winter sea. Perhaps, Morgan thought wildly, this madness was hereditary.

Come!

The voice. Stronger this time, driving away all thought except obedience. With a cry, he flung himself out of the cot, no longer able to resist the siren call. The compulsion took a hold of him now, drove him out of the hut into the gray stillness of false dawn. The storm had spent itself. Wind and rain no longer lashed the shore. The world held its breath, waiting.

Waiting for what? Morgan thought.

In an instant he knew. It waited for him. Rubbing his arms briskly to ward off the predawn chill, he followed the dirt road down to the docks. Every step brought Morgan closer to *her*. He ignored the downed branches, shattered trunks, and other detritus that littered the road, and began to run. He had no choice.

And yet, there was a sense of promise to this call, a hint of mystery unveiled. If he was going to end his life sea-mad like his father, he would at least receive something in return, a gift from the dark waters that had been his true home these past eighteen seasons more truly than the insular huts and close-minded folk of Mourktar. He understood that now, and the notion filled him with equal parts terror and fascination.

At last, he reached the end of the dock, sweat soaked and gasping for breath. He cast about desperately, hoping to catch some glimpse of the mysterious creature that haunted both his waking and dreaming, proof that he had not simply lost his wits. *She* was there, floating idly to the left of his family's dory.

Even from a distance her beauty stung him with its purity. The skin of her green-tinted face was creamy and smooth as marble, and her delicate features set his fingers twitching, so much did Morgan long to trace the curve of chin, nose, and throat. Long blue-green hair, though matted with moisture above the water, floated tenderly over the outline of her body.

Morgan would have dived into the chill sea that very moment to be with her, had she not opened her full-lipped mouth and spoken.

"Greetings, Man-child, son of Kevlyn. I feared that you would not come in time."

Her voice was sweet and clear, her intonation fluid, making it sound to Morgan as if she sang every phrase.

Questions filled his head to bursting. Who was she? How did she know him? Why did she call him here? As he hurriedly tried to decide which one to speak aloud, he realized that the compulsion was gone. His thoughts were his own.

He looked at the mysterious creature again, noting for the first time the thick webbing splayed between the fingers of her hands as she easily tread water. She tilted her head slightly to the side, obviously waiting for his response.

Morgan said nothing, letting the moment stretch between them, letting the rhythmic slap of water against dock, the wail of early rising gulls, and the faint rustling of the coastal wind fill the void her compulsion had left inside of him.

He was angry, and not a little frightened. This creature

had used him, manipulated him, and when at last he spoke, his voice was full of bitterness. "Of course I came. You gave me no choice."

She laughed at that, though he heard no humor in it, only a tight quaver that sounded suspiciously to his untrained ear like sadness.

"There's little choice any of us have now, lad," the creature said softly, almost too softly to be heard. Then louder, "But you must forgive me, Morgan. These are desperate times. I sent out the Call; you came. And a truer Son of Eldath never walked or swam upon the face of Toril."

Now it was her turn to stare, deep-colored eyes locking on to his. Morgan felt his anger drain away, only to be replaced by he didn't know what—embarrassment? Shame? He felt like an ungainly boy under the weight of that otherworldly gaze.

"H-how do y-you know my—my name?" he stuttered quickly, trying to focus the creature's attention elsewhere.

The sea woman chuckled, her amusement plain to hear, and said, "You mortals wear your names as plainly as a selkie does her skin. It is child's play to pluck it from you—if you know how to look for it." Her smile faded. "Ahh, but I see that I am being rude. Forgive me, again, for it has been a long time since I have spoken with a mortal. I am Avadrieliaenvorulandral. You may call me Avadriel. I am Alu'Tel'Quessir, those folk your ancestors called 'sea elves,' and I need your help."

Morgan sat on the dock, stunned. Alu'Tel'Quessir. Sea elves. Morgan had only dreamed of ever seeing such a creature, and here he stood, talking to one in the flesh.

"You need *my* help?" he asked incredulously. "But lady—"

"Avadriel," the creature interrupted. "I gave up such formalities centuries ago."

"Avadriel," he continued, choosing to ignore the implications of the sea elf's last statement. "I'm but a fisherman."

Clearly, Morgan thought, this beautiful creature who floated up out of the depths was mistaken. Soon, she would realize this and return to her watery realm, leaving him alone and feeling the fool. At this moment, he did not know which would be worse.

"A fisherman," Avadriel scoffed. "You are far more than that, Morgan. You are one of the few mortals left who can hear the Old Song.

"Yes," she continued, noticing his look of confusion, "the sea has set its mark upon you, even if others of your kind fear and distrust you because of it. That is why I have come."

Here were words straight out of a bard's fancy, the young man thought, but could he laugh them away, dismiss them as so much nonsense, when they came from the mouth of such a creature? Morgan's world had spun out of control since he first saw her. He felt caught in the grip of some implacable tide, carrying him to the depths of a black abyss. Yet, Avadriel's words rang with the truth, and her presence gave him something to hold on to, an anchor in an otherwise tumultuous sea. Gravely, he nodded, too afraid to speak.

Avadriel shot him a half smile and said, "It is good to see that the children of the sun are still brave—though I fear even bravery may not be enough to save us. You see, Morgan, a great evil has awakened deep within the blackest abyss of the sea, leading an army of its dark minions. Already this force has destroyed Avarnoth. Many of my people . . ."

The sea elf faltered, and Morgan saw the pain she had been hiding burst forth, marring her beautiful features. He looked away, not wishing to intrude. After a few moments, she continued—her voice a tremulous whisper.

"Many of my people made the journey to Sashelas's halls, but it will not stop there. This evil grows daily, and it will sweep across the lands of Faerûn like a tidal wave, destroying everything in its path."

Something in her voice made Morgan look up. Avadriel looked pale, her face drained of color. He was about to ask her what was wrong, when a large wave pushed her hair aside, revealing a deep gash across her right shoulder. Flesh, muscle, and vein were ripped apart, exposing thin white bone.

Morgan cursed softly. "Lady—Avadriel, you are wounded!"

He was angry; at himself for not noticing sooner, and at her for concealing such a thing.

How she had managed to carry on with such a grievous injury was beyond him. Hurriedly, he searched about the wooden wharf for one of the small dinghies used to ferry fishermen to boats anchored away from the limited space of the docks. He soon found one tied off near a set of rusting crab traps. Adroitly climbing down a rickety rope ladder, the young fisherman cast off and rowed the battered dinghy toward the wounded creature.

"Do not concern yourself with my well being, Morgan," Avadriel protested weakly as he neared. "My message is far more important than my life."

Ignoring the sea elf's instructions, for he had already concluded that her life was far more important than his own, the young man drew close to Avadriel and gently pulled her into the rude craft, careful not to further damage her wounded shoulder. The sea elf was surprisingly light, and, despite her initial protest, offered Morgan no resistance. Carefully, he laid her down, folding his sweater under her head for a pillow and covering her naked body with a weather-worn tarp.

Avadriel's skin was cold to the touch, and her once bright eyes began to glaze over. Even so, she reached out to him with her webbed hands, turning her head to reveal three gill slits running through either side of her delicate throat. He bent down to her, fascinated as the slits sucked noisily in the air.

"Morgan . . . you . . . must listen," she whispered unevenly. "There is something you must . . . do . . . something . . ." Her voice trailed off into silence.

At first, he thought she must have died, for her gill slits had stopped opening, but his fears were allayed when her chest began to rise and fall shallowly. Avadriel was sorely wounded, but by the gods, Morgan thought, she was alive.

Quietly, he sat down in the small boat. The early morning wind raked his now bare arms and neck. His thin, short-sleeved undertunic offered him little protection against the seasonal cold. Morgan ignored the chill, however, and began to row. There were several shallow sea caves not far from the docks. He would take Avadriel there, away from the prying eyes and fearful minds of Mourktar's inhabitants. He would tend to her wounds, and when she awakened, he would travel to the ends of Toril for her. He remembered her impassioned plea. He was needed.

Blood. The scent of it filled the water, thick, heavy, and rich. T'lakk floated idly amid the waving kelp strands, savoring the heady aroma, sucking it in with each flap of his gill slits. It stirred something deep within his hunter's heart, an ancient hunger, older than the sea itself. He waited, letting it grow, letting it build, until the hunger sang within him—tooth and claw and rending flesh, a savage, primal tune.

Quickly, he shook his green-scaled head, refusing to go into the Place of Madness. Though it cost him great effort, the creature focused his senses back on the hunt. He still had work to do, and the master would be displeased if he failed in this task. Three long clicks summoned the other hunters from their search along the rocky sea floor. Balefully, he eyed each one as they arrived, satisfied that they approached with the proper humility. He would brook no challenges now. Not when their quarry lay so close.

He smiled grimly, revealing several rows of needle-sharp teeth, as the assembled hunters scented the blood. A quick signal sent them arrowing through the water to follow the trail. Soon, T'lakk thought gleefully as he swam after his companions. Soon the Hunt would be over.

Morgan sat in the damp cave, watching the measured rise and fall of Avadriel's chest as she slept. A battered lantern lay at his feet, perched precariously between two slime-covered stalagmites. Its rude light licked the jagged rocks of the cavern, revealing several twisted stone shelves surrounding a small tidal pool.

He had arrived at the bank of sea caves just as the morning sun crested the horizon, grateful that he was able to reach shelter before most of the village boats sailed through the area in search of their day's fishing. Once he had maneuvered his small craft deep enough into one of the caves to shield it from sight, Morgan had gently lifted Avadriel out of the dinghy, placed her on a low, relatively flat lip of stone overhanging the tidal pool, and set about binding her wound as best he could.

Now he sat stiff-necked and attentive, anxiously waiting for the sea elf to awaken. The silence of his vigil was broken only by the slow drip of water echoing hollowly in the enclosed space. His grandparents would be frantic by now—though Morgan knew that his granda would no doubt have sailed the boat out to sea, not willing to miss the day's fishing, thinking all the while of ways to box his grandson's lazy head. Still, he thought in the foreboding chill of the cavern, he would gladly suffer a great deal more than his grandfather's wrath for Avadriel's sake.

As Morgan kept a cold, damp watch over the sleeping sea elf, he marveled at how much his life had changed in such a short time. Yesterday, he had given no thought to the world beyond the coastal waters of Mourktar. Today, he found himself hiding in a cave with a wounded sea elf, ready to leave behind everything for the beauty of a creature he'd never thought he would actually see.

When Avadriel finally awoke, several hours later, the water level in the tidal pool had risen, lapping gently around her body. She sat up with a start, looking rather confused and frightened, until her eyes met Morgan's. He smiled, hoping he didn't look as foolish as he felt, and approached her carefully, determined not to turn his ankle on the slippery rocks in his eagerness.

If he had expected a long litany of thanks and gratefulness, he would have been disappointed. Though there was a softness about the sea elf's face, a gentle hint of a smile in answer to his own, her words were abrupt and as hard as steel.

"You must leave at once," she said. "Before it is too late."

Morgan stared at Avadriel once again. He didn't understand—didn't want to understand. He only knew that his place was by her side.

"Leave?" he asked incredulously. "But Avadriel, you're still hurt. Perhaps once you have healed a bit we could travel together."

He tried to keep the wistfulness out of his voice, failing miserably.

"If only that were possible, Morgan, but we don't have that much time. You must go to Firestorm Isle and tell the wizard Dhavrim that Avarnoth has fallen. An ancient evil is free once again. Its black army is even now poised to strike at Faerûn, and the wizards must be warned." She paused, then added, "Please, Morgan. I need your help."

Silently, he cursed the luck that separated him from his heart's desire the moment he had discovered it. It would be difficult to leave, but Morgan knew that he would do it. Too much was at stake.

Avadriel smiled then, as if reading the young man's thoughts, and drew herself closer.

"Thank you," she said simply, and brushed her lips lightly over his.

Morgan closed his eyes at her touch. Avadriel's scent surrounded him, intoxicating in its subtlety. Their lips met each other's again, firmer this time. A wave of desire crested through him, wild and strong as a riptide. The world faded away in the wake of that desire, leaving only the ebb and flow of bodies.

After a time, Avadriel pulled away.

"Morgan," she whispered softly, sadly into the shadows of the cave.

He nodded once, and wiped a blossoming tear from her eye.

"I know . . . it's time." With that, he stood and climbed into the waiting boat. "I shall return as soon as I can."

Slowly, he rowed out into harsh light of day.

❧ ❧ ❧ ❧ ❧

With a grunt of effort, Morgan let the rhythmic slap of oar on water carry him through another hour of rowing. The sea surged and foamed around him, threatening to turn aside the small force of his craft. Spume sprayed his face as the boat's bow bounced hard against the trough of a rolling black wave. Insistent burn of chest and arm muscles long-since spent, harsh gasp of salted air into lungs, sting of wood chafing raw skin—these were his offerings, sacrificial prayers to the gods of his people.

They ignored him.

Slowly, he made his way across the churning water, more by force of will than anything else. When his energy flagged and the oars seemed to weigh as much as an iron anchor, he summoned a picture of Avadriel's face. The memory of her lips on his, the salted taste of her tongue, renewed his determination. Too much lay at stake, for his heart and his home. He would not fail.

By mid afternoon, the heat of the sun had dried the sweat from his body, and his tongue felt thick and swollen, like a piece of boiled leather. With a deep sigh, he pulled up the oars and gave his knotted muscles a brief rest. Shielding his eyes from the sun's glare, he scanned the horizon.

Several years before, he had stolen out with a few friends and sailed to the wizard's island on a dare. Though none of the intrepid band of explorers had set foot on the island, Morgan alone sailed his ship around the rocky shore of that forbidden place.

Even now, amid the burning heat of the sun, he shivered with the memory. Dhavrim's tower had stood stark and terrifying, thrusting up from the coral of the island like the tooth of some giant whale. As Morgan had guided his craft around the island, he couldn't help but wonder if the wizard would send some deadly spell arcing out from his demesne to punish the trespassing boat.

The upsurge of a wave snapped Morgan out of his reverie. He still had a fair distance to row before he reached the island, and he felt as if time were running out.

By late afternoon, when the sun began its lazy descent, a calm fell over the waters. Morgan quickly wiped his brow and surveyed the silent scene. The sea lay placid and serene, its gently stippled surface resembling nothing so much as the facet of a blue-green gem in the sunlight. In the distance, he could make out a small shadow, a black pimple on the horizon that could only be Dhavrim's tower. Before Morgan could even celebrate his good fortune, he caught sight of something that tore an oath out of his parched throat. There in the distance, dark and ominous, a roiling wall of haze bore down on him.

Terrified, Morgan renewed his efforts, hoping that he could reach his destination before the line of fog enveloped him. The sailors of his village called such unnatural weather the Breath of Umberlee. It often lured unsuspecting boats to a watery grave. Even the beacon fires set upon the cliff walls of the Alamber coast were often not enough to save the doomed vessels.

With a determined grunt, Morgan bent his back to the task once again. Whipcord muscles already pushed beyond their limit protested mightily, but he pressed on. Time seemed to slow in that silent moment, until he felt as if he were trapped in some artist's sketch. He continued to row, of that he was sure, but the island did not seem to draw any closer. At first he thought himself dreaming, until the first patchy cloud of fog rolled across the bow of his craft, followed soon after by more until the fog drew close around him like a thick blanket. Desperately, he cast about for sign of the island, for any landmark in the sea of gray that surrounded him, but to no avail. Even the sun, which had lashed at his skin with its fierce rays, hung muted and dim, a hidden jewel in the murky sky.

Filled with frustration and not a fair bit of rage at the unfairness of it all, Morgan shouted fiercely at the blanket of fog, "Damn it all! I will not fail. I can not!"

Savagely, he beat his fist against the oarlock and continued to hurl invectives at the fog, at the gods, at the wizard in his thrice-damned castle, but most of all at himself, for agreeing to this fool's errand in the first place.

The answering cry of a gull surprised him so much that he stopped his railing in midsentence. Again, its wail cut through the fog, echoing in the gray murk, followed by a white streak and a light thump as the creature landed on the bow of his craft. Startled by the gull's appearance, white-crested and intent, Morgan didn't even wonder why such a creature should fly out so far from shore.

"Heya, silly bird," the young man said pitifully. "Fly away before you become stuck like a poor fisherman's son in a fog bank."

The large gull simply cocked its head slightly and regarded the young man with a serious gaze.

"Go!" he shouted finally at the stupid creature, letting frustration and anger creep into his voice.

The bird ignored his command and continued to stare at him. Finally, with a soft chirrup, the gull flapped its wings and hovered gently a few feet from his craft. It was then that Morgan noticed a small crystal clutched in the bird's grasp. The jewel began to pulse slightly as he stared at it, softly illuminating the gloom around him.

The bird landed again on the boat, casting a knowing glance at Morgan, before it lifted off once more, now flying a few feet in front of the craft. Surprisingly, the light from the crystal pushed some of the fog away, allowing him the opportunity to see a few paces on all sides.

Confused, but unwilling to pass up this odd gift, Morgan dipped oars to water and followed the gull and its gleaming treasure. Hours passed—or minutes—it was difficult to measure the passing of time in the gray waste that surrounded him, and still the young man rowed after the witchlight. Without warning, he burst through the spidery maze of fog into the fading evening sunlight. In front of Morgan loomed the great white stretch of Dhavrim's tower, set only fifty feet or so from the shore. A few more quick strokes brought him scraping onto the rock-strewn beach.

Offering a quick prayer to any god within earshot, he gratefully stumbled out of the boat, stretched knotted muscles, and pulled his craft safely onto the shore. Now that he had arrived on the wizard's island, fulfilled part of Avadriel's wish, he felt hopeful. Perhaps the sea elf had chosen correctly, he thought, as he basked in the pleasurable warmth of sun-baked sand. The simple fisherman, braving wind, wave, and fog to deliver a desperate message. He liked the sound of that, and despite the all-too-real urgency of the situation, he could not help but think himself a hero.

The crash of surf on shore reminded him of the reason for this journey. Anxiously, he studied the stone structure, searching for some entryway. In the fading light of day, the wizard's tower looked more weathered than forbidding. Thick lichen and moss covered parts of the cracked stone structure in mottled patches, and even from this distance he could make out the long, thin stalks of hearty scrub vines twining up the tower's base. Gone were the mystical guardians and arcane wards that had populated his adolescent imaginings, replaced by the mundane reality of sand, rock, and sea-blown wind. Smiling ruefully at his fancies, Morgan the fisherman headed up the path toward the black tower.

And found himself face-to-face with death.

He had little warning, just a slight scrape of sand and the span of a heartbeat in which to react, before he was struck by a powerful blow. He hit the ground hard, felt the air explode out of his lungs. Gasping and dazed, he struggled to his knees, only to find himself staring into the heart of a nightmare. It stood nearly six feet, covered in thick green scales that glistened wetly in the dying light. Deep scars pitted its humanoid face, nearly closing one large eye completely. The other eye fixed Morgan with a baleful stare, its cold black orb seemed to pull what little light remained into its depths.

The creature took a step forward, opened its slightly protruding jaw. Still kneeling on the ground, Morgan could make out row upon row of needle-sharp teeth, no doubt eager to rend the flesh from his bones. He wanted to scream, but the wind was still knocked from him. Instead, he forced himself to his feet and stumbled desperately toward the wizard's tower. If he could just make it from the sandy footing of the beach to the tower's path, he would have a chance to outrun the creature.

Morgan felt the beast's claws rip through his shirt, scoring the flesh underneath, just as the path came into sight. He twisted to the side, avoiding the creature's next strike—and tripped. The last thing he saw before his head exploded into light was the outline of claws against the sky.

By the time the world resolved itself back into color, the sun had set. A pale half moon bathed the island in gentle illumination. By its light, Morgan could see a figure standing over the smoking corpse of the nightmare creature. The figure, obviously a man by the suggestion of a beard visible from this distance, prodded the ruined body with the end of a long staff. The smell of burnt flesh wafted off the corpse, fouling the sea air.

"Ho, I see our visitor has come back to us," the strange man called out, ending his grisly examination.

Morgan's voice caught in his throat as he tried to reply. Dhavrim Starson—for who else, he reasoned, would he find standing on the shore of the wizard's island—resembled nothing of the legendary mage. Short and fat, with a deep-jowled, ruddy face and scratchy salt-and-pepper beard, he looked like nothing so much as a drunken wastrel whose appetites had long since consumed him.

The wizard wheezed heavily as he lumbered toward the fallen fisherman. Morgan watched in morbid fascination as the man's prodigious girth stretched the fabric of his generous blue robe with each step. Only Dhavrim's white staff, inlaid with spidery runes that flowed like molten silver down its length, betrayed the wizard's true power.

That, and his eyes.

Cold and gray, charged with the promise of a hundred storms, they held the young man frozen beneath their ancient gaze. Morgan felt himself pulled within their depths, felt the weight of the wizard's gaze as it measured him, searched him, then cast him aside.

"Can you stand?"

A voice. Calm. Reassuring.

Release.

He felt his body once again, reached for the pudgy hand extended before his face.

"Y-yes, th-thank you," Morgan stammered. He looked once more at the corpse lying in the sand. "What . . . what manner of beast was that?" he asked unsteadily, not really sure if he wanted to know the answer.

Dhavrim followed the young man's gaze. "Those who wish to appear learned call it a sahuagin. Those who truly understand it, simply call it death." The wizard paused for a moment and turned to look at Morgan once again, one silvered eyebrow arched expressively. "The real question, however, is why it followed you here."

Morgan hesitated before answering. Wizards, he knew from the old stories, were unpredictable and quick to anger—this one most of all. For a moment, he was once more that headstrong youth who sailed a small boat around the mage's isle, fearfully waiting for the wizard's wrath to fall.

I don't belong here!

The moment passed, and Morgan mustered his courage enough to speak—he owed that much to Avadriel.

"I bear a message from the sea elf Avadriel," he said in what he hoped was a firm tone.

Dhavrim's expression grew grave.

"Go on," he replied simply.

The wizard stood in silence as Morgan finished recounting his message.

The young man wondered what the wizard could be thinking, but was loath to interrupt the mage's rumination. The silence grew, charging the air with its intensity like the moments before a lightning storm. Morgan's skin prickled as he watched Dhavrim grip his staff tighter.

Abruptly, the wizard spun and began to march back to his stone tower.

"Come!" he barked commandingly, "there is much to be done this night."

"Wait!" Morgan called to the retreating figure. "What of Avadriel? If these . . . sa-sahuagin . . ." Morgan stumbled over the unfamiliar word before continuing, "followed me, then they must surely know where she is. We have to help her."

"Avadriel is a warrior and daughter of a noble house. She can take care of herself," Dhavrim replied, not stopping. "But if what she reported is true, then all of Faerûn is in danger. A great war is coming, and we must be prepared!"

Morgan ran after the heavyset wizard, the thought of Avadriel being torn apart by sahuagin driving everything else from his mind.

"She may be a warrior," he shouted at Dhavrim, "but right now she's gravely wounded and alone, while those creatures are out there ready to tear her apart."

He watched in disbelief as the wizard, only a few steps ahead of him, ignored his plea. Avadriel would be killed and the fat coward refused to do anything about it.

Wizard or no wizard, he thought acidly, I will make him come with me.

Increasing his pace, Morgan caught up to Dhavrim and jerked hard on the wizard's meaty shoulder.

"Listen to me!" he shouted.

And instantly regretted his decision.

The wizard rounded on Morgan, his eyes flashing dangerously in the moonlit sky. Horrified, Morgan took a step back as Dhavrim pointed the glowing tip of his staff right at him—and began to laugh.

"By the gods, boy," Dhavrim managed to wheeze in between chortles, "you've great heart, you do. There are few warriors who would dare brave the wrath of Dhavrim Starson." Another wave of laughter racked the wizard's frame. Seeing the young man's obviously confused expression, Dhavrim sucked in a huge gulp of air and tried to calm himself. "You've wisdom, too," he continued, "though I doubt you know it. Avadriel is perhaps the only witness to the strength of the enemy. Such information is undoubtedly critical."

Morgan stood in stunned disbelief as the wizard, still quietly chuckling, raised his arm and called out a name. A few moments later, a familiar white form hurtled out of the night to settle upon Dhavrim's pudgy arm. The wizard whispered something to the gull, then Morgan watched the night reclaim it as it flew away.

"It is time we were off, boy," Dhavrim said softly.

He started down the path toward the beach, leaving Morgan to wonder briefly at the quicksilver nature of wizards.

Dhavrim stood at the stern of the boat and whispered a word into the deepening night. To Morgan, sitting anxiously in the small craft, it sounded like the dark hiss of sea foam—ancient and redolent with power. The boat surged forward and cut across the waves, eventually piercing the thick wall of fog. Another word brought light, pale and ghostly, pulsing forth from the silver-shod tip of the wizard's staff. The mage-light shredded both fog and night. In its path, Morgan watched Dhavrim scan the horizon, grim and rigid as the unyielding stone of his tower.

Despite himself, he could not suppress a shiver of fear. The wizard's words had frightened him. War. It was coming, and the tides would run dark with blood before it was over. Damn it all, he thought, everything and everyone he knew was threatened by a danger he could scarcely comprehend, let alone fight.

Especially Avadriel.

That's what frightened him the most. The sea elf wounded and alone, while a host of Umberlee's darkest creatures hungered for her flesh. If she should die, he knew that the world would seem empty. Geas or not, he loved her.

This was madness, he thought bitterly. Perhaps his father had it right, sailing into the moonless arms of the sea, silent and alone. Perhaps some forms of madness were better than others.

Lost in the darkness of his thoughts, Morgan was surprised to hear Dhavrim's voice cut through the night. "We're close now, lad. Keep watch."

With that, he extinguished the light from his staff.

They had traveled through the thick bank of fog, and the moon shone once more in the sky. By its light, he could make out the ghostly silhouette of the sea caves just ahead.

As they drew nearer, Morgan's blood ran cold. In the pale light, he saw several figures creeping around the rocks near Avadriel's cave. Their movements seemed stiff and awkward, but even at this distance he could identify them as kin to the creature that had attacked him on Dhavrim's island. He reported this to the wizard.

"Aye, lad, I see them," Dhavrim replied. "Wait until I give you the signal, then cover your eyes."

Morgan nodded silently and waited as the dinghy drew closer to the sea cave. His heart pounded heavily in his chest. The names of several gods came to his lips, but he was too scared to utter a prayer. What am I doing here? he thought.

"Now!" shouted Dhavrim.

Hastily, Morgan drew both arms over his eyes. Even with this protection, his vision flooded with light. Just as suddenly, it disappeared. The boat rocked and he heard a splash, followed by the wizard's voice.

"Row hard for the cave and bring Avadriel out. I'll keep the foul creatures occupied."

All thought stopped as Morgan struggled to obey the voice. Quickly, he set the oars to water and rowed toward the cave. Off to his side he could hear the sibilant hiss of sahuagin and the fierce cries of Dhavrim, but he forced them out of his mind. When he reached the sea cave he called out for Avadriel.

A small voice answered, "Morgan? What are you doing here?"

"Quick, Avadriel, you must get in. I've brought Dhavrim, but the gods-cursed sahuagin are everywhere."

She jumped into the boat. Morgan found it difficult not to crush her to his chest. Avadriel was alive, he thought, though their survival depended on his strength and the power of an inscrutable wizard. Desperately, he turned around and rowed back out toward the wizard. In the wan moonlight, he could see the evil creatures lying in crumpled heaps upon the rocks. Dhavrim leaned heavily against his glowing staff, a beacon of hope amid the broken sahuagin bodies.

Relief flooded through Morgan. They were safe. Steadily, he propelled the boat back toward the wizard, thinking all the while of what his life with Avadriel would be like. He couldn't help but smile as she drew her body closer to his. He turned toward her, ready to speak his heart, when the water in front of the boat began to froth.

Suddenly, the last sahuagin slavered out of the churning water into the boat. With a cry, Morgan pushed Avadriel back, drew one of the oars out of the lock, and swung it at the beast.

It glanced off the creature's thick hide with a dull thud.

The sahuagin hissed loudly and brought its scaled arm down upon the oar, snapping it in half. Morgan watched helplessly as the beast made a grab for Avadriel. Desperately, he took the splintered haft of the oar and jammed it into the creature's chest. This time the wood pierced the beast's scales, sliding past muscle and bone. The sahuagin roared in pain and lashed out wildly, raking Morgan across his throat, before the boat overturned.

As Morgan struggled feebly to the surface, his throat a corona of agony, he cast about for signs of Avadriel. In the distance, he could still see the glowing tip of the wizard's staff, obscured by the crest of a black wave. His limbs grew heavy, as if they were weighted anchors, threatening to pull him down, and his head spun from loss of blood. Disoriented and in pain, it took him a few moments to realize that he no longer needed to keep himself afloat. Silently, Avadriel had come up from behind to support him.

Morgan tried to turn and see her, but his sluggish limbs would not respond. Instead, Avadriel gently laid him on his back, and carefully held his head above the water. He watched her in silence for a few moments, marveling at the way her eyes absorbed the crystalline light of the moon, before speaking.

"The sahuagin?" he gurgled from the ruined strip of flesh and cartilage that remained of his throat.

Avadriel touched a webbed finger to his lips.

"Hush, Morgan. The beasts will trouble us no more."
She paused before saying, "Twice now, I owe you my life."

He tried to protest, to profess his love before the darkness that danced at the edge of his vision claimed him forever, but a spasm of pain racked his body. All he could do was let out a single, frustrated gasp.

The sea elf gently stroked his forehead, and, as if reading his mind, spoke gently into the night.

"Do not worry, my love, I, too, hear the calling of my heart." She looked away, but not before Morgan caught the look of pain and sadness that creased her face. "Come, the wizard has recovered the boat. It's time to go."

As she turned her face back toward him, Morgan stared deeply into her eyes. He nodded, understanding flooding his awareness.

"May Deep Sashelas bless you until we meet again," Avadriel whispered before touching her lips to his.

At that contact, Morgan felt his pain flow out of him, leaving only a steady, measured sense of peace. Water enfolded him, circling him gently like the protective arms of a lover. They had succeeded, he thought dully, as his body slid through the depths. The wizards knew of the sahuagin invasion, and Avadriel was safe. Smiling, Morgan floated down into the dark waters of oblivion.

And beyond.

Published for the first time in this volume.

EMPTY JOYS

R.A. Salvatore

I have to listen to those little voices in my head. Whenever my editor calls to tell me that it's time for a "Realms of . . ." short story, I sit back and let the little voices talk to me—in this case, those of Artemis and Jarlaxle. I usually don't like writing short stories, but with these two characters, the chore seems less daunting. After writing *Servant of the Shard*, it became apparent to me that Artemis and Jarlaxle could carry a book, perhaps many books, and these yearly stories are allowing me to better define where I want these two to go. I have fun visiting with them each year; I hope you do, too.

—R.A. Salvatore, June 2003

R.A. Salvatore has been writing
professionally for sixteen years, with
more than thirty books under his belt,
including more than a dozen
New York Times best-sellers. His score
of FORGOTTEN REALMS novels have sold
more than eight million copies.

EMPTY JOYS

Artemis Entreri looked down the sloping rocks to the distant fishing village on the shore of some lake he did not know. Small waves rippled in, gently rocking the many ships and sending their tall masts into a hypnotic sway.

Usually impervious to such fits of introspection, Entreri allowed himself to follow that dance for a bit, to ponder the unlikely circumstances and unlikelier companion that had delivered him to that spot.

With four decades of life behind him, and nearly three of those spent surviving alone in the harsh underbellies of Calimport and other cities, it struck Entreri as curious and ironic that, into middle-age, he found himself being guided by the machinations of another.

Was it a testament to Jarlaxle's persuasiveness that he was allowing himself to be tugged along that strange road, or was it, perhaps, some inner need of his own, unrecognized and unexamined?

What was Jarlaxle offering to him? Adventure? Entreri had known that for most of his life, and most of it had not been of his choosing, but rather had been foisted upon him by circumstances dangerous and troubling.

Wealth? To what end?

Never had Entreri desired anything substantial of material value, unless one counted the possessions of his trade that he even then carried, particularly his signature jeweled dagger on his right hip, and the fabulous sword, Charon's Claw, on his left.

The assassin noted the approach of his dark elf companion Jarlaxle, and shook the thoughts from his mind, and he wouldn't lie to himself sufficiently to deny that he did so with some measure of relief.

For deep within, Artemis Entreri understood what it was that Jarlaxle was giving to him, and despite his rational objections, the loner survival instinct shouting most prominently among all of his emotions, he would not reject that one gift: friendship.

Jarlaxle held his wide-brimmed and outrageously-plumed hat in one hand as he casually strode toward Entreri, revealing his angular drow features and bald head in all their ebon-skinned beauty. His traveling cloak was thrown back over one shoulder in a dignified, almost aristocratic manner, and it flapped out in the breeze behind him, accentuating his lithe elf form. So thin and agile was he, with no weapon visible, and yet he exuded a confidence and power, a simple physical presence, beyond that of any man Entreri had ever known.

He was carrying a new item, Entreri realized as the drow moved closer. At first, the assassin had thought it a simple walking stick, a broken branch collected along a wooded trail, but as Jarlaxle neared, Entreri began to see the beauty and craftsmanship of the cane. It was made all of silvery metal, the head curved forward and was carved into the likeness of an alert ferret, head craned in ready posture. The eyes were two black gems—and flawless ones, if Entreri knew Jarlaxle.

What a pair of opposites the duo must seem, Entreri mused, considering his own appearance, with boots often mud-caked and cloak weather-beaten. But as he considered that, the assassin did a cursory inspection of himself and had to wonder just how much his traveling companion was beginning to wear off on him.

His black hair was pulled back in a tight ponytail and he had shed his bulkier and oft-torn leather surcoat for a shirt of fine fabric and quality, that he kept unfastened several inches down from the collar. More than a fashion implement, though, the shirt, furnished by Jarlaxle, was sewn with fine strands of enchanted metal threads that could turn a blade at least as well as the bulkier leather.

Entreri was looking trim and fit as well, at least as much so as he had been over the past decade. Jarlaxle was keeping him on his toes, keeping him constantly on the move and in practice.

And perhaps there was something else contributing to that fitness, Entreri knew, and he couldn't help but wince a little bit as he considered it. In one of their last encounters, Entreri had utilized his vampiric, life-stealing dagger on an unusual creature, a shade, and in that strike, something of the essence of the creature had apparently found its way into Entreri's being, as was evidenced by the slightly grayish tone his skin had taken.

Jarlaxle had professed ignorance to what it might portend, and Entreri had no idea at all, and so he had chosen to simply ignore it all—except on occasions when he took a moment to consider his present state.

"They are in their cave," Jarlaxle informed his companion, referring to a ragtag band of highwaymen they had followed into the foothills.

"Why do we care?"

"Must I explain every adventure to you, detail by detail?" the drow replied with that grin of his that always promised Entreri that they were going to get into serious trouble.

Jarlaxle, freed from the confines of the Underdark by his decision to turn his mercenary band of dark elves over to a lieutenant, seemed to desire life right on the edge of disaster.

Entreri wasn't sure if that was a good thing or not.

They were living fairly well, in those times they sat still long enough to realize the spoils of their adventures. They traveled from town to town, putting down no roots, taking jobs—usually as bodyguards or bounty hunters—as they found them. Every so often, circumstance forced a tactical retreat—it didn't take long for Entreri and Jarlaxle to wear out their welcome, after all—but on most occasions, it seemed to Entreri that their constant movement and hunting for adventure was more the realization of Jarlaxle's agenda than the pressing pursuit of any authorities.

"You truly want us to join in with a band of highwaymen?" Entreri skeptically asked. "Are we to climb through their ranks, position by position, by proving ourselves worthy in the eyes of their self-appointed leader?"

"You live for sarcasm."

"I am being tutored by the best."

"At least in that, unlike in other matters, you admit your inferiority, then."

Entreri had no answers, and didn't even bother to fix Jarlaxle with a scowl. The dark elf would only find some witty answer for it, anyway, and would hardly be either threatened or bothered.

"We need not stay with them for long," the dark elf explained. "But they have some good food—of that I am certain, and I tire of our rations. Besides, this group might well lead us to some greater ally or adventure; we will never learn unless we seek."

Entreri didn't bother to argue, and fell right into step as Jarlaxle started away, moving toward the road they both knew the highwaymen to be currently working.

Sure enough, within an hour, the two came upon a clear area of trail, lined by only a couple of trees, and there they were predictably accosted.

"Stand where you are!" came the order from the boughs of one of the trees.

"It took you long enough to discover us," Jarlaxle called back.

"There are a dozen bows trained upon you!"

"Then at least four of your fellows are holding two, which would leave them quite ineffective, I would wager," said the dark elf.

"You are a wealth of information," Entreri remarked.

"Impress them with intellect."

"Tell them everything we know," Entreri corrected. "And perhaps our life's tale that brought us to this point. What next, Jarlaxle? Will you draw them a map to your mother's house?"

Jarlaxle's lips curled at the amusing notion of sending a stream of surface dwellers trotting happily to House Baenre in Menzoberranzan.

Entreri dropped his arguing and glanced around, to note that several of the bandits were about, a couple with bows and all scrambling for a better angle on the pair. The one who had verbally accosted them dropped down from the tree, then, and started forward, sword in hand.

Entreri measured the balance (or lack thereof) of that step, and figured that he could have the man dead in three moves, should it come to a fight.

"Strip yourself of your weapons, your coin, and even your clothing," the man demanded in a falsely haughty voice, a tone of sophistication that did not match reality, both the friends knew, and one designed to convey superiority over his slobbering fellow robbers. "Perhaps my friends and me will let you walk away."

"And I," Jarlaxle corrected.

"Aye, yourself as well."

"No no, you said 'my friends and me,' but the proper—"

"Let it go," Entreri interrupted.

"Quit yer whispering!" the man demanded, reverting to an accent that seemed far more fitting to one of his lowly and uneducated stature. "Now go ahead and start dropping the goods."

"Now, now, friend," said Jarlaxle. "We come not as enemies, and surely not as victims. We have been watching you and your fellows for some time now, and have decided that a joining of our resources might prove a valuable alliance."

"Eh?" the man responded, his face blank.

"Oh, wonderful," Entreri remarked.

"They have not shot their bows yet, have they?" whispered the dark elf.

"All owing to the brilliant diplomacy of Jarlaxle, no doubt."

"Enough o' that, both of ye!" the highwayman yelled. "Now I'm warning you for the last time to start dropping the goods!"

"It will be the last time if I choose to cut out your throat, to be sure," Entreri replied.

He saw Jarlaxle explode into motion before he ever finished the sentence, and heard as well the *twang* of bows.

But Jarlaxle was the quicker, pulling a black disc from his mightily magical hat, spinning it (and hugely elongating it in the process), then throwing it down at their feet, creating an extra-dimensional pocket, a portable hole.

Entreri and the drow dropped in as the arrows zoomed overhead.

The human assassin landed easily, dropping fast into a crouch, while Jarlaxle, with hardly a thought, it seemed, caught himself with levitation and lightly touched down beside him.

Up came Entreri, up and forward, and Jarlaxle threw himself against the hole's front wall and turned fast, cupping his hands in front of him and offering Entreri a boost. The assassin light-stepped onto those delicate but surprisingly strong fingers and Jarlaxle hoisted him.

He came out of the hole in a dead run at one very surprised highwayman.

Entreri fell into a roll, threw himself over sideways, then scissored his legs around the highwayman's, tripping him up. The man had barely hit the ground before Entreri was over him, that devilish jeweled dagger at his throat.

"Tell them we are your friends," Entreri said, and when the man hesitated, he pushed the dagger's tip in, just a bit.

But enough for him to activate the enchanted weapon's life-stealing ability.

The would-be robber's eyes widened with horror as he

realized that his very life force was suddenly being sucked out of him.

"Tell them," said Entreri, and the man began to shout for the others to stand fast.

Entreri pulled the man up roughly and rolled around behind him, using him as a shield against any of the archers. He saw Jarlaxle float up out of the hole then, standing perfectly still and perfectly calm.

"Drow elf!" one of the others yelled and they all began firing their bows, lines of arrows streaking at the dark elf, who didn't flinch in the least.

Every arrow went right through him—or right through the illusion of him that he had brought forth from the hole.

"Are you quite done?" the drow asked, when at last the firing subsided.

"Very well, then," he added when there came no response, and no further arrows.

Entreri stood up and pulled his captive to his feet before him, then roughly shoved the man away and flipped his dagger back into its sheath in one fluid motion.

"We wish to join your band," the assassin remarked, "not thin your ranks so that there might be room for us."

Entreri's attention went back to the hole, where another Jarlaxle was floating up to stand beside the illusionary. He looked out wide to both sides, to see the archers nervously fumbling with their bows, though none offered a shot.

"Have they learned?" came a call from within the hole.

"They seem willing to talk first, at least," Entreri answered, and a third illusion of Jarlaxle drifted up from the hole.

When a few moments passed and the archers still made no move to fire, a fourth image of the dark elf appeared, and immediately began inspecting the other three, nodding his head admiringly before he finally made his way to the side of the hole, stepped onto solid ground and lifted the extra-dimensional device.

The three images began to slowly fade.

"Very well then," Jarlaxle said, moving to Entreri and

the befuddled and terrified would-be robber. "Lead on."

"I-I will have y-your weapons," the man stammered, trying futilely to sound as if he was back in control as his fellows closed in.

"In your throat or your chest?" Entreri asked.

The man gulped audibly and said no more about it.

Entreri sat on a ledge, nearly twenty feet up from the floor of the cave that his newly-adopted band of cut-throats used as their lair. It was a large and airy chamber, and the band had been quite adept at adding homey comforts. Many beds sat on the different levels of the shelved main cavern and there was a complete cooking area, with a well-constructed fire pit, counters, and cabinets. Numbering fourteen, with the addition of Jarlaxle and Entreri, the rogue band had plenty of space.

There was only one separate chamber, used by Pagg, the band's leader, a tough if somewhat simple ruffian with more scars than Jarlaxle had magical devices.

Even with the comforts offered by the cave, it didn't take Entreri long to come to wonder why in the world the band had decided upon that particular location for their base. They were off the main merchant routes, and the only towns around were poor farming and fishing communities. Even if they cleaned out every village within a twenty mile radius of every valuable, the robbers would still be poor.

Entreri watched with amusement as a game of dice continued on the main floor of the cave. Jarlaxle was playing, and winning of course, as was evidenced by the continuing growls and complaints of the others.

Entreri shook his head and wondered if the drow would push his winnings far enough to start a terrible row—and Entreri honestly wished that he would. They had been among the band of ruffians for the better part of two tendays, and Entreri was growing dreadfully bored. He had been out on the road twice with Jarlaxle and some others, and once they had even managed to overtake a merchant wagon, relieving the terrified man, a baker, of his goods. The ruffians had then moved to murder the man, but Jarlaxle had stopped them, explaining that doing so would only incite the wrath of authorities.

Entreri could hardly contain his grin as he recalled that moment of terror for the poor, trembling baker, when Jarlaxle had turned to him and elicited a promise that he would not tell anyone about the theft.

After tasting one of the man's creations, a sugary cookie, Jarlaxle had then gone one step further, insisting in no uncertain terms that the man surrender his previous life and join in the group at the cave.

And there he was, Entreri mused, working away by the fire pit on some new creation to satisfy the unusual creature who most surely terrified him beyond anything he had ever known.

A shout of victory from below turned the assassin's eyes back to the game, where Jarlaxle had apparently lost a rather large pot, to the delight of the three people rolling against him and their four watching friends. A short time later Jarlaxle lost yet again, and he put his hands up in defeat and walked away from the game, moving to the ladders and climbing up to sit beside his friend.

"And when all is counted, Jarlaxle makes just a bit, while giving the others the satisfaction that they finished strong," Entreri reasoned.

"That and the hope that their luck will continue when next we play," the drow agreed.

"This is as sorry a band in as worthless a land as I have ever known," said Entreri.

"Ever do you see the dark side of it all."

"As compared to?"

"I have learned much of the region from our dice-rolling friends," said Jarlaxle. "And there is fat Piter McRuggle," he added, motioning down at the hardworking baker. "A fine and useful chef."

"All we need are a few women, and why would anyone leave?" came the assassin's predictably sarcastic reply.

"Well, there is Jehn, and of course Patermeg," Jarlaxle

reminded, speaking of the bands two female associates, one a weather-beaten human and the other a half-orc—and reflecting much more of her orc heritage than her human side. "An inspirational pair."

"To anyone aspiring to celibacy, one would suppose."

Jarlaxle laughed, but Entreri was hardly in the mood to follow that lead. Both he and the dark elf turned as a figure moved by. it was Pagg, the group's leader.

"You two'll be out on the road later this tenday," he instructed. "And far off to the south. I'm hearing that there might be another caravan coming through. Ye'll get to prove yer mettle and yer worth."

He walked on by, and neither Entreri nor Jarlaxle even bothered to follow him with their gazes.

"He keeps hoping that he'll find another wealthy hit," said the drow. "Akin to the one that put him in the position of leadership in the first place."

Entreri nodded his agreement, and did glance over at the departing Pagg. The man had risen to prominence among the ruffians with one particularly profitable haul—the only profitable haul the ragtag bunch had ever realized. Pagg had led them to intercept a merchant caravan moving from Sundabar to Silverymoon, and buried among the more mundane goods the thieves had found one wagon laden with actual treasure.

That had been a long time ago and a long way away, however, as the band had then been fervently pursued by some of Sundabar's quite capable authorities. When the dust had settled, their numbers depleted, their leader dead, the remaining thugs had allowed Pagg the position of leadership, and he had taken them . . . nowhere.

Entreri, no stranger to thieves' guilds and the workings of noblemen, figured it was only a matter of time before Pagg angered the wrong group and got his band exterminated.

"Perhaps when we set out tomorrow, we should just keep walking," Entreri remarked.

Jarlaxle looked at him curiously, as if he was missing the entire point of it all.

"Well," the drow began, "I cannot leave baker Piter

trapped here with these uncouth and uncivilized creatures." Both looked down at the poor man, working furiously as always, over by the fire pit. "And I assured him that I would supply him with better equipment—a proper oven, even."

"You feel responsible for him? If it weren't for you, the thugs would have murdered him on the road."

"To the loss of all the world," Jarlaxle dramatically replied. "For truly the man is an artist with the spoon."

Artemis Entreri just snorted and looked away.

The next day, Jarlaxle was back at his gaming area, surrounded by eager gamblers. Dice rolled and cheers erupted repeatedly, and when Entreri finally found his curiosity piqued, he moved closer to see what might be going on.

"Quick Cut and Snatcher are coming in with a catch," one filthy wretch said to him.

The stupid nicknames such lowly thugs always seemed to place on each other never ceased to amaze Entreri. He hardly paid attention other than that quick musing, focusing instead on events at the dice area.

Entreri's eyes widened as he saw more coins there than he thought the entire band could possibly possess, piles and piles of gold and silver, and even a few jewels. He started toward Jarlaxle, thinking to ask what might be going on, when he realized suddenly that those piles, most of which were in front of the rogues, had to be a portion of Jarlaxle's wealth!

The notion of Jarlaxle actually losing to those fools was beyond comprehension, and that led Entreri quickly down a different path of reasoning.

He finally caught the gaze of Jarlaxle, who smiled and shrugged, as if helpless, and motioned with his chin, albeit subtly, toward the narrow cave entrance.

The one escape from the lair.

Entreri moved back from the gathering and the shouting, found a few handholds and deftly went up onto the lowest ledge. His attention was diverted before he could even begin to focus back on the surprising game, for he heard a commotion over by the door.

Several dark forms appeared in that opening, and as they entered, Entreri recognized a couple of the missing ruffians—the stupidly nicknamed men who had been sent out on the road that morning—along with a pair of new additions: two young women, plainly dressed and obviously terrified.

Daughters of fishermen, Entreri realized.

The thugs pushed them forward into the open area, and all interest in gaming fell away fast as the band came to recognize their newest playthings. They surrounded the girls. Even Jhen and Patermeg came out to inspect the prize, with ugly Patermeg pawing the two girls rather lewdly, to the hoots and howls of the appreciative audience.

"Wonderful," Entreri muttered when Jarlaxle came over to stand just below him. "And I will bet that our compatriots found a king's treasure trove on the cart with those two. Or perhaps we can ransom them off to their families for a goat, or even a fat pig."

"A win is a win," Jarlaxle chimed in, and Entreri stared at him incredulously.

"Did I just notice you losing a rather large sum of coin to these dolts?"

"The coins are only shiny metal unless one has a place at which to spend them," the drow replied.

Entreri didn't even try to search for the reasoning behind that statement.

"Wonderful life, this," he muttered. "So much hardship for a pittance and the empty joys in reveling in the misery of others."

"Empty joys?" Jarlaxle echoed, and when Entreri looked at him, the dark elf seemed like a smug and judgmental mirror reflecting back upon him.

Unwilling to acknowledge that sly retort, however truthful, in any positive way, the assassin just shook his head and stood as if to leave.

"My friend," said Jarlaxle, "it is a cave, with but one

easily defended exit. Where are my coins and jewels to go?"

Entreri started to offer a smug retort, but he stopped short as Jarlaxle's intent became clear. One corner of Entreri's lip curled, as close to an expression of intrigue as he had been able to muster on his typically dour face in some time, something the grinning Jarlaxle obviously didn't miss.

"They are a dozen," the assassin reminded his black-skinned companion. "Seasoned and skilled."

"Have you so lost the will for a challenge?"

It was Entreri's turn to smirk.

"No," he replied. "In traveling with you, I simply have not found a worthy challenge placed before me."

Jarlaxle glanced upward at the higher ledges, and Entreri took the cue, moving to one of the rope ladders and scaling to the highest ledge, where he quickly gathered up one of the ropes used for sliding fast back to the main floor.

Jarlaxle, meanwhile, ambled over to the gathering, where the two terrified girls were being prodded and pushed around as the thugs began to sort out the order of the coming assault. At one point, Patermeg, out of jealousy or just her typical nastiness, balled up her fist and punched one of the girls in the face, knocking her to the ground.

"Don't ye ugly her up!" one of the men complained.

Patermeg stormed over anyway and kicked at the girl.

Or started to, for a howl from above turned them all that way, to see Pagg standing on the high ledge, staring down at them, his face locked in an expression that none could immediately decipher.

Until he fell forward, quite dead before he ever hit the floor.

The bandits all watched that descent, and so none noticed the sudden movement up above as another form came leaping off that ledge, angling out to the side. Entreri released the rope perfectly as he went, launching himself into a long and fast-descending swing, angling down in a great swoop that brought him sweeping right at the gathering.

The assassin slammed in hard against the first thug in line, his knees tucked at a perfect angle to shatter the man's hip and send him sprawling to the floor in agony. Letting go of the rope and drawing forth his dagger and sword, Entreri fell into a wild roll and charge, slashing and stabbing every which way as he cut through the group.

Charon's Claw, his magical blade, began issuing forth its stream of ash, leaving black lines hanging in the air that only added to the confusion.

Around went Entreri, coming to his feet and turning a circuit, launching a backhand stab with his dagger and cutting down one fool with his sword—and nearly cleaving the man's head in half in the process.

He knew that he had to move swiftly, that he and Jarlaxle had to take down at least half the remaining cutthroats before any organized defense could begin to take shape, but even as he started to gain true momentum, even as he found his footing so that he could offer more substantive and devastating strikes, he found his blade deftly deflected by a perfectly timed parry, and he had to throw himself out far to the side to avoid a countering thrust.

As he squared up in a defensive posture, he heard a whistling noise, and despite being pressed hard by three of the killers, including both women, he glanced back at his companion.

Jarlaxle, surrounded, was spinning his cane over and over in his hand, and it was the item that was "singing" like some strange musical instrument. The octave raised as Jarlaxle increased the spin, bringing the walking stick in diagonal swoops back and forth to either side of him.

A sword came hard at Entreri and he brought Charon's Claw across in a parry, then slashed it back the other way, releasing a wall of black ash. He rushed around to the right of the ash, sword swiping and building a perpendicular visual barrier.

Entreri stopped short and pivoted back the other way, ducked low as he quick-stepped, then turned back and plunged right through the first of his ash barriers.

Patermeg was still looking to her left, to the far end of the second wall, when he burst out right beside her, his dagger stabbing deep into the side of her chest, his sword going across the half-orc female's torso to poke her opposite shoulder, keeping her sword at bay.

Entreri twisted the dagger and called upon its life-stealing abilities, then tore it free and hopped forward over the crumbling Patermeg, engaging Jhen and the other in a sudden and furious exchange.

The whistling continued from across the way, and was accompanied by a series of grunts, shouts, and squeals that Entreri could not ignore. He glanced back to see the ring of thugs about Jarlaxle collapsing, bandits grabbing at their bellies, at their faces, and falling away, stung hard. Entreri's scan of Jarlaxle registered the truth.

As the walking stick twirled, the drow was fast tapping his little finger against one of the ferret eyes, and that was setting loose a needle dart to fly forth from the other end. A stream of the tiny, stinging (and no doubt poison-coated, judging from the spasms of those being hit) missiles flew forth.

Entreri focused completely on the task before him, slapping aside Jhen's sword and that of his other attacker. He had an opportunity to strike at that man, but held his defensive posture, and when both blades came at him side-by-side a moment later, he swiped his sword across and up, taking them both high.

Entreri fast-turned inside that parry and slashed Charon's Claw back down, painting the air black before his turning and dodging attackers.

And they were face-up before the wall of ash, apparently expecting Entreri to burst through it or come running around either end.

Except that the pivoting Entreri had been on the near side of the ash wall when he'd created it, and so was behind them, watching with some amusement.

Jhen, to her credit, got it first, and she gave a scream and spun wildly around. She ducked the swinging Charon's Claw, but the sword wasn't aimed for her anyway, and instead went across and lopped the head from the male thug, who still stood staring stupidly at the ash.

No, for Jhen, Entreri had reserved his jeweled dagger, taking her right in the face as she conveniently ducked low.

The assassin pulled the blade free and looked back to see Jarlaxle with only a pair of thugs remaining, and both of them taking refuge behind the two captured girls.

A third man was sprinting for the door, but Jarlaxle reached into his innate drow magic and placed a globe of impenetrable darkness over that opening. The man ran right into the globe, and from within its dark confines came a crash and a grunt.

"He has most of my coin, I fear," Jarlaxle calmly said, as if intending to spur Entreri to motion.

But the assassin just stood and watched the standoff with amusement, wondering if Jarlaxle would barter for the lives of the innocent girls.

Jarlaxle stood calmly, his only movement that of his walking stick, still spinning before him, rocking back and forth.

"Empty of darts?" Entreri asked in the drow language, guessing correctly that the others could not understand.

"Not quite, though the poison is depleted," Jarlaxle replied.

That prompted Entreri to glance around at those fallen near to the drow mercenary, most squirming on the floor weirdly.

Drow poison, Entreri recognized, a paralyzing and debilitating mixture.

"And so I should be ready to take this pair, I suppose?" Entreri asked.

"Yeah stop yer blabbering and let us go!" one of the thugs demanded, and to accentuate his point, he brought his short sword up against the throat of one of the girls.

Entreri watched Jarlaxle's delicate movement, a slight turn to put himself in better alignment with the rogues.

Entreri gave a shout and charged forward.

Jarlaxle's walking stick clicked twice in rapid succession and the poor girls screamed.

But both men fell back from them, each hit in the face by a stinging needle. One recovered quickly, to his credit, while the other, a needle buried deep into his eye, thrashed about on the stone floor.

As for the other, he would have been better off had he not recovered, for as he reached back for the girl, she was suddenly thrown aside, her place taken by Artemis Entreri.

The man responded with a thrust of his sword, but the assassin parried it once, twice, thrice, moving it to a lock between his dagger and sword, where a twist and flick of his wrists had the blade flying free.Before the man could even respond, before he could plead for mercy or surrender, if that was his intent, or before he could punch out with his bare hands, if the fool had that in mind, Entreri was suddenly up against him, both the assassin's blades buried to the hilt into his chest.

A sudden shove dropped him dead to the floor.

And still the girls were screaming. And still many of the others joined in, or flopped about on the floor.

"We should be leaving," Entreri suggested, turning around to regard his friend, who was standing calmly again, leaning on his walking stick.

"Indeed," Jarlaxle agreed, motioning to the cave opening, where his globe of darkness was now gone, and gone, too, was the man Jarlaxle claimed had taken much of his coin. "To the hunt?"

"What about them?" Entreri spat with obvious contempt, as he regarded the two shivering girls.

"Our rescue would be less than complete if we did not escort them to their homes," the drow answered, and it seemed to Entreri as if both the poor girls would just fall over and die. "And there is Piter, of course," the drow added, and he called loudly, "Piter?"

The fat baker came out from around a rock near the back of the cave.

"Come along then, friend," said the drow. "I am afraid that I cannot deliver a proper oven to you here, so we must settle for depositing you back in your shop where you belong."

It occurred to Entreri then that he and his companion had garnered no spoils from their two-tenday adventure, and indeed, if they could not catch up to the fleeing thug, had apparently lost some coin. He took out his frustration on the face of one unfortunate rogue who was trying to rise against the pervasive pull of the drow poison, kicking the man hard in the face and laying him low.

"Be at ease, my friend," said Jarlaxle. "You are a hero! Does it not fill your heart with joy?"

Entreri's returning expression could not have been a better combination of venom and incredulity.

But of course, Jarlaxle merely laughed.

"He is reveling in the adoration of gratitude?" asked Kimmuriel Oblodra, the handsome and slender drow psionicist whom Jarlaxle had placed in charge of Bregan D'aerthe.

"That one?" Jarlaxle replied with a chuckle. "He is too suspicious and angry to allow himself such pleasantries. I really must find him a woman who will help him to release his tensions."

"By killing her?" the other dark elf said with obvious contempt.

"He is not as bad as that," said Jarlaxle. He glanced back in the direction of the small fishing community where Entreri was waiting, though of course the buildings and the assassin were long out of sight. "There is hope for that one."

"With the right teacher?"

Jarlaxle turned back to Kimmuriel and asked, "Is there any better?"

The other drow respectfully bowed.

"How did you find the walking stick?" he asked as he straightened.

"It is slow in the loading, but was quite enjoyable in action. And effective, yes."

"I find your demands pleasantly challenging," Kimmuriel replied, and he held out one hand, dangling an eye patch and holding a wide-brimmed hat that perfectly resembled Jarlaxle's own. Jarlaxle removed his hat and swapped it with the new one after only a cursory inspection, then spent more time in comparing his own eye patch with the one he was trading, even ensuring that the stitching was identical.

"They will offer me new opportunities?" Jarlaxle asked.

Kimmuriel looked as if he might pout, and the other drow retracted the doubt with a burst of laughter. Had Kimmuriel ever disappointed him in that regard, or in any regard, for that matter?

Almost as an afterthought, Jarlaxle pulled the plume out of his newly-acquired hat and handed it over, plucking his old plume back and slipping it into his new hat's band.

"I have grown fond of the beastly bird it summons," Jarlaxle explained.

"But did you not fear that the man beside you was figuring out your various tricks?" Kimmuriel replied. "Was that not the point of this exchange?"

"Entreri is a clever one," Jarlaxle admitted. "But we have thrown him off any advantage he might have gained with this trade, even though you have not yet prepared my new bracers."

"And if you are wrong?"

Jarlaxle's face grew very tight and threatening, but only for a second.

"I will find him a woman," the drow decided with a wide and confident grin. "That will take the sting from his dagger."

Kimmuriel nodded, and Jarlaxle, so enamored of his sudden plan, didn't even bother to get a complete report of the goings-on in Menzoberranzan from his trusted drow friend, but just turned and skipped off back toward the town.

With a thought, literally, the powerful Kimmuriel Oblodra was back into the Underdark.

Leaving Jarlaxle alone to plan his next escapade with Artemis Entreri.

The Hunter's Blades Trilogy

New York Times best-selling author
R.A. SALVATORE
takes fans behind enemy lines in this
new trilogy about one of the most popular
fantasy characters ever created.

THE LONE DROW
Book II

Chaos reigns in the Spine of the World. The city of Mirabar
braces for invasion from without and civil war within. An orc king
tests the limits of his power. And *The Lone Drow* fights
for his life as this epic trilogy continues.

Now available in paperback!

THE THOUSAND ORCS
Book I

A horde of savage orcs, led by a mysterious cabal of power-hungry
warlords, floods across the North. When Drizzt Do'Urden and
his companions are caught in the bloody tide, the dark elf ranger
finds himself standing alone against *The Thousand Orcs*.

R.A. Salvatore's
War of the Spider Queen

Chaos has come to the Underdark
like never before.

New York Times best-seller!
CONDEMNATION, Book III
Richard Baker

The search for answers to Lolth's silence uncovers only more complex questions. Doubt and frustration test the boundaries of already tenuous relationships as members of the drow expedition begin to turn on each other. Sensing the holes in the armor of Menzoberranzan, a new, dangerous threat steps in to test the resolve of the Jewel of the Underdark, and finds it lacking.

Now in paperback!
DISSOLUTION, Book I
Richard Lee Byers

When the Queen of the Demonweb Pits stops answering the prayers of her faithful, the delicate balance of power that sustains drow civilization crumbles. As the great Houses scramble for answers, Menzoberranzan herself begins to burn.

INSURRECTION, Book II
Thomas M. Reid

The effects of Lolth's silence ripple through the Underdark and shake the drow city of Ched Nasad to its very foundations. Trapped in a city on the edge of oblivion, a small group of drow finds unlikely allies and a thousand new enemies.

The foremost tales of the FORGOTTEN REALMS® series, brought together in these two great collections!

LEGACY OF THE DROW COLLECTOR'S EDITION
R.A. Salvatore

Here are the four books that solidified both the reputation of
New York Times best-selling author R.A. Salvatore as a master of fantasy,
and his greatest creation Drizzt as one of the genre's most beloved
characters. Spanning the depths of the Underdark and the sweeping
vistas of Icewind Dale, Legacy of the Drow is epic fantasy at its best.

THE BEST OF THE REALMS
A FORGOTTEN REALMS anthology

Chosen from the pages of nine FORGOTTEN REALMS
anthologies by readers like you, *The Best of the Realms* collects your
favorite stories from the past decade. *New York Times* best-selling author
R.A. Salvatore leads off the collection with an all-new story
that will surely be among the best of the Realms!

Starlight & Shadows

New York Times best-selling author Elaine
Cunningham finally completes this stirring trilogy of
dark elf Liriel Baenre's travels across Faerûn!
All three titles feature stunning art from award-
winning fantasy artist Todd Lockwood.

New paperback editions!

DAUGHTER OF THE DROW
Book 1

Liriel Baenre, a free-spirited drow princess, ventures beyond the
dark halls of Menzoberranzan into the upper world.
There, in the world of light, she finds friendship, magic,
and battles that will test her body and soul.

TANGLED WEBS
Book 2

Liriel and Fyodor, her barbarian companion, walk the twisting streets
of Skullport in search of adventure. But the dark hands of Liriel's past
still reach out to clutch her and drag her back to the Underdark.

New in hardcover – the long-awaited finale!

WINDWALKER
Book 3

Their quest complete, Liriel and Fyodor set out for the barbarian's
homeland to return the magical Windwalker amulet.
Amid the witches of Rashemen, Liriel learns of new magic and love
and finds danger everywhere.

The richness of Sembia yields stories within its bounds...and beyond.

LORD OF STORMWEATHER
Sembia
Dave Gross

Thamalon Uskevren II thinks he has a long time before he'll inherit Stormweather Towers and the responsibility such inheritance brings. When not only his father, but also his mother and mysterious servant Erevis Cale disappear, Tamlin will have to grow up fast. To save his family, he'll have to make peace with his brother and sister and face a truth about himself that he imagined only in his wildest dreams.

TWILIGHT FALLING
The Erevis Cale Trilogy, Book I
Paul S. Kemp

Erevis Cale has come to a fork in the road where he feels the pull of the god Mask and the weight of a life in the shadows. To find his own path, he must leave the city of Selgaunt. To save the world, he must sacrifice his own soul.

The Rogues

Travel into the shadows with this new series.

THE ALABASTER STAFF
Edward Bolme

An item of great power draws the attention of even more sinister forces.
In the ancient streets of the Old Empires, a young thief finds out
the hard way that some things are better left unstolen.

THE BLACK BOUQUET
Richard Lee Byers

Give a man a potion, and you empower him for a day.
Give him the formula, and he could rule the world.

THE CRIMSON GOLD
Voronica Whitney-Robinson

Thazienne Uskevren leaves behind the streets of Selgaunt to challenge
the Red Wizards of Thay, but even the priceless Crimson Gold might
not be reward enough when all Thay rises against her.

December 2003

The Avatar Series

New editions of the event that changed all Faerûn…and the gods that ruled it.

SHADOWDALE
Book 1 • Scott Ciencin

The gods have been banished to the surface of Faerûn,
and magic runs mad throughout the land.

TANTRAS
Book 2 • Scott Ciencin

Bane and his ally Myrkul, god of Death, set in motion a plot to seize
Midnight and the Tablets of Fate for themselves.

The New York Times best-seller!
WATERDEEP
Book 3 • Troy Denning

Midnight and her companions must complete their quest by traveling
to Waterdeep. But Cyric and Myrkul are hot on their trail.

PRINCE OF LIES
Book 4 • James Lowder

Cyric, now god of Strife, wants revenge on Mystra, goddess of Magic.

CRUCIBLE: THE TRIAL OF CYRIC THE MAD
Book 5 • Troy Denning

The other gods have witnessed Cyric's madness
and are determined to overthrow him.